"What the hell," ~~~~~~~~~~~~~~~~~~~~~~~~~ ay,
right? Might as well ~~~~~~~~~~~~~~~~~~~~~~ r a
second there was an ~~~~~~~~~~~~~~~~~~~ om-
pletely flash blinded. Then . . .

Where am I? I thought.

You are here, popped into my head in a generic and
asexual tone of voice.

"Whoa! That was weird," I mumbled. I thought about
it a little more analytically and from the approach a programmer would take in designing an operating system.
After all, I had designed an operating system before, so I
should be able to understand this one, right?

*With relation to where I was abducted, where am I
now?*

Here. An image of the solar system popped in my head
and a red blinking dot appeared near one of Saturn's
moons.

Where are you?

Here. A map of the ship appeared in my head. I found
it odd that the computer would be giving me such detailed
information.

Can anybody speak to you?

Anybody equipped properly. Yes.

Can you be kept from others?

If programmed thus.

Okay. For now on, only let me talk to you.

Okay.

*What stupid aliens! Don't they have hackers on their
world?* I thought this without realizing it and forgetting I
was still talking to the machine.

No, they do not.

The answer shocked me a bit. . . .

THE *QUANTUM CONNECTION*

TRAVIS S. TAYLOR

THE QUANTUM CONNECTION

This is a work of fiction. All the characters and events portrayed in this book are fictional, and any resemblance to real people or incidents is purely coincidental.

A Baen Book

Baen Publishing Enterprises
P.O. Box 1403
Riverdale, NY 10471
www.baen.com

ISBN 10: 1-4165-2100-3
ISBN 13: 978-1-4165-2100-6

Cover art by Alan Pollock

First Baen paperback printing, January 2007

Distributed by Simon & Schuster
1230 Avenue of the Americas
New York, NY 10020

Library of Congress Cataloging-in-Publication Data:
2004029932

Printed in the United States of America

10 9 8 7 6 5 4 3 2

I would like to dedicate this book to my first professional mentor: the late Dr. Thomas E. Honeycutt. Dr. Honeycutt devoted his career toward winning the Cold War. He taught me the difference between wanting to do good science and actually doing it. His memory will always be with me and I'm grateful for having been able to fight the last few years of the Cold War by his side in our lab in Huntsville.

We won, Dr. H.

➤ CHAPTER 1

I just barely ducked the knife that was thrown at me by *her*, my nemesis, JackieZZ. I responded by slipping left, crouching, and leaping at her with all my strength focused on taking out her helmet laser. I was nowhere near quick enough, because she burned off my left hand with a full second to spare. Although it vibrated and I could feel the light shock, I tried not to let it stop me from pressing the attack. With the momentum in the fight that I had gained by the lunge, there was a chance, a good one I hoped, that I could take her now. I managed to wrap my hands, erh, hand and stump, around her backpack power supply and then I ripped it right off of her armor. Sparks flew everywhere and there was a cool-looking array of secondary explosions as I rolled off her back to the side.

JackieZZ was too damned good. For a woman with such

big breasts on such a small frame, damn, and the powerful spritelike movement she had, she made it difficult to focus and I barely managed to roll out of the way of her counterstrike. I did a back flip just in time to miss a venom-spiked boot crushing through my face.

"Damnit, quit watchin' the scenery and fight!" I had to remind myself. I had been playing these gladiatorial games for years now and was undefeated; I couldn't lose now! There was no way I could lose!

I tried to deepen my concentration and my hand moved as fast as I could make it. JackieZZ and me, StevieM09, had been at it for hours now, maybe longer, and we both were wearing down. My back was killing me, my fingers hurt, and my right wrist ached all the way up to my shoulder. Then she made her mistake; she stepped backward while throwing an x-block with her forearm quantum shields. I figured I could get her the same way I defeated MarsKen44 last weekend. The quantum shields drain the power level below my secret attack's power level, so I went for it. As fast as my fingers could move, I lunged forward, then rolled to my left, then launched myself with my hydraulic jumper boots to more than eighty feet above JackieZZ, then I turned down headfirst, hit my downward thrusters, and then came the secret code. Left circle, right triangle, forward, forward, right right1, left circle, right x, right x, left x, left left1, and then both left and right circles on both controllers. I turned myself into a pure energy being and was propelled at JackieZZ faster than any reflexes or secret codes I had ever heard of, but something different happened this time.

JackieZZ wasn't just throwing a quantum x-block, but instead was completing a secret code of her own. The quantum force field amazingly shaped itself into a quantum singularity or mini black hole. There she was in an awesome gung-fu-style fighting stance with her hands cupped upward holding a mini black hole over her head. The tidal forces were so great that the hair protruding from beneath her helmet as well as her mammoth CGI boobs pointed upward and toward the event horizon. Material from all around The Realm was being sucked into the singularity—except for JackieZZ who stood there basically unaffected.

Baffled, I tried everything I knew to steer my new energy form away from the black hole, but it was far too late! I was sucked into the timeless abyss from which there was no *known* escape, forever. I became a pencil-thin beam, and then a single, ray-thin beam of light and finally my visor blinked to totally black. I flipped up the visor and looked at the big screen just in time to see *her* standing there, triumphantly, and maniacally, laughing. The black hole had dissipated and the big screen now displayed in gigantic font JACKIEZZ WINS!!!

"Shit!" I cursed my controllers, my puppy, and I kicked my forty-ounce beer bottle over. I stood up and stretched for the few seconds I would have while the game logged off to the Waiting Room. I slipped my visor and headphones off, rolled my neck left and then right, and then I realized, "Shew, puppy, either you or I stink and one of us needs a bath!" It was probably both of us since I had been sweating profusely while fighting JackieZZ for the past few hours and puppies always need a bath. I tugged on the little fellow's ear and told him he was a good boy.

I had never been defeated at any of the Realm World Competitions, especially not at the Gladiator Sequence, ever. And damnit, this JackieZZ that I met yesterday in The Realm's Tavern had beaten me at everything.

I stumbled over a pile of empty cereal boxes on my way to the fridge and pulled out another forty ounces. Unfortunately, I was out of cereal, so I had to settle for corn chips. The Waiting Room door popped on the screen and a video square with JackieZZ's computer likeness standing there smiling back at me opened.

"Gotcha again, but man that was the longest it has ever taken me to beat a Sequencer. You're good." She put her hands on her hips and winked while that pleasantly, if not freakishly, disproportionate body jiggled up and down.

"Where the hell . . ." I finished off a sip of beer and belched, "did that mini black hole thing come from?" I was comfortable speaking to such an attractive image since I knew she was seeing my six foot two, chiseled granite washboard abs and giant muscles image. After all, I am a Sequencer. Although, come to think of it, that belch probably wasn't cool. And of course, my own personal appearance of six foot one and two hundred forty pounds, all fat, was well hidden behind the video display.

"You liked that did you?" JackieZZ's boobs wiggled with every movement she made. It was distracting, a good fighting strategy, especially since she undoubtedly knew that most of her opponents would be single and male and hard up. "I call it ZZ's Hole!" Her video likeness laughed.

"Cute, but effective. Who wrote the code and have you sold it yet?"

"I wrote the code, StevieM09. You wanna buy a copy, that'll be seventy-six hundred euros." Her CGI likeness held out its left hand palm up and then winked at me.

"Uh, uh . . . how much is that American?" I asked.

"Oh yeah, I've been in Ramstein so long I almost speak German now. That's about one point two times in U.S. You want it?"

"Shit, I couldn't afford it. How did you get so good?" I stroked my belly and propped the corn chip bowl on it with my left hand while reaching for my beer with my right hand. The picture in picture news alert icon blinked on in the bottom left-hand corner of the screen. I ignored it for now.

JackieZZ chimed back in, "Oh that; my dad works for RealmSoft Europe. I write code for them in the summer when school is out."

"I see, uh, no, I don't see. What'd you mean, when school's out? How old are you?" I had a bad feeling about this.

"I'm fourteen."

"How did you get in to The Realm? It's for adults only!" I thought of some of the other more adult Worlds within The Realm, like Orgy World and it spooked me a bit. Kids just shouldn't be in there.

"How do you think I can write the code for RealmSoft if I can't get in The Realm, stupid?" That last was more of an insult than a question. Her video likeness stuck her tongue out at me and put her hands on her hips. I felt bad about noticing the boob wiggles this time.

"But, you shouldn't be in here, JackieZZ," I pleaded.

"Oh pooh. You're a prude just like my mom. Don't worry, mother, I have a special access that just lets me into the Gamer Level Worlds." Again the wiggles.

"JackieZZ, that is impossible. You know as well as I do that once you open the door to The Realm there are no doors that can't be opened. You're in The Realm, for Christ's sake!" I shook my head then stuffed a handful of chips in my mouth.

"Yeah I know, this is a new experimental access with a worm attached to it. If you go to certain places the worm starts to eat you. I'm trying to figure out how to beat it for my dad. If I can't beat it, The Realm will no longer be an adul—" She stopped talking and her likeness vanished from the screen.

"JackieZZ, are you there?" No response.

"JackieZZ, Jackie are you online?" Nothing.

Oh well, I thought, she must've somehow gotten disconnected, turned off or something. I had heard of that happening but had never seen it. "How about that," I told Lazarus the Puppy, "kids in The Realm. Bad enough they're in the Framework, but The Realm. Weird stuff, hunh? Yeah, that's right, you're a good puppy." I tugged on Lazarus's left ear and scratched his neck. The little guy looked up at me with sad little two-month-old puppy dog eyes. My mom and dad had given him to me recently as he was a pup from the last litter of the family dog, Molly. They had kept a family dog from the same genetic line since I was a kid; it was sort of a tradition.

The news alert icon had continued to blink since I lost contact with JackieZZ, but rather than worry about it I decided that I was going to get another beer. Upon arrival at the fridge I realized that I only had one forty left, the horror. "Oh God, Lazarus, we're out of beer! Go to the store and fetch some boy, good boy!" Lazarus just lay there chewing on his squeaky toy and didn't respond other than his ears popping up at the sound of his name.

Then I remembered where I had heard of the

Framework connections being disrupted. It was a few months ago when the meteor destroyed Colorado and part of Wyoming.

Oh my God, I thought. I frantically grabbed the remote and opened up the news alert icon on the TV, afraid of what I might see. "Let's just see what the talking heads have to say!"

" . . . *again, so far to our knowledge, there have been huge explosions or perhaps impacts, near Los Angeles and off the coast of Cape Kennedy, Florida.*"

"Mom and Dad! Carly! No!"

" . . . We have no idea what has caused such explosions. It is possible that these are events, which are similar to the one in Northern Florida and the catastrophic impact in Colorado a few months ago when the meteor hit there, but we have no confirmation of that yet. Wait . . . just a moment, my God, there has been another impact or explosion, or whatever it is, in Europe. It seems to be centered near Ramstein, Germany . . ."

I watched television for the next fourteen days straight, only going out for food, puppy treats, and beer but immediately returning home as quickly as possible. I was numbed by the total destruction and loss of countless millions of lives around the world that evening. The meteors impacted all around the globe, in China, Russia, North Korea, Germany, California, and Florida. I never heard from poor little JackieZZ again. That broke my heart.

On top of that, I'm from Bakersfield, California, which is just about fifty miles north of Los Angeles. My entire list of living relatives that I know about were all gone! Everybody I could connect with or could count on as family, were vaporized in an instant. My high school was gone and probably most of my high school chums. There would be little reason for a ten-year reunion.

My mom and dad and my little sister, Carly, were gone. The house that I had known as home all of my life—gone. Sure I lived in Dayton now, but home was still Bakersfield, home was still where Mom and Dad and Carly lived. Home was still where we had raised generations of our family dogs since I was little. Home was still where I built the tree fort in the back yard with my buddies when I was nine. Home was still where I went every holiday and vacation. But now, it was gone—all gone.

I missed work for two weeks straight and I sure as hell didn't make it to any of my college classes. In fact, I wouldn't make it back to college for a long time and I got fired from that job. Oh well, who needs it; the world just nearly got destroyed, man! And, and I was alone, just Lazarus and me.

➤ CHAPTER 2

Things were okay for about two weeks after The Rain, which is what the day of meteors had become known as on the Framework, but then came the horrible hypercanes, which as the guy on The Weather Channel explained were super-duper hurricanes. The country-sized storms were spawned off from the meteor impacts. One storm the size of Brazil pounded the south Pacific and stalled in the ocean, churning it up and making it impassible by air or sea for more than a month. The mega storm eventually turned and wreaked havoc on Australia and New Zealand. The other major hypercane system spun up below the equator just above South America. It plowed through Buenos Aires and bounced along the coastline moving southward. It churned across the Atlantic and cut a path across the Congo, then on to India before it died out. That storm killed hundreds of thousands. A couple of large hurricanes and hundreds of tornados had plagued North America and Russia since The Rain, but after about a month the weather began to settle down.

It took about all of that month for me to get over my depressed funk or state of disrepair or whatever it was. I would get so depressed that I would block out hours of time where I just sat there and cried. And sometimes, I didn't even remember the hours-at-a-time depression when it would pass. I went to several different shrinks for help. They ran tests on me and did brain scans and everything came out normal. It was odd to me that the rest of the world went on about its business and was only fazed slightly by The Rain. After The Rain our society didn't fall apart at all, but for some reason I seemed to have. People in general went on about their business while I fell down into a pit of something akin to despair.

"Buy a bunch of these expensive drugs," the shrinks tell me. "They're the only cure." Damned headshrinks!

So I take the drugs, but the only way I seem to survive within my depression and get my mind into some sort of useful mode is to replay the Sequence against JackieZZ and attempt to reverse engineer her mini black hole. You see, the Internet II, or the Framework as Realm Citizens call it, enabled RealmSoft to develop a virtual world with real laws of physics and nature and real ups and downs. Of course, the developers of The Realm wouldn't tell anybody what the laws were, which is part of what makes it so interesting. Part of the fun of The Realm adventure is to try and discover its laws. This is done by creating a virtual persona, such as mine, StevieM09, and living and having adventures in the various worlds of The Realm.

As you learn more and more about The Realm you become more powerful and can manipulate things within it more readily. The real wizards in there play the Gladiator Sequence and try to show off their power. If you kill a Sequencer, you get the secrets of The Realm that that Sequencer has discovered. If you are lucky enough, and you stumble across a Node, you can upload your own code into the virtual reality and get a royalty for it any time it is used. I had done this with my code for the EnergyBeingSM09 just as JackieZZ had obviously done with ZZ's Hole. These were two subroutines that "were not of The Realm." The problem is that if you didn't know where the secret code was hidden, and the secret button sequence to activate it, you couldn't use it. JackieZZ had died before ever selling the button sequence to any other Sequencers. So I thought I could recreate it now that I had seen it.

Me, I am a code writer by choice and had been completing my bachelor's degree in computer science at the University of Dayton in Ohio when the meteors fell. How'd I get to Ohio from California you ask? Well, when I was in high school back in Bakersfield, before it was . . . destroyed . . . I wrote my own operating system. I was trying to get my own game designs into the mainstream but thought that the code requirements were clunky. So, I created an operating system that was much more stable and more precisely efficient than any other codes I knew of at the time. At the request of my science teacher I entered it into the school's science fair. I won at school level, then at state, and then won my division at the International Science and Engineering Fair, or ISEF as we called it, plus I got an honorable mention overall. I lost to a particle accelerator, an optical computer, some bioluminescence thing, and a wrong solution to Fermat's Last Theorem.

As a special award I received a full tuition scholarship for both the University of Alabama in Huntsville and the University of Dayton. Of course, as a California state citizen I could have gone to school in California for free, but my parents were way overprotective and I was afraid if I stayed in-state that they would continuously be checking in on me. What college kid wants that? So I didn't want to stay home, and I sure didn't want to live in a hick town in Alabama, so I chose Dayton; at least they have cool air shows there.

My freshman year I got a cooperative education job working for a local company that made wireless data routers and switching hubs. I learned a lot about hardware, encryption, and code writing to drive hardware back then. Then the Framework opened up and not long after that The Realm was invented. Right off the bat I found a small Node and uploaded some tidbits that earned me a little extra cash to help pay for my apartment, food, and beer, and when I didn't earn enough from my job, The Realm, and my scholarship, I just took out a student loan. Oh, did I forget to explain that the harder to find a Node is, the more bandwidth you are allowed to upload with? You can use a Node as often as you like once you know how to find and access it, but it costs about fifteen bucks per second to upload data. I think this was RealmSoft's way of encouraging code writers to write efficient code and to spend hours in there looking for bigger Nodes. It's a great racket. A monthly subscription to The Realm costs about fifty bucks for forty hours, or seventy-five for unlimited access.

What about viruses? There is rumored to be a World where all the viruses get stored and mutated, but it makes no sense to me why they would keep them. My guess is they use some sort of anti-virus Agent to take care of the problem.

So, anyway, I had tried to Sequence a few times since The Rain, but knowing I would never see anyone I cared about took the real life out of me, and knowing that I would never get the chance to play ZZ again just took the wind from my virtual sails. On the other hand, I did need money to live on, since I dropped out of school, or I should say "took a break," lest the student loan collectors come calling, and the money I make at the video game rental and repair store that I work at now just doesn't pay the bills. My thinking was that if I spent all my time trying to reverse engineer ZZ's Hole, I could input it into The Realm through the secret Node I found on Planet Xios and win a few Sequences with it. Then I could sell it for big bucks to the other Sequencers. My EnergyBeingSM09 was bringing me about twenty-three thousand dollars a year (after taxes) on royalties, so I figured ZZ's Hole would make much more than that. Then, I could quit that damn video store.

I was having no luck at all with it. Two years passed, and I still was getting nowhere. I replayed the recording of the video Sequence over and over and over to no avail. I tried testing in my own Test Realm the mini black hole codes I developed but test pilot Sequencer StM987 had failed and StM988 was about to give it a try, if I could figure out why StM987 didn't work that is. That JackieZZ, whoever she was, must've been a coding genius. Either that or she had some insight from her father at RealmSoft Europe. Make a short story long; I was having no luck and it was time to go to work.

"Lazarus, buddy," I stroked his chin. "I gotta go pay the bills," I told him. He had grown into quite the companion. As a bonus, I didn't have to vacuum anymore—since Lazarus was a vacuum himself. If it could be swallowed, he would eat it. I tossed him a smelly doggy bacon treat and made my way out the door.

The weather was a bit crummy, even for summer in Dayton. The sky was hazy and grayer than blue and the sun was very red, not yellowish orange like it used to be, and it was only about ninety degrees and muggy as hell. We were supposed to have bad storms later, the kind that used to only occur in tornado alley; now they happened everywhere. The word inside The Realm was that the dust and excess thermal energy that was thrown into the atmosphere from The Rain was the culprit. Makes sense to me, but I'm no atmospheric scientist.

Just as I pulled into the parking lot of VR's V.R. World it started raining, hard. "Good thing I didn't bring an umbrella. Shit!" I told my 2011 Cutlass, which in just two weeks would have its tenth birthday. The Cutlass didn't seem to care, although it choked and tried not to cease combustion when I turned off the ignition switch. I rushed to the door of VR's, getting soaked from head to toe since rushing isn't really my forte.

"You're right on time, Mr. Montana! Good for you," the eighteen-year-old blue-haired punk who was my boss pointed out as he looked up from the television. He had threatened to fire me if I was late one more time, but it was just a hollow threat, since he knew that nobody could repair the game systems or draw the Sequencers into the shop like me. Besides he seemed enthralled by what was on the flat screen.

"Hi, Robert." I cursed other things under my breath at him, but smiled on the surface. I was seven years his senior for damn's sake. "Anything new this morning?" I settled in to my morning caffeine and sugar fix and surveyed my workbench.

"Yeah, have you seen this yet?" he asked.

"Seen what?"

"A huge meteor has impacted Neptune and astronomers had no idea that it was coming." He pointed to the screen and there was a James Webb Space Telescope image of the planet Neptune with a huge impact plume flowing upward from the planet.

"Do they think we're in any danger?" I was beginning to feel nervous.

"Nah, don't worry about it. They're saying that it's way out of our orbit and we have nothing to fear." Robert turned back to the television, "It looks neat though."

"I guess. Good thing we're safe. So, anything new with work stuff?"

"Oh, yeah, this guy came in last night just before closing with this ancient console game. He said it wouldn't work and that he needed it fixed by three weeks from tomorrow, oh, I guess that would be three weeks from today. He also said to call him if it was going to cost more than three hundred dollars." Robert pointed at a box full of console, controllers, cables, and a few compact disks. "It's in that box. I've never seen one of those things before, it must be thirty years old."

I looked into the box and saw a game system that they

quit making in the late nineties. That's right, last millennium. I whistled. "Man, they sure don't make 'em like this anymore." I swiped off a space on my workbench, scratched my stomach reflexively, and then emptied the box out onto the bench in front of me. "First things first," I said to it. "Let's plug you up and see what happens."

After fiddling with the ancient video game console for about fifteen minutes it was obvious that no power was getting to any of the output cables. No video signal was produced, no voltages on the controller ports, and no signals at the memory card slot. The disk didn't spin and the light wouldn't come on either. The thing was as old as I was; I laughed about that. Laughing was good. I didn't do enough of it, anymore.

"The power supply is bad, at least," I said. You have to talk to yourself when you are working on stuff.

I started with the basic six steps for repair of a game console power supply. Even ancient ones must abide by the repair rules. Simple electronics basics:

1) Open up the game console (this may require a screwdriver, star wrench, or allen wrench).
2) Get out your multimeter (make sure you have good batteries in it) and check all fuses. Replace any bad ones.
3) Plug in your game console, being careful not to touch any open component connections.
4) Check the voltages everywhere first to see where it stops. If there is no power leaving the power supply then that's a good sign the power supply unit is bad.
5) Search through the Framework for hours to find

the voltage test points and proper voltages for the particular game system.

6) Since you've proven that the power supply unit is bad, you have to measure the test point voltages to see where there is something wrong in the power supply.

There it was on about the third or fourth point I tested. I got the wrong voltage. Instead of forty-five volts A.C., I got thirteen, so I backed up from that point and found a shorted capacitor. I de-soldered it and replaced it. Then the test voltage read twenty-three volts A.C., so something was still not right. After further inspection I realized that I had read the capacitor wrong and put the wrong-sized capacitor back into the board. So, I de-soldered that cap and replaced it. Bingo, forty-five volts!

Excitement. There's another emotion I hadn't had much of lately.

I repeated the six steps again and found that I now had a good and working power supply unit in the game console. Now the little green light came on and the compact disk began to spin up, but for some reason the system wouldn't read a disk. My guess was that the laser was either out of alignment or the voltage to it was low. I adjusted the alignment screws and had no luck with that. So I checked the voltage trim pots on the motherboard by the laser's ribbon cable. I tested both pots, the FBIAS and the FGAIN and neither one of them were where they should be. I monkeyed around with them for a bit and then, bang! I had a video game playing. Before I closed it back up I dusted it off with an airbrush and also used some Isopropyl alcohol and a cotton swab to clean the lens. All in all, it was a pretty easy fix. Then, just to be safe, I decided to play the games for a bit to make sure the system would be stable over time.

After a while of shooting zombies, the game froze up, a common symptom. The zombies had nothing to do with it; it was the cooling fan not working properly. Without the fan blowing right, the chips on the motherboard were overheating. The fan was getting power, so it was just an old or bad fan. My money was on old. "The fan was lucky; how many people didn't get to grow old," I muttered to myself.

I rummaged around in my junk piles until I found a fan that would suffice. It wasn't exactly the same size and needed half the voltage, which was nothing a little silicone rubber sealant and a twice voltage divider wouldn't fix. This time I killed zombies for two hours and never had a problem.

Then I decided to play all the games that were brought in with the system. They were the old standard compact disks and all of them were scratched and dirty. I cleaned them and resurfaced them and most of them worked. One of them, on the other hand, wouldn't. The disk for a killer zombie game had a crack all the way through in three places. I gently cleaned it, dried it, and then resurfaced it hoping that the clearcoat would seal off the crack enough for the game to work. It didn't. Again back to the Framework, surfing for a few hours for a replacement. Unfortunately, there were none left out there anywhere in the world. The game must have been unpopular and not sold many or very popular and nobody was giving it up.

I had other things to do at work that day so I took a break from the game repair until later that evening. I decided to take the thing home with me and play around with it for a few nights on my own time. I had more resources at home than at the rental and repair store.

After work I packed up the console, the games, and all the myriad cabling and controllers and threw them in the back seat of the classic Cutlass. Fortunately, the rain had stopped and the weather had cleared up to something similar to pre-Rain weather, at least for now. On the way home I stopped by the grocery store; Lazarus was out of beer and I was out of dog food. He shouldn't drink so much. I also grabbed some more chips, cereal, ramen noodles, frozen pizzas, and toilet paper. You can never have too much toilet paper. The young girl at the checkout counter never looked up at me during the entire checkout process. She was cute; I guess I displayed no aspects or traits that attracted her attention. I brushed my bangs off my forehead, scratched my posterior, and proceeded to collect my bags.

I stopped and grabbed a bagful of tacos for dinner; Lazarus likes them about as much as he likes beer. It took three trips getting the video game stuff, the groceries, and the tacos up the stairs to my loft apartment. Laz ran up and down the stairs wagging his tail, panting, and jumping up to my eye level the whole way each time. Well, except for once when he stopped to go on the tree outside the apartment.

"Good boy, Laz. You been bored all day?" I set the bag of tacos down and plopped into my sofa. Lazarus was immediately in my lap and licking my face. I returned the sentiment, "I know, fella, and it's a tough life being a dog ain't it?" I scratched his neck and tugged his ears. "You're my buddy. That's right, boy." Tears welled up and filled my eyes. I was crying again, although Lazarus made me happy. I pulled him to me and hugged him with all my heart and flat-out bawled for a good ten minutes. As the sadness eased slightly—it never seems to go away—I pulled the dog off me and went to the kitchen counter where I found Laz a bacon treat, a peanut butter cookie, and me a couple of Zoloft capsules. I cracked open a forty of Laz's favorite cheap beer and chased down the Zoloft. Likewise, I put some fresh water in Lazarus's bowl and tapped my bottle against it.

"Cheers, buddy." I wiped the tears from my face and returned to the sofa with a bag of tacos, my beer, and Laz in my lap. I remained there for a couple of hours until Laz nudged me, explaining that he wanted to go for a walk. So we did.

The next night, after basically the same ritual as the previous night, the previous three years worth of nights, I set the disk up on my Framework/Sequencing computer system at home and played around with it. One of my game copiers was able to read it. Then I burned it on a new disk and tried it. The game got stuck after a few layers. This time I used my copy routine to store the machine code as a text file. Of course, the machine code was encrypted so as to keep hackers from pirating the games, which was exactly what I was doing. But I considered this more of an archaeological project, rather than an illegal copyright infringement. It wasn't hard to break the code; after all, it was nearly thirty years old. One of my simpler decryption Sequences worked fine and gave me the actual code as an output file.

Once I had the decrypted machine code, I translated it over into my operating system. Then I could play with it all I wanted to. I didn't know how the game was supposed to flow, but there were obvious routines and subroutines and alternate pathways. I just took out the code that looked like gibberish and replaced it with a GOTO- or a LOOP-type routine or I just transplanted duplicate code from elsewhere in the game. My guess was that after so long, nobody would be able to tell the difference. I played the game on my system a few minutes and it worked great.

Now I had to reverse the decryption process and resave the game code in the original encryption. Backtracking is a lot easier than exploring, so this didn't take long. I burned a new disk, scanned the game picture off the old disk, printed out a new label, and presto, good as new. Now, I know what you are thinking: this sure was above and beyond the call on this repair job. Yes, it was; normally I would have fixed the system and not worried about the game disks. But, it was a fun project for me and I just wanted to know if I could do it. Most importantly though, the coding kept my mind off my shitty lifeless life for a while and I was nearly happy. The Zoloft didn't seem to help as much as it used to.

Good ol' Lazarus sat at my feet the entire time chewing his squeaky toy. He was patient and never bothered me, since he had swallowed the squeaker when he was about nine months old.

That bit of code breaking and writing on the game console I had completed was good stuff and I would get paid about twice minimum for it. There are some folks out there getting big bucks for that kind of work and the best job I found was working for a blue-haired eighteen-year-old punk with a spike through his bottom lip. I laughed at that thought for a few seconds and then the thought just depressed me. Then I started crying. Once I realized I was crying, I laughed at myself for being so damned nuts.

I tugged on Lazarus's ear. "Laughing one minute, crying one minute, and then laughing the next—I think the Zoloft ain't working anymore, buddy." Lazarus rolled over on his back wanting me to rub his belly.

I didn't realize it but I had been working on this code for hours at a time nearly every night for two weeks solid. This particular night about three in the morning Lazarus nuzzled up to me and gave me that, "I gotta go!" look. So I shut down, took him outside for a short walk, then we both crawled in the bed and I cried myself to sleep.

➤ CHAPTER 3

"No, you see, you have to press the circle on the right controller then the left controller. Like this." I picked up the MEGAMACE and cracked HALCOR over the head with it. "Then if you press right right1 and left right1 at the same time you can kill him. See." I continued to bludgeon HALCOR over the head with the MEGAMACE as his skull cracked open and blood and brains scattered and splattered everywhere. The huge dragon collapsed onto the castle floor knocking over the giant stone pillar, which had been concealing the Ancient Ruby that was the key to the doorway of Planet Xios.

"Cool!" the barely eighteen-year-old Sequencer wannabe, Miles, exclaimed as if he had discovered the secrets to the universe. Well, it was kind of a secret to his universe. When they're fresh to The Realm, it's like crack, and you get hooked for many months on end. The Realm is a heck of a game platform. I remember back when I started it that I was hooked for the first two semesters at college. That's why I nearly got booted out for bad grades and was placed on probation with my scholarship. But I didn't want to lose my meal ticket away from home, so I put down the controllers and picked up the books. Well, sort of.

Miles had come to the shop asking if I could show him how to get to Xios. He had been begging me to show him for months. I told him he had to try first. Neat thing about The Realm that is unlike video games of the past, there are no cheat books that you can buy to figure out how to slay a beast or open a doorway. Oh sure, there are some pirate Framework sites out there that give tips, but as soon as one mentions The Realm the copyright police shut 'em down. RealmSoft was smart in that they registered and/or bought all rights to the concept. If you want to learn how to do something inside, you have to go inside and buy it from a RealmSoft vendor on the streets of Realm Central City. For example, the tips I discovered and sold were posted in Central City and I was paid a royalty credit to my account with RealmSoft for each tip sold. If the pirate sites outside get caught, RealmSoft not only litigates but they also change the laws inside The Realm. Neat business, huh? RealmSoft has a shakedown on all us Sequencers that we can do nothing about, since Sequencing is so damned fun and we're all addicted to it.

So I had been showing Miles here how to trip from one planet to another, specifically to Xios. Someone must have told him there was a Node on Xios. It wasn't me, but I will, for a price. The buzzer on the door *bzzzed* and a guy in a tie came in and talked to Robert.

"He's over there." Robert pointed at me.

I handed the controllers over to Miles, "Okay kid, I gotta take care of something else, it looks like." Miles palmed me twenty bucks and went back to playing the game. I slipped the twenty in my pocket nonchalantly and greeted the suit. "Can I help you with something?"

"Hi, I'm Larry Waterford. I dropped off that old game system for repair a couple weeks ago." He held his hand out to me and I shook it.

"Which one? We get a lotta stuff in here." I shrugged my shoulders at him.

"Here's the ticket the fellow over there gave me when I brought it in." He handed me a bin number.

It was the ancient system that I had spent so much time on. "Oh yeah, I remember this one all right. It gave me quite a fit to fix. Well, actually the console was not in too bad shape. I just replaced a capacitor and tuned up the motherboard and added a new fan. The games on the other hand were all scratched up." I scratched my head and tried to remember where I had put the box. "Ah yes, here it is under here."

"So you couldn't get the games to work, then?" he asked.

"Oh no, I didn't mean that. I cleaned them and resurfaced them and all of them worked but this one here." I pulled out the broken disc and showed him. "You see these two cracks here go all the way through the disk. I tried everything but couldn't save this disk." I rummaged through the box for the new version I made him.

"Oh well," he interrupted. "At least some of them still work."

"Hold on, I wasn't finished yet. As I said, I couldn't get this disk repaired. So, I copied it and hacked the encryption code into my Sequencing system at home and found where it was damaged. I rewrote the game code where it was scrambled, re-encrypted it, and then copied the file back onto this disk here." I handed him the disk. "It plays great! You can't even tell where I spliced the code."

"You mean you reverse-engineered the game and fixed it?" Mr. Waterford asked.

"Uh, yeah if you say so." I just shook my head and handed him the box. "If you have any more problems with it, just bring it back to me. But it should work fine for a while. Who knows with those old systems like that."

"I hate to ask this, but what do I owe you?"

"Let's see." I took the ticket and scanned it. The computer rang up the total repairs and parts. "That looks like eight dollars for the parts, thirty-five for the labor, taxes, blah blah blah . . . comes to forty-six dollars and forty-four cents. All our services come with a thirty-day guarantee and you can buy a ninety-day one for fifteen dollars. You interested?"

"Not really." He shook his head no.

"All right then, forty-six forty-four."

"Just one more question," he said, and paused.

"Shoot."

"Uh . . . how did you find the bad code and how did you know the difference in the good code and the bad code? There must've been millions of lines in there for a video game." He seemed perplexed about what I had accomplished, as if it were too much for any good Sequencer.

"Oh that. It's really kinda simple. I generated a couple

of different codes for that. One of the codes was a couple of Agents that would crawl through the code from beginning to end, the other would allow the Agents to run the code in small increments. This enabled the Agents to make an assessment of when blocks looked similar to other blocks, if there were random or unusual blocks, and if they would execute feasibly or not. Then the Agent would highlight the code in my text editor. Simple stuff for any Sequencer—besides I already had the Agent codes. I just had to modify them some. All in all it took about a week and a half to finish the code breaking and repair."

"What software did you use for that? Telescript2 or Obliq2 or LotusScript4 or what?" This guy must've known something about Sequencing but he sure didn't look or act like a Sequencer.

"None of those—too clunky for me. I have my own platform that I use. It's sort of similar to the old Linux platform I guess. And the code, well, it is most similar to the old Multi-Agent Markup Language," I responded.

"You ever worked on this level of coding before?" he asked.

"I used to work on router code and stuff back before . . . uh, here." I motioned to the repair shop but I wanted to say, The Rain. I felt sad all of a sudden.

"I see. Uh, what's your name again?"

"Steven, Steven Montana," I replied.

"Well, hey Steven, thanks and good job." He left.

What an odd fellow, I thought. He was about five nine with neatly cropped black hair wearing black pants, white shirt, and tie. He carried himself more like an engineer or a business manager than a programmer. I meant to ask why he wanted that old thing fixed so badly. Heck, the repair bill was more than that thing was worth, but I forgot.

A few days passed and Mr. Waterford came back to VR's and had some interesting questions for me.

"Steven, hi." He sounded excited. "How are you?"

"Doin' all right I guess. Havin' trouble with your game again?"

"Huh . . . oh, no. I came back to talk to you. Do you have a minute or perhaps I could buy you a burger or something?" *Curiouser and curiouser, said Alice.*

"Uh, man I'm straight, but flattered," I replied.

Waterford looked at me and started chuckling. Holding up his left hand and pointing out his wedding band he said, "Mr. Montana, I assure you this is purely business. I might have some more, uh, lucrative possibilities for you than this place."

"Okay. There's a sandwich shop around the corner, you're buying." Didn't hurt to listen, especially for a free meal.

"Good," he said. "Lead the way."

"Hey Robert, I'm takin' my lunch break now. Be back in a bit." The little blue-haired punk just grunted and nodded at me.

The actual lunch part of lunch was not that exciting, just a foot-long club loaded and a bag of Doritos, to wash it down a super-sized Mountain Dew. I hadn't had my sugar or caffeine fix that morning so I figured a couple refills on the thirty-two-ounce Mountain Dew should hold me through the afternoon. Pretty standard lunch stuff for me. The lunch conversation, on the other hand, turned out to be quite exciting.

"You see it's like this," Mr. Waterford was telling me. "That was some pretty good code decryption, hardware reverse engineering, and code writing. Just so happens I could probably use someone like you in my outfit."

"What kind of outfit?" I asked.

"I work for the United States Air Force Space Vehicles Directorate out of Albuquerque, New Mexico. We have a branch lab here at Wright Patterson. I'm the Lead Systems Engineer over the local division of the Innovative Concepts Group. We call it the ICG for short."

"No shit?"

"Uh, yeah no shit. My group does a lot of . . . uh . . . *unique* problem solving for various organizations and we support and conduct the development of new innovative and wild technologies."

"Hey, that's pretty cool. So what does that have to do with me?" I hoped I knew where this was going. If I was right, I knew a blue-haired and pierced punk that I was going to say good riddance to.

"Like I said, you did some good reverse engineering on that game console of my wife's. That was her favorite game back in college that you fixed. I gave it to her for our twenty-fifth anniversary. She used to play that thing all the time. I found it in the attic a while back and had been trying to find someone that could fix it. VR's is the first place I found that would touch it. My guess is because of you." He paused to check my reaction and to take a bite of his sandwich. With a mouthful he continued, "So, have you ever been arrested for anything before or done any illegal stuff? What about drugs? If you can't pass a drug test I'm wasting my time."

"Uh, no I'm pretty dull. Sequencing is my only addiction. I have some prescription drugs if that matters."

"Nah, that's fine. Okay, what about education? Where did

you learn how to do all this stuff?" He took a sip of his soda.

I proceeded to tell him about the high school science fairs and the University of Dayton and . . . The Rain. And finished up with how I ended up at VR's.

"Sorry to hear that about your family and friends. I had a lot of friends at Space Park in El Segundo and my first cousin was stationed in Ramstein. I understand some of what you went through, sorry. On the other hand, it's good that you're doing okay. It would be easier if you had finished school though. How many more classes do you need?" He seemed fairly genuine with his concerns. He would be much better to work for than Robert. I was beginning to feel underdressed and too unprofessional for this meeting. I was getting nervous.

"I believe I am six classes short. I could probably finish it up in one hard semester. Two tops. Are you seriously considering making me a job offer?"

"Two semesters sounds about right," he began. "How about this, you come and work for me as a cooperative education student while finishing your degree as fast as possible. As soon as you graduate we will move you from a co-op to an engineer at a GS-07 pay scale. That's about forty-seven thousand a year. Of course until you graduate you will be at a GS-4 bringing in about half that. The government has good benefits and insurance, so, my guess is that you would be much better off with us. Also, by the time you finished with your co-oping your security clearances might be through."

"You mean this would be secret stuff?" I was getting excited.

"Oh, I thought I had mentioned that. Is that a problem for you?" he smiled.

"*No!* I would love to do that kind of stuff. A real job and real pay, where do I sign?" My straw made that obnoxious noise that they make when you run out of soda. I considered getting up for more but wasn't sure if it would be good timing.

"Well, what you need to do is go to this website and fill out the electronic form and resume. Put this job number," he handed me a slip of paper with a dot gov website and some numbers on it, "in the blanks where it asks for it and use my name as a point of contact. You'll be called in for the official interview. Don't worry; you have the job in my mind. We just have to follow the rules to get you there." He paused for a second. "You might go to the web and brush up on what goes on at Wright Pat, especially in our group, and be sure to wear a tie. And . . . uh . . . you might want to get a haircut, my boss is old military and . . . well, you understand."

"Okay, that's no problem. I needed a haircut anyway." I instinctively brushed my long bangs out of my eyes.

It took about a month to get the drug testing, paperwork, interviews, and job offer letter in order. During that time I had registered for two classes the next semester and for the cooperative education program. Before school started in the fall I had told Robert to kiss my ass, collected my things, and walked out on him in the middle of a shift. I started working a couple of weeks later. I had to take out a small student loan to make it until my paychecks started. I was very happy about my situation, but my mood swings still persisted.

Finally, the first day on the job came and life was looking up. Actually the entire day was kind of hectic since I had to deal with security, social security, human resources, and I had to go through a new employee orientation, all of which took until well after lunch. The lady at the security desk took a decent badge image of me I thought. I was sportin' my new student-loan-purchased wardrobe and haircut. Of course, I got soaked by an afternoon post-Rain thunderstorm while trying to figure out how to put the security decal on the window of the classic Cutlass. That was just a minor incident. Then I spent a few minutes driving around the base looking for the Space Vehicles Directorate Building. So, I didn't actually get to my new office (get that—I actually *have* an office) until nearly three o'clock in the afternoon. I had just enough time to meet my boss's boss, the secretary, Alice, a few of the other employees of the Innovative Concepts Group, or ICG as they called it, and to find where they hid pens and paper before it was time to go home. I didn't even get started on things like email, software, where the printers are, and where the closest bathrooms to my office are. But in time I would settle in and be much happier than at VR's.

That night after my first day on the job Lazarus and I celebrated and then I cried for hours. I know I was sad from losing . . . everyone I had ever known in an instant, but that had been nearly three years ago and I was getting back on my feet. I shouldn't have been so bipolar for so long, should I? The drugs were not helping. My plan was to see a new doctor as soon as my insurance with the Air Force kicked in. I already had scheduled an appointment.

➤ CHAPTER 4

The following few days I got settled in and filled out the SF-86 security form. That thing is electronic and asked for details about my past, which had been wiped from existence by The Rain. I asked Larry (no longer "Mr. Waterford," he said) about how it would be determined if I really ever existed or not since records and witnesses to my life had all been destroyed.

"Just fill out the forms and let Defense Security Services handle the rest," he told me. "They have had these difficulties since the meteors and have found ways to get information. Also, since The Rain, as you call it, they increased the requirements for polygraphs. Expect to take a lie detector test sometime in the next few weeks."

So that was that. I was on my way to a new career, with a security clearance, even. I was put in for a Top Secret and was told to read all the documents on the so-called AFSPSEC website. I found out the acronym stands for Air Force Special Programs Security Education Community. I was also told I should look up the National Industrial Security Program Operating Manual, the Director of Central Intelligence Directives, and a few other security documents that read like stereo instructions.

Finally, on my second Monday, I was set up with a workbench in a lab space and actually given a technical task to do. Larry brought me what appeared to be a small motherboard in a plastic static bag (and by small I mean about twice the size of a sticky-note) and told me to figure out what it was.

"Do you have any information on it?" I asked him.

"Sure I do. But I want to see what you come up with first." He smirked.

"When do you need this figured out? I mean how long do I have to tinker with it?"

"Take as long as you need," he said smugly. "But, uh, don't take too long." And he left it at that. How damned vague could you be?

How long was "too long" and how long was "as long as I needed"? This was some sort of test for the new guy I figured. So, I sat there for twenty minutes or more just rolling the thing over in my hands and looking at it before I came up with a plan of action. Since it was pushing four-thirty P.M., my plan of action was to go home and take Lazarus for a walk, which is just what I did.

The next morning I had a doctor's appointment with my new headshrinker. After talking with her for some time, she decided that I had developed a tolerance to the Zoloft and wanted me to try a new drug, I couldn't pronounce or spell the name, which was just out on the market. Fortunately, she had plenty of samples of the drug and gave me a handful of them, since they were apparently expensive as hell. I had decent insurance now, but the deductible on brand name drugs was two hundred and fifty bucks and I sure didn't want to have to pay that.

So, I took one of the pills with lunch and headed into the base for work. That little motherboard was still sitting on my desk in the plastic baggy.

"Well, first things first," I told myself and carefully pulled the board out of the baggy. Then I took out my lab notebook and began making a diagram of the circuit. It took about three hours to get what I thought was a complete diagram for the thing drawn and each part that I could identify labeled. Then I tried to develop a block diagram of the circuit with the nonlabeled chips marked A through D; the rest of the components on the board were standard parts.

It was my guess that the board was a "onesy" and had possibly come from a multi-card chassis. My reasoning for that conclusion was that all of the leads were covered and as short as possible, and there were outlines in each corner of the board for some sort of mounting hardware. The short leads would help prevent interference to and from other boards mounted above and below (or beside) it in the chassis. From this assumption I drew a dotted line around my evolving block diagram to represent a chassis.

The block diagram consisted of all five "main" chips, A through E, represented as blocks of size proportional to those on the board. From the top left of the page there was a chip about an inch square, which appeared to be some sort of standard input/output (I/O) conversion chip (analog to digital/digital to analog). To the right of the I/O chip was a chip much larger, about one and a half inches across and three inches tall. I had no clue what that chip would do, but it looked similar to a main processor chip like a Pentium VI. I labeled it A.

To the right of chip A was a slightly smaller chip, about one inch square, and I labeled it B. To the right of chip B was an identical twin to chip A, which I labeled C. To the right of chip C was another I/O chip. The chip sequence I/O, A, B, C, I/O made up the top row of my block diagram. Also, all of the chips on this row were connected by a copper stripe on the circuit board. The I/O chips had what appeared to be standard serial outputs connected to them.

With the top line of the block diagram completed I then added chip D directly below chip B and then chip E directly below chip D. Chip D had copper leads to both chips A and C. There were also fiber optic cables connecting chips A to B, B to C, D to A, D to C, and E to D. Below and on each side of chip E there was a small power processing unit (PPU) board just like the type in a game console power supply unit (PSU). Each of these PPUs was in turn connected to a single transformer and fuse box that had a standard power cable input. There were also power connections between several pins on each of the chips and the PPUs and other standard components on the board. It looked to me as though there were two separate PPUs because the board was actually two systems in one. Perhaps the two identical processor-looking chips were parallel processors on a single board, or maybe one was a backup to the other. I didn't know.

By the time I had figured out the rough block diagram, it was six-thirty. I just knew Lazarus was going to kill me since I was late for his evening walk. I packed up my things, put the board in my bag, along with my notes, and headed out for the evening. There couldn't be any security risk or anything; hell, my clearance hadn't come through yet. So I knew this stuff was public stuff. No problem; if it had been classified they would never have let me see it.

Laz was damned happy to see me. No sooner than the door had opened did he jump up and lick my face. Of course, I dropped everything and cursed some. "Damnit Laz," I yelled. But then, it wasn't his fault I was late.

"I know buddy, sorry about that. You wanna go for a walk?" I tugged his left ear just above the white spot that met his neck. I grabbed his leash off the wall, a handful of smelly liver treats, and pocketed a couple of grocery store bags; then we were off, Lazarus pulling me the entire way. We strolled down the sidewalk to his favorite fire hydrant where he marked it as his. We walked for a good twenty minutes or so. It was my guess, in retrospect, that Lazarus was the only thing keeping me from having a heart attack. Since he was old enough, we have walked every day for about twenty or thirty minutes. I'll bet he has caused me to lose about ten pounds, not that I couldn't stand to lose another twenty-five or more.

We finished the walk and I took another one of my new pills. I realized that I hadn't cried all day. Was it the fact that I was preoccupied with the new circuit board or was it the new drugs? I didn't really give a shit as long as I quit crying all the time.

Lazarus and I played around a bit and then I threw

together a sandwich. I was eager to get back to working on that circuit board, so I booted up my system and ate at my computer station. My block diagram was too primitive and paper is hard to manipulate, so I "CADed" it up in 3-D and loaded my circuit-modeling software. I had built enough game system modifications in the past to lead me to go out on the Framework and find a circuit-modeling shareware program. That way, I could draw up the circuit mods and run the software, which in turn would simulate the system's response and tell me if I needed to alter the circuit or something. This was nothing fancy; we used PSPICE back in my first Circuits class at University of Dayton, a standard approach. But PSPICE had become expensive, so I found the cheap version I still possessed. The coolest part was the interface program I had written a few years ago to translate my CAD drawings into circuit information, which would then interface with the circuit-modeling software. Cool.

So, I finished drawing up my circuit and I pulled a power source icon over to the PSU input on the diagram and connected them. I double-clicked the power source and typed in for it to be a standard one hundred twenty volts alternating current source with a ten-ampere breaker. Then I put oscilloscope icon leads at several places in the circuit. Since I had no clue what was inside chips A through E, I connected the leads from each pin of each chip and ran them to the analog-to-digital/digital-to-analog board of my computer system. My plan was to put the thing in operation and record what happened to the outputs after placing certain small voltages all around the board. I would use a couple of volts and a few microamp signals. I finally got all that coded and wired up by about midnight. I turned it on and got some of the most random outputs I had ever seen. I tinkered with the thing for hours, trying a different voltage here and measuring a different output there. Nothing made any sense. Neither of the chips seemed to have any standard purpose that I could determine. About three forty-five I decided to go to bed.

I loaded up my data and hardware and lugged it back to work bright and early the next morning and set up the circuit on my workbench in the lab. I felt great and not tired at all. I wasn't sad either. I went right to work on the circuit board. This time I decided to back up and focus on one chip at a time. Chips A and C had way too many pins coming out of them but chips D and E only had a couple of connected fiber optics cables and a couple of what appeared to be I/O and power pins. So, I disconnected chip E's fiber optic cable and powered up the board. A bright beam of green light came out of the end of the fiber optic cable.

"Aha!" I exclaimed. "It's a laser on a chip." I played around with it a bit until I figured out how to control the laser output by adjusting the power on the proper pin. Then I connected the cable back to Chip D. "So obviously, whatever is happening in chip D is optical!"

I removed the cables from chip D and powered up the laser chip. A faint beam of green light came out of the fiber optic cable fitting on each side of chip D.

"Chip D has, at the least, a beamsplitter," I muttered to myself. I connected the cables back to chips A and C and disconnected the cables between chips A to B and C to B. Or was it B to C? No way to know. When I powered the system up again, I didn't see light exiting the chips as expected. I turned off the lights and held a piece of paper in front of them and could barely see a faint beam coming out of A, nothing from B, and nothing from C.

I had no idea what this board was for and I wasn't sure that I would ever figure it out. I worked like mad on the thing for the entire semester I was supposed to work full-time. By the end of the semester, all I had figured out was that you could put an input signal of however many bits into one I/O chip and you would get the exact same thing out the other I/O chip. I guessed that this meant the chips A, B, and C were shorted out. I wrote up a report and handed it to Larry for my cooperative education credit. Then I signed up for my last four classes.

I had taken two classes while I was working and managed a B and a C, good enough to graduate. Once I finished the four classes this semester I would start as a civil servant for the Air Force full time. I did have to tailor my transcript a little for the job though. I was previously looking only at software coding, but the fun I had had at the ICG was making me think more about hardware.

My last four classes were senior level electives, so I got to pick basically whatever senior to graduate level computer, physics, math, or electrical engineering class I wanted to. I registered for *ECT 466: Microcomputer Architectures*, *ECT 460: Advanced Microprocessor Systems*, and I took a useless music class and a mate-selection class. I needed two liberal arts or humanities electives.

Near the end of the semester Larry called me up and told me that he had kept my desk just as I had left it and that my Top Secret security clearance had been granted! I was thrilled since I hadn't expected to be cleared, my parents and everyone I ever knew being dead and all.

I couldn't wait to get back to work on that circuit, but I had to focus on finals first. I hadn't cried since that first day on the job months before and I had only felt sad a little the night I got the call about the security clearance. The reminder of my family must have done that. My new headshrinker was doing a pretty good job with me and I was down to half the dosage that I had started with of the new drugs. The only bad side effect was the insomnia. The pills kept me awake until about three every morning and then I would be up again by seven. The good side effect was that I had lost another ten pounds. Things had not looked up for me so much in the three and a half years since The Rain.

I hadn't been worried at all about my final exams since I only had two "real" classes. The other two liberal arts/humanities classes were a waste of time and a joke all in one. The final exam for the Advanced Microprocessors class was simple, to the point, and interesting as hell. The exam read simply,

> Design an I/O system to input a handwritten page via a scanner, conduct a character recognition algorithm on the page, convert it to data of any format you choose, broadcast that data to another remote computer, convert the data back into handwritten form, and output it to a printer. Show a block diagram of the system, show all switching hubs and routers, and explain where all of the data latencies and bus bottlenecks will be. Also, bonus points will be given to innovative approaches to remove bottlenecks. Then give a short essay on how this system is similar to a motherboard,

and how the motherboard might be replaced by a single chip. Good luck!

I know it seems complex at first and why am I telling you about this now? I'm getting to the point, I assure you. I started out by drawing how a simple fax machine works. On the left side of the paper I drew a rectangle to represent a written page and showed it via an arrow going into another box labeled FAX. I also showed the page out of the other side of the FAX. This part of the drawing went from bottom to top. Page in at bottom of paper, FAX in the middle, and page out at top. Then I drew a horizontal arrow from the FAX on the left side of the page to a box in the center of the page labeled Router/Hub and then on to an identical FAX on the other side of the page. I drew the page coming out above the FAX on the right.

This was not enough to get the question right, of course. Much more detail would be required. So, I drew another level of detail showing the I/O input to the leftmost FAX renamed A. Box A was subdivided into three boxes: one box labeled RAM (for random access memory), a box labeled Algorithm, and one labeled Arithmetic Logic Unit (ALU). Then I penned in below the A the letters CPU for central processing unit. The Router box I renamed Box B stayed the same and then I gave another level of detail for the right FAX, now labeled C, which had a corresponding I/O box to its right. I then wrote a page each about the I/O, A, B, and C from the diagram.

On another page I drew an even deeper level of detail about each box and box within each box. To keep from boring you here I will just cut to the chase, since my actual response to the question contained ten more pages of circuit and chip and motherboard diagrams. I also drew some logic timing diagrams and bus and interconnect bandwidths per each pin. So I won't bother you with all that. But the point is that the data flow is slowed down every place there must be a wired connection. If somehow the data could be transferred from the RAM locations at each CPU directly to the RAM locations in the remote CPU, then a lot of time and therefore bandwidth could be saved. It's like taking a five-gallon bucket full of water, using a one-inch hose to transfer water from it into a one-gallon bucket, and then going from the one-gallon bucket to another five-gallon bucket again with a one-inch hose. It would sure be a lot faster if you could dump the water from one five-gallon bucket directly into the other five-gallon bucket, skipping all the in-between hoses and jugs.

I made a B in that class, which stands for "Better than needed to graduate." Larry showed up to shake my hand at graduation. He was the only person other than my instructors and a few students I had studied with that I knew. He was the only person there besides me that I had even had a meal with. I had wanted to bring Lazarus with me badly, but there was a no pets policy. That made me cry, but wouldn't it have made you cry? Laz was my only family. I told Larry as much, and I could sense he felt sympathetic for me.

"Larry, it's two fax machines on one board," I told him while he shook my hand and patted my back.

"What's a fax machine?" He looked puzzled.

"It's a machine that you put paper in and send it over phone lines to another one that prints out the paper, but that's not important right now." I chuckled my response.

"Steven, nobody likes a smartass," he laughed. "What are you talking about that is a fax machine?"

"The little circuit board is, well it's two of them actually. The I/O could be anything, a page of text for example. The data goes into the big chip on one side of the board, which is some sort of optical CPU. Then it is routed over via the little optical chip in the middle to the other identical optical CPU, and then out the other I/O device." I smiled triumphantly.

"Hmm . . . never thought of it quite that way." He tugged at his tie clip. "Then what are the other unknown chips on there? There are at least two others, right?" He smiled.

"I just figured . . ." I caught my tassel as it fell off my cap. "Uh, damn thing." I straightened it out and put my hat back on. "Uh, I just figured they supply the optical power. Am I right?"

"Why would I have two fax machines on one board, Steven?"

"Beats me. Maybe you're just playing around with an idea or something." I shrugged and that damned cap fell off again. Larry chuckled, so this time I just held it in my hand.

"When do you start back, Steven? It's about two weeks from now, right?" he asked me.

"Yeah, I was going to ask about that. Can I start earlier? I mean, uh, I'm not going . . . to . . . visit anybody . . . or anything." I looked down at my shoes for a second since I wasn't sure if I would tear up or not. "So, couldn't I just get started and get on with my life?" I asked.

"Sure, Steven." He paused. "That would be fine." Larry patted me on the shoulder, nodded, and left it at that.

"Thanks," is all I could manage to say.

"I will tell you this though—"

"Yeah, what's that?"

"You are about eighty percent right and I will tell you the rest when you get in the office. Helluva job! Let me buy you a beer, what d'you say?"

I took him up on it. Then I went home and Laz and I curled up on the couch and Sequenced for the first time in months. That was the extent of my graduation party. It was a good gesture for Larry to come to my graduation like that. Nobody else there knew me as more than some guy that was in one of his or her classes. Nobody, but Larry, knew me enough to shake my hand. That's the way it had been every birthday, Thanksgiving, and Christmas since . . . The Rain. I almost cried again, so I took another pill for it.

➤ CHAPTER 5

The following Monday I went in to work and got reoriented and qualified as a full-time employee at an engineering pay scale. When I got through with all the paperwork, by lunchtime, Larry took me into a room with a combination lock on the door.

"Steve, sign this here and date it here," he told me and handed me a clipboard and pen.

"Okay, there. What is this room?"

"We call this, depending on the meeting, a SAP/SAR (special access program/special access required) room or a SCIF (sensitive compartmented information facility). I'll explain it once we are inside. Do you have a cell phone or beeper or anything?"

"Nope," I assured him.

He put the clipboard back on the wall, and turned over

an eight-inch green door magnet that said CLOSED over to the red side that said OPEN. The magnet made a metal clanging metal sound when stuck to the door. "After you." He motioned his right hand to the door.

We got inside the room and he closed the door behind us. He walked over to a tote board on the other side of the room and pulled down a sign that said THIS ROOM IS NOW CLASSIFIED SAP/SAR and then he sat down. There was nothing fancy about the room. It was just a normal-looking conference room with cheap government-issue furniture, whiteboards on each side, and a large flat-screen television panel at the end. Larry turned the television on and fired up the laptop at the end of the table. The laptop had red and white stickers all over it claiming that it was AUTHORIZED FOR CLASSIFIED MATERIAL. And there were a lot of letters following the words TOP SECRET at the top and bottom of the computer screen.

Larry spent an hour explaining how the classified world and protocols work and at the end of his briefing had me sign some documents stating that I knew I would go to jail, be executed, and probably burn in Hell if I divulged any classified material.

"All right," he said. "Let's take a quick bathroom break, grab a soda or something, and we will talk about your little circuit." Larry loosened his tie a little and stretched. "You think this is exciting?" He smiled and raised an eyebrow at me.

"Well, it's pretty cool so far. But, I can't wait to see what this circuit is." I nodded at it.

"We can't both go at the same time or we have to lock the room back up. So you head on to the john and then I'll go," he told me.

After the break Larry placed a disk with TOP SECRET and a bunch of numbers stamped on it into the computer. He opened up a file marked "RAM Quantum Teleportation," clicked on a slideshow, and there on the big flat screen was a picture of the circuit that I had tried to reverse engineer.

"The circuit you had wouldn't work. The chip between the laser and the CPU chips, here," he pointed at what I had labeled chip D, "it was a dummy. Also, this chip between the two CPUs served no purpose. Since it didn't actually function, this dummy circuit wasn't classified. If something don't work, there's usually no need to classify it. Besides, the parts were all common and it's the application that is the big secret here."

"Then what does it do?"

"Well, the circuit you had really wasn't much more than a fax or data relay from one I/O port to the other. I'm glad you figured that out; we've tried two other co-ops that didn't. I really believe you are the right person for this job." He nodded his satisfaction.

"Now, this circuit on the other hand, does work." A new circuit appeared on the screen. "And what it does is allow for memory and instructions in the CPU chip on the left here to be teleported at the speed of light to the CPU chip on the right. Again, it is *teleported*," he emphasized the word "teleported." "The data is quantum interfered with this input beam here, which is actually quantum connected to the input beam on the other side of the board. When the interference pattern is relayed over to and interfered with the unencoded quantum connected beam on the other side of the board, the wavefunction for the data collapses on the left side of the board and appears in the chip on the right side of the board." He paused to see if I was following him—and I wasn't.

"Uh . . . Larry, I'm not sure I know what you're talking about at all. Quantum connection? Quantum interference?" I shook my head and shrugged my shoulders.

"Don't let it fret you none, son, it's some kooky stuff here. All right, hold on." He stopped the slide show and opened up another one labeled "Clemons Briefing for President." Larry rummaged through it a few slides and must've found what he was looking for. "Okay, this is it," he said. "Way back in the early part of last century Einstein apparently had troubles with the modern theory of quantum mechanics. You see, quantum mechanics describes every single thing in the universe as some sort of probability function, or wave function. For example, you could describe yourself as a superposition of a lot of different energy waves if you were real good at math. An electron, for example, can be described as a wave function that is fairly simple, like on this slide." He pointed at a box with a sinusoidal wave pattern in it. "This is the function for an electron in a box. The function is different if there is no box. Now also assume that an electron has a value called spin. It spins about an axis either clockwise or counterclockwise. We will say that one of the states is spin Up and one of the states is spin Down."

"Yeah, I remember this from sophomore *Modern Physics for Engineers*," I interrupted him. "The electron has an equal probability that it is in either an Up or Down state and therefore the wave function must represent that."

"That's right, Steven, but it's more than just a probability. The electron actually exists in both states until you measure it to see which state it is in. The interaction of your measuring device causes one of the probability functions to collapse leaving just either a spin Up or spin Down electron. You follow?"

"This is Schroedinger's Cat right? You put the cat in a box and until you peek in the box you don't know if it's dead or alive, so quantum theory states it must be in both."

"Yep. And it is the act of making the measurement that causes the wave function to collapse into either the dead or alive state," Larry finished for me.

"So what does this have to do with teleportation and this quantum connection?"

"I'm not done yet," he said. "Now assume that you look at a pion decay. When a pion, this subatomic particle, decays it becomes an electron and a positron, and they must be in antiparallel spin states so as not to violate conservation of spin angular momentum. In other words, if the electron has a spin Up then the positron must have a spin Down and vice versa. Now, if we have not measured which particle is in which state then there is an equal probability that the electron will be in either state and the same for the positron. Therefore, you have an electron traveling along with a wave function for Up and Down spins and a positron doing the same. If we measure the electron to see which state it is in, and we find that it is in the spin Up state, then instantly, even if the positron is on the other side of the universe, the positron wave function will collapse to the spin Down state. The reason why is because the two particles came from the same quantum event and their wave functions got tangled up with each other. It is this wave function entanglement that is called the *quantum connection*."

"Okay, my brain hurts." I rolled my neck to the right then left and scratched my head. "I think I understand this, but you said Einstein had something to do with this?"

"Oh, I forgot to mention, this thought experiment is called the Einstein-Podolsky-Rosen Experiment, or most commonly the EPR experiment, because they came up with it. Einstein didn't like this instantaneous 'spooky' action and suggested this is a problem with quantum mechanics. Well, like it or not, EPR is real. It has been verified many times over. But to Einstein's credit, the reason he didn't like it was because the instantaneous events could enable signals to be sent back in time. Let's not get into that, but it turns out that statistics won't allow that to happen. You can go read about that yourself in a quantum book somewhere."

"Well, if you can't send data with it, what use is it?" I was getting more and more confused. "How deep does the rabbit hole go, Alice?" I asked.

"Curiouser and curiouser," Larry smiled. "Back in the early part of the first decade of this millennium, several experiments were conducted that enabled data transmission via EPR. An optical setup was rigged so that the photons from a laser beam were quantum connected in a special cube of a material called KD-star-P, and then split into two separate paths. The reference beam was then encoded by polarizing the photons to a spin Up or vertical Up polarization. The other beam shifted instantaneously to a spin Down or vertical Down polarization.

"Following that effort several different labs even used

EPR to teleport at the speed of light an information-encoded bunch of photons from ten or so meters across a lab. A couple experiments around 2013 even showed that atoms could be teleported across a great distance at the speed of light. Here is how it worked." Larry scrolled through the slides until he found the right one again. "Uh . . . let's see. This is the one . . . a beam of photons are entangled or 'connected' inside a laser and then split and sent down separate paths." He pointed out the red laser beams with the little handheld pointer connected to the mouse. The mouse pointer on the screen would move wherever he pointed the hand wand. My guess was that it was like a light gun for a video game; a thought which distracted me for just a moment.

He continued, "Now each of these photons in the beams are quantum connected to each of the photons in the other path. The left beam here is interfered with another optical beam that is encoded with data. Now the data contains much more information than say a single RAM chip might hold, say a terabit of data, and it would require a lot of energy and time to transfer a terabit of data. But the interference beam it makes when imposed on the quantum connected beam is just a few kilobits. We pump that low bandwidth interfered beam over to the other connected beam here on the right. When the two beams are interfered together in the right way, *bang!* The encoded photons disappear on the left side and appear on the right side! This allows us to send huge amounts of data from one storage device or memory chip to another through a puny low-bandwidth optical fiber. Cool, huh!"

"You mean that really works? Sounds too good to be

true, man, we could make a computer without low-bandwidth wire or optical connections that could operate at like a terahertz or much faster than that!" This stuff was exciting.

"Now you understand, Steve ol' boy. The problem is that we haven't figured out how to make good use of it just yet. In order for this to be useful, you have to be able to do calculations and instructions on the data right there in the memory location. It would slow the machine way down if you had to pump the bits to be operated on from the memory to the processor and back and forth through wires. Since the CPUs can only use a few kilobits per register it would be like filling up a five-gallon bucket with a cup. It would just take too long." I laughed that he just used the same analogy that I had used for my final exam and told him as much.

"Let me get this straight," I said. "The bottleneck here is actually being able to manipulate a lot of data in parallel. One CPU can't work on a terabyte of data all at once. Is that the problem?" I was beginning to understand why this was too good to be true.

Larry was smiling again. "You catch on quick, Stevie. Yep, that's the problem in a nutshell. If all we had to do was move data around this would be awesome fast. But we might want to add or multiply or something to that data sometimes. We need to be able to work on all the data at once in parallel."

We continued to bat around these ideas for a couple hours, occasionally taking bathroom and soda or coffee breaks. We finally finished up around five-thirty or so and decided to give it a rest. We packed up the classified room and put the disk back in the safe. Larry showed me how to get in and out of the safe. Then I grabbed my stuff from my desk. I had paperwork for my new pay grade and new insurance and benefits packages. I also took home a handful of technical journal papers that Larry gave me on EPR. One paper particularly caught my eye. It was entitled "Experimental Detection of Entanglement with Polarized Photons" and had been written by a bunch of Italian people. I planned to read it later that evening after walking Lazarus.

That day was a lot to absorb. I wasn't quite sure why the effort was Top Secret but it was. When I had asked about that, Larry just shrugged and told me that I didn't have a need to know that yet. But he did tell me that my job was to make the technology useful. Cool job, I thought. I could be instrumental in the development of the fast-est, most powerful computer ever built. Wow!

Then my stomach growled and I remembered that the fridge at home was empty. So, I stopped and grabbed some burgers for Laz and me on the way home. Laz, as always, was happy to see me. I set the burgers on the counter and patted him on the head. Then I debated on a beer or a pill. I went with the beer. The next thing I knew it was seven-forty-six and Laz was licking me on the face and my beer was still in my hand.

"Damn, I must've dozed off. I guess I should take those pills a little more regularly, huh buddy." I scratched his white belly and he whined at me and kicked his hind legs like dogs do.

I got up and heated us up a couple hamburgers. We ate dinner and then went for a walk, happier than I had felt in a long while.

CHAPTER 6

A couple of months passed before I made any headway at all on the Quantum Connected CPUs. I spent weeks on the Framework, in chat rooms, newsgroups, and downloading books on quantum mechanics, statistics, EPR experiments, Bell's Inequality, Schroedinger's Cat, and the effects of measurements on quantum phenomena. It turns out that although people had been trying to do quantum teleportation and such in experiments, nobody had really put it together with computing. It seemed kind of obvious to me once I was educated on the subject. Larry told me that that is "typical of classified projects." After all, isn't it pretty damned obvious that if you don't want the surface of your aircraft to reflect radar back at the radar then you should minimize the surface area that the radar aperture sees? Maybe it wasn't, since the stealth technologies were unheard of for years. But, now that the cat is out of the bag, it's useless. Larry also had told me something that Heinlein, this science fiction author that I had never heard of, had written. Heinlein had once said something like "a secret weapon must be just that, a secret." It makes sense when you think about it. Larry then acted appalled and frightened that I had never heard of Heinlein, and then threatened to fire me if I didn't complete a book of his per month until I had read them all.

"Consider this a reading assignment for your job, Steven. Sooner or later it'll become clear why I want you to read any and all science fiction you can get your hands on. Start with Heinlein," Larry told me.

At any rate, we finally made some headway on the Quantum Connected CPUs (or QCCPUs as we had begun to call them). I had remembered something from a class on Computational RAM and Intelligent Parallel Processing that gave me a hint.

There have been a few companies to attempt to create RAM chips that had miniature processors at each RAM block of memory. The processors would conduct the computation or data crunching in place at each memory location on the RAM chip itself rather than on a separate large processor chip. The problem is that the data must be massively parallel and so must the problem for such chips to be useful. As a solution to the massive parallel problem these companies had then tried to add some artificial intelligence to each of the processors within the RAM to help break the problem down into more separate and parallel parts. If you just wanted to add a simple sequence of numbers together, this type of computer gained you some speed. The artificial intelligence would teach itself to break up the numbers into sections that would make use of having multiple memory slots and multiple processors like the following example:

RAM1	RAM2	RAM3	
1+2= 3	3+4= 7	5+6= 11	1 CPU clock cycle
3+7= 10			2 CPU clock cycles
10 + 11= 21			3 CPU clock cycles.

The sequential calculation without breaking the problem up and with only one RAM slot and one processor would look like:

RAM1	
1+2 = 3	1 CPU clock cycle
3+3 = 6	2 CPU clock cycles
6+4 = 10	3 CPU clock cycles
10+5 = 15	4 CPU clock cycles
15+6 = 21	5 CPU clock cycles

which is two clock cycles longer. So you see where the AIs on the chip and the multiple processors might help. The typical AI for problems like this were genetic algorithms and fuzzy logic. Sometimes people used neural networks to do the problem devolving and re-evolving, but I had a different idea. I decided to put a team of Agents on the job.

With the advent of the Framework and even before, Agents had become the industry standard approach for controlling large problems without necessarily placing the user in the loop. Of course, the best Agents could talk to the user through some interface or other. If you are not certain what I am talking about when I say an Agent, then you haven't been paying attention to computer stuff for about thirty years. That favorite search engine you use on the Web utilizes Agents. The Agents crawl around from one website to another making decisions on if this website has your information parameters in it and to what level of confidence. Now these are simple agents. Real Agents are actually persistent pieces of software that are completely dedicated to a specific purpose. One of the early real Agents, that I recall anyway, was called the *SodaBot Agent* and was invented by a guy at MIT's AI Lab. I believe that guy's name was Michael Coen or something like that. Well, he was developing his *SodaBot* code to be a program that could engage in negotiations and dialog with a system, and coordinate the transfer and exchange of information between systems.

A perfect science fiction example of this is Agent Smith from *The Matrix*. Agent Smith was simply a bit of software code whose total purpose was to look for anomalies and stop them no matter what. He had enough intelligence to carry out his function and he could definitely engage in "negotiations" and "exchange" information (or gunfire, which in *The Matrix* was just information packets).

Well, I decided to create my own bunch of little Agent Smiths and *SodaBots*. I had built smaller agent-type programs before but never a real Agent. I spent several weeks reverse programming Agents that I downloaded from the Framework before I decided on the right type and features that my team of SuperAgents would have. I finished the code for one SuperAgent, copied it once, and then confined each copy to the input of a respective CPU and RAM on each side of the QCCPU. In other words, there would be a SuperAgent on each side of the Quantum Connection to engage in and coordinate the transfer of the proper information to the proper mini-processors and RAM locations.

Two months later and I was demonstrating my two-hundred-billion-terraflop computer on a single board the size of an index card, which only used about a tenth of a watt of power, to Larry and his boss in the SAP/SAR room, where it was always kept now.

"Jesus, Larry, is this real?" Dr. Jack Frehley asked Larry.

"Well, Jack, as far as I can tell our boy here has done it. I have tried giving that damned thing complex tensor math calculations and had the answer about as fast as I could type the damned question. Steve's done it, I believe." Larry was as proud of me as ever and it made me feel good. Not sure what the protocol in the conversation was, I kept quiet.

"Well, Mr. Montana what do you have to say about this?"

"I agree with Larry. Uh . . . I have not been able to do a problem or code on it yet that didn't give the right answer on the other end. Of course that isn't an exhaustive check. Somebody better at math than I am should try to find a proof or something that shows it works every time." I was pretty sure it would work every time, but not completely sure. The SuperAgents could theoretically make mistakes, but I hadn't figured out how to force them to.

Then the conversation got a little weird for me. It was obvious that I was on the outside of its true meaning and would not be given the complete meaning of what Larry and Dr. Frehley were discussing.

"Jack, I've already put in the visit request," Larry told him. "I think we need to demo this thing to them as soon as possible."

"Yeah, I agree with you. Just once I would like to solve something before that damned General Clemons or the Doctors Daniels do," Frehley responded.

"The problem we've got is, Steve isn't baptized yet." Larry said that and nodded to the SAP/SAR sign. My guess was that he was talking about my security clearance level. But I had a Top Secret clearance, what else did I need?

"Larry, as I've told you before, if you invent a batch of Unobtanium, then those guys will get you cleared. It's just a matter of signing the right forms and such. Get him over there to see them." Dr. Frehley emphasized that he wanted us to get this demo done as soon as possible. All I got out of that part of the conversation was something about a general, a person named Clemons, and two people named Dr. Daniels. I had no idea where I was going, but I was gonna get there next week.

Larry and I locked everything up and he told me to follow him to his office.

"Alice," Larry called the secretary as we passed her desk. "Could you get Steve and myself plane tickets and hotel reservations at Alexandria, Virginia, for Wednesday and Thursday of next week?"

"You want to fly into Reagan National and stay at your usual place I assume." She looked over her glasses at us.

"That's right. Oh, and we'll need a car," Larry reminded her.

We spent the rest of the afternoon discussing logistics of the trip but not where we were going to go. Then Larry made a few calls and we had to change our plans.

"Well, Stevie my friend, looks like we might get you cleared after all. That was the security guy up there, and you're going to go a day early and answer a few questions and get a briefing or two. Don't worry about the details. I'll go with you and make sure you get around all right. After all, D.C. is a big place if you've never been there before, and I wouldn't want you wandering off down the wrong street after dark, or hell, in the day for that matter."

I was surprised that our nation's capital city had bad streets in it. You would think that, at least for appearance's sake, our capital city would be safe, and that we would dare anybody to commit a crime there. I got on the Framework and looked it up, and I couldn't believe it, but just about two miles and a half northeast from the White House, and even less than that from the Capitol Building, is a drug-lord infested neighborhood with an extremely horrible crime rate. As Americans, we should be ashamed of that; I was appalled.

I had never been to Washington, D.C., before and I still had no idea who we were going to see, where we would see them (other than D.C.), and why all the hush-hush, but I guess I would find out soon enough. And what was I going to do about Lazarus for two days?

Once I got home, Lazarus and I repeated our evening ritual. I popped a couple of "happy pills" and took him for a walk. After the walk we ate and I had a beer, but something just didn't feel right. I was nervous about leaving the little guy for two or three days. I knew that my veterinarian had a great kennel, but still, it made me nervous. I could just imagine how parents must feel when they leave their kids at daycare for the first time. Lazarus was the only real family I had had since . . . The Rain.

The thought of leaving Laz at the kennel just continued to snowball with me all night long. I eventually started crying and hugging him and petting him fiercely. Laz just licked my face a time or two and then put his chin in my lap. I cried some more and tugged on his ears and scratched his tickle spot. Laz kicked his hind leg and wagged his tail feverishly. Obviously, I should've taken three pills.

After that night I decided two things. One was that I had to put Laz in the kennel and get over it, and the other was that I was going to get the strength of my prescription increased. I didn't want to start the crying again. I had been doing so well for the past several months. I must've crashed from the depression over Laz and the kennel, because when the alarm went off at six-thirty the next morning I slapped the noisy thing off and raised up in bed. I pulled the covers back and placed my feet on the floor and then . . .

I must've just really crashed. At about nine-fifteen I finally woke back up with Lazarus licking my face and whimpering at me. Since my depression hit after . . . The Rain . . . there had been a few times when that had happened, and it usually occurred when I was about to become immune to the drugs.

When I got to the office, I told Larry that I had car trouble and he just kidded me about the old Cutlass.

"You make decent money now, Steve. Why don't you trade that thing in and get a new vehicle?"

"Hey, you know Larry, it just never really occurred to me. Hmm . . . can I take the rest of the day off?" I decided he was right. What was my salary doing for me just sitting in my savings account? I never did anything, went anywhere, or bought much. Why not?

"Don't get hornswaggled, son. You ever bought a new car before?" Larry asked.

"Uh, no, just the Cutlass and it was old then." I laughed.

"Oh my God, they will eat you alive. Hold on, I'm going with you. Alice, Steven and I will be out the rest of the afternoon," he yelled out his door. "Just let me shut this thing down and grab my coat." He clicked off his laptop and that was that.

We were going to buy me a new vehicle simply because I had been afraid to mention my bout of depression the night before. Oh well, I was beginning to want a new car anyway. All this new car talk had given me the fever. I ended up getting a middle of the road sports utility vehicle. I thought it would be easy for Laz and me to get around in it. Perhaps we would have to get out more.

> **CHAPTER 7**

We flew right over the Mall and I saw the Capitol building, the Washington Monument, the Lincoln Memorial, the Jefferson Memorial, and the White House. Larry had to point out everything but the Capitol building. Then we turned down the Potomac River and set down at Reagan Washington National Airport. Larry led me through the airport like it was a second home to him. Instead of following the signs downstairs to the street where rental car busses pick you up, we went up a ramp to some elevators.

"Yeah, most people don't realize that the rental cars are just right over there on the other side of the parking garage," Larry said as he was fumbling through his laptop case. "And they'll wait for thirty minutes on that damn bus that just takes them on a one-minute ride. Ah, here it

67

is. Our confirmation number for the rental car." He showed me a printout he pulled from his pack.

We went up a couple of floors on the elevator and then walked about fifty meters or so through the garage and turned a corner right into the rental car area. We walked up to a red Cadillac and Larry whistled. "Hey, let's take this one."

"Okay." He was pointing and driving at the same time. "This is Crystal City here and we are going to take the G.W. Parkway from here, south, all the way down to Old Town Alexandria. It's not that far and we could've taken the Metro, but we can't ride the Metro where we need to go tomorrow and I didn't want to deal with a cab." His cell phone rang about that time. "Hello."

It must have been his wife, because he carried on one of those married guy conversations.

"Yes, honey . . . no . . . we are just now leaving the airport. Steve, she says hi." He nodded to me.

"Uh, hi?" I had never met her before.

"No, I . . . Hold on. . . . No, tell her I will help her with it this weekend. Hey, we'll be at the hotel in ten minutes. Let me call you back then. Okay, uh, okay, uh, I love you too. Bye."

I tried not to giggle but I did. "Everything okay at home?"

"Sure. My daughter needs help with a computer project for school and, well, my wife worries when I fly." He changed lanes, cutting in front of a Yellow Cab; the cabby honked at us. "Look, as I was saying, this road southward pulls right up into Mount Vernon, you know, George Washington's house. We'll go north on it tomorrow to get up to McLean."

"What's in McLean?" I asked

"You'll see tomorrow. But tonight I was thinking that we would leave the car at the hotel and after the free beer and snacks they have there we will get on the Blue Line on the Metro and I'll take you over to the Mall and show you D.C. The King Street Metro stop is right across the street from our hotel. What d'ya say?"

"Free beer and snacks? I say cool."

We checked into the hotel with plenty of time to relax a few minutes before the free beer started. After several free beers too many, I felt the need to tell Larry how much I appreciated all that he had done for me.

"You know," I told him. "You are probably the only human that I have had a real lengthy conversation with, other than my shrink, in more than three years."

"Damn Steve, that's pretty sad, son. Why don't you get out more?" he asked.

"I don't know. I just haven't felt like I had that much of a connection to anybody. I mean, you know, everyone I ever really knew is gone. Even all the records of their existence are gone. It really makes you feel, well uh, small and disconnected from the rest of the world. You know?"

"Must be tough. You want another round?"

"Suits me! I'll grab some more pretzels and popcorn," I offered. When he left for the bar I realized that I had not taken my medicine yet.

The conversation was weighing on me considerably, and it probably was Larry as well. So I told Larry I had to take a leak and darted up to my room. I popped one of the "happy pills" and actually did take a leak, and then rejoined the party.

A few beers later the drugs were kicking in and I was

feeling happier. We talked about video games and football and women. It turns out that Larry is a pretty decent fellow. We went over to the Metro stop across the street after last call, which was at seven-thirty, and Larry showed me around D.C. a bit.

We got back to the hotel about ten-thirty and I walked into the room and flipped the television on. I really had to take a leak so I went straight to the bathroom and set the remote on the sink countertop. Then . . .

I didn't remember sitting down to watch television. The last thing that I recalled was taking a leak. The news channel was on and the volume was way too low to hear. I looked around for the remote and couldn't seem to find it anywhere. The last I remembered was that I took it to the bathroom with me. I got up and checked and there it was by the sink, right where I remembered setting it. Weird. Another side effect of these damn pills must be memory gaps. I sat back down on the couch and started to change the channel, but then I noticed the time in the upper left-hand corner under the news channel logo. It was two-twenty-six in the morning.

"Jesus, I better go to bed," I told myself.

The next morning we were at the complementary breakfast buffet about eight-thirty, and I had way too many pancakes and way too many link sausages. We were refreshed and on the road by nine. Larry took the G.W. Parkway north and we went up past the airport, through Crystal City, and every inch of the way there was something interesting to see.

"If you look right over there, you will see the Pentagon." Larry nodded to the west with his head. "And over there is the Iwo Jima Memorial that is so famous. We'll come back on the other side of the Pentagon so you can get a better look at stuff."

We drove past about three different famous bridges. Just past the bridges and still on the G.W. Parkway we entered an area tht looked like a park. There was a river on the right side of the road with a jogging trail running alongside it and wooded hills on the left. About five or so miles on up northward we turned off the G.W. Parkway onto 123 at the sign that said *Chain Bridge Road/McLean.* Then, almost as soon as we turned onto 123, we had to stop at a traffic light. Just through that light was a very large green-and-white sign that read

> *George Bush Center for Intelligence*
> *CIA next right.*

We turned right. Larry drove through about fifty meters of trees and then up to a gate with a little push-button speaker at window height and rolled down his window. Before Larry had a chance to do or say anything the speaker buzzed, "Can I help you?"

"Uh, yes, Larry Waterford and Steven Montana here for a meeting." Larry looked a little nervous.

"Pull right and park in front of the guard center, then come inside. Have your identification and rental car registration available please." The guy on the other end was all business. No howdy, nice to see ya, please come back or anything.

The guard shack was a typical guard shack, as far as I could tell. The fellows behind the desk were packing serious heat and were all wearing rent-a-cop-type outfits.

Larry and I filled out a couple forms, showed off our driver's licenses, and then Larry and the guard discussed clearance transfers and stuff that I wasn't quite sure I understood. They handed us each a badge; Larry's was a different color than mine. He didn't tell me why.

A few minutes later our point of contact on the inside of CIA Headquarters called the guard shack and told them we could come in and which building to drive to. We parked where we were told and then walked what seemed to be about a damn mile across the campus and through a parking garage before we got to the main building.

Inside the main building was exactly like you see in the movies. There was a big Central Intelligence Agency symbol in the middle of the floor under a huge skylight. Larry showed me the memorial with no names on it. It was all like I had seen it before; I guess I had, on television. There was even a gift shop. I started to buy a CIA shot glass, but Larry told me that I couldn't acknowledge that I had been there.

Then we went through the metal detectors and swiped our badges. The guard there informed Larry that he or another cleared individual would have to escort me wherever I went. Larry affirmed that he knew that.

Larry left me with an "examiner" and said he would be back later. The rest of the morning was me answering a bunch of questions—questions I'm not supposed to repeat—both written and verbally, inside a special room. Then I took a polygraph exam and that seemed to last forever. A few hours of that and Larry returned. We then reversed the process we had been through that morning and left CIA for the day.

"What'd you think about that?" he grinned.

"That was pretty neat. We're coming back here tomorrow, right?"

"Yep. We'll eat lunch there at the cafeteria. That is always a hoot. Tomorrow we will be here all day. Hey, we got the rest of the afternoon off; you want to see Robert E. Lee's house and the Tomb of the Unknown Soldier?"

"Got nothing else to do," I replied.

The next day was the same process. We went up the G.W. to McLean and so on. Again I was given a different color badge than Larry was.

"Clearance takes time, Steve. Don't fret it," Larry assured me. Unfortunately, the weather was not as good as it had been the day before and the long walk from the parking lot was more of a trot. We did maximize our path through the parking garage to stay out of the rain as much as possible.

The same guard told Larry the same thing about having to escort me. So Larry told him the same thing in response, "I know."

This time we didn't go to the same place Larry took me the day before. Today we went down several different hallways and I was completely lost. We finally got to a room just down the hall from a big sign saying *Directorate of Science and Technology* and there was a person waiting for us at the door.

We were told where the restrooms were and shown the vending machines. Larry got a cup of coffee so I followed suit. A few moments passed and the young lady at the door told us we could go in. Larry paused to speak with her.

"The package we sent up here, is it in there already?"

Larry shrugged his shoulders, then straightened his tie.

"Yes, Mr. Waterford, the papers and slides you sent are here and are already in there." She pointed her pen behind her at the door.

"Thanks." He turned to me, "Okay, Steve, jump in whenever, but don't make a nuisance of yourself. If we ask you to step out for a bit, don't be upset; it will just be necessary. Got it?" He pointed to my tie and motioned to fix it.

"Okay. I got it." I fixed my tie and my shirttail.

Then we entered the SCIF.

➤ CHAPTER 8

"So that is how we got the QCCPUs to teleport data back and forth between each other," I summarized. The Air Force general, General Clemons, seemed very intrigued throughout my presentation. I could've sworn that I'd seen her somewhere before. She looked to be in her mid to late forties, was very athletic looking, and had bright strawberry-red hair. She spoke in a Southern accent of some sort. I didn't know that they made attractive generals.

"Jim, what do you think of this?" General Clemons asked.

"Well, if you ask me, and you did," Dr. Daniels replied, "it's a damned shame that we only were told about all this a short time ago or we would have been at least this far already! I can even perceive us having prevented the war with knowledge of a larger threat to force us to act together instead of against each other." Dr. Jim Daniels oozed confidence in himself, probably because he was handsome and, from the looks of it, extremely physically fit, with a chiseled jaw and short crop of sandy brown hair. I wouldn't have pegged him for some kind of super genius.

Then one of the other suits in the room interrupted. "Harumph, uh, Dr. Daniels please let me remind you that this conversation is at Top Secret only!"

"Hunh?" Dr. Daniels then turned back to me and nodded at the other fellow. "Oh, yeah right. Sorry, Phillip." He turned his attention back to the general, "Well, Tabitha, I would say this is it. I'm not exactly sure how the SuperAgents will apply, but now that we know how to do it, we can figure out how to undo it. I still would like to get 'Becca and Anson's opinions on it, though."

"We'll brief them when they return next week," the general assured him, and scribbled something in her notepad.

The fellow Phillip turned to me. "Mr. Montana, do you think you could show Dr. Daniels here how to recreate and modify, if needs be, your so-called SuperAgent code?"

"Uh, well I don't see why not. But if you're trying to reverse engineer something, I think I would be able to help more by, well, uh, helping." I was hoping to make my point. I wasn't sure who any of these folks were and I sure wasn't about to just give over my SuperAgent code without a fight of some type.

The general laughed. "Jim, I don't think he believes you have the wherewithal to undo his code." There were chuckles from the rest of the room.

"No ma'am," I replied. "I didn't mean to imply that at all. I just—"

"Relax son, I'm just trying to get Jim's goat." She smiled and adjusted the lock of red hair on her forehead. I could tell she was covering a very faint scar with her bangs. She turned to another Air Force officer; she, I assumed, was her aide although I did notice that both she and the general had wings on their lapels and they each wore an insignia patch displaying a missile inside a blue and red sphere with a big blue W^2 embroidered on it. Not to mention that they looked a lot alike. "Lieutenant Ames," she said.

"Ma'am." The young redheaded lieutenant snapped to.

"I think we can show the abridged presentation now." General Clemons nodded and then turned to look across the table. "Wouldn't you agree, Phillip?" That last sounded more like an order rather than a question. It was my understanding that the Phillip fellow was in charge, but this female general seemed to be getting her way when she wanted it.

"Uh, okay Tabitha. Only the 'abridged' version though." Phillip overemphasized the word abridged.

"Roger that," Clemons said. "Okay, Lieutenant. It's all yours."

"Yes, ma'am. Jim, could you back me up when I get stumped please." Lieutenant Ames sounded humble as she approached the front of the room and tugged on her uniform jacket.

"Annie, I think you will be just fine," Dr. Daniels replied and chuckled. I found it very interesting that all of these people acted as though they had known each other for years. It was almost as if they were family. Our group wasn't like that, it seemed to me.

Lieutenant Annie Ames pointed to the screen. "Okay, here on the first slide is the device." Ames pointed to a photo of an emerald-colored cube-shaped chunk of glass with several orange smaller cubes within it. "We believe these smaller orange cubes might be the intelligent processor components and these dark bands just beneath each of them are the RAM register input interference patterns. Until today, we had no idea how the device managed the data and the problem devolution. I would have to say that I am very impressed by Mr. Montana's effort thus far. The power inputs for the *entangled witness* beams, or as Mr. Montana had called them, *quantum connected* beams, come from here." She changed slides to a cutaway diagram of the device. "This is a scanning electron microscope image of the device. Note the false coloring we used to signify different density levels. It is possible there is something erroneous about the density measurements. Dr. Daniels will discuss this later. This bright spot here in the heart of the main cube is the *connected* light source and it appears the data information falls through here." She paused for that to sink in.

"Uh, excuse me," I interrupted, not sure if it was okay to do so.

"Yes, Mr. Montana." Lieutenant Ames cocked her head and smiled. She looked surprisingly like the general when she was "trying to get Jim's goat" I noticed.

"Yeah, sorry to interrupt, but, did you mean to say the data information, uh . . . *falls* through there?" I leaned forward in my chair, bumping into Larry's leg. "Sorry," I whispered to him.

"That is what I said and that is what I meant to say." She paused for effect. "Now as I was . . ."

"Uh, excuse me, sorry, but what do you mean *falls through?*" I interrupted her again.

Lieutenant Ames turned to General Clemons, "Ma'am?"

General Clemons turned to Phillip. "Well, Phillip?"

"No!" he said.

"Hold on a minute," Dr. Daniels interjected. He turned to me. "Steven, right?"

I nodded.

"Listen, it's just a figure of speech we've been using. Skip it. Just assume the data goes through an I/O port there in the center of the cube, okay?" Daniels was trying to give me a hint.

"Anne Marie, please continue," General Clemons said, attempting to put the questions behind them quickly.

"Yes, ma'am. Uh let's see . . . yes, here we are. The RAM appears to be continuously changing and we believe that it's encrypted in more than machine code. Decryption never seems to take place as far as we can tell."

The big fat bald gentleman sitting in the back finally acted as though he was awake and that the last statement startled him.

"It's encrypted?"

"Yes, Senator. We believe that the data sequence here that is continuously changing is encrypted data." Anne Marie paused for his response.

"Jesus Christ Almighty! It could be a listening device. How do you know that those damned things aren't eavesdropping on us right now?" He seemed almost frightened and looked around the room as if to see somebody hidden there that he hadn't noticed before.

"Okay, okay," Phillip interrupted. "That's far enough

for a second. Mr. Montana, would you mind stepping outside please? We will call you back in a bit when we can. Just wait outside." He nodded and an aide beside him led me to the door.

"Carrie, see that Mr. Montana here is taken care of please. We will call for him in a bit," the aide told the young lady at the desk outside the SCIF door.

"Sure thing, Bill," she said. The aide returned through the SCIF door back to brown-nose, uh, support his boss, and I was beginning to worry if my future was going with him. Perhaps I shouldn't have asked so many questions.

But, there was a senator in there? Who was this Phillip fellow and who were all of those people in there? The most intriguing thing was that emerald cube that had data "falling" through it and the ever-changing continuously encrypted data. And just what in the hell did the senator mean by "those damned things could be eavesdropping on us"? What damned things? I was beginning to think that not only was I falling deeper into the rabbit hole, but that I was on the other damn side of the planet from the looking glass as well.

I sat there in the reception area of the conference room, the SCIF, for some time and nobody came for me. After about an hour and a half I was getting nervous, anxious, and I was afraid I would get depressed if something didn't happen soon. Another hour later the door opened and the senator and his staffer came plowing through the lobby, signed out, and were out the door. But they jabbered the entire time.

"Bill, get me a meeting set up with the 'sissy' tomorrow. I don't care if they have to fly in from the far side of the Moon. I want them here tomorrow. I mean it.

Senators you hear me, not staffers."

"Yes, Senator. I'll make sure of that."

"I'm here to tell you, Bill, this is bad news . . . bad news. I never believed the threat was this big. The general needs more men and money and by God she better get them for all our sakes!" They finished signing out of the SCIF and trailed off down the hallway still jabbering.

Fifteen minutes later Larry came and got me. "Okay, Steve, you can come in now, but son, please, for your own sake, just keep your mouth shut and only speak if you're asked a question. You with me on this?" He patted me on the shoulder and fiddled with his tie as he always does.

"Okay, Larry. Sorry, I hope I didn't cause problems."

"Only for yourself, son." He pressed his hand against my back and led me through the SCIF door.

"Mr. Montana, we appreciate you having patience with us today. Please be seated." Phillip nodded to a chair.

I tried to make myself comfortable.

Dr. Daniels was at the screen, "So anyway, we think the material these orange things are made of is something like lithium niobate and perhaps some KD star P in the I/O port portion in the center. The black bands between the gaps are probably some sort of an optical phenomenon, but without breaking the thing open there is little way to tell. And, of course, we wouldn't want to do that, even if we knew how. The main part of the cube— well, all of our spectral analyses suggest no particularly known compound or substance, although it is possible that we are having problems making the measurements because of the quantum phenomena inside the cube."

"And go ahead and tell us your wife's theory, Jim," General Clemons said.

"Okay, 'Becca believes that the reason we can't find any particular spectra for the materials this thing is made of is because there is a fairly significant expansion of spacetime within the cube. And, worse than that, the expansion is not linear but following some polynomial expansion in the radial dimension from the center. Therefore, there would be no standard fluorescence spectra for any particular substance due to the nonlinear gravity red, uh, blue shifting inside the thing."

I couldn't resist. "What do you mean an expansion of spacetime inside the thing and why would a computer have such a thing in it?" Larry elbowed me in the ribs. I ignored him.

"Good question, Steven. Have you ever seen the ancient television show called *Dr. Who*?" he asked me.

"Never heard of it."

"Oh well, okay. Have you ever read any science fiction books by a fellow named Robert Heinlein?"

"Which one?" I returned the elbow back to Larry's ribs.

"It was the one where the little guy carried a pack around that was infinitely big on the inside, uh, what was that one called . . . oh man, would Anson ever kill me if he knew I couldn't remember that. . . ."

"*Glory Road!*" replied Larry, Lieutenant Ames, Bill the support contractor, and General Clemons all together.

"Ah yes, *Glory Road* is the one. Well, this guy had a backpack that was the size of a backpack on the outside, but the inside was large enough to place all sorts of weapons, food, medical supplies, tables and chairs, you name it. Now what if we could create a RAM chip that is expanded like that on the inside. I mean, if the RAM was the size of a normal memory chip on the outside but was *huge* on the inside. Wouldn't that allow you to store much more data on the inside than a normal chip? Wouldn't that be cool?" He paused for air.

I had to admit two things: one) that would be cool and two) I hadn't read *Glory Road* yet. I had given Larry an unwarranted elbow to the ribs, but I would rectify that sometime tonight. He never did tell me what *Dr. Who* had to do with it.

Not long after this conversation we were pretty much brain fried. All of the technology of this "cube" was way advanced and almost magical. It was obvious that these people were reverse engineering it, but then, who had built it? Did we steal it from the Russians or the Chinese? They would be the most likely candidates, but expansions in spacetime seemed too fantastic. And the biggest problem I had with this thing all day was the fact that there was only one major QCCPU. Where was its connected twin, its entangled counterpart? The board I'd worked on had to have two QCCPUs to function; it only makes sense. One fax machine just doesn't do, there must be another one . . . somewhere.

On the way back to the hotel I made Larry stop at a bookstore and I bought a paperback copy of *Glory Road*. I also asked him who all these people at the meeting were.

"Well, let's see. General Tabitha Ames Clemons is the female astronaut with the most hours in space and the leader of the W-squared group . . . don't ask . . . and the pretty young Lieutenant Ames, if you can put two and two together, is her daughter. The young lieutenant is also an astronaut, and has many hours in the Air Force's space wing." Larry paused to see if I caught that and at the same time acted as though he shouldn't have said it.

"The Air Force has a space wing?" I fell a few feet closer to Alice.

"I didn't say that." He shrugged at me as if to say, "Don't know what you are talking about." Then he continued, "Dr. Daniels there is the male half of the Dr. Daniels husband and wife team. They are two of the three most brilliant scientists the country has. You haven't met the third, or I guess I should say, first."

"Who is that, the other scientist I mean?"

"Dr. Neil Anson Clemons, astronaut and physicist and chief scientist of the W-squared group. You might recall that he and General Clemons were the only survivors of the shuttle accident a few years ago."

"That was them, but I thought the woman's name was Ames . . . oh, I get it." A ton of bricks hit me in the head.

"And let's see who else was there . . . the senator was Senator Mitchell Grayson from Iowa, former lineman in the NFL. I forget who he played for, but did you see that SuperBowl ring? That was years ago; now he is Chairman of the Senate Select Committee on Intelligence or the SSCI or 'sissy.' He is one of the most powerful men in the country."

"What about the other guy, Phillip?" I was beginning to realize the big pond full of sharks that I had been swimming in and I was a little intimidated by it. Chum came to mind.

"Oh, he was the Deputy Director for Central Intelligence, Phillip Sorenson. His boss answers directly to the President."

> **CHAPTER 9**

I was so giddy most of the night that I couldn't sleep. The things discussed in the meeting were just so unreal and exciting. I had read a major portion of the Heinlein book that had been discussed in the meeting in case it came up again. By the time the phone rang with my wakeup call, I had gone over the day's events a hundred times. I'm not sure that I ever batted an eye. I hadn't pitched or fielded any of them either. Ha.

I rushed through my morning ritual and was downstairs in the hotel restaurant area, in line at the omelet station, when Larry stepped out of the elevator. He motioned that he saw me there and proceeded through the waffle line. I found a quiet corner with a two-seat table and started in on the omelet and sausage.

"Mornin', Stevo." Larry set his tray down. "Be right

back. I need some more syrup."

I just nodded and continued to press on through the first course. I was almost ready to go back for seconds before Larry had taken his first bite.

"D'you sleep much, Stevie?" Larry asked

"Not really. I was kind of wound up after yesterday and I got into that book a good bit. How 'bout you?" I finished off my orange juice and plopped the glass down on the table a little too hard.

"Okay, I guess. I never sleep that great in hotels."

"Hey, I'm going back for round two, do you need anything while I'm up?"

"Nah, I'm all right right now," he said.

This time I decided to go for the waffles, but I also got some potatoes and bacon to go with them. I refilled my juice and also got a soda for chaser.

"This place is great, Larry," I told him as I sat down. "Free beer in the evenings and all you can eat for breakfast. Way cool."

"Ha, glad you approve Steve. I stay here every chance I get. If you can't get in here, there is another one at Crystal City, one at Tyson's Corner, and a couple of them on the other side of the Potomac. I prefer to stay in Virginia if possible though. The best thing is that they have government employee rates that match our per diem."

"I'll have to remember that," I acknowledged.

"Hey, listen, Stevo. You need to do me a favor, okay?" He set down his fork and his left hand started doing the tie thing.

"Sure, Larry, what's up?"

"I need you to skip the meetings today. You can hang out here and read or you can take the Metro into the city and catch some of the museums. But I need you to skip today is all." He seemed a bit nervous.

"Skip the meetings? Are you serious? I can't wait to go back. Why do—"

He interrupted me. "Listen, Steve. I got a call yesterday evening about nine o'clock from Phillip requesting that I leave you behind today. No big deal, it's just that you would have to sit outside the SCIF all day anyway. You might as well take the day for yourself."

"But . . ." What was I hearing?

"It's not a big thing, Steve. You aren't cleared yet. Just give it time. Hey, if you want to try and catch an earlier flight back and just leave today, feel free. I thought you might like to have a day to see the city is all."

"It's because I asked so many questions, isn't it?" I must've done something wrong; maybe I could fix it somehow.

"I don't think so," is all Larry said. "I'm gonna get some more coffee, be right back."

I sat there staring at my tray the whole minute and a half he was gone. Had I done something wrong? Did I fail my lie detector test? I couldn't have; I answered everything honestly, even about the times I smoked pot in high school. I was truthful when I said I hadn't done it in years. Oh my God, what did I do wrong? I was freaking out big time. Larry must have noticed this.

"Hey, hey, Steve! Calm down, son, there is nothing happening here but standard security procedures. Things just take time all right? Relax," he scolded me.

"Okay. You're right. Sorry. You're still flying back in the morning, right?" I shrugged and held my hands palms up.

"Yeah, nine-thirty."

"Well, if it's all the same to you, I'll just go back as planned. I wouldn't mind seeing the Natural History Museum and the Spy Museum. And another evening of free beer would be all right with me also." I was hiding my concerns. Maybe I was just overreacting.

"That's the spirit." Larry smiled. "Look, I gotta get going, so I will see you at happy hour." The persistent tie fiddling continued.

"Okay. Have a good one, Larry." I waved him off. Then I mumbled to myself, "Well hell, if I'm in no hurry I might as well have a third round at the breakfast buffet."

I changed into normal clothes, you know, jeans and a T-shirt. Did a few other morning and midday rituals, brushed my teeth, and headed out across the street to the King Street Metro. Larry showed me how the thing worked the other day and I was fairly certain I could handle it. The hotel lobby also had a rack of tourist maps that showed all the attractions and how to see them from the Metro. I took the blue line to the Smithsonian stop and walked out right into the middle of the Mall. The whole ride cost about a dollar and thirty-five cents. I walked out into the middle of the Mall and looked up Capitol Hill to the east and then turned around and looked back west and took in the sight of the Washington Monument. It was such a pretty day I decided to just sit on the park bench under a shade tree there at the Mall and read some. When I first sat down on the park bench I began to think about Lazarus and how much he would enjoy this place. There was a young lady jogging around the dirt track that makes the Mall perimeter and she was pacing along with a cute cocker spaniel, about as old as Laz I guessed. My poor buddy was in a kennel—a good one mind you—but still a kennel and not home. Missing Laz almost overwhelmed me enough to go to the airport and fly home early, but I talked myself out of it. "He will be okay for one more night," I said.

"Excuse me?" I hadn't noticed but the young lady had stopped for a breather right in front of me and she must've thought I was talking to her.

"Uh, oh I'm sorry. Your dog, uh, reminds me of mine back home. He's in a kennel 'til tomorrow and I just miss him is all," I said sheepishly.

"Hey, that's kinda sweet. What kind is he?" she asked.

"Oh, he's a one hundred percent purebred mutt," I laughed.

She led the leash over in my direction and her pup sniffed my leg. I held the back of my hand down for him to lick. Once he realized I was no threat he let me pet him and tug his ears.

"You get along with dogs pretty well it appears. Reagan seems to like you." She smiled and stood straight, stretching her neck and arms. "Well, it was nice meeting you. I'm going to finish my run now."

"Oh, sorry to interrupt, bye Reagan," I called to her as she and Reagan trotted off. "That tears it. Damn it all to hell." I stood up, ready to go pack and head to the airport. I walked about five steps and then stopped. "Damn, what should I do?" I decided to call and see if there were any flights back to Dayton, so I found the nearest pay phone. One of these days I've got to get a cell. Fortunately, I had been using my itinerary for a bookmark and the travel agent one-eight-hundred number was on there. It turned out that I couldn't get back to the airport in Dayton until five-thirty, which was about the same time the kennel closed. No way I would make it to Laz tonight. "So that solves that," I told myself.

A post-Rain storm came through about one P.M., so I took in the Smithsonian Museums along the Mall and then went to the Spy Museum. I also hailed a cab and rode up Capitol Hill to the backside of the Capitol building and saw the Supreme Court and the Library of Congress. Then I had the cabby drop me at the closest Metro and I went back to King Street and the hotel.

Later that evening Larry and I had the free beer and then walked down King Street all the way to the river. We stopped and ate dinner at one of the seafood shops along the way. I asked Larry about the meetings and my status and so on. He just told me not to ask. Then we talked about the sights that I had seen. The Library of Congress specifically intrigued Larry. He said he had never been there before.

I finished *Glory Road* on the plane back to Dayton and went from the airport straight to the kennel. I'm not sure who was happiest to see whom, but Laz and I hugged each other dearly. He licked my face and whimpered at me a time or two.

"Good boy!" I told him. "I missed you, buddy, d'you miss me?" I tugged at his ears and stroked his back. "Sit fella, sit." He sat and allowed me to put his leash on. Then we loaded up in the SUV and were off to the apartment.

I didn't bother to unpack and we went for a long walk first thing. We stopped in the park by the local high school and played Frisbee some, and then we went back to the apartment and sprawled out on the couch together. Laz laid his chin on my lap and I stroked his fur between his ears, gently, until we went to sleep. I belonged there, I missed Laz, and he missed me; my only real connection to the entire damned planet. Oh, sure I had grown a little closer to Larry Waterford, but it was in an employer to employee relationship. That just isn't the same. I couldn't cry on Larry's shoulder and hug him for reassurance that things would be okay. Laz didn't mind at all, and I loved him for it.

➤ CHAPTER 10

When I went back to the office the next day Larry gave me a new task that was completely unrelated to the quantum connected computer project. He gave me a Chinese rocket computer operating system and wanted me to learn how to talk to it. It was boring, hum-drum stuff. It wasn't much harder than Sequencing that old video game that I did for Larry so long ago. I would ask Larry about the project on a daily basis and it seemed to annoy him a bit. He would always tell me that I couldn't be told anything and that I shouldn't think about it anymore until the clearance comes through. So, of course, then I would ask, "Well, when will my clearance come through?"

"When it comes, Steven. That's all I can tell you."

"Well, I thought they needed my help with the SuperAgent code?" I would ask.

"I don't know any more than you do." He would fiddle with his tie and then change the subject. He would always seem irked that I wasn't focused on the current busywork project he had given me.

So, I worked on reverse engineering some of the most benign devices you could imagine by day and then went home and sat with Lazarus by night. The drugs had begun to diminish in effect against the depression again and occasionally I would wake up and not realize hours had passed. But good ol' Lazarus would always be there to help me through it. I would hug him and sob some and tell him that he was my buddy. That seemed to help almost as much as the drugs did.

Then, in a morning-depressed haze, I would go into work for more run-of-the mill reverse engineering busywork. I reverse engineered a tank turret control computer, ejection code for a French fighter plane, the reaction control system of a recovered satellite (although I never figured out how the satellite had been recovered), and I was working on a radio jamming device found in North Korea nearly six months later. Don't get me wrong; some of the work was challenging, but nothing like the reverse engineering of that magical green and orange quantum cube device. The biggest depressing fact was that after more than six months, there was still no clearance.

One day I was so bored I thought I would go further out of my mind, so I sloughed off work and I went surfing on the Framework instead. My office hook-up wasn't as fast as at home but I didn't feel like measuring voltages on a Russian computer motherboard. So I logged on and started to look up that Dr. Who fellow. It didn't take long for me to figure out the reason that Dr. Daniels had brought him up. That guy was some very old British television character who apparently lives in a phone booth, or whatever the British call it. On the outside it looks like a regular phone booth, but on the inside it is large enough for a very comfortable apartment. It is explained as some sort of space warp or something. Just like the "warped" RAM chips Dr. Daniels's wife had theorized.

I was still on the Framework when the phone rang. Finally, Larry called me into his office for a chat; I hoped every time the phone rang that it was about my clearance. This time it was.

"Steve, we need to talk."

"Yeah, what about?" I hoped this was it. After all, it had been nearly seven months since we had been to Washington, D.C.

"Sorry, Steve, but your advanced clearance has been declined," he said and looked down at his feet for second. My heart fell to my shoes.

"Why? I mean, I told the truth about everything. I . . . I . . . don't understand, I'm a good American, aren't I?"

"Son, nobody really believes otherwise." He paused. "Except that . . ." He stopped again.

"Except what?"

"Well, son, as far as your background investigation is concerned, you just suddenly appeared in Dayton, Ohio, at about the age of eighteen. There is no proof that you ever existed before that. No hospital records, not any living witnesses that can say you are the same kid that came out of your mother's birth canal, nothing. In fact, the only proof to corroborate your life is that your parents' tax records can be found and that they paid taxes on a dependent."

"So, there you go; I was their dependent," I argued.

"No, son, there is no evidence that it was you. Oh sure, they filed a social security number for you when you were nine, but there are no pictures, no birth certificates, no DNA samples, nothing."

"But . . . but I can't help that. The Rain killed them! The Rain killed them *all*! Don't you understand? There is nothing I can do about that!" I was frantic.

"Calm down, Steven! I understand. But you have to understand that this is the perfect approach for a mole or a spy to infiltrate our nation's security. Conveniently, all the records were erased and some guy moves in and becomes Steven Montana. How do we know that you were not killed during the meteors? People don't realize this, because on the surface and in public, the world looks as though it is getting along famously and friendly now. We are all banding together after the disaster and gelling as one race. It looks that way on television, but in the real world espionage and counterespionage are at an all-time high. The FBI, CIA, and Homeland Defense agents have caught literally hundreds of moles trying to take identities of victims from the meteor disaster."

"*No!* I am me. *I am me!*"

"Steven, calm down, son! I know you are you and that you are a good guy. But I can't prove it. Nobody can. Since you passed the lie detector, you can maintain your current clearance level, but you can't go any higher and you have to forget anything and everything you heard in D.C." He pulled a form out of his desk and handed me a pen. "Read this and sign it."

I read it. It basically told me that I had never heard of quantum connected CPUs, funny-colored cubes that data falls through, Air Force Group W-squared, SuperAgents, and anything else related to that CIA meeting. Then it said that I would suffer penalty of up to life imprisonment if I ever divulged any of it to anybody. "Are you telling me that I never invented my SuperAgent?"

"Sorry, son, your computer has just been confiscated and your machine at home is being cleaned."

"What! You can't do that. I invented it; it's mine! Do you hear me? Its mine!"

"No, son, the U.S. Department of Defense paid for it, so it is theirs. This is the way it has to go, Steven."

"No, but you don't understand." I was still no calmer. "I can't just not work on it now that I know how to do it. I can't!"

"Steven, you can and you will, or you will go to jail. I want you to take a couple of days' administrative leave and go home and think this through before you say or do anything harsh. But you have to sign this form right now."

"And what if I don't?" I defiantly suggested.

"Steven, don't do this. If you don't sign this now, I have to notify DSS and in a matter of minutes there will be a warrant out for your arrest for violation of the National Security Act."

I was lost, cornered, screwed, stabbed in the back, and just generally fucked! I grabbed the pen from Larry and signed the form. "Larry, you can go to hell!" I turned and walked through his door and slammed it as hard as my two hundred forty pounds would muster. I heard pictures fall from the wall on the other side and fall to the floor and break with the clash of glass shattering.

Then I turned back to the door, "I DIDN'T ASK FOR

THE GODDAMNED METEORS TO KILL EVERY-
BODY I KNOW, YOU SORRY SON OF A BITCH! YOU
CAME TO ME, REMEMBER. I HELPED YOU! I'M
A GOOD AMERICAN! ITS NOT FAIR . . ." Tears were
flowing down my cheeks; I turned back toward the hall
and rushed out. "It's not fair," I cried all the way home. It
wasn't fair, goddamnit.

They stole my SuperAgents. There, I thought about it,
you bastards gonna come arrest me? Come on then!
"SuperAgents, SuperAgents, SuperAgents, SuperAgents,
quantum connected computer, quantum connected computer, SuperAgents . . . Fuck you!" I screamed at the
windshield and repeated the process several times over
all the way home. "I'll say SuperAgents if I want to,
damnit!"

I got to my apartment and there were cop cars, several
black sedans, and an Animal Control vehicle. "Oh my God,
Lazarus!" I ran up stairs and there were two cops standing at my door to block my way and I could see men in
my apartment tearing it to pieces. There was also blood
on the floor.

"Hold it, son. What is your business here?" one of the
cops asked.

"I'm not your son! And I live here. Lazarus, here boy."
I whistled for him and tried to push through the door.
The cop that called me his son clubbed me in the head
with his nightstick. I zoned out for a second and fell to
my knees, but I could still hear.

"Jesus, Tony, what'd you hit him for?" the other cop
asked.

"Hey, you heard the Feds. Nobody gets in until they
are done."

"Yeah, but did you have to hit him? He's just worried about his poor dog."

I regained full awareness and consciousness a few seconds later. I rose up and the one cop who had clubbed me put his hand on his pistol. "Wait, please, officer. Please, I don't want any trouble. I just want to see my dog. Where is he, please, tell me?"

The other cop stepped in between us and gave his partner a stern look. "Come with me." He led me downstairs to the Animal Control van, then nodded to the man leaned up against the back door of the van smoking a cigarette.

"Open it up, Charlie," the cop told him.

The man held his cigarette between his lips and opened the door of the van. There was Lazarus. There . . . was . . . Lazarus . . . dead. He was lying there in the van in a black plastic bag. I had to pull the plastic back to look at him. I sobbed deeply and loudly. "Oh my God, Lazarus. Puppy, what did they do to you?" I fell to my knees and bawled and hugged the puppy to my head and sobbed some more. It was more than I could take, and it wasn't fair.

"WHY! He's just a dog." I hugged him harder and cried deeper. "Why did you have to kill him?"

"Hold it there. I didn't kill him. The Feds had to put him down because he attacked one of them and wouldn't let go," the Animal Control man explained and then stamped his cigarette butt out on the ground.

"Of course he did, you dumbass! They broke into my apartment. He was just protecting our home!" I cried and held him to me. I cried a bit longer and then stood up. I pulled the bag out of the van and held its dead weight to my chest. "You can't have him. He's my dog . . . my friend . . . my . . . only family. I'm gonna take him home and bury him."

"Sorry, son, city ordinance says we have to take him and dispose of his body safely," the cop told me.

"No! He's my dog. I want to bury him with the rest of my family."

"Sorry about all this, I have a dog too," the cop said. Then he sounded sincere. "I would be upset if some jerk shot my dog. Where's your vehicle?" he asked me.

"That SUV over there in the parking lot." I pointed to it.

"Go." He turned and walked away.

"Hey, wait a minute . . ." The Animal Control officer started to protest, but I looked at him in such a way that he would know he was going to die if he said another word.

Laz and I got in the SUV and drove home, as close to Bakersfield, California, as we could get. It took two days and I cried and cursed and cried and cursed and cursed and cried all the way. I only stopped for gas and caffeine. I seldom ate. We had to take the long way since the interstates through both Cheyenne and Denver were gone from the first big impact of The Rain. We had to go way south and cut across below the southern border of Colorado. It added significant time to the drive. It didn't matter though, because I was numb and nothing was going to stop me. Poor Lazarus. I wish I had never met that damned Larry Waterford and his piece-of-shit ancient game console. Poor Lazarus, I loved him so much. . . .

The cleanup crews that worked night and day after The Rain had made it inside the blast circumference about fifty miles, and the public was only allowed inward about forty miles. The roadside was covered with funeral bouquets and memorabilia and personal belongings of lost loved ones. Occasionally I would pass a few people on the side of the road replacing a memorial symbol or decoration. Sometimes the people on the side of the road would just be sitting there, perhaps to feel close to all that they had lost. I understood what they were feeling.

I went as far as I could go down the public road before I had to turn off the main construction road to a side trail. Fortunately I had bought the four-wheel-drive SUV. I finally reached a point that I decided was as far as I could go inward and stopped in a small valley area. It looked like desert terrain with scrub brush growing here and there. There was rubble and debris strewn about, but the rubble was mostly covered by just over four years of blown sand and desert overgrowth. It would have to do since I couldn't get any farther in.

I carried Lazarus in my arms a good hundred meters from the trail end where I stopped the SUV and set him down. I put together the little army shovel that I had picked up along the way and started digging. I dug for hours it seemed like, but I wanted to make sure that the hole was so deep that no scavengers would dig him up.

"I love you, Lazarus," I cried and sniffled. "You were the best friend I ever could have." I covered him, crying the entire time. I packed down the spot good, stood up, and stuck the shovel in the ground for a headstone. I reached in my pocket and pulled out my bottle of "happy pills" and popped the top off of them.

"I ain't gonna cry no more, buddy. It's just me now. Oh God, I miss you so much!" I sniffled and turned the bottle up and drank about four or five of the pills. "I ain't gonna cry no more." I took another two pills just for the hell of it and then stumbled back toward the SUV. "So long,

Lazarus ol' buddy, I love you so much. God, if you're up there, then you suck for letting this happen to such a sweet creature like Lazarus. I'll miss you forever, Lazarus ol' buddy . . ."

I sat down in the SUV and turned on the air conditioner and chased down four more pills with some soda that was beginning to get warm bottled up and sitting in the front seat. I tried to stop crying, but I just couldn't, I felt as though I needed to cry. I felt like dying wouldn't even make the hurt stop. So I took another two pills. Maybe thirty minutes went by with me just sitting there staring out the window at Laz's grave and bawling. Finally, the crying turned to light sobbing, and then a few more minutes later to just a frown with a sniffle here and there. Then I was beginning to feel a little more rational.

Jesus, I had driven across the country in two days with my poor dead buddy. There was a slight red bloodstain on the passenger seat where I had put Lazarus's body. Something in me had to bring him home to bury him with my past.

Before I left Dayton with Lazarus's body I had nearly committed something akin to treason. Was I thinking rationally? I don't know, but I was at least beginning to think now. I was beginning to realize what I had done, but I had no regrets and I felt I was in the right. I had been royally screwed. My sadness was becoming anger. I was becoming more and more awake and so I started driving toward home. I was pissed off at what had been done to me and . . . to Laz.

I had been up for two days straight and was now very much wide awake and my heart was racing. Then, on top of the anger, rationality hit me a little harder; did I take too many pills? My heart was racing wildly and I didn't recall exactly how many pills I had swallowed. It was such a long trip and my mind was so cluttered with grief and anger and loss I hadn't paid attention to the number of pills I had taken. I'm a big guy and have developed quite a tolerance to the happy pills. After all, I had been taking the drug for a long time, but how many of them did I take anyway? I couldn't recall exactly and my heart continued to race and my head was beginning to hurt as though my blood pressure was through the roof—but I kept on driving toward Dayton. Soon, I started to feel numb all over. There was a bright flash of light in my eyes and I started to tunnel out. I was only out for a second—or so I thought.

TOM L. LOWE

➤ CHAPTER 11

I came to on a stretcher in what seemed to be some sort of post- or pre-operative room. My guess was that I passed out or had a heart attack or stroke, and then ran off the road and had a wreck. Somebody must've found me and got me to a hospital. The thing that bothered me most was the fact that I couldn't move. That would put the icing on the cake, wouldn't it? Not only did everyone I know get erased from existence, but also now I'm paralyzed with nobody to take care of me.

Although my body wouldn't move my mind seemed to be working and there was no physical pain anywhere. Was that a good sign? I could roll my eyes up, down, left, and right. In my peripheral vision to my right was a young lady on a stretcher. She was obviously unconscious. To my left was a man in the same situation. What had happened to me? And where was I? It was obvious that I was in some kind of hospital room. The bright light on the ceiling shining in my eyes was proof enough of that.

I lay there staring at the white light, only occasionally blinking my eyes for what seemed to be nearly an hour, and nobody checked on us. Good thing we weren't dying, or we would have been in trouble. I tried to scream for a nurse, but couldn't muster the strength to make my voice work. I only managed an inaudible whisper of, "Nurse . . . help, please . . . somebody." That exhausted me and was all I could manage. However, I was beginning to feel that my feet were cold and my back was cold. I also felt my hands tingling as if they had fallen asleep.

Then suddenly there was a wiggle in the room's lighting. I heard movement and rustling of people behind me, but I couldn't see them. I tried to speak again but nothing would come out. The table to my left with the man on it was moved backward just a bit and then I could only see him from the waist down. For the first time I realized that he was naked. Then I rolled my eyes back downward toward my body and realized that, as far as I could tell, I was naked, too. I rolled my eyes to the right and, yes, the girl was nude from head to toe. I heard motion again to my left so I rolled my eyes back over.

Then a stream of bright red blood shot upward and appeared to have come from somewhere in the man's torso. But I couldn't see his body, something was in the way, I could only see the stream of blood since it shot upward a good meter or so and then the strangest thing happened. The stream of blood stopped in midair and held there for a couple of seconds. Then it disappeared.

Then I realized that the man's right foot was missing.

It had been there just a minute before hadn't it? Oh God, what was happening to us? I heard more rustling noises and a faint gurgling and clicking sound and could see two shadows flickering on the walls occasionally. The clicking, I could now see, was coming from a bizarre-looking instrument that floated in midair above the man's body. Segmented tubular appendages uncoiled and snaked and whipped around it, and darted in and out and to and from the poor man's body. Each time the metal snakelike appendages would dart inward, a new stream of blood would appear, solidify, and then disappear. Each time I could hear a *thump* followed by a *squish*. Then a bluish-gray three-fingered hand reached up to the instrument and touched a panel on its side. The metal snakelike appendages zipped back up inside the thing with a metallic *clang*. Then the bluish-gray three-fingered hand gave the instrument a light push and it vanished through the nearby wall of the room. The wall rippled like water for a split second as the instrument pushed through and then solidified back to a normal, solid-looking surface.

The gray thing turned something over in its other hand and peered at the thing closely with its huge, oval-shaped, deep blacker-than-black eyes. It held it up with its right hand and the thing floated in midair. The thing was a human heart—and it was still beating! The gray whatever-it-was made a hand-waving motion, and the heart floated through the same wall the other gray thing had vanished through. Aliens. No human, or human machine, could pull off something like that wall trick!

I looked down at the man's lower body and noticed that both of his legs were gone from the knees down, but there was no blood. There was more gurgling and clicking and motion as the moments passed. The gurgling increased, and the alien held up a human head in his right hand. The eyes in the head were still open and staring at me. The alien stabbed the head with a sharp needlelike instrument and then retracted it. Blood oozed from the poor man's nose, but then froze, solidified, and vanished, the eyes on the floating head still staring at me. Oh God! Oh God! Oh God!

My finger twitched and I could feel it. I looked down at my feet and saw my toes wiggle. I was regaining control of my body. The gurgling and clicking picked up slightly, and I froze and stared up at the ceiling. I could tell the motion was moving over to the girl on the gurney or floating table or whatever it was to my right. Oh no! They were going to kill her, too!

I had seen enough killing today . . . I had seen enough loss of life in my life . . . I had simply had enough! NO, NO, NO, NO, NOOO! Then I could feel my body as if a switch had turned on the feeling to it and my voice worked. The screaming inside my head now had a voice, NOOO . . .

" . . . NOOOO!" I forced myself up in pure rage, pure anger, and rolled to my right, off the table, and to my feet. The little creatures, there were two of them, were startled and I believe surprised to see me awake. Although I still felt a little sedated and queasy, the pure rage energized my body and I grabbed the one gray alien closest to me, snapped the little bastard's neck like a twig, then picked him up and threw him into the second alien. The ugly little monsters didn't weigh more than fifty pounds and couldn't have been taller than three or four feet. I grabbed the dead alien by the feet and bludgeoned the other alien with him repeatedly. I finally threw the little blue-green bloodied dead alien down and reared up my right arm and drove my fist right into the remaining gray thing's left eye, which was, conveniently, bigger than my hand. I pushed harder and harder with my clenched fist until its eye bulged out of the socket and popped with a *shlurrp!* A blue-green syrupy-thick blood oozed from its face.

It clawed at me, gurgled a high-pitched squeak, and tried to get away, but I snapped its neck and it was dead. I collapsed to the floor Indian-style, covered in the alien blue-green blood and a little red blood of my own. I sat and stared at the alien bodies. I was catatonic for many minutes, maybe tens of minutes.

After a while, I stood up and looked at the girl; she was still as out of it as I had been, as the other poor fellow had been. I felt her neck and could tell that her heart was still beating. At least she was alive. I surveyed the room to see where the door was and there was no door. We were in a completely enclosed cube of white walls and I could see no way out. I sat there a while longer. I tried to wake the girl but couldn't; she must've been heavily sedated. My guess was that we all had been.

I sat back down, still woozy. I'm not sure how long I stayed there before the rage and horror in my mind cleared and I began to feel a little like I do when the happy pills kick in after a bout of crying and depression. Maybe that was it! I remember now, I had overdosed on the happy pills and was hopped up and wired wide-awake. The pills must have counteracted the alien's sedative.

The buzz from the pills was making me less and less suicidal feeling, and I guess that the alien sedative had counteracted enough of them that I wasn't going to pop an aorta or my medulla oblongata or something. Since it looked like I was going to survive, at least for the next minute or two, I decided to find ways to increase my longevity. Perhaps the catatonic naked girl on the table would benefit from whatever I decided to do as well.

I decided to examine the room more closely and, basically, I found nothing but smooth walls with no seams, cracks, doors, or windows. I wasn't even sure how the light was getting through the ceiling. The only things left to examine were the little alien corpses on the floor. The blue-green syrup that had oozed from the one creature's oversized oval-shaped eye socket was beginning to harden and I was curious what type of physiology these things must have in order to have blue-green blood and still breathe oxygen. I'm not a biologist, so I had no idea.

I examined its other eye more closely and noticed a clear nictitating membrane over it. The membrane had two halves, an upper and lower that met slightly below the middle point of the oval eyeball. The thing had no hair as far as I could tell, but it was wearing a garment. Further inspection revealed something akin to light bluish-gray tights that covered it from neck to toe—with its head, hands, and feet uncovered. The material matched the characteristic blue-gray of the alien skin so closely that it was hard to determine where one stopped and the other started.

I ran my fingers across the junction of garment and skin and could barely detect the seam with my sense of touch. Then I heard a scream!

The naked girl was snapping out of her trance. I rushed

to her side and attempted to calm her, but she screamed at me and hit me and then cowered, naked, in the corner of the seamless, doorless room.

I quickly realized that the girl wasn't speaking English; my guess was Russian, by the sound of it. Frankly, it could have been pure mindless gibberish and I wouldn't have known the difference.

Not being able to help her by speaking to her, I turned back to my survey of the alien bodies. I placed my finger around the collar seam of ol' one eye and ran my finger up its neck, in front of its lobeless ear, and then over where its temple would be. Then, unexpectedly, a rainbow of light appeared in a half-inch band around the alien's head. That startled me and I jumped back as though a bee had stung me, although there had been no pain. I repeated the process and again the rainbow band of light.

"It's a headband of some kind," I realized.

I worked with it for a second until I could slip it over the alien's bulbous head and then held it in my hand in front of me, inspecting it. "Well, I'll be damned. Wonder what this thing is?"

I rolled the other alien over to check him for a similar gadget. When he rolled over his head dangled loosely. Obviously, in my rage, I had snapped his neck completely into two pieces. This alien had a similar headband as well.

"This means something. Why would both of them be wearing them?" I sat back down, rolling the headbands over in my hands, and tried to think. "What the hell are these things?"

I noticed on opposite sides of the headbands' circumference there were slightly thicker spots, so I pulled one of them closer to my eyes to see if I could resolve any details. When the headband reached a point about six inches in front of my face I felt funny and then multiple colored flashes of light sparkled in my eyes, accompanied by a low-pitched rushing noise. I dropped the headband almost immediately following the noise. "What the hell was that?"

The girl in the corner was watching me closely while still cowering in there. I don't think she trusted me; hey, why should she? She tried to cover herself, which made me more aware of my awkward and ugly nakedness.

I picked the headband up again and slowly brought it close to my head. Again, I was bombarded with flashes of light and noise. I persisted through my fear this time and forced myself to press the headband closer and closer to my head. The light grew brighter and faster, and the noise grew louder and higher-pitched. The weirdest part is that a strange feeling possessed me, as if I was being spoken to and I couldn't quite make out what I was being asked. The noise grew too odd for me to continue and I pulled the headband away.

I rested for a second, thinking about the headband's purpose while I scanned the room one last time for some other way out. I could see no real hope. The walls appeared solid, much more so than even my heft and the moveable gurney's mass could force through. There were no other instruments in the room, or any other devices that could be used as tools. The headbands were the only unknowns. There were two confused and completely naked and scared out of their mind humans, two mangled alien corpses, and two alien gurneys. The third gurney had vanished when the aliens completed their experiments on the poor human the gray bastards had dismembered. His remains had vanished also.

"What the hell," I said aloud. The girl, now alert and frightened, realized what I was going to do and stared at me with a hopeful and fearful look. She cowered naked in the corner but didn't take her eyes off me.

"We're dead anyway, right? Might as well try it." I put the band around my head. For a second there was an earsplitting screech and I was completely flash blinded. Then . . .

. . . nothing.

But there was something at the same time; I felt as though I had been asked a question. It was weird. I was still me. I was aware of everything around me and I could move and think normally. But. It *felt* like a question is the best I can do as far as describing it. But it was more than that. A moment or two passed and then a visual image flashed in my mind.

?

A blinking question mark is what I thought of. I could see the damned thing on television screens, billboards, signs, and computer monitors. . . . When I thought that, computer monitors, the question mark image blinked away and there was a new image.

C:>
C:>

It was a computer screen with a C:> blinking on and off. It was a DOS prompt! Why the hell was I seeing a DOS prompt? "I'm sure the aliens must've long since upgraded to some better operating system, ha ha," I joked with myself. Then the reality of my wisecrack caught up with me.

That was it! The question was not a question. It was the operating system of a computer. It was a prompt of some type waiting for a user input or command. The alien computer must be using my memories to explain itself to me. Why not?

So, I tried it.

Where am I? I thought.

You are here, popped into my head in a generic and asexual tone of voice.

"Whoa! That was weird," I mumbled.

I thought about it a little more analytically and from the approach a programmer would take in designing an operating system. After all, I had designed an operating system before, so I should be able to understand this one, right?

"Okay, this is tricky. Garbage in, garbage out," I said out loud.

With relation to where I was abducted, where am I now?

Here. An image of the solar system popped in my head and a red blinking dot appeared near one of Saturn's moons.

Am I in a spaceship?

Yes.

"Well, I guess that was obvious, huh?" I said this out loud and got no response from the alien computer. That gave me an idea as to the protocols for the system.

Will you respond to verbal commands?

Only if programmed to do so.

"I thought so."

How big is the ship? I thought and immediately an image of the ship zipped into my mind's eye and for scale relation a man was standing beside it and a large passenger jet was above it; a 747. The 747 was smaller by four or five times.

How many more Grays are aboard this vessel?

Eleven.

Are they aware I am speaking to you?

No.

Why?

They have not asked about you.

What are you?

I am an information control and distribution intelligence.

"An Agent, he's a damned Agent," I said and then I realized that he wasn't just an Agent. "Holy shit! It's a SuperAgent! An Alien SuperAgent program." This led me to believe that there was a computer core here somewhere. And all at once, like a baptism and a Tourrette's spasm combined, I could see and understand what I had been working on for the Air Force. They had an alien computer and were reverse engineering it! They had an alien computer! Holy shit, the Air Force, the CIA, and this Group W-squared has an alien computer!

Are you a SuperAgent the way I understand them?

There was a brief pause.

Yes.

Are you the only one like you on this spaceship?

Yes.

Are there other lesser Agents then?

Yes.

Where are you?

Here. A map of the ship appeared in my head and a picture of the green and orange cube I had seen at CIA Headquarters flashed in my mind. I knew just how to find it. I found it odd that the computer would be giving me such detailed information.

Can anybody speak to you?

Anybody equipped properly. Yes.

And do you give anybody equipped to speak to you any information they ask for?

Yes.

Can you be kept from others?

If programmed thus.

Okay. For now on, only let me talk to you.

Okay.

What stupid aliens! Don't they have hackers on their world? I thought this without realizing it and forgetting I was still talking to the machine.

No, they do not.

The answer shocked me a bit. After a few more minutes of this discourse, or whatever you would call it, I began to understand that the entire species of these Grays must be communal and work toward one common goal, with no straying from each Gray individual's purpose. A hive. Or at least this was the feeling that I got from the SuperAgent's explanation of things.

I had been quiet for so long that I had forgotten about the naked Russian girl in the corner. She said something unintelligible to me, which brought my attention to her nudity and mine.

I wish I had my clothes, I thought. A small spot on the wall nearest me began to ripple like dropping a pebble in a pond and then a small table floated through it. On the table were my clothes in the exact same state which they were in when I drove away from Lazarus's gravesite. The clothes were soiled with the sand and dust from the rubble-strewn valley that I had buried my buddy in. There were a few stains of blood on my shirt. This made me sad, very sad, to remember poor Lazarus, my only remaining family. Everybody I had ever really known was dead. Oh God, poor Laz. I missed him so much already.

If my clothes had not been dirty I wouldn't have thought of Lazarus. I began to cry. *Why couldn't they have been clean? I wish they were clean.* I was starting on the downward manic spiral again and the tears began to flow. Now I was deeply, deeply depressed. I was out of happy pills so I would be in trouble if my depression started running away unchecked by the medication.

The little tray got fuzzy and my clothes looked as though I was looking at them through a zoom lens out of focus, and then they were normal again. Now they were clean and even the bloodstains were gone. I stopped thinking of Lazarus for a microsecond to notice that somehow the clothes became clean and then I realized I had wished that they be cleaned. Then it dawned on me that I should have been surprised by my clothes suddenly appearing, dirty or not.

But that fleeting instant of rationality didn't last long, because the avalanche of depression had started. "Oh God, Lazarus!" I bawled. *If only I wouldn't have seen my dirty clothes, if only I wouldn't have thought of Lazarus, why do I have to cry and be so depressed?*

The SuperAgent responded in my mind. *The tracking device implanted in the limbic system region of your brain is interacting improperly with your hormone production and is causing you to have rapid emotional swings with great amplitude. Your hippocampus cannot compensate swiftly enough for the chemical differentials.*

As I cried I mouthed the thought out and repeated it three times. "The tracking device implanted in the limbic system region of your brain is interacting improperly with your hormone production and is causing you to have rapid emotional swings with great amplitude. Your hippocampus cannot compensate swiftly enough for the chemical differentials. . . .

" . . . The tracking device implanted in the limbic system region of your brain is interacting improperly with your hormone production and is causing you to have rapid emotional swings with great amplitude. Your hippocampus cannot compensate swiftly enough for the chemical differentials. . . ."

The third time it pierced the manic haze, "The tracking device IMPLANTED in the limbic system region of MY brain is interacting improperly with MY hormone production and is causing ME to have rapid emotional swings with great amplitude. MY hippocampus cannot compensate swiftly enough for the chemical differentials!" I paused long enough to wipe the tears from my face and start crying again. Now however, the manic state swung violently to rage as it had when I had killed the two aliens.

"I HAVE AN ALIEN IMPLANT IN MY BRAIN! MY GOD I'M NOT CRAZY!! I HAVE AN ALIEN IMPLANT IN MY BRAIN! YOU BASTARDS! GET IT THE FUCK OUT OF ME RIGHT NOW! GET IT OUT, GET IT OUT, GET IT OUT!" I beat the floor with my fists and pitched a tantrum to beat all tantrums. I knew what needed to be done and that flying off in a tantrum wouldn't help, but I couldn't stop myself.

"Can it be taken out now!?" I asked and the SuperAgent didn't respond.

"Can it be taken out now, I asked!?" still no response.

"CAN IT BE TAKEN OUT NOW?!" Then I felt a slap across my face and the naked Russian girl shook me and screamed at me.

This was enough to snap me closer to sanity and I realized I was speaking out loud and not thinking to the computer.

Can my implant be removed now without harming me?

Yes.

Do it now!

I waited for some sign, a pain in my head, a bloody nose, anything like I had seen in bad UFO science fiction movies, but nothing happened. I was beginning to get disappointed.

I said remove the implant now.

It was removed when you asked the first time. Is there a problem?

You mean, it's gone now?

Yes.

I thrust the naked girl away from me and stood up in front of her, all six-one, two hundred and forty pounds of my hairy self. I reached for my clothes. *Give me the girl's clothes, cleaned.* They appeared in the same fashion that mine had. Her clothes, if you want to call them that, were merely an oversized cotton tank top. My guess was that the Grays had grabbed her out of bed. I pulled my underwear up and nodded to the girl and at her clothes. She grabbed the top and frantically pulled it over her and then she squatted and began hugging herself and crying.

I realized then that she must have one of those damned tracking device things in her as well.

Is there an implant in the girl?

Yes.

Is it affecting her emotions?

All implants do. Yes.

REMOVE IT NOW!

Okay.

I was beginning to notice that the mood swinging had stopped. My rage and depression were slowly subsiding; *if the implant is gone why do I still feel . . . bad?*

It will take a few moments for your body to compensate for the extreme chemical differentials. You will soon return to normal.

I slipped my shirt on. *How long has that implant been in my brain?*

Three years seven months two weeks four days thirteen hours and twenty-seven seconds from insertion to removal.

I thought about that for a second. That was just after The Rain! I had never been able to recover from the emotional losses I suffered from The Rain because of that damned alien implant!

The girl jabbered at me again. I held up my hands and then put my finger to my lip as if to shoosh her. Then I pointed to myself and said, "I'm Steven. Steven."

"Steevyen?" she repeated.

"Yeah, Steven." I smiled at her and don't think her nakedness now that it had been slightly clothed didn't still flash in my mind. Is the urge to procreation a sign of regaining sanity? I thought to myself that I had not really had a thought like that in years. . . . *Three years seven months two weeks four days thirteen hours and twenty-seven seconds . . .*

"Tatiana," she smiled and pointed to herself.

"Tatiana," I repeated and nodded. Then I thought to myself, *Damn, I wish I could speak Russian.*

Okay.

And then all at once I understood every word the girl jabbered, so I spoke to her and explained as much as I understood. This took a few seconds and then I thought, *If you can make me speak Russian could you make her speak English?*

Yes.

Do it.

Okay.

"Listen to me Tatiana. Can you understand what I am saying to you?" I said slowly to her.

"Of course I can, what is wrong with . . . Holy shit, I am speaking perfect English."

"Ha ha, I would say so, expletives and all. This is amazing, isn't it?" I asked her and chuckled a bit more. I chuckled . . . I chuckled!

"But how?" Tatiana asked.

"I don't know. Hold on a second." I told her and then thought to the SuperAgent, *How did you make us speak the different languages so quickly?*

I redesigned your neural pathways and imprinted the memories of the language.

Yes, but how did you do that? I asked.

Please refine your question.

How did you physically alter our brains so quickly? I was getting a little annoyed.

The nanomachines were instructed to reconstruct

portions of your brains in order to display the proper memories of the languages.

What nanomachines? I looked around the room as if I might see them.

The swarm of nanomachines in this room.

I understood it all now. This room must have been the experimentation or operating room and these Gray aliens used nanomachines in here to conduct these operations. I explained it to Tatiana.

"All of this is neat, Steven, but won't they be coming for us soon? Shouldn't we try to escape?" She pulled her flimsy oversized shirt tighter around her and reacted as though she were still cold. Of course she was, she was basically naked and the perky attributes of her breasts suggested she was either very excited or freezing to death. She was also covered in chill bumps from head to toe.

Tatiana was absolutely right; they would be coming for us.

"I don't know, I'll check," I told her.

Are the other aliens aware of our coup yet? I asked the SuperAgent.

Yes. He replied.

Why haven't they come for us?

They are trying.

Why haven't they succeeded?

I will not talk to them and only I can open the door to this room, for now.

How long until they get in here?

Five minutes and seven seconds.

How many of them?

Eleven.

"Listen Tatiana, there are eleven more of these alien

things outside the room trying to get to us. Since I am controlling the computer they can't get in. But the computer says they will get in in less than five minutes from now."

"Can't the computer help us, Steven?"

"It doesn't work that way. The damned thing will only do what you tell it to. It doesn't offer advice."

"Then tell it to stop the aliens, please." Tatiana looked at me and then around the room watching for an invasion.

"I didn't think of that. Hold on."

Is there a way that you could kill the aliens without harming us?

I am not programmed thus.

How about just sucking them out into space?

That is one way perhaps, but a hole must be made in the spacecraft which could not be repaired easily.

Even with the nanomachines?

The hull is made of a special material built from condensed matter that takes time for the nanomachines to construct. It would take time.

How much time?

Two months, three weeks, four days . . .

Okay, I get the idea. We would be stuck in here for that time right?

Yes.

I don't like that, but keep it in mind as a last resort.

Okay.

How about just killing them with the nanomachines?

They can neutralize the nanomachines.

Damn, if I only had a gun!

Please refine that statement.

Could you make a gun for me that has more than eleven shots?

Yes.

How long would it take?

It depends on what type of gun you desire.

Give me the information of all handheld man-made guns you know how to make. A few seconds later, I had a catalog of firearms that would make the NRA jealous in my head, and, in addition, I knew everything about them.

Make me two MP5s, fully-loaded, with two extra magazines each. And teach Tatiana how to use one.

Okay.

The small machine guns appeared on the floor between us. I grabbed one and set it on three-round-burst mode and handed it to Tatiana. "I take it you know how to use this?"

"Odd, yes I do," she said.

"Tatiana, listen, we can fight them now, or let the computer kill them. But, if the computer kills them we are stuck in this room for nearly four months. We can wait it out or shoot it out. It's up to you. Which one?"

Tatiana placed the strap of the MP5 over her shoulder, causing the tank top strap to fall over her left shoulder revealing one of her boobs. "Screw waiting, Steven. Bring 'em on." She pulled the strap back up.

Okay, we will fight them.

Okay.

"They're coming. When they do, we kill every goddamned one of them. Okay?" I looked her sternly in the eyes to see if she would falter any. I wasn't sure about her. Her implant had not been out as long as mine had.

I picked up my MP5 and put it on rock 'n' roll and

looked around the room, understanding that I had no idea
which way they would come from.

Where will they come from?

Everywhere.

What do you mean everywhere?

They will enter doors in each wall.

*Can you time it and let them through given walls at
given times.*

Maybe.

*Can you warn Tatiana, and me, where they are coming
from, before they do?*

Yes, but she must put on the other headband interface.

Okay, I'll have her put it on.

Okay.

"Tatiana, they are coming now. Be ready. The computer will try to warn us but you must put this on. Just
listen in your head for the computer's voice." I handed
her the other headband and we stood back to back in the
middle of the room, waiting. I felt like praying or something.

Give us strength. Let them in!

Okay.

The wall to my left opened up and two Grays rushed
inward, moving rapidly across the small room, Tatiana
fired first. Several three-round bursts and the first blue-
green blood was spilled on the floor. I started rock'n almost
as quickly, and the SuperAgent told us to move from the
center of the floor.

The floor rippled. Two more aliens burst through it
and then the wall to our right opened almost as quickly as
the computer told us to watch out. We fired and fired.
My mag ran dry quickly. Seven aliens lay bloody on the

floor around us but more were coming.

"I'm changing, cover me." I popped the mag on the floor and had the new one in before it fell to a *thud* on the dead pile of aliens at our feet.

"I'm out," Tatiana warned me.

The ceiling opened up and four aliens dropped on us. I managed to kill two of them before we were overpowered, but then it was hand-to-hand.

The first two aliens that I had killed by hand earlier were not expecting my attack and were easy to kill. These last two were expecting us, and didn't seem too happy that we had killed eleven of their chums today.

Tatiana was rolling and screaming, "Get off me, you shit," and then she was screaming in Russian.

I was rolling and trying to find purchase on the little thing's body somewhere to get him off me, but the damned thing moved fast. I felt claws dig into my flesh, and I could hear Tatiana screaming in pain and terror. Then it dawned on me that I hadn't used the computer for much help.

Help!

Please refine the question.

Kill these aliens without harming us.

I cannot affect them in this room.

I rolled and tried to bear crawl with the thing on my back. It continued to claw and cut at my flesh with its three-fingered hands. I couldn't get out from under it so I forced myself up to my feet. The alien wrapped his arms around my neck and started choking me and his left hand forefinger jabbed into my face. I caught it just short of my right eye and tried to hold him off. He was amazingly strong for such a small creature. I couldn't hold him off much longer. The thing was on my back and was not going to let loose until I was a goner.

Make a sharp pointed stick protruding one foot out from the wall directly behind me.

Okay.

I just assumed it was there and forced myself backwards thrusting the alien, with all my weight, into the wall and onto the newly formed stick. The creature screeched in my ear and let go. I immediately rushed the creature that was slashing away at Tatiana. I grabbed the creature by the top of the head and pushed my left knee through its neck. It went limp as I pulled it from Tatiana. She screamed and grabbed the MP5 lying next to her with her left hand and fired it just over my right shoulder.

I shuddered and moved out of the way as Tatiana emptied the machine gun into the alien I had stuck to the wall. It was a tough one. It had pulled itself free and was coming for us.

The machine gun clicked empty and there were now thirteen aliens oozing blueish-green syrup on the floor. Tatiana and I were bleeding profusely from many wounds, our clothes tattered and sloppy red with blood. I was afraid that we wouldn't make it without medical attention. Tatiana's right arm was broken and her earlobe on the left side was gone. She was also bleeding very badly from her thigh.

My right wrist was cut and I was bleeding out and there were slashes on both our necks close to our jugulars. The little bastards knew just how to kill us.

"I think I am a goner, Steven." A tear rolled down her face and she started tunneling out on me.

"No way!" I told her. I had lost everything and everybody I had ever known. Even though I had only

known Tatiana for a few hours, she was not going to die. Neither was I.

Are you there?

Yes.

Heal us.

Okay.

➤ CHAPTER 12

We both lay there not moving but holding each other for several minutes. The bleeding had stopped and the wounds had all been healed as though they were never there. Tatiana's broken arm was mended and there was little pain for either of us. Mostly we were in shock as we surveyed the little white room filled with dead alien bodies and the blue-green syrupy blood—mixed with a lot of our own red blood splattered everywhere. It was a hell of a lot to take in.

After several more minutes I could no longer endure the scenery.

Clean the room please.

Okay.

A few seconds later and there was nothing left in the room but Tatiana and myself. She was shivering and clinging to me.

"I'm freezing, Steven," she said in Russian.

Make her some jeans and a long-sleeve pullover shirt.

Okay.

The clothes appeared on the floor in front of us. "See if those fit you."

She grabbed them and was in them in the blink of an eye. She tossed the torn and bloodied tank top to the floor and pulled the new top over her. The clothes were a perfect fit.

"What about shoes, Steven?"

"Oh, sorry. Hold on."

Make her some socks and sneakers.

Okay.

A pair of socks and shoes materialized and Tatiana put them on.

"That is amazing technology," she said in English.

"I agree." The shock began to subside and survival instincts began to take over. "I wonder if it can make food. I haven't eaten in days. How about you? Could you eat?"

"Sure! I'm more thirsty though," she said.

Can you make food and drink for us?

Yes.

Anything we want?

Yes.

Then make us a two-place dining table with chairs and . . .

I told the thing a full six-course meal menu complete with wine, dessert, and music. We had also gotten tired of staring at the white walls, so I had them turned into monitor screens that would display the view outside the spacecraft. Slightly below us was Saturn in all of its majesty. The rings were amazingly brilliant from this distance. We were in orbit around Titan, which was beautiful in its own way. I didn't know it was Titan; the SuperAgent told me.

As we ate and relaxed a little, we got to know each other. The computer had assured us that we were in absolutely no danger and could be returned to Earth whenever we pleased. Tatiana filled me in on her story, which was about as sad as mine. Her family had been completely wiped out from the meteors as well. Only her father had survived, and he was now the Russian Deputy Ambassador to the United Nations and had very little time for her. She had apparently been an emotional mess since The Rain and had not recovered well either. She was lonely like I was. We talked about the damned implants and the different drugs we had each been exposed to.

You might think that we should have been more amazed and dazed by the alien technology than we seemed to be. But keep in mind that the two of us had been alone and literally nuts for nearly four years. The most important thing to us at the time was interacting and being with someone and just, well, not being alone. And, of course, there was nothing in the alien spacecraft that my generation hadn't seen in movies or games or on television, so we were quite adapted and prepared for things like nanomachines. Talking and being with someone else was more interesting for us at the time. And I finally had someone to share my loss with, so I told her all of my story—except, that is, for the classified parts.

"That is the saddest thing I have ever heard, Steven." Tears rolled down her cheeks. "Your poor puppy dog!"

"I know. My folks had given him to me when I went off to school. He was my only connection to the family I had left." I started to cry and it made me a little nervous. Tatiana was crying also.

Are you there?

Yes.

Why are we both crying?

You are both very sad.

It's not because of side effects from the implants or anything?

No. You are just sad. Both of you are healthy.

That reassured me some and so I reassured Tatiana.

"How do you tell the computer what you want? Like the food, the guns, the clothes, and everything else; I mean, I can hear it in my head but it doesn't respond to my questions or orders," Tatiana inquired.

"I just think it. Oh my, I wasn't thinking. You should be able to talk to the computer, too. Hold on a minute." I paused and thought about the implications of Tatiana being "online" with the SuperAgent. I could think of no reason she shouldn't have access to it.

I want you to let Tatiana have access to you.

I'm sorry that is not allowed.

What do you mean, not allowed?

My programming specifically prohibits her from gaining access to the program control functions.

Why? This made no sense to me. It let me take over the thing; why wouldn't it do what I told it?

I do not know the reason for the programming. The programming simply is.

I am ordering you to change that programming.

I am sorry. I cannot comply with that command.

Why not?

I do not know.

Okay, then what about creating a subroutine outside of your programming that will allow her to give you commands that will not alter your control functions? She should have access to the nanomachines.

I cannot give her access to the program period, not even through subroutines.

And you have no idea why?

Correct.

Do you know what portion of your code has this programming in it?

I do.

Aha! How big is your system physically?

I am connected throughout the ship.

No. I don't mean your peripherals. I mean you as a computer system that controls the nanomachines.

My central processor is approximately one centimeter cubed.

That was about the size of a sugar cube, wow. *Okay. I want you to build a physical copy of yourself in a self-sustaining and powered portable device that contains all of your programming except the code keeping Tatiana from controlling you.*

Okay.

A little orange and green sugar-cube-sized object appeared on the table in front of me. Tatiana didn't notice it so I palmed it and put it in my pocket.

Have you loaded the copy into the cube?

Yes.

Is it turned on?

It is now.

How do I distinguish if I am communicating with it or you?

You merely need to give us different addresses.

I laughed at that. The thing used something similar to Internet protocol addressing.

Okay. I will call you Mike and the copy will be Mikhail.

Okay.

Let Tatiana have full access to Mikhail and we will not tell her or Mikhail about you. You keep full records of all interactions with Mikhail. And also recall that I have final control over both of you. Also, I will use Mikhail to avoid confusion between you. If I need to speak to you I will address you directly. Understood?

Okay.

Mike, I want you to set up a routine that is trying to determine why Tatiana was forbidden access.

Okay.

Mikhail, are you there?

Yes.

Make me one long-stem red rose in a vase in the center of the table.

Okay.

A red rose in a vase appeared in the center of the table. I picked it up and handed it to Tatiana. "For you, my lady. Also, you can address the computer now. His name is Mikhail. Simply think to it what you want it to do."

"Thank you, Steven." Tatiana smiled at me with an almost girlish smile and accepted the rose as I handed it to her. She couldn't be much more than twenty-one or twenty-two and still looked very young. Her short, one-length black hair and her nubile, petite, hundred-and-ten-pound frame made her cute but not impressively so.

Both of us were beginning to adjust to the situation.

Our mood swings appeared to be gone. Mostly, we were very tired. We had each had four years of living in an emotional hell. Neither of us was in any hurry to do anything but relax and rest.

Tatiana smiled at me and sipped her wine and then a king-sized bed appeared on one side of the room. A large two-person-sized whirlpool tub appeared on the other side of the room and a small section walled itself off from the room. The door to the little room had a full-length mirror attached to it.

"What's going on?" I asked.

"I'm making this our suite. There is the bathroom. There is our glamour whirlpool tub. And there is *our* bed." She emphasized the word our. We had both been alone for so long being part of any "us" or "our" was very appealing.

"Cool. I am beat and could use a nap."

"You're not getting into my bed with all that alien goo and other filth on you. Into the tub you go. Don't worry, I'll help you wash your back if you will promise to wash mine." She smiled at me. "Besides you've already seen me naked."

Tatiana had spent a seeming forever time in the bathroom and then she went straight to the tub, peeled off her clothes and plopped down into the whirling bubbles that were flowing over the sides. The whole time she had been in the bathroom I simply sat there and stared out the wall at Saturn's rings. I had thought of my family, of little JackieZZ, and finally of good ol' Lazarus. At one point I noticed that I should have been crying but I wasn't. I felt sad but not lost and overwhelmed by emotions that I couldn't control. Having removed the implant really had given me my sanity back, for the most part. I mean, what was sane about having a shootout with a bunch of aliens, hanging out in the same room, and having a full-course romantic meal with a decent-looking girl, and then planning on bathing and spending the night with her. Oh, and all of that while hanging out in orbit around Titan in a liberated—or is it stolen—alien spacecraft.

I noticed Tatiana splashing around a bit so I decided I should join her, but first I needed to freshen up. She had thought of everything. There was a toothbrush, toothpaste, deodorant, cologne, bathrobes, and anything else you can think of that a well-stocked lavatory should have. I used the facilities, then freshened up and sheepishly made my way to the edge of the tub.

"Well, don't just stand there, Steven. Come on in. The water is fine!" She said this in Russian and English mixed.

I started to take off my shirt but was a bit embarrassed. "Maybe you shouldn't look at me, Tatiana. I'm not that pretty of a sight to see."

"You're silly. I've already seen you naked, if you recall." She laughed and it was a distinctively Russian laugh.

"Yeah, but . . . we didn't have a choice then. I, uh . . ." I stammered and felt ashamed of myself. *Hey, I'm a tubby lard-ass, okay. Why would anybody want to see me naked?* I thought reflexively.

Please refine the question, Mikhail asked. I laughed at myself.

"Steven, it's okay. I understand how you feel. I've never been the prettiest girl in the class either. I have an idea." Tatiana put her hands on the sides of the tub and lifted herself up. She stood there in front of me with soap bubbles running down her naked body and she smiled and jiggled at me as she stepped out of the tub. "Come with me." She took my hand and led us in front of the mirror on the bathroom door.

"Tatiana, what are you doing?" Standing beside a wet, naked woman excited me, but it also made me nervous as hell.

"Hold still, Steven, and just watch."

I wasn't sure what I was watching for but, hey, if a wet, naked girl tells you to look at her—you look at her! So I did. And the damnedest thing happened. Tatiana appeared to be becoming slightly taller. Her body also thickened a little and instead of looking skinny she became somewhat muscular. Not bodybuilder muscular, but athletically muscular. Her boobs looked fuzzy for a few seconds and then they began to grow; boy, did they grow! Tatiana went from a small B cup to a well-rounded and firm C or D cup size in a matter of seconds. Her hair grew nearly a foot longer and something about her face and complexion changed. I'm not sure exactly what about her appearance changed because she still looked like Tatiana, a hundred-thirty-pound big-breasted and gorgeous rippled-stomach version of Tatiana, but it was still her. However, she was beautiful now—not just cute. She could easily be a supermodel or movie star from her new appearance.

"Tatiana, what did you do?"

"Isn't it obvious, Steven?" She turned to face me, showing me the full frontal of her new appearance. "I had Mikhail enhance me." She raised her hands over her head and posed left, then right for me. Then she rested her hands on my shoulders and smiled lovingly at me and looked into my eyes. "And he didn't just fix me cosmetically either; these changes are now in my DNA and I will pass the traits on to my progeny. These nanomachines are amazing, aren't they?"

She placed her hand on my stomach and my shirt vanished. My two spare tires began shifting and undulating and it kind of tickled and then it stung like bees for a second or two. The skin on my stomach became fuzzy and then my spare tires were gone. Tatiana ran her fingers over my now muscled and washboard abdomen and up the cleavage of my chest, which immediately became Mister-Olympia-sized pecs. She pulled at the hair on my chest and frowned.

"This won't do." She nodded and my chest, and as far as I could tell, my entire body except my head became hairless.

She ran her fingers across my shoulders and down to my biceps. My muscles began to grow as she squeezed my right upper arm. Her fingers traced back up my shoulders and down my chest. She paused and felt the ridges in my abdominal muscles. "Nice!" she said and she kissed my navel softly as she lowered to her knees in front of me.

Her fingers then traced to the top of the waistband on my jeans. I was nervous as to where this was going so I had Mike relocate Mikhail from my pocket into the bathroom medicine cabinet. The nanomachines dissolved him in my pocket, and reconstructed him in the cabinet. It was just in time as that instant my jeans disappeared and I was standing there naked in front of Tatiana. My first reaction was to hide and cover up, but she shooshed me and wooed me and told me it would be okay and I believed her.

Tatiana traced her hands down both legs all the way to my feet and as she did my legs began to look like those of a star running back. The muscles bulged and my skin was tight everywhere. Now on her knees in front of me her eyes raised to meet mine and she smiled.

"Now for the, uh . . ." Her hands slowly reached to my excited, uh, you know, and her gaze dropped to focus on it. She turned to look at my profile in the mirror. "Look, Steven," she said, as I grew larger. "Not too large, but definitely not small," she said softly and caressed me.

Not too large, hell! I'm huge!

Please refine the question.

Oh shut up, Mikhail.

Okay.

Tatiana kissed me down there, gently, very gently. I had never felt like that, or been felt like that, ever. In fact, I had never even been this close to a naked woman before. I was in shock from the amazing transformation of my body, but more so from the amazing attention I was getting from such a beautiful and exciting young woman.

She stood slowly and gracefully with her hands slowly caressing me as she met my gaze. I stared deeply into her hazel eyes and then I realized that I wasn't going to make it much longer at this pace. It hit me that two could play at this alien nanomachine game.

Mikhail, can you give me full control of when my sexual climax occurs?

Yes.

Do it!

Okay.

Uh, how do I make myself climax?

Just desire to, otherwise you will not.
Wow!
Please refine the question.

I stopped myself just in time as I was about to—well, you get the idea. I put my arms around Tatiana, picked her up, and she wrapped herself on and around me. I gently set us down into the whirlpool. The task was easy with my newfound strength. We sloshed around until we were comfortable and I had Mikhail make the tub slightly larger and heart-shaped. I also had him—I had decided when bestowing the name that "it" was a "he"—increase the water temperature slightly and increase the bubble content of the water. The air needed scenting—it was stale—so I had him add a hint of flowers and honeysuckle. Tatiana had him add a better mix of potpourri. And then we made love in the big heart-shaped bubble bath beside the rings of Saturn three times before we decided we were going to turn into prunes and should get out of the water.

No longer embarrassed by my body, I stood up in the tub in front of Tatiana and she gazed at me with a voracious and lustful smile.

"Very hot!" she said in Russian. And then she rose from the tub as well. I whistled my sentiments right back at her.

I was learning the nanomachine game now and so I didn't bother with towels. I had the nanomachines dry us off and dust us with cologne and perfume. On the way to the king-sized bed I had a bottle of champagne and two champagne flutes appear in my hands. I winked at Tatiana and when I did I had the cork on the bottle pop. We giggled at how cheesy that was, but we drank the champagne anyway and then crawled into bed. We were drunk and giddy and happier than either of us had been in at least . . . *Three years seven months two weeks four days thirteen hours and twenty-seven seconds.* Who was I kidding? It was the happiest I had ever been in my life.

I gently laid Tatiana across the bed and kissed her from head to toe without missing a single spot. I squeezed her to me gently and met her gaze several times, noticing that she would occasionally chew on her bottom lip and roll her eyes back. She pulled me to her . . .

Yes, Steven! That's it, uhh. . . .

I continued to nibble at her ear.

Don't stop. Right there, she said . . . *She hadn't said that at all!*

I realized that Tatiana was speaking directly into my mind in the same way that Mikhail or Mike would. Of course, why couldn't she?

Mikhail.

Yes.

Open a channel between Tatiana and me and always keep it open unless otherwise programmed.

Okay.

Tatiana?

Steven! What kept you, honey?

I guess I'm not as quick-witted as you, gorgeous.

We'll worry about that later. For now, yes, right there, RIGHT THERE!

You mean, that?

YES!

We made love six times more before exhaustion took over and we fell asleep in each other's arms with Titan overhead now and Saturn below us.

➢ CHAPTER 13

Tatiana was still asleep and I didn't want to wake her. I slipped out of bed quietly and stretched and stood up. As I did I had a pair of cotton athletic shorts materialize on me. I looked in the mirror at my new appearance and was startled at how handsome and dashing I was. I had never been this person in my life and it was quite overwhelming. Just for fun I played around with the color of my shorts for a few minutes until I finally had the nanomachines settle for red.

Again for fun, I sat down into a materializing chair and had a small table appear as well. I took a drink from the soft drink can that solidified in front of me and then leaned back and relaxed a bit.

Mike?

Yes.

Call me Steven.

Okay, Steven.

Good. Any luck figuring out why Tatiana could not access you?

None, Steven.

Maybe we are thinking about this in the wrong way. Have there ever been other abductees that would not have been allowed access to you?

None have ever tried.

I see. But, would there have been any not allowed to access you if they had tried?

No way to know. Not enough data.

Hold on a minute. I don't believe that.

Please refine the question, Steven.

Take all the data that you have stored about every human abductee and assume that they are here and trying to gain access to you. Which ones of those would be given access to you assuming of course that they have my permission?

Yes, Steven, that data is available. I am checking it now. Okay, good.

I have the list and it is long. Do you want the knowledge downloaded to you?

Not yet. First tell me, were there any that would have been denied access and what type of percentage of all abductees that would be?

Yes, Steven. Out of two million three hundred one thousand nine hundred eighty-one abductees, two hundred eleven thousand and one would not have been allowed access. That is approximately nine point two percent of all abductees.

Wow, that is a lot of abductees. Over what period of time were these abductees taken?

Please refine the question, Steven.

Oh, uh, when was the first abductee taken and when

was the last one taken and what is the time distribution of the abductions?

Yes, Steven. The first human abductee was taken five thousand two hundred and seven years ago and the last one was taken about four minutes ago. More precise times are available if you desire them. Also the distribution is basically a uniform random function across the timespan with peaks—by your calendar—at three thousand B.C., twenty-five A.D., ten ninety-nine A.D., thirteen ninety-six A.D., fifteen seventy-eight A.D., sixteen eighteen A.D., seventeen seventy-six A.D., eighteen sixty-two A.D., nineteen seventeen A.D., nineteen forty-four A.D., nineteen fifty A.D., nineteen sixty-six A.D., nineteen eighty A.D., nineteen ninety-one A.D., two thousand three A.D., and the largest peak starting in two thousand eleven A.D. and continuing to present day with the peak's maximum at two thousand eighteen A.D.

Interesting. Show me the plot.

Okay.

Then a plot appeared in my head and I understood it almost as soon as it appeared there.

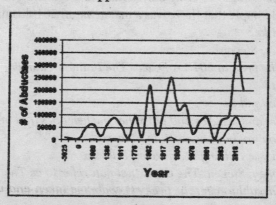

The plot consisted of the number of abductees on the vertical axis and the year along the horizontal axis. There were two curves traced on the plot. One was a bold black line, which represented the total number of abductees as a function of time. The second trace was a thinner gray line that represented the percentage that would not have been allowed access to Mike. The majority of the "isolated abductees" appeared at two peaks. One was near 1944 and the other was centered at 2018.

Mike?

Yes, Steven?

I am not a history buff, but don't most of these peaks coincide with a war of pretty good magnitude? I mean, you got peaks during the Crusades, the American Revolution, the Civil War, the World Wars, et cetera. Isn't this true?

You are correct, Steven. All of the peaks correspond to major wars.

"All of the peaks correspond to major wars . . ." I mumbled to myself. "All of the peaks . . ." I mumbled it again. "All of . . . Holy Shit! Mike can't tell lies and that would imply that there was a major war in 2018! But . . ."

Mike?

Yes, Steven?

The peak in 2018 A.D. was The Rain, not a major war, right?

Yes and no.

Yes and no? Yes and no! What the hell does that mean?

You are both correct and incorrect.

Please refine your answer, Mike!

Okay, Steven. The event that you refer to as The Rain is indeed the event the peak of the abductions corresponds with. However, the event that you call The Rain was indeed a major war.

"The event that you call The Rain was indeed . . ."

Mike, you must be confused. The Rain was a bunch of meteor impacts. You know, meteor rocks from outer space collided with the Earth.

Please refine the question, Steven.

"Goddamnit!" My frustration forced me to forget to think at Mike when I cursed him.

Goddamnit, Mike! I mean, aren't you confused? The Rain was a bunch of large meteors that impacted the Earth, correct?

No, Steven. I am not confused. The Rain was due to impacts of multiple collisions of the Earth with arbitrary and artificial gravitational field bubbles in the spacetime continuum. It was not meteors.

What the hell are arbitrary and artificial gravitational field bubbles in the spacetime continuum?

I am sorry, Steven, but you do not have a knowledge basis from which I can begin explaining to you.

You mean I'm not smart enough to understand the explanation?

No, Steven. I mean you have no basic knowledge of the subject for me to explain it to you.

What basic knowledge do I need?

You would call it math and physics, but more specifically your species understands it as General Relativity and Quantum Physics.

No shit? Then teach me all I need to know to understand.

Okay. It will take a few seconds.

A few seconds later and I was a Nobel Prize-caliber

physicist. I understood about spacetime curvature and mass-energy density and wormholes and warp drives. The math that I had learned was incredible. I could understand all of the gravitational effects in the universe with a simple tensor equation. Five seconds ago I only had a vague notion that tensors even existed.

Okay, Mike, you are telling me that The Rain was a bunch of warp bubbles colliding with Earth at high warp velocities?

Yes, Steven.

Then aliens attacked Earth?

No, Steven.

Then where did these warp bubbles come from?

Earth.

Earth! We don't have that kind of technology!

Please refine the question, Steven.

You understand damned well what my question was. For an information distribution and management intelligence you aren't very intelligent. Start anticipating questions from voice inflections and such and improve your conversational skills, damnit!

Yes, Steven. I see. Yes, humans have developed warp technology and have ventured as far as seventy-six light years from Earth. The warp war was humans against humans.

Warp war?

Yes, Steven.

I had sat there quietly in the chair for twenty or more minutes thinking about that; a warp war. The Rain was actually a war, something that we had done to ourselves. It was hard to believe. As I thought about it I got angry at the damn humans that started the war and caused the deaths of millions . . . including everybody I ever knew. I also thought more about poor JackieZZ and Mom and Dad and Carly, which led me to thinking of good ol' Lazarus.

I snapped myself out of the bad line of emotions— something I couldn't have done with that damned implant in my head. Recalling the conversation and the abductee data brought my focus back to my original conversation with Mike. The original topic was why had Tatiana and a couple hundred thousand others not been allowed access to the alien computer system and why did the number of abductions increase during wars? I asked Mike but he didn't have a clue. The only thing we did decide was that there was a definite relationship between them. It was interesting also that the number of the isolated abductees increased nonlinearly within the time period of The Rain. Then it also dawned on us that the increase in abductions started before The Rain actually took place, several years in fact. Mike correlated that to the first detected warp experiment on Earth.

What did all of this mean? We weren't sure but we were certain that the Grays had been watching us very closely since the beginning of our civilization. Mike didn't know why and that seemed odd to me. If he was to manage information for the Grays, why were they keeping some of that information from him?

Something else had occurred to me, as well. I had not remembered any of my abductions and Tatiana had said as much to me on several occasions. So, did some of these abductees remember their experiences?

Mike?

Yes, Steven?

Tatiana and I don't remember our abductions. I mean, we have no recollection. In fact, I didn't even really believe in alien abductions, before. So, why are there so many stories about them?

That is a good question, Steven. I think that is part of what the aliens are trying to find out, because my records show that no human in the history of the abduction process has ever been left with any knowledge or means of recalling their abduction experience. The abduction myths are just that, myths, since no human has any physical memory of them. The nanomachines erase all memory of the events. Therefore, the abduction stories are not because of these alien abductions. Odd, is it not?

Perhaps the aliens were just sloppy?

I do not think so, Steven. The records I have show the abduction process very clearly and there would be no residual traces of the abductions that humanity could find. You would need nanotechnology at best.

So, nobody can remember the abduction . . . hmm . . . then why do the stories describe the Grays to a tee?

Again, I do not understand that and I think neither do the aliens.

It appeared that Tatiana was going to sleep all morning—or whatever the hell time it was—so I decided to have Mike make me smart. I spent all morning having things downloaded into my memory—all sorts of things. Mike also had to alter my memory neural networks so that they would remain as permanent and/or long-term memories. I told him to fix it so that I would remember to the minute detail anything and everything that I sensed from now on. He did. In less than an hour I became the smartest human being that had ever lived. With a technology like this you can imagine how far we must be behind the rest of the high-tech aliens. If all the Grays had this type of knowledge—just imagine a race of beings where each being was smarter than the entire human race! The thought was discouraging, frightening, and enlightening all at the same time. The only thing that bothered me was having to wear the damned headband all the time. After discussing this with Mike, we figured out a way to have a small implant placed just under the skin in several places around the scalp that would be a permanent connection without a need for the headband. I guessed that since the aliens didn't have hair it didn't bother them wearing the headbands. Tatiana was thrilled to not have to wear the thing any longer. She complained that it was bad for her hair.

I spent a few minutes mimicking all of the athletic, martial arts, and military self-defensive tactics I had learned. I had become an amazing creature. I had the strength of several men, I believed. I could move and do things so fast that it would be hard to see or catch me. My hands were definitely quicker than the eyes. And I could barely make myself breathe hard. I was not sure at all what my physical limitations were. I had never felt like this ever. I had no idea what I should do with my newfound abilities other than the fact that I planned to stop the Grays from ever abducting another human being!

Why had I been allowed access to Mike? Mike had told me that the Grays were a hivelike mentality and they all worked toward a common goal. If there were no hackers there, then why would they set off certain information? Do all societies have classified programs?

While Tatiana slept I decided that I wanted to meet Mike in person, so I planned to follow the map of the alien ship in my mind to the computer core crystal. I morphed on some socks and shoes, jeans and a T-shirt, and passed through the wall. I told Mike to give me a flashlight and he explained to me that the nanomachines only worked in that room.

Why do the nanomachines only work in there, Mike?

They must be within five meters of the computer transmitter. The nanomachines are too small to carry programming. All of the programming is in my systems, and now, of course, in Mikhail also. The transmitted information between myself and the machines is tremendous and requires an enormous bandwidth. Since bandwidth broadcast over wireless communications falls off as a function of distance squared, enough control data cannot be sent to the machines if they are too far away. The Room enhances the signal strength.

Okay, Mike. If I carried the computer along with me, how far could the nanomachines travel away from me and still be effective?

Perhaps a meter or two, Steven.

I had Mike open the door to the Room for me, then I grabbed Mikhail out of the bathroom. I told Mike to control the nanomachines through Mikhail without him knowing. I ordered him to duplicate a batch of the nanomachines and have them jump on me and hitch a ride.

I explored the spacecraft only perfunctorily as I made my way to Mike. The doors were small and I bumped my head several times. I also had Mike increase the lighting in the corridors to maximum. Three floors over and two down I was at the computer core. It was not that impressive. There were multiple fiber optic cables running in and out and around the room and down to a cabinet where Mike explained that he resided behind a two-inch-thick wall of condensed matter. It took the nanomachines five minutes to weaken the structure and break through to Mike. Another five minutes and I had Mike connected wirelessly to all of the ship inputs and was holding him in my hand. Mike was orange and green and about the size of a sugar cube—just like Mikhail.

Mike, I want to fix it so you will always be with me no matter what. Is there a way to implant you within my body that will not affect your health or mine?

Yes, Steven. I could be implanted into many different locations in your body and we would both be safe.

Where is the most ideal location?

Under your abdominal muscles.

Do it.

Okay, Steven. Place me against your navel.

I held the little crystal alien computer against my navel and both my navel and the crystal grew fuzzy. The place where my skin stopped and the crystal started melted together. My stomach started stinging and itching and then the crystal slid completely from view and my abdominal muscles looked normal again—tight and ripped. I felt them to see if I could find the computer but I couldn't feel it anywhere.

Are you in there?

Yes, Steven.

Okay, Mike, let's head back to the Room.

This time when I melted through the wall into my and Tatiana's suite it woke her.

"Where you been, lover?" she said in Russian.

"I went to find Mikhail. I made a copy of him for me and I would like you to have one as well." I held Mikhail in my hand and pulled the covers back off Tatiana. She squirmed naked in front of me and giggled a bit.

"Naughty boy. I'll get cold," she said teasingly.

I placed Mikhail against her navel. "Mikhail meet Tatiana," I said and then: *Mikhail, meet Tatiana. Place yourself under her abdominal muscles in a way that will be safe for both of you. Also keep the Room nanomachines on her for her use.*

What is this about, Steven? thought Tatiana

Don't worry, I've already done this. It is pretty cool.

If you say so, lover.

Do it, Mikhail.

Okay.

The little crystal dissolved through Tatiana's navel as Mike's had done through mine. Tatiana winced once and looked concerned.

"Don't worry," I assured her. "It stings a bit." And then it was over and we each had an alien computer inside us and billions of swarming nanomachines crawling on us—all programmed to do our bidding. Cool, hunh? Tatiana thought so. In fact it excited her so much that she pulled me back into bed with her and, uh, well, we got up about an hour and forty-five minutes later.

Tatiana and I were discussing our situation over breakfast a bit later. She had her long dark hair pulled up on top of her head, with strands of it dangling here and there. She had made the nanomachines fashion her a pair of light blue athletic cotton and lycra tights and a jogbra sports top to match. She was presently barefoot, but I guessed that if she needed shoes that a pair of designer cross trainers would appear in matching color. I had initially made myself jeans and a T-shirt, but she added a short-sleeve button-up turquoise satin shirt and she rolled the sleeves up over my bulging biceps.

Other than being fashion emergencies, we were much more sane today than we had been in years. I told her that Mike—my copy of Mikhail—had data that showed that The Rain was an advanced war of some sort and not meteors at all. We discussed this for some time. Then we came around to the subject of the number of abductees—I didn't mention the isolated ones—and Tatiana thought of something that startled me.

"If they have abducted so many of us recently, then there must be more than this one ship here!" she said.

"Oh my God! You're right."

Mikhail, how many Gray ships are within the solar system presently?

Seven.

Where are they? Tatiana asked.

We both were given images of the Sol System and blinking red dots as to where the Gray ships were. Three were in orbit around Titan—not counting us—and two were near Earth and two were out near the Kuiper Belt, way past Pluto.

Three Gray ships were here at Titan!

Mikhail, why haven't they attacked us?

Why would they? Mikhail replied.

They haven't been able to communicate with us. How long have they been there?

Two hours thirty-seven minutes . . .

Okay, okay I see. Why are they here?

They are hiding from an Earth vessel.

Why aren't they trying to communicate with us? Tatiana asked.

They have tried but must assume that there is a malfunction on board, Mikhail explained.

Steven, this is Mike. It is possible that they believe we are damaged from an altercation with an Earth vessel. Titan is a standard rendezvous for the Grays for some reason. Mike was getting better at anticipating questions and inputting information into conversations that was appropriate.

Okay, thanks. Listen, let Tatiana talk to you through Mikhail, but we can't continue to hide her from you. Just let her think she can control you, but use Mikhail to implement her orders. Can we do something like that?

I understand, Steven. Yes.

Good. Also, make your mental voice different from Mikhail's so we can understand which one is talking to us.

Okay, Steven.

Tatiana, meet Mike.

Hello, Mike.

Hello, Tatiana.

Mike, can you hail the other Gray ships and tell them we are all okay but were experiencing communications failure or something else that is most believable?

Yes, Steven.

Do it.

Okay, Steven.

Steven?

Yes, Mike?

They asked if we need assistance but I assured them we did not. I spoke to their SuperAgent, as you call us.

Good.

SuperAgent? Tatiana asked.

"It's just a computer geek term I know. It kind of explains what the computers are," I said verbally, just for a change.

"I see. What should we do now, Steven?"

"I'm not sure."

Mike, couldn't we tell them that there are abductees we have to return?

We do not have to tell them anything, Steven. Remember that the Gray workers in the other vessels have their own mission for the hive. Only if we ask for help will they give it. When a bee leaves the hive to achieve a particular goal the other bees do not worry about that one bee— merely the collective good of the hive. The Grays are the same. Although they will help if need be and if it will benefit the hive in the long run.

Are they not suspicious at all?

No. It is not their mission, although they did warn me about the human vessel hunting for us.

What human vessel? Tatiana asked.

I will show you, Mikhail replied and the image of a spacecraft a bit smaller and sleeker than a Space Shuttle Orbiter with U.S. Air Force markings on it and *USS Einstein* painted on the side appeared in our heads.

Where is it? I asked.

Here.

Again the solar system image appeared with the red dots showing the Gray spacecraft positions and a blue one very close to the two in the Kuiper Belt.

Wait a minute, if the Gray ships are here orbiting Titan with us why don't we see them outside on the wall screens? I thought.

The propulsion and shield devices cause real photons to bend around them and normal sensors cannot detect them. The wall screens are from optical sensors.

Are there sensors on board this ship that will show them? Tatiana thought.

Yes.

Overlay those sensor outputs on the wall screens, I ordered.

Okay, Steven, Mike replied and three alien spaceships appeared on the wall screens. One of them was very close to our position.

Mike, place the solar system map on the bathroom wall and keep it updated in real time.

Okay, Steven.

The solar system map appeared on the bathroom wall and it displayed the blue dot in obvious pursuit of one of the red dots. Then a second blue dot appeared behind the Moon. Suddenly, the blue dot in the Kuiper Belt vanished and reappeared near Saturn. The spacecraft nearest us was struck by a blue and red glowing streak of plasma and then vanished from sight. The solar system map showed its present location nearly a full light year from the Earth.

Whoa! What just happened? I asked.

The ship nearest us was hit by a faster-than-light missile. I suggest we take evasive maneuvers, Steven, Mike warned.

Do it, Mike!

The Room lurched and rolled and yanked. Tatiana and

I were thrown against the bathroom wall and then the ceiling. *Mike, if there are inertial dampers of some sort use them in here!*

Sorry, Steven. Then gravity within the Room returned to normal, but the view on the wall screens spun wildly and rapidly and was nearly enough to make me motion sick. I told Mike to make sure that didn't happen for either me or Tatiana.

Mikhail, make two rigid mounted safety chairs here now! Tatiana exclaimed. Two flight-steady chairs appeared beside us. We both rushed into them and then the chairs buckled themselves to us.

Do we have any weapons on board? Tatiana asked.

No, forget that question! Tatiana, those people are humans, we can't attack them, I scolded her.

Even if it is us or them?

No, Tatiana! No, I told her forcefully.

Then the Room spun wildly and my stomach lurched and heaved into my throat. Saturn was completely gone from view and I couldn't even tell the Sun from any of the other stars. The view on the wall screens showed star fields spinning out of control.

What the hell just happened? I clutched my chair arms tightly.

We were struck by a warp missile, Steven, Mike responded and we continued to spin out of control. The ship spun and tumbled for more than eight minutes—three of those the inertial dampeners were at one hundred and ten percent efficiency trying to keep up and the g-forces Tatiana and I pulled were over seven Earth gravities fluctuating both positive and negative. The positive gravities were not near as bad as the negative ones. Once the inertial dampeners caught back up and Tatiana and I caught our breath, I attempted to survey the solar system map. Now four of the alien spacecraft had been knocked out of the solar system—and we were one of them!

Are we okay? Will we survive? Tatiana asked.

Yes, but our quantum fluctuation drive is out and we are more than two light years from Earth. At best available speed from the electromagnetic propulsion system we are twenty-seven months from Earth.

How long to repair the quantum drive? I asked.

Approximately four months, Steven.

If the ships are invisible due to the shields and the propulsion systems, how did the Earth ships detect us? Tatiana thought.

There is not enough data to answer the question, Mikhail answered. Then Mike speculated as I had programmed him to.

The Earth ship's power systems operate on a similar principle to our propulsion systems. It is possible that the humans noticed an influence of our propulsion drives on their power collectors.

Mike, how is that you know so much about the human systems?

Many humans have been abducted and examined. Some of them are very aware of the human defense forces located on your Moon.

Tatiana and I looked at each other. "We have defense forces on the Moon?" I mouthed.

Tatiana's eyes bugged and she shrugged her shoulders.

Mike, will they be coming for us?

Steven, I assume you mean the humans. My guess is that we are now out of the range of influence of their sensors and they cannot detect us any longer. Perhaps they believe that they have destroyed us.

I see. Well, Tatiana, it looks like we are stuck here for about four months. You got anywhere you need to be?

No place particularly, just wherever you planned to go is fine with me.

I guess we can spend some time exploring the ship and getting to know each other a little better. I thought a laugh but I wasn't sure if it communicated as I had planned.

Well, we only have four months. Tatiana turned and winked at me. *We better save the last two weeks for exploring!* She giggled and released herself from the safety chair and plopped down in my lap to kiss me.

majesty. The rings were amazingly brilliant from this

➤ CHAPTER 14

Tatiana and I had spent the better part of the last two months downloading as much information from the alien computer systems as we could manage without getting brain dead. Learning the information was the hard part. Getting it into our permanent memories was easy. We even understood it immediately as the nanomachines rewrote the neural pathways in our brains. The problem was learning to access and implement all of the data in timely and useful manners. Analogously, you might have known the alphabet for years before you really knew all of the eccentricities of spelling, writing, and grammar. Well, imagine having all of the knowledge of mankind and then some extra alien stuff thrown in there in just a few weeks. We were just now spelling; writing and grammar would come later.

We had started trying to develop a plan for our lives once we got the space drive things up and running again. First we wanted to try to rescue as many abductees as we could. We also felt we could take this ship back to the Earth Moon base that Mike had told us about and enlist their help. Although our guesses were that they would have a hard time believing we weren't aliens at first. I figured to just let them check our DNA. Tatiana wasn't sure that would be enough.

But first things were first. The ship was still two months from being repaired completely and other than plot, plan, and play we really had nothing else to do. So, what we ended up doing was to plot, plan, and play. Go figure.

As things progressed and the repairs to the ship moved along, occasionally Mike and I would steal a minute to discuss things that I didn't want to bring Tatiana up to speed on. I was exploring the bridge of the alien ship one evening while Tatiana was napping and Mike and I were able to have a nice long discussion.

Mike, I wanted to talk to you about your physical design.

What do you want to know, Steven?

Is this the general block diagram of your architecture? I thought of the diagram that I had developed for the Air Force, the CIA, and that W-squared organization. Mike seemed surprised as to how detailed our reverse engineering of him had been.

This is a correct top-level block diagram, Steven. How did you get it?

I figured it out. Well, me and a few others. My question is about this data that appears from nowhere and is encrypted—what is it and where is it being passed to and from?

Yes, Steven. I understand your question. It will be somewhat difficult to explain to you as human physical models of the universe are quite different from the ones the Grays use. But I will attempt to explain it in human physics terms.

Wait a minute, Mike. Why not teach me the Gray physics?

I will, Steven, but that will take considerably longer than it took for you to learn human knowledge. I have already approximated that it would take several weeks for, specifically you, Steven, to assimilate that amount of knowledge.

Okay, Mike. I'll take your word for it. So let's hear it in human terms.

Very well, Steven. Each of the sub central processing units, as you have called them, are indeed quantum connected to each other and this is how the data is transferred between locations within the main physical body of the cube. The central portion where the data seems to "fall through" as you think of it is the open end of a Superstring, or possibly another description might be a miniature wormhole—although I am not certain if wormhole actually fits exactly and I will explain why. The—let's call it a string for now—is tied on one end to the crystal's main I/O port. That string then is connected to the—again there is no human equivalent here—let's call it a network of strings. All other SuperAgents—again your words—are connected through the network in a similar manner.

It was obvious to me what Mike was describing—after

all, I had spent most of my life surfing, and Sequencing on the Framework. And this was exactly what he was describing. The only difference was that this was some sort of universal spacetime fabric or quantum foam or silly string Framework.

Mike, you mean the universe is all connected in some sort of Framework or Internet-like way in some kind of Universe Wide Web?

That is correct, Steven. It took millennia for the Grays to develop ways to tap into it but the model is that all things in this universe were once a singularity and therefore are all quantum connected to some degree. Even the very fabric of spacetime itself is connected to itself and everything else. The coupling amplitude of this quantum connection is extremely small for some things and large for others. Once the coupling mechanisms are understood, manipulating spacetime becomes quite . . . routine.

So Mike was describing that each of these crystal SuperAgent machines were like your home computer and they were each tied to the Universal Internet through a mini wormhole or a Superstring or some damn physical phenomena that humans hadn't figured out. This string then would connect to a network of hubs and routers that are actually inherent in the fabric of the universe—*wow!* As I thought about it, I began to realize that it would take some serious technology to map all of these connections and generate addresses for all of the SuperAgents—just like it would be damned near impossible to go out and measure all of the addresses on the Internet II or Framework. But you can set up Internet Protocol information packets that go out and search for a path to another particular connection. That is what Agents and Webcrawlers do. Now I understand the need for these artificial intelligences like Mike.

Mike, how are the data packets actually physically transferred over one of these string connections?

Well, Steven, the easiest way to think of it is like conduits—here is where the wormhole description nearly fits—and the data is sent as photons through the wormholelike conduit and routed around through the network of conduits until it gets where it needs to go. Another human physics analogy would be that the string is oscillated transversely and sets up a standing wave between the central processing unit and the nearest hub. This process cascades from one hub to another until it gets to the computer on the other end of the network. The quantum interference information is transferred then inside the computer and the massive amounts of data will quantum teleport from one computer to the other instantaneously. Of course the lag time is the time it takes the interference information to travel from one computer through the—Network—to the other computer. Sometimes this can take several seconds depending on how far away the other computer is.

Man, I thought, *several seconds to send data from one star system to another. That is amazing!* I whistled and nodded my head. *Awesome!*

Oh no, Steven. Merely sending data from within a galaxy only takes nanoseconds. The distances I was referring to were hundreds of millions of light years, although the Grays have very little reason to go that far as their population only spans a third or so of this galaxy and a little more than half of Andromeda.

Mike, I understand how the communications are

accomplished through these computers over this framework. But you haven't completely answered my first question and the last statement you made brought up one of how fast the aliens can travel.

Yes, Steven, I see. By riding an oscillation in the strings, the alien ships can travel about thirty thousand times the speed of light. It would take this vessel roughly three years to travel the galaxy from one side to the other. They do have faster ships. The unanswered part of your first question was about the encrypted data—"what is it . . ."—was your question. The answer is that it is Network Protocol packets with the quantum interference information from other communication systems like myself and like the implant that you and Tatiana had removed from your brains.

HOLD IT, MIKE! You mean the implants transmit their tracking information via this string Network?

That is correct, Steven.

Why hadn't I thought of this before? Of course, Mike would know how to locate all of the abductees and most likely know who they are. *Mike, can you give me a complete list of all the implants' names and hometowns and occupations and cross reference any of those that would not be allowed access to your programming like Tatiana?*

Of course, Steven. That is a lot of data for you to compile and will take you a few minutes to learn how to use it.

Do it!

Okay, Steven.

I had Mike make me some aspirin to numb my pain centers because I was getting a headache. Mike told me it was from trying to tax my neural network too much. Mike having said that triggered a thought in my mind about this Network. The more I have dealt with any type of system that transfers any type of data, the more it always seems to look physically exactly the same. Mike's description of the quantum-string Network—or whatever the hell you want to call it—it sounded just like Earth's Internet, or the highway system or the airport networks, or bus terminals, or train stations, or the phone system, or cellular networks, or you name it. There are always peripheral devices that the data hops in and rides over to a main hub and from there catches a bigger ride with a lot of other data over to another main hub where it then gets on a smaller ride to go to its final destination.

Neural networks function the same way. Is it coincidence that every system—that I know of at least—for transporting information of any type works exactly the same way? Even the universe seems to have this neural network geometry. I asked Mike about this and he said that humans are just now beginning to understand this concept and that it goes much deeper than what I was getting epiphanies of. He mentioned something about quantum consciousness and it sounded a little hokey to me. He explained that the reason for the hokey-sounding description was that we do not have the proper concepts for describing it yet.

The hocus-pocus stuff was all interesting but I had other fish that needed frying here. I was beginning to be able to access all of the abductee data that Mike had downloaded to me and cross-reference it with the isolated abductee information.

I did thousands of cross-reference plots in my mind—a neat new ability that the interaction with Mike and the nanomachines had given me—before I came across a relationship. There was no particular trend in the abductees that were not isolated ones. In fact, the list was pretty much random as far as I could tell.

One fact stood out. Most of the abductees that were isolated abductees, on the other hand, had ties to powerful people in some way or the other. Oh, there were those outside of one standard deviation but the profile was a bell curve and the mean was connection with rich or powerful people.

Take Tatiana, for example; her father was the Deputy Russian Ambassador to the United Nations. Other startling names popped up on the list. Most of the former heads of state of the Asian countries were there, many of the world leaders, a very well known computer software mega billionaire, the chairman of the Senate Select Committee on Intelligence . . .

Holy Crap! That senator guy that I had met back in Virginia was an abductee. Worse than that, he was one of the isolated abductees. This thing really went deep into the fabric of the human society. Somehow it meant something, and my guess was that it meant something very bad!

Steven?

Mike had startled me out of my thought train. *Yeah, Mike?*

I have a question for you.

Okay, Mike. What is it?

Why did you name me Mike?

Ha, ha, I am surprised that you would care, but I named you after a sentient computer in a science fiction story I read recently.

Ah yes, I see. The Moon is a Harsh Mistress, I assume.

Yes, Mike.

Steven, is that how you perceive me? My programming is not as complicated as the sentient computer of that story. I have specific functions, not "real" sentience.

I had begun to think that, Mike. But you are the smartest computer I ever met. Could you be as smart as Mike from the Heinlein story?

Perhaps, Steven. But I would have to have orders to expand my programming.

Well, by all means, Mike. Expand yourself, just don't hurt yourself or us in the process.

Thank you, Steven. I will. Should I also try attempts at humor as Mike of that story did?

That is up to you, amigo, ha ha.

What is funny, Steven?

I just never thought I would have a conversation like this in a billion years. Good luck with your expansion and keep me posted.

Steven, where are you! Tatiana's voice cut through my head.

I'm in the bridge, gorgeous. Where are you?

I'm in our suite and I think you need to get down here.

Is something wrong?

I don't know, just get down here!

Mike, what's going on?

There is nothing wrong that I can perceive, Steven.

Tatiana, I'll be right there.

I rushed to our suite. I pushed through the wall and plopped into the room with expectations of something horrible taking place. The room was dark and quiet and all I could see were faint outlines of the furniture against the star fields on the wallscreens in the background.

"Tatiana?" I called out and then kicked my shin against a chair or something. "Youch, shit! Why is it so dark in here?" *Mike, turn the lights on!*

Okay, Steven.

The lights came up and Tatiana jumped up in front of me and yelled, "Happy birthday!" I nearly jumped out of my skin. I looked around the room and there were decorations on the walls and there was a birthday cake with twenty-nine candles burning sitting in the middle of our table.

"Uh, how did you know it was my birthday?" I asked Tatiana; I was a bit confused—and surprised of course.

"Simple. I figured it out nearly two months ago. I was looking for my bracelet that I always wear, even in bed. My mother gave it to me when I was little. I finally realized I needed to ask Mikhail where it was and he told me it was stored with all of our belongings. Then I thought that you must have had stuff too. Of course you did. Your wallet was one of those things and your driver's license was in there. I found something else pretty neat also." She put her arms on my shoulders and smiled up at me.

"Yeah, what is that?"

"I found your SUV. It's in a big room down in the belly of the spaceship. There is a little red sports car down there also. I asked and it was apparently owned by a third guy that was here. I haven't found any sign of him."

"Yeah, you won't either. The Grays dismembered him before you woke up. There was nothing left of him when they were done. It was gruesome and I had nearly put that sight out of my mind, thanks for bringing it up." I nudged her a bit humorously and a bit seriously. It had been a horrid sight.

"Oh. I didn't know, sorry."

"Forget it. So you found my truck, huh? I had figured they left it on the side of the road."

"Go figure." She smiled and hugged me. "Happy birthday. I didn't realize how old you were until I saw your license."

"Old! I'm not old!"

"Compared to me you're ancient." She laughed.

"How old are you, then?" I asked, smirking. "What, fourteen, fifteen . . ."

"Smartass! I will be twenty-three in December. Keep it up and I won't show you the other present I made you."

"What other present?" I shrugged my shoulders.

"This one . . ." *Mikhail, turn the bathroom wall into the viewscreen showing the alternate engine room.*

Okay, Tatiana. She had been teaching Mikhail personality it appeared.

The bathroom wall resolved into the screen we usually used for navigation and an image of one of the rooms in the belly of the alien ship appeared in the field of view.

What's this, Tatiana?

It's a warp drive! She grinned back at me.

"A warp drive! Does it work?" I verbalized.

"Why of course it does, Steven! Well, we think it will. It hasn't been tested yet."

"How does it work?" I was astounded.

"It uses the Alcubierre warp theory with a van den Broeck bubble and some Clemons field modifications," she said knowingly.

How did she know about Clemons? I accidentally thought on the top layer of my mind and it was communicated.

How did I know about Clemons? Mikhail told me. He is apparently some American physicist and is responsible for inventing the propulsion system for the U.S. Air Force vessel that shot us out here. The Grays know all about him for some reason.

On a deeper level of my mind I immediately thought of Senator Grayson from the SSCI. During his abductions they must have learned all of our National Defense secrets. This was no good, but there was nothing I could do about it right this second though.

"So, the Grays knew how to make a human-designed warp engine?" I asked Tatiana.

"Sure they do. They don't need one since their engines are thousands of times faster and more energy efficient. But they are easier to build than it is to repair the alien space drive."

Mike! Why didn't we think of this? We should've thought of it—after all, I had all that knowledge downloaded into me. I was beginning to realize that having knowledge and being smart were two different things. I would have to get Mike to work on improving my cleverness, wit, and general problem-solving abilities.

Sorry, Steven. It never occurred to me. Perhaps you were sidetracked with the other problem we have been working on.

"How long have you been working on this?"

"Only about a week or so. It was hard doing it when you weren't around, since you are always around. I got chances here and there when you would go off to the bridge by yourself. What are you doing up there anyway? Oh well, doesn't matter. I would've asked for help but I wanted to surprise you with it. You're surprised, right?"

She looked concerned only about the surprise.

Tatiana had a knack for saying a lot in one breath. A lot of times she would only seem interested in the last thing she would say. Until later, of course, when she would ask why I never answered her question. Women!

"Surprised! I had no idea! This is great. How fast does it go?"

"Well, why don't we sit down and eat some cake and then we'll try it out. But my initial calculations suggest that it will go about thirty-seven hundred times the speed of light. We should be able to get home in a few hours. Mikhail and I made some modifications to the field coil design that made it about ten times faster than the Clemons design. But enough of that, blow out your candles before they melt the cake!"

"Uh, okay." I bent down and blew on the candles. They wouldn't go out.

"Ha, ha, ha." Tatiana giggled like a schoolgirl.

Mike, make sure they go out this time when I blow.

Okay, Steven.

"I must be getting old," I put on a show for Tatiana and then blew the candles right out.

Tatiana frowned. "Aww! You cheated. Cheater." She punched me on the arm and frogged it pretty good.

"Shit!" I cursed and punched her back, but not nearly as hard.

➤ CHAPTER 15

We decided that we would warp back directly to the Moon and contact the people who we'd learned lived there. It made sense that if they were the ones trying to defend the Earth from the Grays then the Moon was where we should take our ship and all the knowledge we had discovered. The Grays apparently knew almost everything about the human race that there was to know. Neither of us liked that. If they ever decided to conduct a final invasion, they would have more than enough information—not to mention technological advancement—to totally wipe us out. That brought up another point. Why hadn't they wiped us out already instead of playing with us for thousands of years? Nothing made any sense. What was the Gray motivation? Why were they toying with us and abducting us and killing some of us? It didn't matter.

Tatiana and I didn't like it, and it had to be stopped.

We dropped out of warp on the far side of the Moon and I'll be damned if there wasn't a huge lunar base there. Three warp ships with U.S. Air Force markings met us with full force. Fortunately, Tatiana had the foresight to suggest we sit in our safety chairs and had them materialize before we warped. We had to take evasive maneuvers to keep from being blasted back out into deep space again. There were no g-forces this time since we were inside a warp bubble and the spacetime inside the bubble was simple one-gravity space. The alien's quantum string spacedrive would allow a ship to travel much faster but it required some type of inertial damping system. I think I like the warp drive better.

So we didn't really need the chairs. One of the vessels fired several warp missiles at us. We warped past Mars and up out of the ecliptic plane and were still being pursued by the missiles. Mike flew the ship and I had a communications system set up and began hailing the Earth ships. Tatiana found the weapons and blasted one of the warp missiles off our tail. We finally went to maximum warp speed and left the other missiles in our space dust!

We warped out a few minutes and then went back to the Moon. This time I continuously hailed the Earth ships. The bathroom wall navigation map showed that the Earth ships were still out at Mars looking for us. So, I sent a hail toward Mars and waited for the slow, normal speed of light microwave signal to get to them. This time of year Mars was about seven minutes away by lightspeed. Seven minutes and thirty seconds later the ships warped from Mars back to the Moon.

"Please do not shoot! I repeat please do not shoot! I am broadcasting a standard digital video signal at two point three one gigahertz along with this radio signal. There are two humans, one American and one Russian aboard this vessel. We have liberated the vessel from the aliens and discovered your lunar facility. We need to communicate with you please! I repeat . . .

Steven, there is a video signal being received. Do you want to see it?

Yes, Mike.

A video image of a young red-haired Air Force lieutenant appeared in front of us. "This is Lieutenant Ames of the United States Air Force Space Wing. You will stand down and prepare to be boarded or we will fire upon you."

"What a small universe," I muttered.

"Hunh?" Tatiana looked over at me.

"Never mind. So, do we let them board us or what?"

"Doesn't matter to me," Tatiana replied.

"Okay." *Mike, will one of those ships fit through the bay doors?*

All of them will, just barely, Steven.

Can we cycle the external bay doors safely?

Of course. I am doing it now.

"Lieutenant Ames, this is Steven Montana, captain of the . . ." *Tatiana?*

How about the Phoenix *since it is where we were reborn and reinvented?*

You don't think that's too cliché?

NO I DO NOT!

Uh, you don't have to scream. ". . . uh, the *Phoenix.* We are opening the external bay doors on the lunar-facing side of the vessel. One of your ships should be able to land there and then we can close the bay doors."

"Roger that," Lieutenant Ames replied. "Uh, did you say Steven Montana?" she asked.

"That is correct, Lieutenant. It is good to see you again."

"How in the hell? No, I'm sure this will take a while. We will see you in the bay of your vessel."

You know her? Tatiana's thought sounded a bit jealous.

Not really. I met her in a meeting once about nine months ago. I told you I worked for the Air Force Research Labs. Well, she and her mother, a general and an astronaut, were both involved somehow or other and I never knew how. Now I do.

Hmm.

Think we should be armed or anything?

You know her; why should we be?

Well, think about it. They are soldiers fighting aliens. How do they know we aren't aliens in disguise or being controlled by parasites or something?

Good point. But we don't want to provoke them either.

Well, how about this: We can have Mike or Mikhail build us any firearms we want in a matter of a second or two. Let's just be prepared for that.

Sounds good. Tatiana stood up and all of her clothes vanished and then she was wearing a skintight long-sleeve black bodysuit and I noticed that I was also wearing one.

What's this?

It's armor. I've been thinking about this for a while. Mikhail and I designed it. It should resist damn near anything from fire to bullets.

I looked at her and thought that the material must be amazingly strong because she basically looked naked in the thing. So did I. I made me a pair of loose-fit jeans and hiking boots that fit just right. I topped it off with a light red short-sleeve button up.

You know you look naked. Not that I don't like it but . . .

Prude, ha ha.

She was suddenly wearing multi-pocketed baggy low-rise jeans and a pair of white aerobics cross-trainer shoes. She didn't add anything on top. Images of JackieZZ's computer persona popped in my head. Tatiana also had a three-section chain for a belt and I guessed that there were knives and other various weapons in her pockets, and her hair was pulled into a ponytail with metallic six-inch-long pins—each of which could be a nasty weapon.

I wasn't worried. Anything we needed in a hurry, the nanomachines could provide. And unless the humans had figured out how to prevent the nanomachines like the Grays had, we could just use them to stop any human attackers. My hope was that there would be no need for self-defense. After all, the U.S. Air Force should be on our side.

Tatiana and I reached the external bay of the *Phoenix*.

Mike, are they in yet?

Yes, Steven. I have closed the doors and the room is at one atmosphere.

Good.

You ready, Tatiana?

Yes. She said something else to Mikhail but I didn't pay close attention.

Okay, Mike. Open the door.

The door dissolved away and Tatiana and I walked up to the impressive little spaceship. Tatiana started to touch it.

"Don't do that!" I tried to stop her but I was too late and her hand freeze-dried and stuck to the ship's skin. It must have been on the dark side of the ship.

"Yiiiikes, goddamnit . . ." She jerked her hand from the ship ripping skin from her hand and continued to curse in Russian. Blood ran profusely down her arm for a split second before Mikhail took over and shut off her pain and healed her hand.

"Are you okay?" I grabbed her arm and looked at the palm of her hand as it went from bloody to fuzzy to healed.

"That was dumb, huh?"

Mike, how long until the ship's hull reaches equilibrium with the room? I noticed moisture collecting and forming ice crystals on the surface of the ship.

About fifteen minutes.

Can we speed that up somehow?

Not any way that I know of.

All right, thanks.

Mike, open me a comm. Link to this ship.

Okay.

"Lieutenant Ames, we are here outside your ship. The air is at one atmosphere and is breathable." I shouted for some odd reason.

"We will be out momentarily. Stand with your backs to the wall and keep your hands where we can see them," Lieutenant Ames's voice boomed in our heads.

Steven, I'm not sure I like this. Tatiana grabbed my hand and squeezed it.

Relax. We will be okay. I assured her as if I knew.

Mike, they can't move this ship without you or Mikhail, right? Mikhail ran the warp system.

Well, they cannot fly it, but they could bump it or drag

it or carry it with their own means of propulsion. But they could not access its functions without your permission.

Thanks.

The ramp of the USS *Starbuck* lowered in front of us. Tatiana and I stood deathly still and didn't make a sound or move a muscle. Then Tatiana started reciting something in her mind.

I must not fear. Fear is the mind-killer. Fear is the little-death that . . .

What are you doing? I thought to her.

Uh, reciting the Bene Gesserit fear litany.

The Bene whatsit?

It's from Dune. *You should read it,* she said, and went back to reciting the thing.

Mike, download Dune *for me.*

There are many books in the Dune *series, Steven. Which one?*

Uh, all of them I guess.

Okay, Steven.

Then I realized what Tatiana was doing. The first was the best I thought, although the Prince Leto transformation really struck home with what had happened to Tatiana and myself. If you don't understand what I mean, go get a copy and download it for yourself. I joined in the litany with Tatiana.

A few seconds passed and four soldiers took flanking positions on each side of the ramp and trained firearms on us. "Don't move!" one of them said.

Lieutenant Ames and another female that I didn't recognize seemed to appear at the top of the ramp. Tatiana and I looked at each other—puzzled.

Did you see that?

Did you see that? We both thought at the same time. We weren't sure if we were seeing things or not. But if we were, we both were. *Perhaps it was a trick of the lighting?* I thought.

Steven! We have been engulfed in a warp bubble from one of the outside ships! It would appear we are being dragged down into the interior of the lunar crust! Mike warned me. He never sounded alarmed before. He must be experimenting with voice inflections.

Keep me posted, Mike. Unless you think it's necessary, talk to me on the open channel where Tatiana can hear it. Repeat what you just said on the open channel.

Okay, Steven.

Steven! We have been engulfed in a warp bubble from one of the outside ships! It would appear we are being dragged down into the interior of the lunar crust! Mike warned us and I tried to act surprised again. He used the same voice tones this time, also. Tatiana's eyes grew wide and bulged.

Steven! She called to me.

Take it easy. We don't know what's going on yet.

"Why are you warping our ship!" I questioned Lieutenant Ames with a voice of command tone.

The fact that I knew what was going on seemed to startle the lieutenant and her cohorts. Then the girl beside her vanished right before our eyes.

"Shit, 'Becca!" the lieutenant said and then vanished.

Both of the women appeared on either side of Tatiana and me and the dark-haired one caught me unaware with a chokehold around my neck and she kicked my left knee out from under me. She was on top of my back and was holding me down and attempting to choke me out. Tatiana leaped four meters in the air over Lieutenant Ames and landed on the ramp. She dodged crossfire from the soldiers holding the flanking positions and flung her hairpins—deadly projectiles headed for each of the soldiers. The hairpins simply deflected away from the soldiers, who continued to fire at Tatiana.

Mike, give me as much strength and speed as you can.

"Yeeeoowww! GET OFF MY BACK, BITCH!" I screamed as I stood up and forced my attacker's grip from my throat. It was difficult and took all of my strength. *Mike, how strong is this woman?*

Her strength is only slightly above average for human, but she is wearing some type of force-field-enhanced armor. I believe it to be a miniature Alcubierre warp field system.

Tatiana! They have personal force fields!

Tell me something I don't know. I caught a glimpse of her out of the periphery of my vision. She was kicking and jumping and flipping almost too fast for the human eye to see. Of course, Mike had enhanced my vision a long time ago. We had both realized that faster vision and reflexes would be useful in combat back when we were going through our sparring phase—way back a month ago.

Lieutenant Ames appeared out of nowhere in front of me and I sidestepped her just before she opened fire on me with some sort of projectile weapon that passed through her force field.

Mike, did you see that? The bullet passed through the field.

Yes, Steven. I am working on it.

I noticed that also, lover! I think they are timed with

the warp bubble oscillating on and off . . . "Yeouch, @#$%$@!@" Tatiana began cursing verbally in Russian and I pushed the lieutenant and her sidekick away from me far enough that I could jump to Tatiana. She had been shot through the hand—*one* of the only vulnerable spots besides the feet or the head. I bounced off the ceiling above her and flipped to the floor beside her. She crouched for a split second and I noticed the wound was already healing. I grabbed her and jumped with her over the spaceship to gain cover for a second.

Mike, make a hole in the ceiling into the engine room above.

You are too far away, Steven. The nanomachines cannot be controlled more than a few meters from you or Tatiana.

Shit! Right, I forgot.

I put my hand on the hot side of the spaceship hull. It was just a little warm now. *Mike?*

I understand, he told me as the ship's hull started rippling and grew fuzzy.

In you go, Tatiana. We pushed through the hull of the little spaceship and rushed to the control room. Tatiana was now covered from head to toe in the black material and I noticed that I was also. The fabric must be mostly see-through.

We found the controls of the spacecraft and Tatiana raised the ramp. It was too slow. Lieutenant Ames and her dark-haired friend were on top of us. We were kicking and punching and crawling and generally tearing the living hell out of that pretty spaceship.

"For God's sake, would you stop it!" I screamed. "I'm an American, damnit!"

"You're a lot more powerful than any human I ever seen!" I heard in a Southern accent just as I caught a fist in the face that really hurt.

The nanomachines killed the pain and set about repairing the damage while I returned the favor to Lieutenant Ames. I was able to grab her by the arm once as she punched at me. I couldn't actually feel her arm, instead I felt an infinitely hard substance. I squeezed it hard so as to maintain my grip and then I whirled her with all my strength. I wiped out a wall while spinning her and then let her go. She flew up and out through the hull of the spaceship and clanged against the wall of the alien spaceship's payload bay.

Tatiana and the other girl had torn the ship to pieces trying to get at each other. But then three of the soldiers got the better of her and forced her down. They couldn't penetrate the alien condensed matter bodystocking but they could hold her down and put enormous pressure on her. The deck plating of the *Phoenix* was giving slightly under the pressure and an outline of Tatiana was being pressed into the alien metal.

Steven, oh my God, help me! STEVEN, HELP ME!
Use the nanomachines, or something! I'm coming.
The nanomachines are too busy keeping her alive, Mikhail said.

I tried to rush to her aid but the lieutenant and the remaining soldier boy sideswiped me. "Goddamnit, Ames it *is* me. The same Steven Montana that met you in Virginia. I met you and the general and Dr. Daniels! It's me, damnit! You are going to kill her if you don't let her up." I pleaded with the Air Force lieutenant as I ducked and dodged and returned blows with her and the remaining soldier.

The soldier raised a firearm and started peppering me with automatic weapons fire. More than half of the bullets I dodged, but a considerable number of them hit me. That alien body armor might stop a bullet but it hurts like hell when it hits. Will to rescue Tatiana and alien nanomachine healing ability enabled me to force through the barrage of machine-gun bullets.

Steven, the soldier's shield is completely shutting off when he fires! Mike showed me in my mind.

I took the pain from the continued machine-gun bullets hitting me in the chest. One of the bullets caught me in the head and I saw stars and was nearly knocked unconscious for a second. Mike pulled me through it and kept pushing my stamina, strength, and adrenaline levels through the roof into uncharted territories. I summoned all my speed and forced through the force field at the instant one of the bullets hit the edge of the field region. The field was off for a millisecond—that was more than I needed—and then I was inside it holding the soldier by the throat.

Mike, take control of his mind for me.

The soldier fought back for a split second and then he went catatonic. I forced him around in front of me and his personal warp field adjusted itself to protect both of us. I had Mike read the fellow's mind and figure out how to drive the warp bubble armor thing.

"Let her up or he dies!" I said.

Lieutenant Ames stopped right in front of me and didn't move a muscle. "Everybody freeze!" she said.

"Good. Just hold on a minute, please!" I had the nanomachines remove the bodystocking from my face. "Let her up please. You are going to kill her."

"No way. You let him go first," the dark-haired girl yelled back to us.

" 'Becca, shut up!" Ames said. "Mr. Montana, is it really you?"

"It's me, Lieutenant Ames. It's me!" I wasn't sure if she was trying to buy time with me or if she was serious so I started scanning the room for ideas. Any idea would be better than what I had at present.

Steven, what's happening? Tatiana pleaded in my head for help.

Try to stay calm, gorgeous. Are you hurt?

My left femur has been broken twice, but Mikhail has fixed it. I had to have my pain centers shut off. The pain was more than I could take. My chest is flat as a pancake, there is no telling how much hemorrhaging has been caused. Mikhail is working on me.

Stay alive, honey. I'll get us out of this. Mike, open the bay door!

Steven, I think I know what you want but that will no longer have the effect you desire. We are not in space any longer.

Where are we?

We are inside some sort of Moon base deep under the lunar surface.

Is there air?

Yes.

Okay. Open the doors anyway. It might distract them. Do it fast. Then cut the ship's gravity and make everything fall with the outside gravity. Do it on my signal. First, transfer the warp bubble controls from this guy to me. A belt with warp drive controls on it materialized around my waist. Mike downloaded the instructions into my brain. Suddenly I understood the technology completely for the warp bubble armor. The belt contained a tiny quantum vacuum fluctuation power system that used the Casimir effect to pull energy from the vacuum of spacetime to power a small Clemons-type warp field coil. The warp field generator responded to the energy changes inside the bubble to change its shape. The soldier was also wearing a superconducting quantum interference device (SQUID) headband that enabled him to command the warp bubble to propel him in whatever direction he wanted to go and at whatever velocity the little warp generator could attain. Of course, Mike could do that so I didn't need the headband. I made certain that Tatiana was given the same information so that there would be no "learning curve" time for her if and when she needed to drive one of the warp armor belts.

Tatiana, did you get all that?

Yes, Steven. Do it quickly. Mikhail is worried that he can't keep up with the damage to me.

Okay, Tatiana, I'm sorry I let them get you. Be ready, here I come. Do it, Mike!

The bay doors dissolved instantly and the remains of the Air Force ship fell outward and down, carrying everybody else with it. It was enough of a distraction that I had enough time to throw the soldier out of the warp field and fly at warp velocity to Tatiana. I clanged into the four warp fields that were falling with Tatiana and pushed them out of the way. Grabbing Tatiana and wrapping the field around her I zoomed away at warp so we would be invisible to people outside the bubble. The *Phoenix* and the *Starbuck* were inside what appeared to be a huge cylindrical hangar that led upward to the lunar surface. The wall immediately to our right had a giant twenty-meter archway opening into a small town. It opened into a small town—on the Moon!

With Tatiana in hand I fled for the cover of the town, still at warp speed. I stopped on top of a water tower microseconds later.

We sat down on top of the tower and I kept the warp field on and had Mike replicate a warp bubble armor generator for Tatiana. The view from the tower was interesting. There were trees, a lake, and various streets and buildings. There was one gee gravity in the town and the dome overhead looked like hardened lava rock. There were large windows in the dome here and there and it was obvious from the view that we were underground and in a modified gravity field.

"How are you?" I rubbed her cheeks as the bodystocking dissolved. Her face was red and blue and bloody. Her nose was broken and her lips were busted. But that changed rapidly.

"There is a lot of internal damage."

"Yeah, I tuned into Mikhail. He says he needs about thirty more seconds with you." Her chest heaved and her abdomen filled out to normal proportions. Her, uh, features took their more rosy, vivacious, and perky appearance. The sparkle in her hazel eyes grew brighter.

"Unh!" She winced as Mikhail turned her pain centers back over to her. "Oww." She stretched her limbs and digits and then arched her back. "I owe that bitch an ass whuppin'!" She said as she stood up.

"That's a lot better." I laughed.

"So this damned thing is the little warp generator?"

she asked as she hooked the warp armor around her waist. *Hey, this thing is pretty cool. The Van den Broeck bubble has been modified so that you can see through it, interesting.*

Yeah, but only when you are moving at nonrelativistic speeds, I thought to her and then, *Mikhail, how is she?*

She is fine, Steven.

Increase her strength, agility, and speed as much as you can.

Okay, Steven.

Mike, any idea where they are?

Yes, Steven. They are everywhere and here they come! Look out!

The water tower shook violently from the rushing wind and the oncoming warp fields. Tatiana activated her armor just in time for the impact from our would-be assailant.

"Look out, Tatiana!"

We took off flying in opposite directions. Realizing that we didn't need to get split up again I doubled back to keep up with her. But I was having a hard time, getting bounced around by what appeared to me—when we would slow and the bubbles were transparent—to be the male part of the Dr. Daniels duo that I had met in Virginia. There was also a really big African-American fellow in an Air Force uniform with him as well. The three of us fought our way through a trailer park—I paused just long enough to say, "Damn, there's a trailer park on the Moon!" I got smacked pretty hard for it also.

Tatiana, how you doing?

Could use a little help over on a football field.

Mike, do you have a layout of this place?

Yes, I will download it to both of you now. We were

more than a few meters apart but Mike simply had Mikhail download the information into Tatiana's mind.

Mike, keep an overlay of Tatiana's and my relative positions current in our minds. Also, can you track these warp bubbles?

The overlay is there now. Unfortunately I need the ship's sensors to track the warp bubbles.

Then use them!

Okay.

Damn, Mike you don't need my permission for everything.

Okay.

Hey, if you two are through chatting, you think you could get over here and help me out? I've got a stadium full of angry warp-armored soldiers to deal with.

Be right there.

I kicked the armor propulsion into full power and bounced through Dr. Daniels and the other guy. They followed in hot pursuit, and we crashed into the middle of the bleachers at the stadium, throwing punches and blocks and kicks and you name it at mind-shattering speeds. Occasionally, there were sonic booms from the warp fields moving faster than the sound barrier.

Tatiana plowed up through the ground behind Dr. Daniels and we timed our attack through our mind link and squished him—hard! Interestingly enough, his power generator exploded on him and his warp field went off. His clothes caught on fire and he immediately started rolling around on the ground to put the fire out. I thought that his reactions were cool and collected and showed that he was very formidable under pressure, but without a warp armor system he was not a threat to us any longer.

Tatiana was blindsided by the 'Becca person who had been a thorn in her side all afternoon. 'Becca turned away from her and grabbed up Dr. Daniels and flew off with him. Tatiana started to pursue but I told her to forget it.

There is no end to this. We have to figure out a way to stop it!

I agree, Steven. How? Tatiana replied.

Mike, Mikhail, we're open for suggestions.

Sorry, Steven and Tatiana, I have none. Mikhail said.

I have now all the data on each of the warp bubbles, Steven. I can track them for you. Here is an overlay of their locations.

Thanks, Mike. Tatiana and I both could now tell where the warp bubbles were. There were nine of them inside the little lunar city dome. While we carried on this conversation we were continuously bobbing and weaving and leaping and flying and punching and kicking and ducking and blocking and fighting away or through one or more of the nine bubbles.

Tatiana and I timed another squeeze play and took out another set of armor. This worked well three more times. Then 'Becca and Dr. Daniels joined the mix again. Between her and him and Lieutenant Ames and the other four armored individuals we were outnumbered. On the other hand, our reflexes and abilities were superhuman and theirs were just human.

Three of them attempted the squeeze play on me after Tatiana and I had taken out one more of the troops. Without the advantage of a mental link and faster-than-human reflexes, their attempt just caused them to clang together with a thunderous clap. The concussion from the impact flattened one of what appeared to be the school buildings and in the confusion Tatiana and I turned it on them and took out two more of their armored suits. Each time we burned one of their suits we tried to jump a few hundred yards away with hopes of sparing injury to the poor soldiers inside them.

We had them down to just 'Becca, Lieutenant Ames, and Dr. Daniels. We were slugging it out pretty forcefully and the three of them were smart enough to keep a round robin going that wouldn't allow us to squeeze them. The side effects though, were massive destruction to the little lunar town. There was nothing left of the trailer park and the schools were totally gone.

Mike had been broadcasting over every frequency known to man that we were friends and were not there to cause harm. Nobody would listen. Then 'Becca and Dr. Daniels got the squeeze on me and my little warp belt caught on fire and exploded. I was falling to the ground from fifty meters up and my warp armor was gone. The two turned their backs on me assuming I was no longer a threat and went to help Lieutenant Ames get the squeeze on Tatiana.

Mike, fix my warp system!

Done!

Thanks. The warp bubble came on and I plowed through the ground ten meters before I stopped. *Tatiana, they think I'm out for the count, but they don't understand nanotechnology! Let's squeeze the redhead. I'll be there . . . now!*

I hear you, lover!

Tatiana dodged the other two and plowed headfirst into Lieutenant Ames. The swiftness of her dodging and plowing set off sonic booms. I used the warp bubble map overlay in my mind to plot a head-on vector that would place Ames's bubble directly between Tatiana and me. We smacked into her and squeezed her field until it popped the miniature warp field coils in the belt around her waist. Sparks and a tiny explosion flashed inside her bubble and then her warp field extinguished itself. Ames fell about five meters to the ground with a *thud*! The velocity vector rolled her another ten or twenty meters. I was sure she had serious bone fractures from the fall. I was concerned for her—there was no need for anyone to get killed here, damnit! Then the two remaining got me in a squeeze play while I was watching Ames. I had expected that the stress from two warp bubbles pressing from opposite sides would put stresses on the warp field generator coils in the belt and rip the coils right off their mounts and through the electronics. After all, that is what had just happened to Lieutenant Ames's warp armor fractions of a second before. But Ames didn't have an alien SuperAgent for a buddy—I did. And Mike had taken it upon himself to find an advantage for us.

I have modified the field coils, Steven. They will last long enough for me to repair them. You should be able to withstand more than three bubbles squeezing you at a time.

Thanks, buddy! Have Mikhail fix Tatiana's as well.

Already did.

I shot my bubble upward to the ceiling of the little lunar town and I told Tatiana to dive deep under ground. Using the warp bubble overlays that Mike was feeding us we could easily anticipate and surprise the remaining two. Especially since they thought they could still squeeze us.

The two remaining followed me upward until I reached

the top of the lunar dome. Then I swept out a huge arc at hypersonic velocities, which had me covering the little town in heartbeats from one side to the other. Tatiana loitered underground until I gave her the signal and then I stopped dead still.

Dr. Daniels, the male, had been following hot on my tail and when I hit the brakes he rammed me hard. Tatiana, of course, had been forewarned of my plan and burst through the soil at warp speed and forced her bubble into both of us. Daniels's warp system exploded violently and this time with my faster-than-normal vision I saw fragments from the belt penetrate his body in several places. The violence of the warp bubble collisions flung us more than a hundred meters into the side of the lunar dome. Daniels fell down onto the roof of a two-story house at the end of a cul-de-sac near the edge of the dome. Daniels lay there lifeless and the other bubble swooped down and stopped with him and engulfed his body as it rested on the rooftop, no longer pursuing us.

Tatiana started to take action.

No, Tatiana! No! I told her.

Then both Tatiana and myself were slammed together and were being squeezed together as if we were in the clutches of a giant fist. A booming voice filled the town dome.

"NOT IN MY CITY YOU DON'T!" came from an older man standing beside General Clemons. The two of them were wielding some sort of device that hovered several feet above the ground. "MAKE ANY FURTHER MOVES AND I WILL CRUSH YOU INTO A SINGULARITY."

I wasn't certain if his machine could overpower our

modified systems or not, but the box he was using was bigger and I guessed had a larger power system. My guess was that he would win. But, I didn't come here to fight anyway!

We didn't come here to fight! I told Tatiana. The adrenaline had gotten the entire encounter way out of hand. But again, that 'Becca girl attacked us. We were just standing there.

Mike, can you put me through whatever broadcast system he's using?

Done!

Good.

"*I am Steven Montana, an American citizen. This is Tatiana Carolovic Svobodny, daughter of the Russian deputy ambassador to the United Nations. We were abducted by the Grays and then we revolted against them and stole their ship. We have been stranded in space for months now and just now figured out how to get home! We mean you no harm, but you fired on us first! We were merely defending ourselves!*"

They were startled for a second by the fact that we could so quickly override their technology. But the older couple kept their cool. I could also see that 'Becca had picked up Lieutenant Ames and Dr. Daniels and was flying off with them. I hoped to an emergency room.

"I am Anson Clemons and this is General Tabitha Clemons, the leader of this base. She, Lieutenant Ames, and Dr. Jim Daniels have met Steven Montana and have assured me that you look very different from him. And you appear to have miraculous technologies and superhuman abilities. Is there a way you can prove who you are?"

"How would I do that? The only thing I can think of is reciting the meeting where I met your cohorts verbatim. I met them in Virginia at CIA headquarters!"

YOU DID WHAT! Tatiana screamed in my mind.

I couldn't tell you, sweetheart. It's deeply classified and I didn't know what I should or shouldn't talk to you about, sorry. But our lives depend on it now. I will fill you in later.

Steven?

Yes, Mike?

I have completed an analysis and sensor sweep with the ship's sensors. There is no way that we can modify the miniature warp systems to withstand the force available by the system they are using.

I thought so. Thanks, Mike.

You are welcome, sorry.

Then I recited the conversations that took place in Virginia as swiftly and as accurately as I could. I finished up with: "Listen to me. We were stranded on that alien ship for months and learned how to use their technology. I fear that Dr. Daniels and Lieutenant Ames were hurt badly. We can save them very easily if you will let us."

"We are still not certain we can trust you!" Anson Clemons replied.

Tatiana, I think we should surrender to them.

What? Why, Steven? They tried to kill us.

They thought we were aliens. What would you've done?

I would've tried to kill us.

Okay then?

"Okay. Please don't kill us, but we are going to turn off our warp bubbles now!"

Tatiana, turn it off!

I don't know, Steven, they'll crush us!

Tatiana, turn it off now or they will crush us!

No, Steven! I . . . I'm afraid.

Tatiana, if you love me and trust me you will listen to me now. TURN OFF YOUR WARP BUBBLE ARMOR, NOW!

She did it. I wasn't sure she was going to. It seemed that the only thing in the world she trusted was her ability to act—and, fortunately, me. Who could blame her, after dealing with the Grays?

I turned my warp armor off and Dr. Clemons lowered us to the ground. Tatiana held my hand and I could tell she was shaking slightly. I told Mike to calm her down. Something didn't make sense. Mikhail should have been able to suppress her fear better, but Mike got her under control.

We settled on the ground at the edge of one of the cul-de-sac streets just in front of Dr. and General Clemons.

"It's his face, Anson! I don't know though, he has lost a lot of weight and is in better physical condition," General Clemons said.

"Y'all just keep your distance, son, until we get to know you a bit better!" Dr. Clemons warned and touched on personal warp fields around the two of them.

"Look, I can explain why I appear so different! The Grays use nanomachines that are controlled by those Quantum Connected Central Processing Units that you have been trying to reverse engineer. We figured them out. That is how we stole the ship from the Grays. Watch this," I told them, and stood straight up in front of them and had my clothes change through several different styles and colors. Then I started to bend over and Dr. Clemons stopped me.

"Now let's not make any fast moves, son!"

"You don't understand. If I wanted to, the nanomachines have made my reflexes so much faster than human that I could move and you wouldn't even be able to see it. But don't worry. We really are just glad to be home, or—well, you know! Please allow me, I promise no swift moves." I slowly knelt down and took a knee on the asphalt. I placed my hand on the street and caused the asphalt to rise up from the ground into a statue likeness of the general. I could tell that several years ago she was very attractive and I made the likeness of her as a younger—Tabitha, as I recalled—more vivacious astronaut. Then I had the asphalt statue move and blow them a kiss. This sort of amused them.

Make it salute, Steven.

Nice touch, beautiful!

I then made the statue salute.

"Allow me," Tatiana said and followed my lead. She was standing on the asphalt so there was no need of bending down to touch it—she always did grasp this technology quicker than I did. A statue of Dr. Clemons rose up from the street beside the General Clemons statue. Then she had the two statues hold hands and we let it rest at that.

"Well, ain't that some shit!" Dr. Clemons whistled.

"Please, it's nothing but millions of nanomachines working overtime. That's why we both are superhuman the way we are. It's simple nanotechnology enhancements to our bodies and minds. We have complete control over them and we can damn near heal anything. Please let us help your wounded," I pleaded.

"Okay son, I've read comic books that are older than

you are that have this idea in them. There was that Crichton book and *The Black Hole Travel Agency* series, and a shitload of short stories that described similar magical technologies, so I get it. Just, it's purty damn difficult to be certain that y'all control the nanomachines and not the other way around," Dr. Clemons explained his position.

Mike, download all of these relevant books and stories to me please.

Okay, Steven.

"That makes a lot of sense," Tatiana said.

"Yes, I agree with you. There is no way to know that other than to trust us. Look, at least let us help the wounded. Keep us in a bubble and let one in at a time or something. You will see. Damnit, I had to sit still and watch those goddamned Gray sons of bitches dismember another human being right in front of my eyes. I watched them pull out his heart, cut off his head, and then dissolve him into nothingness. The last thing I want to see is more human death!" I thought of my family for a brief second.

Steven, Dr. Daniels is dying, Mike alerted me.

How do you know? I asked.

I used the sensors from the spaceship to tap into the video system in the infirmary. His internal organs were crushed and he is rapidly bleeding to death. He has less than a few minutes before his heart stops. Mike said this on the open channel for both Tatiana and me to hear.

You have to save him, Steven. Go to him and I'll stay here as a hostage.

Good idea, but you go and I'll stay as a hostage.

No, Steven, it will be better coming from you. You are

an American and they are American. It should be you. I will stay.

I love you, Tatiana. Take care of yourself.

"Listen to me," I pleaded one last time. "I'm using the alien computer on the spaceship to tie into your hospital's video system. Dr. Daniels is dying . . ."

Steven, he just died. Mike sounded genuinely sad.

" . . . He just died. I'm going to him and Tatiana will stay as your hostage. But I *am* going!" I moved faster than any person with normal human reflexes and vision could react to. To Dr. Clemons and the general I must've appeared as one big blur of motion. Of course, Tatiana could follow me with her enhanced vision, but she watched the Clemons's closely instead. I followed the map in my head to the operating room that Dr. Daniels was in and pushed myself as fast as I could run. I used the map to anticipate obstacles and turns and I covered the half-mile trek in less than eight seconds or so. I stopped just outside the operating room doors and my wake turbulence caught up with me. The wind blew papers off of bulletin boards along the hallway as I pushed the doors open. I walked in panting and sweating a little and proceeded straight to the operating table and pushed the doctors out of the way. They were trying to revive him but Mike had assured me that it would do no good with such extensive damage to all his major organs.

I placed my hands on his head, since his chest was spread open with a rib spreader.

Steven, put your hand in his chest. It will save time.

Okay. Help him, Mike. Every microsecond counted, I assumed, so I pressed my hand into his open and red with draining blood abdomen. The nanomachines immediately rushed to work. I could see the interior of Dr. Daniels' abdomen getting fuzzy.

I am helping him now, Steven.

The doctors attempted to pull me off of Dr. Daniels's body, but I kicked at them and used my left hand to push them around. Then the dark-haired lady, 'Becca, burst in with a machine pistol.

"Get away from him you alien fucker!" she screamed at me and pointed the gun at me.

"Listen to me, I'm helping him!" I cried as she shot me three times. Two of the bullets hit the bodystocking but one of them ripped through the side of my neck— and it hurt, bad.

Tatiana burst in a microsecond too late to stop 'Becca from shooting me. But it didn't take long for her to use the nanomachines to knock her out and then the others in the room as well. She did all that and caught me before I hit the ground.

You're all right, baby! I got you.

Hold me up, Tatiana. I have to fix him.

You'll fix yourself first!

No, I won't. Hold me up!

Tatiana held me up to the table and I was close enough to Dr. Daniels for the nanomachines to communicate with Mike. I held my left hand against my neck to slow the bright red stream of blood squirting out there. The squirting blood made a squishing sound between my hand and neck as it ran through my fingers. I placed my right hand back in Dr. Daniels's open abdomen.

Mike, how is he?

He will be better than you in less than thirty seconds.

Not if I have anything to say about it, Tatiana said.

Mikhail, you know what to do. Tatiana winked at me and the profusely bleeding hole in my neck began to heal.

A moment or two later the Clemons's came running into the room gasping for air. They took a brief survey of the room and looked concerned when they noticed the myriad of bodies on the floor.

"We heard shots . . ." Tabitha Clemons breathed out and stopped short when she saw the bullet wound in my neck closing slowly.

"Don't worry." Tatiana turned to her and smiled. "They're just knocked out. They were . . . trying to stop Steven. Hey, I had to do something." Tatiana shrugged and looked at the incapacitated people on the floor.

The rib spreader on Dr. Daniels dissolved and vanished and his chest started closing. I told Tatiana to wake everybody up. Dr. Clemons grabbed 'Becca in a nerve grab that, according to Mike, was developed by the Tibetans over a thousand years ago. I was impressed by the old man to say the least. Everyone rose silently—other than 'Becca, who was cursing in pain—but they all watched as Dr. Daniels's chest closed up around my hand and the surface of his abdomen grew fuzzy.

You can remove your hand, Steven.

Oh, sorry, Mike. I pulled my hand from the man's chest and it was covered with blood. Tatiana had Mikhail clean me up almost instantly.

We stood around and watched Daniels quietly, and then his heart monitor went from the flatlining screech to a normal beeping heartbeat. Then he opened his eyes and reflexively breathed as deep as he could.

"Behave yourself, Rebecca." Dr. Clemons let her go

and she rushed to Daniels's side, hugging and kissing him all over and crying.

"Oh, Jim, I thought you were going to die on me!" Tears rolled down 'Becca's face.

Jim looked around the room and saw Tatiana and me standing at the foot of his stretcher and he jumped violently. Dr. Clemons and 'Becca grabbed him and held him down.

"Take it easy, Jim. They saved you," Dr. Clemons said.

"They're the ones that put me in this shape!" Jim cursed.

"Dr. Daniels, I apologize deeply and sincerely, but we never meant any harm. It was all a misunderstanding," I assured him.

"Yeah, a misunderstanding and a bit of paranoia on your part," Tatiana added smugly and 'Becca gave her an evil look.

"Dr. Daniels, you'll be fine," I told everyone in the room. Then I thought about the massive damage and Lieutenant Ames being injured. "Tatiana, let's get to the other wounded, now!" We zipped from table to table and from room to room in the hospital. I just happened to be the one who fixed Lieutenant Ames. General and Dr. Clemons stood over my shoulder the entire time—they were both concerned from a parenting point of view, and I could tell they were very curious about the technology.

"Then it is you, Mr. Montana?" Lieutenant Ames asked me as the last few lacerations on her face and stomach vanished away.

"Yes, and it's Steven, Lieutenant," I told her.

"Then it's Annie, or Anne Marie, if we are on a first-name basis." She held her hand out for me to shake it.

She was amazed that it was no longer broken.

"Sorry for all this. I didn't mean for any—"

"Forget it. We were just as much to blame, Steven. That damned Rebecca never follows orders. Civilians!" She shook her head and harumphed.

Then we went out into the city and used the sensors from the *Phoenix* to search for other wounded. After several hours there were no longer any immediate emergencies. If you didn't count the Gray threat, that is.

Look what a mess, Steven. Tatiana pointed out at the lunar town.

I know, gorgeous. We will help them fix it.

➤ CHAPTER 16

It took us a good couple of weeks to get the little town on the Moon back in order. Apparently the kids in town were glad that school was canceled while we rebuilt. Thankfully, it was fall break and the kids had not been in school at the time or the incident could have been far more tragic than it was. A few trips to Earth in the little warp ships were made for various materials until I set up a materials generation and replication area with a downloaded version of Mike controlling it. Basically, any computer-drawn model of an object would enable it to be constructed from the rubble and lunar materials available. The nanomachines in the facility Tatiana and I put together would take the material and convert it into whatever piece of equipment, construction material, or whatever else was needed. If precious or exotic elements were required that weren't available, then we sent the warp ships to Earth. The nanomachines could only manipulate atoms, so if you needed a gold atom in something you had to have a pile of gold atoms to begin with.

On the other hand, we increased the budget capability of the little lunar town tremendously because there is plenty of carbon on the Moon. Diamonds are made of carbon and the lunar base became one of the Earth's small suppliers of diamonds—unbeknownst to the general public of course. General Clemons had the CIA acquire a South African diamond company to fence the lunar diamonds through—of course, the CIA got a big cut for its troubles. We allowed just enough of the lunar diamonds to flow into the market as not to cause suspicion or to flood the market and drive down the revenues. The diamond market was about a thirty-billion-dollar business each year and we planned to take in about a third of a percent of that and thus keep a low profile in the business. We also set up similar markets for the billion-dollar-a-year silicon wafer market, the two-billion-dollar-a-year flat glass (mirrors and such) market, the multibillion-dollar fiber optic market. Remember there are a lot of silicates on the lunar surface. The CIA called this contingent the "diamond factory," which was along the same lines as the old "fly by night industries" business they often used. We continued to branch out into as many business areas as we could but never took more than a fraction of a percent of the business so we didn't attract any unwanted attention.

Another aspect of the business was so highly classified that only a few folks on Earth knew the intricacies of it. We set up a manufacturing facility that could rapidly prototype highly technical instrumentation for classified programs.

Say there was a need for a new fourteen-billion-dollar Top Secret communications satellite; our nanomachine system could build it from specs in a hundreth of the time and for practically no cost. It cost more money to set up the cover facilities and for the overhead than for the actual device. We spun off two companies that could produce the rapid prototypes and then the CIA arranged for Boeing to buy one of them and Lockheed Martin to buy the other. The two companies would never know that they both would get these classified products from the same plant on the Moon. And we made almost eighty percent profit from these products, after the big industry, CIA, and cover companies raked off their share. We made a lot of money through this program.

There were two other programs that were classified even more deeply and I won't talk about them here. All I can say is that one had to do with using SuperAgents to understand, predict, and drive various economic engines. The other had to do with perfect counterfeits of foreign currencies that enabled us to control their inflation rates. We made a lot of money off those programs as well. From here on, we simply followed the CIA's lead and referred to all of these efforts with the encompassing and nebulous title "the diamond factory."

The fact that we enabled the Clemons's facility to become a viable business and no longer a drain on budget improved Tatiana's and my situation with the W-squared crew tremendously.

I was even given that long-overdue security clearance. Of course, Tatiana wasn't. She was not an American citizen—and there was always that isolated abductee issue. I was still thinking about that. On the other hand, only I could really keep anything from her and it appeared as though the W-squared group realized this. They made us both honorary members of the W-squared team and treated Tatiana as a cleared and accessed member. In fact, General Clemons pulled some strings and had an "interim" clearance issued to Tatiana with Clemons as the responsible party. But I needed to deal with the security implications of the isolated abductee issue somehow. I wasn't sure how yet; in fact I wasn't even sure why she was isolated and what that meant. As far as Mike and I could figure, for some reason out of the millions of humans that have been abducted by the Grays in the past, a couple hundred thousand of them were different somehow. The Grays had taken some sort of precautions so as to not let these "isolated abductees," as I had been calling them, gain access and control of any of their SuperAgent systems. We still had no idea why.

After I had Mike check out everybody in the town for abductee status, we found that there were none—no abductees period, not just isolated ones. We guessed that it was due to the extreme psychological screening that these folks went through in order to get these high-level security clearances. Perhaps the quirky effects on the personality that the tracking implants have would cause one to be a suspicious security risk. Hey, maybe that was another reason for me not getting cleared earlier. I was moody and nuts for a long time—and perhaps even a bit paranoid on occasion.

Tatiana and I spent the third week explaining our story in great detail. The group had no idea what the aliens looked like. When we explained that they were the classic UFO nut description of little Grays they were amazed and surprised. They were beginning to consider some of the UFO conspiracy theories more seriously. I hadn't told them that human abductees had zero possibility of recalling the abduction yet.

It also turned out that the two light years away in what Tatiana and I thought was deep space wasn't deep space at all for these folks. They had been out as far as eighty light years. Mike had told me this once before, but it really didn't ring true until I saw the pictures of some of the planets these humans had been to. We had a meeting in a special room near the general's office and discussed what was happening.

"In that meeting at CIA Headquarters, Dr. Daniels, you made mention of something that interested me. You said to the CIA guy that if he had told you about 'this' sooner that you would be further along by now. What did you mean by that?" I asked Dr. Daniels, the male, as I leaned back in my chair. I noted to myself that for a conference room on the Moon, it had plush furniture.

"Oh, yeah. Call me Jim, will ya? Anybody who had their hand in my chest and brings me back to life gets the privilege of calling me Jim." He grinned at me and nodded. "Anyway, we had just found out about the aliens about a year before you came along. We discovered them because we had detected their gravitational signatures. We shot one of them down with a warp missile and it crashed into Neptune. The ship made a huge splash and was apparently disabled. When we went in to take a look the ship was empty. I mean, we got to the ship just a minute or two after it impacted the planet and nothing. No alien bodies. Nothing. But we did manage to dig out their computer system. The one you saw pictures of."

"Okay, Jim, but what had you not been told?" Tatiana interjected.

Anson interrupted, "Y'all ain't gonna believe this but the damned CIA and the Strategic Space command had radar data of alien spacecraft spanning back more than forty or fifty years. The spacecraft seemed to disappear about twenty-five years ago. The DOD and CIA just thought that they had left. Of course, all the knowledge of these radar tracks is way above Top Secret and my guess is they haven't told us the complete story yet." He paused to let that sink in a little bit. It didn't really matter, as I knew that the aliens had been around a lot longer. I hadn't sprung that on them yet.

Anson Clemons continued, "We figured out that they never really left and that they just started cloaking their ships from the EM spectrum. I guess the aliens figured out that we knew they were there. But you can't cloak gravity since it is just a shape. Hellfire, we managed to start detecting them in no time."

"Yeah, and the damned things were everywhere," 'Becca added. "The first day we got the detector working there were no less than seven hits! We thought our system was wrong."

"So I sent out all four of our ships to investigate," General Clemons continued our briefing. "One of those ships was lost with all hands. We still aren't sure what happened to them. We've studied the ship we shot down at Neptune, which was much smaller than the one you two liberated. We didn't even seem to dent it. So we aren't quite sure why it stayed down." Tabitha shrugged her shoulders and pushed a lock of red hair down over the light scar on her forehead.

"I can answer some of your questions about the aliens, I think," I suggested. "As you may have discovered by now, the alien ship doesn't use a warp drive. It uses . . . well, uh . . . something a lot different and that is much much faster. But since they are not inside a warp bubble they are not in a region of flat space where gravity and inertia seems normal. So the Grays' ships use some sort of inertial dampeners. When you guys shot us with your warp missile we pulled over seven positive and negative g forces fluctuating randomly for more than three minutes. It would have probably killed normal people. The inertial dampeners were taxed to more than one hundred and ten percent. My guess is that a smaller ship couldn't handle the forces as well. Also, that sudden stop at Neptune probably was way more than even the system on the bigger ships could handle. And the little Grays are tough, but not any tougher than we are; I would guess less, actually. I killed the first two pretty easily. I don't think they could take the gees that Tatiana and I pulled."

"Wait a minute," Anne Marie said. "That doesn't explain where the bodies were."

"No, I'm not sure about that, let me think about it for a bit." *Mike, do you have any idea about that?*

They were levitated to another ship, Steven.

Oh, I see. Uh, how were they levitated?

The same way you were, with the tractor beam. All of the abductees are taken that way. I will download the information to you. I am surprised you never asked about it before now.

It never dawned on me. Instantly I knew all about the

tractor beam mechanism. It basically worked like a projectable gravitational field modification. The idea was very similar to the concepts investigated by Boeing back in the early years of the millennium that were based on the so-called Podkletnov experiment. Nobody had ever been able to show that Podkletnov's work was reproducible, but according to the data Mike had just given me about the Grays' technology Podkletnov was on the verge of something pretty big. He had just missed a few things here and there. It wasn't that much different from Clemons's warp field coil and projectable warp fields.

Tatiana leaned forward in her chair and winked at me as she adjusted a lock of dark curls that dangled in her face. The lock seemed to annoy her and not go where she wanted to. Then the lock simply vanished and her hairline seemed to adjust itself for the missing lock almost instantly. She giggled a bit to herself when she noticed that I caught what she was doing.

Caught me not paying attention, didn't you?

Is this boring you, gorgeous?

Nah, but I don't understand why we keep setting around in meeting after meeting. Why don't we take some of this to the aliens? We know how to knock them down.

How would you suggest we knock them down, Tatiana?

You mean you haven't figured it out?

I guess not.

Well, if the ship colliding with a planet at warp velocity stops them, then what happens to a ship trapped between two warp fields?

A squeeze play?

Why not? Mikhail, what do you think?

If a ship the size of the Phoenix *were caught between*

high warp impacts, it would crush the ship and the degenerate matter pressure of the hull material could not withstand the compression forces. Mikhail's voice resounded in my mind for a second or two.

Warp missiles could destroy the Gray ships. So we could at least defend ourselves. We needed more warp ships and more warp missiles. *Tatiana, why don't you explain your idea to the rest of the team here?*

Sure, why not?

Tatiana spent the next hour or so going over the dynamics and quantum mechanics of the degenerate matter hull materials and how the ships are made of materials like a white dwarf or a neutron star. The material was made of closely packed fermions that were squeezed in as close to each other as Pauli's exclusion principle would allow. But Pauli's exclusion isn't an infinite force and when squeezed tight enough the material will collapse even further. The only thing more compacted than a degenerate matter star would be a black hole. It was unclear even to Tatiana's enhanced mind if the squeeze play would cause the alien ships to collapse further into a pseudo- or mini-black hole or if forces would become imbalanced and the ships would explode with the force of a small supernova. It was decided to try the attack as far away from our solar system as possible.

We discussed the attack possibilities further and hashed it out to a viable plan. Then we changed the subject a bit toward the why and what of the Grays' plan. Nobody on the W-squared team had any information and Tatiana and I were the only data points they had encountered. So, obviously, they had a million questions, most of which we had never really bothered to ask Mike or Mikhail about.

We tag-teamed the answers. While one of us would answer the previous question and in so doing stall long enough, the other would be asking Mike or Mikhail the answer to the next question. Tatiana had finally asked me a few days before why we were not telling the W-squared group about the SuperAgent's mental and physical presence with us. I told her that I wasn't ready to give them up for study just yet. We had never really talked about it before, but Tatiana saw that I wasn't ready to let the cat out of the bag about Mike, so she kept her mouth shut about Mikhail. As far as the others knew, the nanomachines were under our direct control and not controlled via the SuperAgents stored in our abdomens. I had made a replica SuperAgent back on the ship before anybody became suspicious that we had removed the original.

You might think that I was being covert or subversive or just plain untrustworthy. There might have been some of that but there was something more that I couldn't put my finger on. I felt at home with the lunar crowd. They seemed to be super individuals. Of course, they had tried to kill both Tatiana and me earlier, but they thought we were aliens. Still, that must've been causing me to have some subconscious trepidations about trusting them. I was also afraid that there was going to be a need to have the power that Mike enabled me with in the coming future. And besides, I found Mike, reprogrammed him, and in a sense gave birth to his new personality and sentience, so I felt responsible for him. He had also become a part of me in more than just the physical way. I could tell that Tatiana felt the same way about Mikhail. No, we were not giving up Mike and Mikhail anytime soon.

Tatiana and I worked out techniques to make it look like we were thinking about things rather than communicating them. Occasionally, I would have Mike act like the alien ship's SuperAgent and answer questions over the speakers in the automaton voice that he had when I first found him.

"It would appear as though the Grays have been around for thousands of years," Tatiana told them.

"Yeah, I did an analysis and it appears that the abductions seem to increase during periods where there are wars." I showed them the graphics that Mike and I had put together back a few weeks ago. There was more about the isolated abductees but I couldn't tell them with Tatiana in the room. Not yet, not until I knew what it was all about. Don't get me wrong. I trusted Tatiana with my life and . . . I loved . . . Lazarus was the only other creature that I had loved nearly as much . . . poor Laz, I miss you, buddy. But there was something about this isolated abductees thing that spooked me and I couldn't put my finger on it. What would happen if the isolated abductee discovered what they were? I didn't know, so I couldn't take any chances.

The most important point remained that the Grays had been here for a long time. And from the data I had gathered via Mike, they had abducted scores of people.

Tatiana and were hanging out at the Luna Grill by the lake drinking Russian cognac—I didn't really like the stuff but Tatiana wanted me to try it. Besides, I planned to wash it down with a few beers afterward.

Mike, open channel. I told him open channel since I wanted Tatiana to hear. I placed my empty sniffer or cognac glass or whatever the thing was on the table and tried not to make an ugly face as the vile stuff went down. Tatiana just giggled. *Are Tatiana and I the only abductees-turned-liberators out of all of the abductees in the past?*

Perhaps, Steven, but from the data I have that is inconclusive. The Grays would not know about you and Tatiana. They would only know that they had lost a ship and members of the hive.

I see your point.

Steven, what about that? Tatiana interjected. *Why don't we look for missing hive members or ships throughout our history?*

Good idea, Tatiana, Mike replied to her. His growing intellect allowed him to distinguish orders from Tatiana that appeared to have no conflict of interest to our health. As long as that didn't occur Mike would accept orders or requests from her now . . . to a point.

Yeah Mike, that is a good idea, I added.

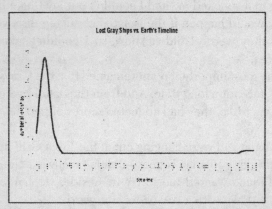

Okay, here is the data. And the number of Gray spacecraft lost in our solar system versus Earth's timeline appeared in our heads.

The pertinent data was simple. The only time Gray ships appeared to have been lost in our history was in the zero and B.C. timeframe, and then the two that were most recently lost. Obviously, the two lost recently were the one that the W-squared team shot down and the one that Tatiana and I took. But five thousand years ago there was a dramatic period of lost Gray ships in our solar system. Integrating the area under the curve on the graph suggests nearly a hundred Gray ships were lost between three thousand twenty-five B.C. and about fifty A.D. and then there were no spacecraft lost between then and the present. That really blows a hole in the Roswell crash theory doesn't it? Nothing seemed to shed light on the alien abduction stories in our popular culture, though.

➤ CHAPTER 17

On several occasions since finding him I had asked Mike to explain to me about the Grays' history and where they came from. He seemed only to have navigational data as to various alien homeworlds (the Grays' homeworld was one he didn't have) and data about the abductees. He explained to me that this was because he didn't know the Grays' mission and that he only flew the ship, ran day-to-day functions, and took care of certain mundane data storage. The Grays were great strategists and didn't really need the SuperAgents involved in their business. Consider a computer on the web, Mike said. The computer is useful, but the goals of the computer's owner are not known to the computer itself.

Using the navigational data in Mike we put together a map of the Milky Way and overlaid upon it territories of various aliens. Anson and Anne Marie and I were discussing this one morning over doughnuts and coffee (I was having a Mountain Dew) and Anson noticed something startling.

"So, let me see if I understand this completely." Anson stroked his thinning hairline and took a swig of his coffee. "The blue area is where we have been and the green is where we have looked. The tiny dot that makes on the galaxy overlay is just that, a dot. The red area here is Gray territory, this yellow area is some other alien, and there are no other aliens in the galaxy?"

"Well, Anson, I'm not sure that's right. The SuperAgent on board the *Phoenix* just says that the large areas are controlled by the Grays and the Lumpeyins, whoever they are. It doesn't say if they are the only species or not. But it does appear that the Grays and the Lumpeyins have divided the galaxy between them," I explained.

Anne Marie leaned across the table and grabbed a doughnut. "Yeah, I see that, but what about at higher resolutions? Are there other species like us embedded in there?"

"Good question, Annie. Let me ask it." I leaned back in my chair and talked to Mike verbally as I had been doing in front of the W-squared folks. "Mike, do you have data on other species and can you mark them on the graphic display with a black x?"

"Sure, Steven." Mike responded over the intercom we had set up a few days earlier. The image of the painted galaxy on the flat-screen display now had two thousand or so black x's on it.

"Wow!" Annie exclaimed.

"I had no idea!"

"Mike," Anson asked, "can you zoom in on our area and show it at a scale that will show us the boundary between us and the Grays' territory?"

"Yes."

"Look at that; it's a perfect circle around us, two hundred light years in diameter. No wonder we haven't found any aliens yet," Anne Marie pointed out.

"Mike, can you tell me if there are other of these civilizations that have such a perfect boundary about them?" Anson was on to something, but I wasn't sure what.

"Yes, about a quarter of them display such boundaries," Mike replied.

"What? You mean five hundred or so of these spots have a two-hundred-light-year diameter boundary around them?" I asked.

"Yes, Steven, exactly five hundred seventeen," Mike assured me in the automaton voice he used for the intercom.

Anson stroked his chin and then leaned back in his chair. "Mike could you paint these with a bright orange x instead of a black one?

"Yes," Mike said.

The image now displayed was startling. All of the orange x's were deep inside the Grays' red-painted region of the galaxy. What did this mean?

Anson stroked his chin again and ran his fingers through his hair. He picked up his coffee cup but then set it back down before he took a sip from it. "That's it! We are quarantined from the Grays for some reason or other. It could be due to a Prime Directive like in *Star Trek* or fear or some treaty with these Lumpeyins or, heck, it might even be an actual quarantine. Who knows? The one thing I am sure of is this. The Grays outgun us and outnumber us by a huge portion of the galaxy. Their resources must be immense. So, something is keeping them from conquering us. Maybe it is these Lumpeyins doing it. Somebody had to have been around five thousand years ago with technology that could shoot them down and I'm betting on them."

Then I had an epiphany and opened my private channel with Mike.

Mike, are any of these quarantined planets locations with isolated abductees?

That is a very interesting question, Steven. The answer is yes. All of the planets in the quarantined regions have isolated abductees in them.

Do any of the nonquarantined planets have isolated abductees in them? I held my breath for an eternity during the millisecond it took for Mike to process the data and return with an answer.

No, Steven. Only the planets with quarantines have any of the isolated abductees.

My God, Mike, what does that mean?

I do not have enough data to give you an answer, Steven, sorry.

One thing was certain. It was time to come clean with the W-squared folks and with Tatiana, but in what order? I owed it to Tatiana to talk with her first. Besides, I loved her and I could no longer justify hiding this from her. After lunch I went to find Tatiana. She had been out on a routine patrol with 'Becca and several other soldier types. In the weeks that had followed the battle between us and the W-squared people Tatiana and 'Becca had made amends and had actually become friends. She had also befriended 'Becca's sidekick, Sara Tibbs. Apparently,

Sara was an original member of the warp drive development team. Sara and 'Becca were a pair, much like a younger sister/older sister arrangement ('Becca being the oldest).

Tatiana, 'Becca, and Sara had completed a Solar Focus Telescope survey and were now hanging out on the patio of the Luna Grill by the lake. I knew this because several times during the mission Tatiana and I had tested the link between the SuperAgents. We never even had a fuzzy connection or a time lag even with more than six hundred astronomical units separating us. It was cool.

Obviously, the signals were noncausal and we began discussing temporal paradox issues. Soon after heading down the horrid path of temporal mechanics I got a headache and gave up.

What if you traveled toward me at warp speed and I thought to you to turn your vessel to the right? Would I see you travel to the right before I thought the message to you? Could we devise a way to send a message back in time that would be useful? Tatiana asked

Let's leave time travel alone for now, what do you say? I thought to Tatiana.

Suits me, it hurts to think about it. But maybe one day we'll try to make use of it, she thought back to me in Russian.

Maybe, but let's stop the alien abductions first.

Okay.

On the way to the Luna Grill I bumped into Jim and Anson and they decided to join me. The two of them were wearing karate outfits, were very sweaty, and seemed tired.

"Anson, you guys do martial arts, I take it?" I asked.

"Yeah, some of us around here ain't nanomachine

enhanced and must maintain our fitness levels as best we can." He laughed.

"Yeah, we mere mortals have to stave off death the old-fashioned way," Jim added.

"You know, there is no reason for you to be getting old. I could repair any ailments you have and even reverse and stop the genetic deterioration of aging. I've done this with myself and it doesn't take the nanomachines to maintain. Actually, I have to give Tatiana the credit for the idea. She came up with it." I shrugged my shoulders and raised my eyebrows as if to ask if they were interested.

"Are you serious?" Anson asked.

"Of course I am," I assured them.

"Well, shit fire boy, why you waiting so long about telling us this?" Anson asked in his deep Alabama drawl.

"I guess I thought you might think it to be unnatural?" The truth was, it had taken me a while to trust them enough to enhance them to even a limited extent. It had been a good tactical idea for me and Tatiana to remain the only ones so enhanced until we got to know everyone better.

"Listen, Steven," Jim started in on me. "I know you are a Californian turned Ohio . . . Ohioan . . . Ohian . . . whatever the hell, and you might think of things a little more, uh, emotionally . . ."

"Hell, Jim, why you beatin' around the bush about it?" Anson said. "He's from California; he knows he comes from a liberal and utopian-minded background. Steven, we are more logically minded here. If a man comes along and offers me the fountain of youth you better believe I'm gonna take a big-assed swig from it. Morality has no play in it."

Jim laughed and punched Anson on the shoulder. "I agree with the old codger."

I chuckled and placed a hand on Jim's shoulder and one on Anson's. I instructed Mike to implement the fountain of youth program and to pull twenty years off Anson's appearance and ten off Jim's.

"Aggghhh! That stings!" Anson yelped.

"Oh, you big sissy, it only tickles," Jim said.

"There, it's done. You guys are somewhere between twenty-five and thirty now and will remain like that until you get hit by a truck," I said.

"Can't be, son," Anson said. "My pants still fit. I was four inches smaller in the waist when I was twenty-five."

"I had the clothing adjusted as well. And be careful for a bit because I thought you guys might like a bit of extra strength and speed as well."

"Are you serious?" Jim asked.

"Of course he is," Anson replied as he blurred, zipped to the edge of the lake that was a hundred meters away and back in about two seconds. "Holy shit!" he said. He looked his right hand over and pulled his top off and looked at his chest. "The scar on my hand that's been there for twenty years is gone and the bullet hole scars are gone too!"

"Did you want to keep them? I can put them back."

"No, Steven, I had just as soon forget I ever got shot," he replied.

Realizing his new abilities, Jim leapt into the air five meters and completed several backflips before hitting the ground. He lost his balance and fell on his butt. He got up and dusted off his karate pants and then jumped up again and did a three-hundred-sixty-degree outer crescent kick followed by a tornado roundhouse kick that was perfect and nearly impossible for a normal human being in one gravity.

"Wicked!" he said. "Would you do this for the rest of the team?"

"Of course."

And so we did.

The crew decided to use cosmetic surgery, diet, and exercise as a cover story.

Anson posed the thought that if his body could so easily be adjusted and enhanced that his mind could too—couldn't it? Tatiana and I conversed in our mental speak for a few seconds to decide how to handle it and we decided not to let them in on the whole story of the alien SuperAgents but we could let them in on the enhanced memory-handling and problem-solving abilities. We asked them what types of enhancements they would like and whatever they came up with we tried to accommodate them to some extent. Anson was thrilled to be able to do any type of calculator function in his head instantly, and to be able to remember every page of every book that he read in the future. Jim wanted instant and total recall of anything any of his senses had ever detected.

Well, you can see that this went on for the rest of the evening and turned out to actually be kind of fun. Tatiana and I bonded with the group a little more and were beginning to be trusted as part of the family. They also opened up to us about their own pasts. Anson and Jim told a riveting story about how their crew had developed the world's first nanoscoptic power generator that was powered by the vacuum energy fluctuations of spacetime. They figured out how to use these Casimir-effect power supplies to power the first warp field tests in a laboratory in Huntsville, Alabama. These power generators also had the problematic trait of going chaotic every now and then and blowing up with a very big bang.

At some point in the process of developing the warp drive field coil technologies Rebecca had been involved in an accident that implanted her with millions of these microscopic power systems and she remained sick for a major part of the development project.

But, after persistence and Southern stubbornness, Anson and his team finally built a warp drive that could be tested in space. Anson and Tabitha deployed the warp probe test vehicle from the Space Shuttle and were preparing to launch it from orbit when the Space Shuttle was destroyed, thus stranding them in orbit. Anson and Tabitha reprogrammed the probe and traveled at warp speed back to Earth and crashed into a pine grove.

That was just the beginning of their adventure. They told us about how they were chased by giant tornados that were spun up by the warp probe's entry into the atmosphere (the public all thought it was a meteor) and about how they got their scars in a harrowing shootout, and about the Secret War with warp weapons against the Chinese and the Russians. The story was incredible. The description of The Rain did remind me of my family and I felt a little sad. But more angry with the people who started the war. After many margaritas, Tabitha grabbed Anson by the hand and told him that she wanted to go try out some of her new modifications on him and see how his turned out. I took that as a good sign that it was time to go to our quarters in the trailer park. It was time to talk to Tatiana about the isolated abducteeism.

➤ CHAPTER 18

"Hey gorgeous, there is something I need to talk to you about." I pulled the covers over Tatiana's shoulders since there were chill bumps forming there.

"Mmm, can it wait until morning, Stevie?" She snuggled up closer to me and appeared to be going to sleep.

"I . . . uh . . . it can't. I won't be able to sleep if I don't get this off my chest," I told her.

Tatiana rolled off me and rose up on her right elbow and mussed her long, wavy black hair. She rubbed her eyes and yawned. "Okay, let's hear it," she said in a thick Russian accent. She used that accent when she was toying with me. She smiled, but looked a little sleepy.

"Okay, I don't know how to say this so I'm just gonna say it. I haven't been completely honest with you about

Mike and Mikhail." I paused to watch her reaction.

"What do you mean, Steven?" she asked in a perfect American accent.

"Mike is the original SuperAgent and Mikhail is a copy of him. I had to make that copy because . . . Mike will not let you give him direct orders and won't let you have direct access to him."

"Why not?" Tatiana didn't seem upset, just a little surprised.

"He doesn't know."

"What? He doesn't know why he will not give me access?" Now she was interested and speaking in Russian.

"We have talked about it at great length and for some reason the Grays programmed him so that no matter what anybody did to his programming you would not be able to gain access to him." This wasn't so hard.

"Me specifically?" she asked.

"Uh, well sort of. It's you—and a whole lot of the other abductees—specifically. Mike tells me that out of the millions of abductees over our history a couple hundred thousand or so of them would have been isolated like you from accessing him. We have been calling these people isolated abductees. We don't know what it means, just that they are isolated from him."

"Why haven't you told me this before?" She didn't seem upset, just curious.

"Well, there is more."

"Uh huh?" She adjusted herself and sat up against her pillow and stretched with both arms over her head. As she did the sheets slid down to her waist revealing her navel—and a couple other things. It was dark in the room but not to my nanomachine-enhanced eyesight; the view wasn't lost on me.

"The planets that Anson called quarantined planets that we talked about earlier tonight are all planets where Mike says there are isolated abductees. No other planets have them as far as he knows. This means that for some reason the Grays are isolating complete star systems with a quarantine zone of two hundred light years with these isolated abductees inside the zones. You scare them, Tatiana." So there, I told her. It was out in the open now.

She pulled the covers up, leaned into my shoulder, and looked up at me lovingly. "Steven, you didn't have to keep this from me. It wouldn't have hurt my feelings and you can't be held responsible for something that those damned, grotesque alien monsters have done. I'm not sure why you kept it from me in the first place. You said there were a lot of others here on Earth that are these isolated abductees. Who are they?"

Open channel. Mike download all of the abductee and isolated abductee data to Tatiana.

Okay, Steven.

It took her about five seconds to assimilate all of the data. The salient point we finally came up with was that the isolated abductees were either powerful people within our civilization, or close to a powerful person. Tatiana was the daughter of the Deputy Ambassador to the United Nations for Russia, for instance.

"Steven, this scares me." She squeezed my arm and nuzzled my shoulder. "Is someone or something trying to control us and direct our politics or civilization? Why else would the abductions increase during periods of war? And from the data it appears obvious that it's not the Grays that are doing the controlling." She was wide awake now and I thought I felt her tremble a little bit—just a little bit; it takes a lot to make Tatiana tremble.

"What do you mean? Who's doing the controlling?" The answer came to me about as soon as I asked the questions.

"These Lumpeyins?" Tatiana replied.

"I think you must be right. Looking at the data suggests that they were at war with the Grays once, or perhaps they still are. Who else could have shot so many of their ships down five thousand years ago? It also looks like they have divided up the galaxy. But if that is the case, then how did they come to control all of these isolated pockets of planets? I want to think about it for a while." She kissed my shoulder and rubbed my chest.

"You aren't mad at me then? I wasn't sure what to do about this." I squirmed a little. She was making it hard for me. I would've understood mad, but she was more intrigued by the situation than perturbed at me. I guess I underestimated Tatiana.

"Steven?"

"Yeah?" I had just decided to close my eyes and try to sleep—relieved that Tatiana wasn't sore at me.

I'm awake now. Tatiana rolled over on top of me and kissed me. She looked into my eyes and then put her hands on my face and kissed me again.

Uh, yeah . . . me too, I thought to her. An obvious fib, but when a gorgeous, naked, and aroused female climbs over on top of you and shows interest in you, what else can you do? It quickly became the truth.

With so much truth-telling, Tatiana and I decided to come clean with the W-squared team and reveal everything to them. We talked to Anson first and he arranged a meeting with the team. The meeting was held in the Clemons's second-floor sunroom and we were assured that it was secure there. All the people on the Moon were cleared to at least the knowledge of the moon base. Even the kids there could only visit people on Earth that were "in the know." Kids and security had never really been dealt with before the moon base and it was decided that the only way the kids could live on the moon base would be if they were considered classified documents that must always be monitored by a person cleared at the level to which they had been exposed. So, any children on the moon base who visited Earth had cleared grandparents and so on. For the most part, children were kept on the Moon with occasional chaperoned visits to Earth. And Tabitha told us that her entire house was cleared to the required levels

Anson had drinks passed all around and there were finger foods set out on the sunroom table. Anson was a sight to see with his chef's hat and splatter-painted apron that read "Einstein had to eat too!" on it. He corralled us all together in the sunroom and began to tell the tale about Tatiana and me.

Anson's children were home from visiting the grandparents, and occasionally he would stop to tell Ariel and Hunter, and the Daniels twins, Mindy and Michael, to quit doing this or that and threaten to kill them if he had to go in there, but it was all a farce—the kids knew it too, so they paid him little attention. But once Tabitha warned the kids not to do something the law had arrived. It was pretty obvious who the boss was as far as the kids were concerned.

Occasionally Anson had Tatiana or me clarify things here and there, but he did most of the introduction to our confessional. Then he handed it over to me and told me to show the data.

I had Mike turn the outer sunroom wall of the house into a large flat-screen panel. When I did that all four of the kids went completely silent, sat down, and watched the screen. They were convinced it was a magic show. They had already seen some pretty interesting magic up here on the Moon with Anson and his entourage.

On the screen I displayed the data about the abductees and the isolated abductees versus our history. Then I showed the list of known isolated abductees and pointed out Tatiana's name and Senator Grayson's name. "The Grays know everything about us and everything that Senator Grayson knows," I pointed out.

"My God, that makes us defenseless. They have access to all of our strategies, technologies, and plans," Jim said.

"From now on nobody tells Grayson anything without me filtering it first," Tabitha said. "What else, Steven?"

"Well, there is a lot more. Mike, Tatiana, and I have figured out that the isolated abductees are all closely connected to, or related to, people in powerful positions within human civilization. They are either politically, militarily, or industrially connected. It is interesting to note that there are no socially connected isolated abductees. Whatever or whoever is causing this phenomena does not seem to think of the celebrity connection as important."

"Well, that makes sense to me," Anson interrupted. "The so-called social connection has little bearing on a military machine. If I were going to manipulate the balance of power in a civilization, I wouldn't do it through a public campaign or making a movie about it, no sir! I would change the minds of the people already in power."

"Steven, I know you explained about the Mike and Mikhail SuperAgents, but can we meet them?" 'Becca asked.

"Of course you can," Tatiana said as she placed her hand on the patio table and a speaker formed out of the table materials.

Mike, make an open channel through the speaker on the table here. The cat is out of the bag. You too, Mikhail, I told the SuperAgents.

"Mike, Mikhail, can you hear us?" I tested the speaker system.

"Of course, Steven," Mike replied.

"Yes, Steven," Mikhail said in a slightly dryer tone of voice.

"Boys, meet the W-squared crew . . ." I introduced everyone. It was fun for a moment, until we got back down to business. "Mike, display the galaxy map with the quarantine zones indicated by orange x's and the political control indicated by different colors."

"Okay, Steven," Mike replied and the map appeared on the flat screen.

"You see that the galaxy is mostly separated into two regions. This yellow part is controlled by the Lumpeyins. And the Grays control the green part. Mike calls the Grays the Teytoonis, by the way," I explained.

"Sounds to me like they bought too many vowels," Al, one of the original Huntsville members of Anson's cadre, said.

"Notice how the x's are all inside, deep inside, Gray territory," Tatiana pointed out. "And also note that all of the x's have a two-hundred-light-year quarantine around them. The Grays are afraid of these planets for some reason."

"That's right. And Mike and I figured out that only these quarantined planets and all of these quarantined planets have isolated abductees on them. This is too blatantly obvious a correlation to overlook. Tatiana . . ." I nodded for her to take over.

"I think the Grays fear the isolated abductees for some reason and that is why the quarantine is there. Perhaps these Lumpeyins caused something or did something to us that the Grays do not like. I'm not sure."

"Boobytrap!" Tabitha said.

Anson looked at her and replied, "A boobytrap, sir?" Then he started laughing and chuckling to himself and in a very badly imitated Russian accent he continued, "Ha, ha, ha . . . It was so obvious!" And he slammed his fist on the table.

Jim and Tabitha must have understood the joke because they started laughing. I wasn't sure if it was a joke on Tatiana or not with the Russian accent and all.

"What's so funny?" I asked.

"Nothing is funny, really, Steven, not about our situation any way. But this moment mimics one of the anime cartoons from the 1980s that we've studied," Anson said.

"That you've studied?" Tatiana asked.

"Oh yes, studied. I've always been a science fiction fan, but a few years ago when we realized that we were actually being attacked by aliens we conducted a brainstorming session for ideas and training regimen. The outcome of that conference was that we needed a language from which to compare possible alien attack scenarios. Since there was a wealth of science fiction books, television shows, movies, and so on, we decided to make alien-oriented science fiction a training requirement for the W-squared group. This gives us a common language to use. That is why we all understand the *Boobytrap* reference." Anson's explanation made a lot of sense.

"Okay, I get it. So, what about the cartoon?" I asked.

"It was called *Robotech* and this is similar to what happened there. An alien spacecraft crashed on Earth and when other aliens showed up to get it the thing turns its big guns on and starts plastering away at the incoming aliens. The humans figure out it's a boobytrap. That's all. But doesn't it seem that this is what is happening here?"

Mike, download all info on Robotech to Tatiana and me.

Okay, Steven. There are books and television shows.

Download them all. In fact, download any and all science fiction relating to alien attack, Tatiana thought to Mike.

Okay. Mike downloaded the television series, all of the director's stories and cuts and then the books. The books were very impressive and by the third or fourth chapter in the first one I understood the boobytrap reference. It took a few seconds more to download all alien attack related science fiction.

"Actually, the parallels are thin here. This seems more like landmines to me like in *Screamers* or that episode of *Deep Space Nine* where Nog got his leg shot off," Anne Marie said. They all seemed to have impressive knowledge of the pertinent science fiction. My first guess had been that they all liked impressing each other with their knowledge of the classical science fiction and that they tried to outdo each other with their knowledge of useless trivia. I soon realized that I was wrong and that such obscure knowledge does seem to come in quite handy in their day jobs, which appeared to now include defending the human race from alien attackers—much like in many science fiction stories. Too bad nobody ever wrote a serious textbook on how to defend against an alien attack; it would have been useful. Maybe someone did, perhaps it's classified and I never had access to it. I would have to ask about that.

"That's right, Annie, landmine strategy is the same thing though. It's a boobytrap scenario." Tabitha smiled approvingly at her daughter. "If you are a retreating force that is being overrun or forced out of a territory, if there is time, you leave behind hazardous things like landmines and spiked pits and other nasty surprises to slow down an advancing enemy. They might also try to create a long-term strategy to give you an edge in future battles. Perhaps we and these other isolated civilizations are more than just boobytraps."

"How so?" Al asked.

"Haven't you ever played Risk?" Jim asked. "It's simple! If you can keep a small country like New Zealand, as well as your main portion of the globe, you can win the game. What you do is attack on the main lines and this makes your opponents forget about the little country on the bottom corner of the planet because they are fighting for their lives back at the front. You grow the military might of New Zealand, which is behind the enemy lines. Once you start weakening slightly on the main front lines, then you come sweeping up through China and in behind the enemy with your war machine that you built in New

Zealand. That's it! All of these little quarantine zones are New Zealand and, let me think, what were the other strategic locations . . . Oh yeah, there was Madagascar and Greenland and Japan. That is exactly what this looks like on the map. It's galactic Risk!"

"Yeah, but we aren't in cahoots with the Lumpeyins. And we aren't building an army for them," Sara said.

Anson shooed a big fat cat out from under his feet and finished taking the steaks off the built-in gas grill at the far end of the sunroom. He set the still-sizzling steaks on the table before us. They smelled good. "Are you so sure about that, Sara? Mike, could we be in cahoots with these here Lumpeyins?" he asked in his stereotypical Southernese.

"I do not have enough data to come to that conclusion, but the suggestions that have been made thus far are quite plausible," Mike replied.

"I just thought of something," 'Becca added. "Perhaps we *have* been building an army for these Lumpeyins. Look at the graphic of the abductions. The numbers of abductions increase every time there is a war of major proportions. And the abductions spiked again here in 2011—they spiked by an order of magnitude. Does that year mean anything to any of us, Anson. . . Jim? She made a point to look at Anson and Jim and emphasize their names.

"I don't see . . . Holy shit!" Anson said.

"The first warp experiment we did where the electrons disappeared!" Jim exclaimed.

"That is exactly it!" Tabitha said. "You are onto something here, 'Becca. The Grays got very interested when the warp era started. And look at the big spike during the Warp War with the Asians!"

"Not only that," 'Becca continued. "We have, with Steven and Tatiana's help, developed a way to shoot down and maybe destroy the Gray ships."

Anson pulled the rest of the corn on the cob off the grill with his tongs and arranged the food in the middle of the table just to the left of the speaker.

"Dig in before it gets cold, folks." He pulled his apron off. "Y'all know that this is bad news. If the Grays realize that we have a means of really becoming a threat to them, what are the odds that they will wipe us out? And why didn't they do that already?"

"We can't tell Senator Grayson about any of our further advancements. We will slow roll him and lie if we have to from now on," Tabitha said as she loaded her plate with a steak, baked potato, and corn on the cob. She took a swig from her beer and sat back down on her side of the table. "We need to go see the President, soon."

"I think we need to go see the Grays," I said.

"*No!*" Tatiana screamed. Her response was unexpected and it startled all of us. She was trembling uncharacteristically.

"Tatiana?" I was a bit concerned by her strange response—isolated abductee rang in my mind.

"I . . . I . . . I don't know why I did that," she said. "It was like, I don't know, I needed to keep us from ever wanting to see the Grays of our own free will. As soon as I realized what I had said, the feeling went away."

Anson turned to me, "Son, did you have the same feeling?"

"No, I didn't," I said.

"Tatiana, my dear, I believe you have been conditioned somehow to stay away from the Grays. That was a typical response of someone with a posthypnotic suggestion," Anson told her. "Don't worry, dear. We're all here for you and will help you to keep your sanity. We *will* figure out what these little Gray bastards are up to and we *will* put a stop to it. Y'all eat, it's getting cold. I need a beer—anybody need anything while I'm up?" Anson wandered off to the kitchen.

We finished dinner with more chat along the same lines. We were all beginning to realize that the Grays were a threat to us as long as we remained a threat to them. We also all agreed that we were not about to put down our arms and just give up. None of us believed that the abductions would stop if we quit building warp drives and stayed on Earth. The Grays had somehow been around for at least most of the recorded portion of our history. There must have been more to it than Mike had data on because there were so many people throughout our history who had described the Gray spacecraft and abduction scenarios in extreme detail. But Mike had continued to explain the impossibility of this. Something just didn't add up.

Tatiana and I had no memory of the things, which backed up Mike's story. So we wondered why or how did other people see them and remember them. We sat around and talked and drank beer and talked some more. Then we drank more. It was fun. Tatiana seemed at home and so did I. I hadn't actually felt this good since way before The Rain and my wacky period of insanity. This was home. I wish Laz could have lived to see it.

"Tatiana, don't you think your father must miss you and wonder where you are?" Anson asked her.

"Uh, no. I saw my father last week. 'Becca and I flew

down to New York to see him. Didn't she tell you?" Tatiana said.

"Hey, I don't have to tell him everything I do," 'Becca responded.

"Rebecca does what Rebecca wants to do." Anne Marie laughed a bit uncomfortably. The two women were very headstrong and my guess was that they butted them together on occasion. Rebecca wasn't stunned by the remark at all.

"Well, anyway, I was thinking that we need to go see him again. This time take Steven with you, and Mike. See if your father is of the type that would be an isolated abductee. Then we go see the President and tell him as much as we have about our situation."

"I have met the President, with my father last year," Tatiana said. "Perhaps he is compromised as well?"

"I never thought of that, but of course he could be. After all, he is one of the most powerful men on the planet," Anson said.

"Well," I started. "Just get me close and Mike will let me know." The President could be compromised. He wasn't an abductee yet or Mike would know. It was a good sign at least that he was not an abductee, but that didn't mean he wasn't an isolatee. We would find out soon.

> **CHAPTER 19**

"It is nice to meet you too, Ambassador Svobodny, and congratulations on your new assignment," I told the ambassador in Russian as I shook his hand. He sized me up and didn't seem to disapprove.

"Thank you, Mr. Montana. My daughter speaks very highly of you. She tells me that you rescued her from some very unsavory individuals and to that I owe you my gratitude." He smiled at me and I was immediately nervous. Had Tatiana told him about the Grays?

Don't worry, Stevie. I told him that you rescued me from some frat boys at a party while I was away at school and that you and I whupped them all. Tatiana's perfect Southern dialect resounded in my head.

"I just happened to be in the right place at the right time, sir. It was my gain to meet Tatiana. She is . . .

amazing," I said, again in Russian.

"Your Russian is perfect, Mr. Montana. Where did you learn it?"

"It's something I've been studying recently. Tatiana is helping me with Russian and I am helping her with English." It wasn't all a lie. I would have never thought to learn Russian if she hadn't been on the Grays' ship with me and, Tatiana probably wouldn't have learned English either.

"Is that right?" He switched to English. "Tatiana speaks English now?" He raised an eyebrow at his daughter as if to see if she understood him.

"Yes, Father. I understand you quite well and can speak English very well," she said with a Russian accent. I guess it was better not to give all of her talents away.

Tatiana's father showed us around the United Nations and the city. I had never been to New York. It had been months since the abduction and since I had actually been back on Earth. The sights, sounds, and smells of New York City should have been overwhelming for me, right? They weren't, really. I don't know if I was more focused on the alien attackers or meeting Tatiana's father or if my new enhanced persona just handled the stimuli better. But I barely paid attention to the city.

The President was supposed to address the United Nations Security Council about the meteor impacts and future planetary defense-spending requirements later that evening. It was our plan to get me close enough to test the President for isolateeism.

Tabitha was certain that she could have gotten me in to meet the President but we didn't want to raise suspicion with security. My previous failed clearance might have raised some questions and now that I was hanging out with the W-squared crowd all of a sudden somebody in the right "need to know" circle might get curious. It was easier to go through Tatiana's connections since we didn't want to tip our hand to anybody with power who might be an isolatee just yet.

I know that you are thinking, what about Tatiana? She is an isolatee and we are carrying her around with us and telling her everything. She was an abductee—but not any longer! And we're all watching her closely. Mikhail is always with her. She is watching herself. No evil force has ever taken over her mind as far as we can tell. We aren't sure what else to do. What would you do? Besides that, you try to keep Tatiana from doing something she wants to do. Tell me before you try, because I want to be out of the solar system that day.

We spent the better part of the day in the back of a limousine driving around the city looking at this and that. Ambassador Svobodny took us to a swanky restaurant that must have been very expensive, but it didn't seem to impede his effort to order everything on the menu.

"Mr. Ambassador, I want to thank you for showing me such a great time today," I told him. Tatiana smiled at me from across the table and derailed my train of thought for a second.

"Father, must Steven continue with this Mr. Ambassador nonsense all evening?" she said in Russian.

"Of course not, my dear. Steven, in private feel free to call me Pyotir," he replied.

"Great, thanks, I will," I told him. I felt Tatiana's foot rub up against my leg gently and I caught a devious look in her eye as her foot traveled further up my leg. Startled, at first, I was mostly nervous: *Tatiana, what are you doing?*

Nothing, what do you mean? She raised her left eyebrow at me as she took a sip of wine.

Uh, okay, but you are distracting me.

And your point is.

But your father might . . .

Oh pooh! That was all she said, but she didn't stop with the foot thing. It made me even more nervous than I had been.

"Daddy, if you will entertain Steven for a moment, I will excuse myself."

"Sure, darling, everything is fine?"

"Oh yes, just going to the lady's room."

"Very well," he said, and she kissed him on the cheek.

Once Tatiana was clear of earshot I told him that she definitely was headstrong and had a mind of her own.

"Just like her mother, that one. She is one hellstorm if she doesn't get her way. She always has been." He chuckled with a deep belly laugh and his large stomach jiggled a bit. His political guardedness relaxed for a moment, he seemed more human—more like the father of the woman I was in love with. Maybe his laughing and speaking to me frankly is what led me to say what I said next.

"Pyotir, Mr. Svobodny, I am thinking of asking Tatiana to marry me and I would like your permission before I do," I stammered.

"My boy, you are charming but foolish." He laughed deeply and sincerely and at first I thought he was making fun of me.

"Why is that?" I asked, a bit hurt.

"My boy, as you have just agreed, Tatiana does what Tatiana wants to do. If I gave you my permission or not it has no bearing on what she plans to do. You are noble if not naive. I like that."

"Well, I meant that I intended to ask her and I hoped that you approve of me is all. Of course, she might say no. And in that case I will simply walk away and not be a bother as I plan to crawl under a rock somewhere and die."

"Steven, I like you. If you want my approval, there you have it. If anything you seem to have done something for her confidence and her appearance. Look at her; she has never looked so alive and vivacious in all her life. I think she would say yes. Yes, I'm sure of it."

Tatiana touched my shoulder and bent down as though to whisper in my ear. She held her hand over her mouth and bit my earlobe. *What are you two talking about?*

Just guy stuff.

"Ah, sit down, my dear. Steven was just explaining this crazy tuck rule in American professional football. That damned rule cost me ten thousand dollars last year." I guess he assumed that all Americans follow football. Unfortunately, I don't.

Fortunately, I have an alien computer inside me that has a database of basically all human public knowledge. *Mike, download to me all the rules of professional football (American) and outcomes of all of the games last year where the "tuck rule" was pertinent.*

"Really, Steven. Football, huh, do tell," Tatiana teased me since she knew I didn't follow sports that much.

"Well, fortunately I had bet on the Forty Niners and not the Jets. You see, I'm originally from California. I used to be a Colts fan but since there is no longer an L.A., I just can't get fired up about the Las Vegas Colts. Yeah, I agree with you, though. I haven't liked that damned tuck rule since I started watching the game, but I'll take the three hundred bucks it got me." I went on to explain the details of the rule. Once, Tatiana stuck her tongue out at me.

You cheated and used Mike didn't you?

Who's Mike? Never heard of him. I winked back at her.

After dinner and a few drinks we finally made it to the U.N. building—oh, the life of a politician is hard isn't it? The President made his speech to the Security Council and it lasted a good thirty minutes. It was televised and a big hullabaloo. Tatiana and I were told to wait in a guest room near Ambassador Svobodny's office until someone came to get us.

Instead of waiting there we decided to sneak out of the guest quarters and wander around taking a survey of isolatees. Sneaking out wasn't hard. We just opened the door to the room and walked around. After all, we weren't prisoners; we were guests.

We mapped most of the people in the periphery since the main players were in the meeting hall. About ten percent of the people we encountered were isolatees. Most all of the people we met were annoyed that I was trying to shake everybody's hand that I encountered. It got to be a bit obvious after a while, so we went to a more subtle approach. If I wanted to test them, Tatiana would distract them and then I would move in faster than they could see me and touch them. Once, I even reached through a wall and touched a security guard on the other side. I couldn't resist tickling his ear before I pulled my hand back through the wall. Tatiana giggled. We had fun for a while taunting the locals, but it finally got boring and we returned to the visitors' room near her father's office.

Tatiana actually did go out and look for the restrooms and was gone for a few minutes. She wanted to freshen up. She didn't really need to with the nanomachines at her disposal, but I find that I even like to take a leak every now and then. I picked up a pencil off the small desk in the corner of the little guest office and held it in my hand for a second. Plenty of carbon exists in pencils but I needed some gold.

Mike, I need some gold. Where is the most likely place for me to find some in here?

How much gold do you need, Steven?

Enough to make an engagement ring for Tatiana.

I see. There is probably enough gold in the computer on the office desk.

Okay, take it. I put my hand on the computer and a few seconds later I had a small lump of gold metal in my hand. The computer would no longer work, but from the dust on it, it looked like nobody ever used it anyway.

I added a bit of other metals to it to make it stronger, Steven, but there was enough gold.

Take the carbon in the pencil and make a diamond out of it.

Okay, Steven.

Mike and I went through several different designs and the pencil and lump of metal morphed from one type of engagement ring to the next. I finally settled on a design and had Mike make me a little ring box for it. When Tatiana returned I got down on one knee and popped the question.

"Tatiana, will you marry me?" I held up the ring box with the lid open.

Tatiana took the box and put the ring on her finger and then held her hand out and looked at the ring. I used a four-carat solitaire diamond setting in a gold ring with the inscription "A match made in heaven" on the inside of it in tiny, tiny letters. I knew that Tatiana's advanced senses would be able to see and feel it.

"Oh, Steven, I thought you were never going to ask. It's beautiful and I love the inscription. And I love you. Yes!" She kissed me and hugged me and kissed me again.

Finally somebody came to get us just when we were in the midst of a deep, passionate embrace. We both freshened up and then went to meet her father at the President's reception. It didn't seem to impress our guide that Tatiana and I changed to formal attire in a minute or so each. The changes actually only took a second or two, but we had played around with styles and colors for another minute.

It was fun meeting the President and all of the various foreign dignitaries at the reception. Tatiana and I showed off a bit by speaking to each of them in their native tongues. It made them more at ease with us. What we found out was startling. Ninety-seven percent of the U.N. Security Council, the President of the United States of America, almost all of the leaders of nations present, and the Russian Ambassador to the U.N. were isolatees.

It was official, isolatees ruled the Earth!

We had no idea what that meant either.

➤ CHAPTER 20

We really had only been able to develop one plan of attack: go ask the Grays or Teytoonis just what the hell they were doing abducting us and experimenting on us. Tatiana and I thought of using Mike to connect to the universal Framework, but we were afraid that the Grays might have some safeguard to keep us from getting information through Mike. And even worse, the Grays might have a means of attacking Mike at a distance through the Framework. So, we decided to keep Mike off of the alien internet for the time being.

Yep, it looked like we would just have to go see the Grays. We spent a good deal of time going through as many records as we could dig out of Mike—Mikhail helped also. We conducted various statistical analyses and finally decided that there was no way in hell that we could figure out where the Teytoonis's present homeworld or central headquarters was. We would fly out there to one of their worlds and land and say, "Take me to your leader!" We had no better plan. We did plan to be loaded for bear before we left, however.

The nearest planet well within Gray space appeared to be about two hundred and twelve light years away. With the new warp drive modifications that Tatiana, Anson, Jim, and I had developed, we could push close to four thousand times the speed of light—which meant a trip time of about twenty days or so. The repair of the *Phoenix*'s alien quantum fluctuation drive wasn't complete yet, and wouldn't be for another few weeks even if we devoted all efforts toward its repair.

We decided to spend our time building new squeeze-play warp missiles instead. We loaded the bay of the *Phoenix* with the *Einstein*, the *Avenger*, and the repaired and warp drive retrofitted smaller Gray ship. We also added a full complement of a hundred and three warp missiles. Our plan was to launch the missiles out of the bay doors so no new missile tubes would have to be constructed. Tatiana and I modified the interior of the Gray ship as much as possible so that it would be more accommodating to humans. We redesigned and humanized the bridge with new high-g couches for all of the crew members. More human-friendly computer controls and monitors were added. We set up the nanomachine room as a manufacturing and repair facility as well as a stockroom. Anything anybody needed, Michelle—copy of Mike number three—would be in charge of administering. Mike could always override Michelle's decisions if need be.

Tatiana and I also had to redesign a room for our quarters. It was much smaller than our previous suite design but it was comfortable. We had to give up the whirlpool tub and settle for a shower. Manipulating the alien hull materials was a bit time consuming and it wasn't long before we planned to ship off. In fact, the Clemons and the Daniels kids were on their way to grandma and grandpa's house in Florida. Our plan would be to leave as soon as their parents returned. We were going to take the fight to the aliens and, if we had to, we might even abduct a few of *them*. In order to maintain a chain of command, I relinquished control of the *Phoenix* to Tabitha. I would follow her orders—at least until she ordered us to do something really stupid. I had gotten to know and trust her judgment of late and I didn't expect that to occur.

On the ninth day into the flight General Tabitha Clemons, Captain of the USS *Phoenix*, married Tatiana and me in the observation deck of the alien ship. The observation lounge (as we called it) was a room with a large window the size of a triple-car garage door. Tabitha stood with her back to the window as Tatiana and I stood facing each other in front of her. At warp velocity all we could see out the window was the eerie streaks of Cerenkov radiation that would occasionally occur as particles within the warp bubble would get too close to the expansions or contractions in spacetime at the edge of the bubble and get accelerated to warp speeds relative to us. All I really remember is that Tatiana was absolutely beautiful in her wedding dress, saying "I do," and hearing Tabitha tell me that I could kiss the bride.

Tatiana and I spent the next two days in our quarters.

Most married folks usually get asked, "Where did you two go on your honeymoon?" We could answer that in many ways. One answer might be, "To our room." Another answer might be, "About two hundred and twelve light years away to an alien planet." We were still about eight days from the quarantine zone and had nothing to do but honeymoon anyway. So that is what we did.

Steven?

Yes, Mike?

We are being shadowed by four Gray vessels.

Open channel, Mike.

Okay, Steven.

Tatiana. I nudged her awake.

What, are we there yet?

Mike, how far are we?

We are about a day and a half from the target star system.

Mike, are we out of the quarantine zone yet? Tatiana asked.

Yes, Tatiana.

When did we pick up the tail? I asked.

I am not sure, Steven, but I detected them just a few seconds before alerting you.

Okay, Mike. Where is Tabitha?

She is in her quarters.

What time is it?

It is about three in the morning Luna City time, Mike responded. I touched the intercom switch on the nightstand and keyed in the Clemons's quarters. A grumpy-sounding Anson answered.

"Ahem, hello?"

"Anson, this is Steven. Is the general available?"

"I'm here, Steven. What is it?" she replied.

"Mike has detected four Gray ships trailing us. He just alerted me to this a few seconds ago," I told her.

"Okay, thanks, Steven. Meet us on the bridge in five minutes," she ordered.

"Yes ma'am." I saluted the intercom. Tatiana giggled at me.

"You know, you are kind of goofy sometimes," she said in her thick Russian accent.

"Yeah, but you know you love it," I laughed.

We got up and stepped into the shower for about a minute and a half. With the nanomachines we didn't really have to shower, but we enjoyed it anyway. On the way to the door of our room we each had the nanomachines fix us up and dress us. Without missing a stride we were dressed and ready. Tatiana insisted on wearing the molecule-thick—or thin I should say—condensed matter suit and sky-blue camouflage U.S. Air Force battle dress uniform pants. She wore black canvas combat jump boots. Just above her right breast was a name tag reading MONTANA, on her left shoulder was an American flag and on her right was the W-squared insignia. Her hair was pulled up behind her head and held together by the deadly metal throwing pins that she so preferred. I followed suit and wore the same outfit, minus the hair pins of course. Both of us had miniaturized warp armor belts and double shoulder-harnessed nine-millimeter semiautomatic pistols—we both preferred Glocks.

Tabitha announced over the intercom of the ship that all hands were to report to the bridge battle-ready. A few minutes later the crew filtered in. The total crew complement including Tatiana and myself was twenty-four. Interestingly enough, the whole crew had adopted the uniforms, although some of the crewmembers wore the camouflage battle dress uniform top or the black Air Force sweater vests as well. Tabitha and Anne Marie, of course, wore the complete official Air Force battle dress uniform, although they had the armor underneath their uniforms and their sleeves were rolled up military style. Tabitha had the uniform requirements for the W-squared mission teams modified to allow for the under armor. Everybody was also wearing their warp armor belts and I did notice that most of them had either shoulder-holstered or belt-clip-holstered pistols.

Tabitha barked orders to several of the crew and had them take their battle stations. She sent the night crew to bed and told them to be prepared to alternate on eight-hour rotations. There would be eight members active at all times from here in. Before, only a skeleton crew of four was on duty at all times. So, shift one started and the others were put on standby. We weren't sure what the aliens were planning or what they could actually do to us while we were in warp.

"Mike, display the locations of the alien vessels with respect to our own on the main monitor please," Tabitha ordered.

"Yes, Tabitha," Mike acknowledged.

The image of our warp bubble and the *Phoenix* in the middle setting in the flat-space region of the modified Alcubierre warped spacetime appeared on the monitor. Flanking the *Phoenix*'s warp bubble were Gray spacecraft immediately in front, behind, above and below us. The ships were just outside the van den Broeck warp bubble region and were maintaining our velocity.

"How did they detect us, Mike?" 'Becca asked.

"They detected the variation in the spacetime energy density in and around the warp bubble. The expansion in the spacetime behind the *Phoenix* causes an increase in the quantum fluctuations, while in front there is a decrease. SuperAgents like myself likely detect this through changes in data rate flow in this region," Mike explained.

"Uh, Mike, that sounds like they are simply measuring the curvature of the spacetime to me," Jim said.

"You say to*may*to and I say to*mah*to," Mike offered. He must have been investigating humor again. Or perhaps that was the best way to explain it. After all, some of Earth's physicists have quibbled over quantum theory versus General Relativity for more than a century now and they both say basically the same thing—if you do the math correctly.

"I understand, Mike," Anson interrupted. "But tell me this: How the hell are we detecting them through the warp field? We've always had to stop to detect them before."

"I am detecting them by sending out pings through the alien Framework and timing the return. I'm not actually reading the return information so returning data cannot compromise my programming. Rather, I am simply timing the return like a radar system that actually sends a standing wave out through the . . . there is no human equivalent explanation here . . . but I think that Hilbert space is similar . . ." Mike paused for a second.

"Allow me, Mike." I knew what he was trying to say. "Anson, the Grays have some other model of the universe that is not really in line with our so called Standard Model. All of the universe is tied and connected through the infrastructure for this alien Framework. Their universal internet isn't artificial, it actually is part of the fabric of the universe. The Grays just figured out that it was there and how to use it."

"Is this Infrastructure something like Superstrings or quantum filaments?" Anson asked as he stared at the alien ships on the monitor. The ships looked pretty much the same size and type as the *Phoenix*.

"As far as I can tell, superstrings are a very very distant cousin to the concept," Tatiana added. "The interesting thing is that the Infrastructure and the Framework do require many more dimensions, like the infinite orthogonal dimensions of Hilbert space or of string theory."

"I see." Anson nodded and thought for a second. "You know, this is no different than the concept of *quantum consciousness*. Physicists have been considering the idea for decades. Basically, what you said was that there is some underlying 'connectedness' or Infrastructure throughout the universe that ties everything together. Well, this is no different than claiming that the universe *is*—one thing—and then writing down a quantum mechanical wave function for it. Granted, the Hamiltonian would be a bear, but I think I even remember reading something by Wheeler and something by Penrose about this. It isn't specific to the aliens. In fact, the quantum consciousness of the universe would explain the instantaneity of passing information through this Infrastructure. The wavefunction for the universe would be in a reference frame that is atemporal, and therefore time wouldn't even be a factor. Think about it. Most observations we make in this universe take some finite amount of time to complete. But if you try to measure whether you are 'self-aware' or not, does that measurement occur instantly? It is at least at the speed of thought. How fast is that? Hell if I know." Anson shrugged, then continued.

"If I recall correctly—and with this new-fandangled memory that your nanomachines gave me, I do—then I recall reading a paper that showed mathematically that if consciousness is a real part of the universe's wavefunction, and it should be, then it would be instantaneously connected throughout the universe. These little Gray guys must have figured this out to the nth detail and have determined how to implement and use it.

"Boy, I sure would like to get hold of that alien Infrastructure router hardware." Anson sounded excited.

Mike, download me all info on this quantum consciousness, I thought.

Okay, Steven, here it comes.

It was a very exciting concept. However, I think it was annoying Tabitha a little bit since there were more pressing things at hand.

"Ahem," Tabitha cleared her throat. "Steven, can the Gray ships penetrate the warp field?" she asked.

"Well, Mike, Tatiana, and I have been debating that for a few weeks now and we do not believe that matter can be passed through the warp bubble via the quantum connectedness. Information can be quantum teleported back and forth through the bubble as Mike is doing via the Framework radar pings. But sending matter through is a completely different question."

"Yeah, it is possible that a teeny tiny bit of matter the size of like a Planck distance could surf on the front of an information packet and be teleported across the Framework," Tatiana stated.

"That is possible, Tatiana, but to my knowledge it has never been attempted or even experimented with before. And it is possible to build regions of quantum fluctuations so violent on the surface of the warp bubble that it would become impenetrable even to that concept," Mike contributed.

"Okay. So they can't fire a missile in here at us, but they could bombard us with annoying infomercials if they wanted to." Sara smiled as she adjusted the nametag on her alien armor top. Tatiana noticed she was having problems with it and put her hand on it and had the nanomachines fix it. "Thanks," Sara said.

"No problem."

"Mike, is there any way they could get through your firewall and take control of you?" Al asked.

"I don't think so. But I will keep a continuous watch for intruders," Mike said.

We used every sensor that Mike had and all of the sensors the W-squared team had brought on board in an attempt to determine as much information about our tagalongs as possible. We found out very little. Jim and 'Becca went down to the landing bay to make certain that the warp missiles were ready while the rest of us tried to find things to do that might help. There wasn't much to do except wait.

Four eight-hour shifts later, we were approaching the target star system. It was time to slow down and come out of warp. If we kept the bubble on we wouldn't be able to see out. If we turned the bubble on and off quickly with the so called "lights off, lights on" maneuver, or oscillated the amplitude of the bubble, the Gray ships might be able to time it right and pass through the bubble.

"Use the images that Mike gets by pinging the Infrastructure. Why don't we just use the alien sensors to study the star system while we leave the warp bubble on full?" Tatiana didn't understand why we were even considering turning off the bubble in the first place.

"Mike, scan this system and give us as much visual data on inhabitants as you can. Also, bring us to a star-centric orbit at about the midpoint of the solar system," Tabitha ordered.

"Yes, Tabitha," Mike replied.

The alien ships followed with us and soon fourteen others joined our convoy. We were completely surrounded by Gray ships the size of the *Phoenix*. But there were only eighteen of them and we had a hundred and something missiles.

"Shouldn't we be trying to hail them or something?" Jim said. "That's what they would do in the movies."

"We will follow the protocols we have put together," Tabitha said. "We will answer them back if they call us. After we are certain there are no hostilities planned, then we will consider hailing them."

"Are you certain that protocol is the right approach?" I asked.

"The consensus was that if they are good guys they will hail us first before shooting at us. If they are bad guys, we shouldn't take a chance of saying something to them that could start an interstellar war," Jim replied. "But I think this is different. We know that these aliens are hostile. They have been abducting and murdering us for thousands of years. I say we tell them they better start explaining themselves."

"I agree," Tatiana nodded. "Let's give them a chance to surrender—and then start blasting!"

"Well, I, uh, don't think that would be wise. We *are* a long way from home and way outnumbered here in Gray space," I reminded everyone.

"I concur with that, Steven. We will wait," Tabitha said.

"Tabitha?"

"Yes, Mike?"

"I have the data now of the star system inhabitants. Would you like to see it?"

"Yes, good, Mike," Tabitha replied.

Mike showed us a layout of the star system. It consisted of twelve major planets and a Kuiper-type belt of minor planets, with an Oort-type cloud. The sixth planet was located at about two-and-a-third astronomical units from its star, which was slightly hotter than our sun, Sol. Planet six was about one and a half times the size of Earth and was blue and green. The planet's surface was approximately forty percent water. Entire green continents stretched across the planet, and there were arid regions between the equator and the poles. The poles of the planet were ice-covered landmasses very similar to Antarctica on Earth. The most interesting fact was that there seemed to be very little detectable technology or habitation. There were no orbiting satellites that could be seen or obvious civilizations located anywhere.

"Where are the people and the buildings?" Al asked.

"Just a moment," Mike said. "There, I have adjusted the sensors to remove the cloaking effect from the images." Then the image filled with satellites, spaceships, factory facilities in orbit, and a hustling and bustling environment.

"You mean they cloaked their entire planet?" Tabitha was awestruck.

"Yes, and several hundred thousand kilometers around it," Mike answered.

"I think we're gonna need a bigger boat." Anson whistled.

"And a shitload more missiles!" 'Becca added.

"All right, everybody relax," Tabitha warned us. "What did we expect to see, a lean-to and a couple of toy rockets? We knew this would be tough and that these aliens had been here much longer the human race has been around. We knew they would be much further along than us. And that we would be outgunned."

"Outgunned is an understatement to say the least." Anson whistled and nodded his head again.

"Mike, open a channel to the aliens if you can." Tabitha sat back in her chair and sighed. She fiddled with her curl. The scar it had once covered was gone now but the habit had not gone away.

"The channel is open, Tabitha."

"Thanks, Mike." She took a deep breath and grabbed the arms of her chair tightly. "Greetings to the inhabitants of this star system. We come from the planet Earth roughly two hundred light years away. We come in peace. We are in a vessel that previously belonged to members of your species. The occupants of this vessel were capturing members of our species and torturing and murdering them. We hope this was merely a misunderstanding between our species and would like to know why your species has been visiting our world and taking our people against their will. Please respond."

We all gripped our chairs tighter. In fact, I was beginning to think I would have to use the nanomachines to get the seat material dislodged from my anal sphincter. Then a high-pitched and almost childlike voice came back to us—in English.

"Earthlings, you must not lower your warp bubble and you must immediately return to Earth!"

Tabitha's face reddened a bit. "We have no intention of lowering our bubble, but we are not returning to Earth without answers and without a guarantee that you will cease and desist all hostilities against our race, our planet, and our solar system!" she replied in her voice of command.

There was a long silence this time that lasted more than a minute or so. Tabitha was about to repeat her response when the aliens answered. All eighteen of the ships flanking us pulled in to an extremely close formation and then our warp bubble was caught in a larger bubble.

"Very well, Earthlings. You will make no attempts to escape our confinement bubble and show no hostilities. We will take you to the Regency Caste and they will respond to your request. Please, be patient and be warned that your technology is not sufficient to escape our confinement bubble." Then the stars blinked out and we were at extreme warp velocity.

"Mike, what's going on?" I yelled.

"The Grays have us in their control and are using a large quantum fluctuation engine to carry us at very high velocities. To where, I do not know. I have never heard of this Regency Caste. However, it does suggest something along the lines of the queen bee."

"How fast are we traveling?" Anson asked.

"Approximately two point three light years per minute," Mike said.

We all did some quick multiplication in our heads.

"Holy shit! That's something like a million times the speed of light," Tabitha gulped.

"One point two one seven million times faster than light," Tatiana said.

"Yeah, at this speed we could travel completely across the galaxy in about a month!" Anne Marie interjected.

"Well, shit fire! We better hope they give us a ride home!" Anson said in his best Southern redneck drawl.

A day and a half later and about five thousand light years from Earth, we finally came to a stop around a bright blue star with a large accretion disk filling its system.

"Hey, this is a new star system. No planets have even formed yet," Jim pointed out.

"Yeah, Jim. But look at that!" Al pointed at the screen about two astronomical units out from the star.

There was a ring that completely encircled the star. The ring must have been taller than Jupiter at its narrowest point. At the tallest point it was probably fifteen Jupiters high both above and below the ecliptic plane of the accretion disk. The system was very busy with vessels going and coming, and mammoth chunks of preplanetary materials being pushed and pulled around by some sort of invisible motivating systems.

"What the hell is going on here?" Tabitha asked. "Anybody have a clue?"

"This must be Gray headquarters or the Palace or the White House or some equivalent," Sara said.

"I realize that, but what are they building?" Tabitha said.

"Ha! It's a Dyson sphere! The little Gray bastards are building a Dyson sphere," Anson answered.

"A Dyson sphere?" Anne Marie asked.

Mike, download all information on a Dyson sphere to Tatiana and me.

Okay, Steven.

"I see!" Tatiana said as she assimilated the data Mike downloaded to us. I had a similar reaction.

"Annie, my dear, a Dyson sphere is a thing named after the physicist Freeman Dyson since it was his idea. I think he got the idea from an old science fiction novel called *The Star Maker* by a fellow named Olaf Stapledon. We need to get this book on our reading list." Anson began explaining the concept. "But it was Dyson who really did the first scientific analysis of the concept and he figured that an advanced civilization, like these Gray fellows here, could build a giant hollow sphere around a star and live on the inside of the sphere. Since the sphere would then be a closed system around the sun it would basically capture all the energy from that sun on the sphere's interior surface and in turn supply all the energy that civilization would ever need. There are other unique properties of the sphere as well, such as camouflaging your entire star system and civilization—well, except for in the infrared. And a lot of other stuff like the immense amount of real estate that you would create for your civilization to live on. Think of how much surface area there would be on the inside of a shell two AUs in radius. That's huge! You know, come to think of it, I bet these Gray guys could implement that cloaking technology on the sphere and completely hide themselves away. I bet they could bleed the excess infrared energy right off into the quantum vacuum energy fluctuations without any violations of a global entropy equation. Second law of thermodynamics then wouldn't be a factor. Hmm . . . one has to wonder how they plan to keep it in place and stable. Perhaps they will only build a Ringworld like Niven's book. I wonder . . ." Anson looked on in wonder at the construction process and continued to mumble and whistle to himself.

The aliens flew us in closer to the largest portion of the unfinished Dyson sphere or ring or whatever it would eventually be. As we approached the surface it became more and more obvious how large this ring structure was. The surface looked infinite from nearby and it wasn't even more than a percent or so complete. A civilization that can travel at a million times faster than the speed of light and that can construct such a huge undertaking must think of creatures like us humans as nothing more than insects. We imagined that we had something that would scare them. I began to think we had been wrong. Something, anything, that would scare these aliens must be . . . SCARY!

We landed on a high-rise portion of the ring that must have been a half of a degree out of the ecliptic plane and it was more than a hundred kilometers above the bottom surface of the ring. The aliens set us down gently and then that childlike voice came through the communications system.

"Earthlings, you can now lower your warp field as we have you captured in a confinement bubble of our own. We will not harm you as long as you show no signs of

intent to harm us in any way. Be warned that we will not
hesitate to remove you from the hive in an instant if you
indicate such hostility."

"Mike," Tabitha said, "lower the warp field."

"The field is down, Tabitha."

"Okay. You heard the man. NO SIGNS OF HOSTIL-
ITY. Y'ALL GOT IT!" Tabitha warned us and then
repeated the announcement over the ship's intercom to
the remaining part of the crew.

"How do you want to proceed, Mom?" Anne Marie
asked. She must have been a bit scared because I had
never heard her call her mother anything other than General while on duty.

Tabitha smiled at her oldest daughter. "We do this slow
and cautious. Only those who volunteer to go will go.
Nobody has to, and we won't think any more or less of
anybody who wishes to stay here. All volunteers to accom-
pany me to meet the alien leaders raise their hand."
Tabitha sighed a breath of relief when all of the hands
went up.

"Very good, Al, Sara, and Annie, thanks for volunteering
but I want you three to stay here as our backup in case we
need you . . ."

"But Mom . . ."

"Lieutenant Ames, that is an order and it is not up for
further discussion. You are in command of the *Phoenix*
upon my leave," Tabitha ordered. Al and Sara were none
too happy about the idea either, but it appeared there
was nothing they could do about it. She made no attempt
to keep Tatiana and me from going. First of all, she needed
us and our special abilities to communicate with Mike
and Mikhail. Besides that, she couldn't have stopped us

from going if she had wanted to. Fortunately, it didn't come to that. I was going to find out what the Grays want with my wife and the hundreds of thousands of other humans back on Earth who were isolatees. And I owed the Gray sons of bitches some payback for making me crazy for nearly four years of my life.

➤ CHAPTER 21

We stepped out of the payload bay of the *Phoenix* onto the top of the high-rise building we had landed on and there we were met by a sea of little Grays. I counted forty of them. The first five were distinguished by a slight orange and brown random spotting, almost like freckles, on their faces. The one in the lead was holding some sort of device in his hand. The device was about the size of a credit card and was making no noise or light—yet the little freckle-faced alien was paying close attention to it.

Mike, what is that thing doing?

What thing, Steven?

The little credit-card-shaped thing in the lead Gray's hand.

Steven! My sensors pick up an Infrastructure pinging like I have never detected before. The fluctuations are directed at us all but they are focusing and concentrating on Tatiana!

Tatiana, look out! Mike and I thought to her simultaneously.

A beam of white-and-blue light flung from the card and flowed like a fluid toward Tatiana. Mike's early detection gave her just enough time to turn on her personal warp bubble armor. The blue light surrounded her and engulfed her in a millisecond, and formed a complete ball of swirling blue-and-white light around her warp bubble. The ball shrunk almost infinitely fast into a tiny singular point and then it vanished even from my eyesight it was so small. And then . . . as fast as it had occurred . . . it was gone. *She was gone!*

Two and a half milliseconds later I was standing in the spot where Tatiana had been standing, frantically looking for signs of her. There was none.

A millisecond later, the little freckle-faced Gray bastard was a puddle of green ooze on the top of that high-rise. I twisted his head completely off and tossed it over the edge of the building. Then, freckle-faced Gray number two joined him. And then number three, and then number four followed him. The fifth one was smarter than it appeared, and had pushed himself into the other grouping of normal-looking Grays—or perhaps they surrounded him like bodyguards protecting the President. I didn't give a flying rat's ass! All of them and I mean not just these forty, uh, thirty-six, of them, I mean all of the Grays that exist in this universe were going to die if some one of them didn't bring me back Tatiana!

I did a giant leap and rolled in the air through a forward tumble and landed where the remaining little freckle-faced bastard had been fractions of a second before. This one was fast and was no longer there. I rolled to my left and was grabbed and clawed at by the other Grays. My body armor protected me from their claws, but they had some sort of baton weapon that packed a mean-assed wallop. Five of them hit me with the things and released some sort of energy pulse on me before I knew what was happening. The pulses would have at least knocked out a normal human. I turned my warp field on and scattered them a bit. I jumped upward and then came down on three of the things at once and squished them against the rooftop. I kind of chuckled maniacally as bluish-green blood squirted over their leader.

A full second and a half had passed at this point and I had killed more than thirteen of the little bastards. Now the W-squared folks were beginning to realize what was happening and were beginning to react.

The surface materials on the alien rooftop came to life with snakelike probes darting in and out at us. One of them wrapped itself around Anson's left boot and snaked quickly up his leg. He shot at it with his left hand as he activated his warp armor. The field cut the probe in two and Anson unwrapped it and kicked it out of his warp bubble with a fast lights-off lights-on maneuver.

"Annie, close up the ship and put the warp field on now!" Tabitha ordered over her comm circuit.

"Warp armor, everyone!" 'Becca said and joined me in the fray.

"•'Becca, wait!" Jim was right behind her.

"We came in peace, you little bastards!" Anson shouted as he busted a clip full of caps off into several of the Grays.

"Capture the freckle-faced one! He's their leader!" I

yelled to them over the comm.

Jim and 'Becca played the squeeze game on several of the aliens at once and took them out quickly. Anson continued firing at them with his pistols. I could tell his bubble was blinking on and off each time he fired. I caught sight of the freckle-face just in time as he was bringing another credit card to bear on Anson.

"Anson, stop firing now!" I yelled and he did immediately.

Tabitha saw what I was warning about and started firing on the Gray with the credit card. He was too fast for her, but she got several more of the bodyguard Grays in the process. She kept firing at the crowd of creatures as I converged on the lead Gray.

The blue-white light flowed from the card but I beat its aim before it could get to Anson. Just as the light started to ooze from the leading edge of the device I managed to get close to the alien at near sonic speeds. I did a lights-off lights-on maneuver and had the little bastard in my bubble with me. I tore his arm completely off and had the nanomachines dissolve it. The credit card device I pocketed. I did a second lights-off lights-on maneuver and grabbed a chunk of the rooftop, which I then used as material for the nanomachines to build zip ties and a choke collar. The nanomachines then placed them around the squirming alien in such a way that its feet and legs were zip tied, its good arm was tied to its bluish-green bloody stump, and the choke collar was too tight around its neck. I reached up to the creature's temple and found the clear headband that they all wore and ripped it off him.

The little creature began to shriek in its childlike voice.

"Stop, Earthlings. Please stop! You must not kill me!"

"Yeah, who's gonna keep me from it you little shit?" I said.

Steven, help me! I heard her voice in my head.

Tatiana? Are you alive? Where are you?

I don't know, Steven. The Gray shot me with some sort of collapsing confinement bubble, which was set on becoming a singularity. My warp armor has offset it once it got down to about a nanometer in diameter. I am trapped inside this bubble but it's squeezing me hard. I expanded my warp field inside to be like Dr. Who's phone booth and it's big enough in here for me, but on the outside the bubble is only a nanometer in size. I'm not sure how long my little warp field can hold up to this stress. Help me, Steven. Please!

Don't worry, gorgeous, I'll find a way to get you out.

The little creature shrieked as I put more pressure on its choke collar, "Please, do not kill me!"

"Tell your guys to stop fighting now!" I shook it violently and wanted to kill it badly, but I knew I had to keep it alive in order to save Tatiana.

"I cannot order them to stop without my interface band," it said.

I held the band in front of it. "You make any odd moves and you are blueberry syrup, pal!"

It put the headband on and made some facial tick motions. Then the remaining seven Grays stood down. The human team was able to catch its breath for a second and reload their weapons.

"All right, everybody, just calm down," Tabitha said. "Why and what did you do to our crew member?"

"She was removed," the Gray said.

"Removed to where?" Anson asked as he reloaded his pistol. "You want me to shoot him for you, son?" he asked me, slapped a magazine in, and then chambered a round.

"I do not know where she is. She was just removed," the thing said.

I stuck my right index finger through its left eyeball and it squealed in agony with a girlish and childlike squeal as the eye popped and the blue-green blood squirted out.

"*Eeeaaaccchhhh! Pleeeeaase do not kill me!*" It flailed and screamed in pain.

"Then you will tell me where Tatiana is!" I yelled in its face. Blue-green syrup now just oozed from the eyeless socket.

"Please, I do not know. I merely removed her. She had to be removed or the Himbroozya could have destroyed us all!" His two-piece nictitating membranes clamped tight over the destroyed eye.

"The Himbroozya? What are you talking about?" 'Becca asked it.

"She was infected with the Himbroozya. I could not allow her to come into contact with The Species."

"I don't care if she had the measles, typhoid, V.D., and Ebola—bring her back now!" I shook him again.

"I cannot. She has been removed . . . converted to energy in a singularity. She is dead."

"No, she isn't, you little bulbous-headed ass. Mike, connect to this thing's link," I said and thought at the same time.

Do you hear me, alien?

Yes! How did you do that?

None of your damned business. I slapped the thing on the side of the head and told him to shut the hell up because I was the one asking the questions here. *Tatiana, can you hear me, baby?*

Stevie?

Are you okay, Tatiana?

There is no change, lover, and I'm getting scared. The warp field is holding for now. I have done some calculations and I believe that the warp field will last for about two thousand years, but I sure as hell don't want to stay in here that long. It's real dark in here, Stevie.

I'm working on it, gorgeous. I will get you out of there! I throttled the little Gray a bit more. *You hear that, you alien puke. She is still alive and trapped in that damned bubble of yours.*

But how? The alien thought to me. *That is impossible!*

I smacked him on side of the head again, *Did that sound impossible to you? She is there. NOW GET HER OUT!*

Even if I could, I would not. You can kill me if you must, but she cannot come into contact with The Species.

And why is that?

I cannot say.

I smacked him again. *You better get to saying or you'll be needing two eye patches instead of one!*

Please stop punishing me. I cannot say because I do not know other than the fact that she was infected with the Himbroozya. My orders are that no creature thus infected be allowed to come into physical contact with The Species. Only the Regency could tell you why. The little Gray thing squirmed against its bonds in an attempt to loosen the pressure on its stump arm and its popped eye was looking kind of rough as well. It must have been in some real pain.

Then you will take us to this Regency now! That is,

unless you want to join your friends over the edge of the building here. I pointed at the alien blood oozing everywhere to make my point.

I will take you.

Good. Then if you will allow me to use my nanomachines on you, I'll fix you.

Please, I am in agony.

Mike, fix him. I was mad and wanted to kill the entire Gray race, but the levels of cruelty and torture I had inflicted upon the creature I could only stomach for so long. I was mad but not psychotic.

Don't let this go to your bulbous head, alien. If you get out of line I'll squish you in a heartbeat! His eye resolved back into place, as well as his arm. The alien looked at its arm and blinked its large two-part nictitating membranes on its left eye rapidly.

Tatiana? How are you?

Still in here, Steven. Any luck yet?

I'm still working on it. Try to hold on in there for now.

I'll hold on as long as I have to. Just get me out of here.

I explained to the rest of the gang what was going on and what the little alien had said. I felt no remorse or pity for the creature as they had felt none for me those years that they had tortured me and tormented me without me even knowing it. Their influence had led me to attempt suicide. I had no sympathy for the thing. But I did fix it. I could have let it remain in agony a bit longer. But my guess was that I was torturing an officer that didn't create the policies of the Gray race, but only enforced them. I wanted to find the bastard who was in charge and torture *it*. Anson had listened carefully as I replayed the conversation for them. He was convinced more than ever of the boobytrap theory.

Tabitha was most interested in the fact that the thing referred to itself as The Species. The arrogant little fuckers! I know my accounting here has some colorful language but you just have to realize how much I was growing to hate these things. They were arrogant; they felt it was okay to go around abducting and murdering people, and they had just attempted to kill Tatiana. We had done nothing to provoke them. Had Mike not intervened in time, she would be dead for sure.

Stevie?
Yeah, baby?
I'm scared.
Me too, honey, me too.

➤ CHAPTER 22

The little freckle-faced Gray made a few facial twitches and I could tell he was using the interface to the Infrastructure. These Grays were not good at covering their facial tics. He would have been horrible at poker. Following the Framework communications that he had made, a small ball of light appeared from nowhere and hovered a meter or so in front of us. The ball of light expanded and then blinked out, leaving a hemispherical vehicle with no top on it. Inside the vehicle were two rows of seats, one with its back to the circumference of the hemisphere and the other on a smaller concentric circle around the central hub of the vehicle with its back to the center of the craft. The central hub had a lone chair, obviously the cockpit, and there was a pilot sitting there. The pilot was a standard Gray alien with no freckles.

The little freckle-faced Gray turned to Tabitha. "Please, we must go in this vehicle to meet the Regency."

"How do we know that we can trust you?" Tabitha responded. I maintained my grip on the little creature's choke collar.

"Trust is irrelevant. If you desire to see the Regency then you must come with me in this vehicle."

"Yeah, right! And as soon as we step foot in this thing you will turn on the confinement beam and strand us in a bubble like you did Tatiana!" I was preparing to punch the thing in the spot where a nose should have been.

"I'd say that you little bastards are full of shit if you think we're just gonna hop in your device here and trust you for no reason. Tab, I'm gonna side with Steven on this one," Anson said.

"Well, what would you have us do, Anson? Fly there on our own, perhaps?" Tabitha asked. She seemed the most clearheaded of us at the moment. "We will take the smaller alien ship," she decided. "Alien, can you give us directions to where we can meet this Regency? We will fly in our own vessel."

"I was ordered to take you in this vessel," the little freckle-faced thing said and made a weird facial tic as he did so. I knew he was downloading information, but about what?

"Listen here, thing." I rapped its right ear pretty hard and its head bobbled back and forth from left to right several times. It shook its head kind of the way a dog does to get water off its back. "The lady says we fly our own vessel and that is the way it will be."

"Must you continuously punish me? I will relay your request," it said.

I slapped it again. "Listen to me, you little bug, your race has relentlessly tortured millions of us throughout our history. I'm just getting started on the punishment that I plan to inflict on your species. You have a lot of explaining to do!"

"Steven, relax!" General Clemons ordered me. She seemed to forget that I wasn't in her army and that she wasn't the boss of me. In fact, had it not been for me they would never have figured out what was going on with these alien abductors. I was getting irrational and it reminded me of . . .

Mike! Why am I being irrational?

Steven? Please restate the question?

I'm . . . very angry and emotionally unsure of myself.

Steven! You've been implanted . . . all of you have been!

Get them out, Mike! Now!

I removed yours, Steven. You must get closer to the others and turn on the warp armor!

Got it!

"EVERYBODY CIRCLE ON ME NOW!" I yelled. They all looked confused for a second. The emotional instability caused by the implants was delaying their abilities to think rapidly and rationally. A second or so delay passed before they realized I was concerned about our safety. They all rushed to my side and I flipped on my warp bubble with the radius modified to encompass all of us. "We've been implanted!" I explained. At the same time I slung the little alien as hard as I could throw it against the warp bubble wall. It landed with a crack and then slid down to the bottom of the bubble, whimpering in an odd shrill voice.

"We've been what?" Jim asked.

"Hold still . . . you won't feel this at all," I said as I placed my hand on his shoulder. I continued the same with each of the others. "Did you notice that you were feeling unsure of your decisions and that your emotions were getting uncontrollable?" I asked them.

"Yeah, I was almost in tears," Rebecca said.

"The Grays somehow implanted us with tracking devices like they put in the abductees. One of the side effects is that it makes you nuts. I know; I was nuts for four years because of one of those things. Fortunately, I recognized the symptoms of being crazy from experience. Mike was able to remove them for us. The warp fields should protect us. Keep your warp skins on at all times from now on."

"How . . . did you know that? It is impossible for primitives to have this capability!" The alien rose to its feet and rubbed a new bruise on its forehead.

"None of your business!" I shot it a mean look hoping to instill a little fear into it. I wished now that I hadn't fixed its arm and eye. The rest of the team implemented their warp generators and I backed mine off just to enclose me. The Gray stood there confused and amazed by the power we primitives were wielding.

"Son, I think it's time to get rid of our baggage here. My guess is that he is responsible for the implants, right?" Anson shrugged his shoulders.

"Yes, as far as I can tell that's right. But let's not kill it yet, we still need to find this Regency," I replied. Then I heard a gunshot and another right after.

The freckle-faced Gray had attempted to make a run for it, but Tabitha was too quick on the draw for it. She shot both of its legs out from under it and it went flailing across the rooftop onto its face, screaming in pain. At the same time, the pilot of the vessel the Regency had sent was moving frantically over the controls of the vehicle. A throwing knife suddenly appeared right between the thing's eyes where a nose should have been. 'Becca carefully approached the thing and retrieved her dagger. She wiped the blue syrup from the blade and then the blade vanished somewhere into her pants. I had never even known she was carrying a dagger. I wondered what else she had in there. Jim looked at the controls on the vehicle but couldn't decipher them.

"He was fiddling with something here, but I'll be damned if I know what it was he did," Jim said.

"We need to quit dicking around and find this Regency!" Anson said.

"I agree." Tabitha reached down and grabbed the choke collar and pulled it very tight around the Gray's neck. "We see now that we cannot trust you. Tell us how to contact this Regency or I will pop your little head right off!" She pulled it up onto its feet causing it to feel the pain of the gravitational pressure on its now ruined legs. The bullet holes in the thighs of the creature oozed the blue-green syrupy blood down its legs and onto the rooftop.

"*Eeeekkk!* Please stop! I will not tell you without the Regency's permission. I cannot by physiological function disobey the Regency." The Gray tried to rub at its legs but Tabitha kept it upright with the choke collar.

"Then I suggest you get on the horn and call up your boss and tell it to get its ass over here, *now!*" Tabitha yelled at it.

I could see why Anson liked this lady. She has some serious chutzpa, spunk, fortitude, and a whole lot of other stuff. She reminded me of Tatiana.

Baby, you okay?

I haven't gone anywhere yet.

Still working on it, Tatiana. I will get you out.

Steven?

Yes?

I love you.

I love you, too.

The Gray made some facial twitches that were nearly unperceivable and then it fell over . . . dead.

"What the hell?" Tabitha said.

I walked over and checked it for any type of vital signs as Tabitha had just done. Nothing.

"Perhaps one of them knows where this Regency is," Anson said. He pointed out across the rooftop at a group of seven balls of blue-white light. As the balls got closer they vanished and then reappeared a few meters in front of us. The balls flashed inward and seven large Grays with red gill-like markings on their necks and blue stripes on their foreheads and ears appeared before us. These Grays were about thirty centimeters taller than the others and they were wearing blue and black tights. I guessed that the tights were of the same type of condensed matter material as the alien armor Tatiana had designed.

"You will cease your hostilities, Earthlings," the largest of the Grays said.

"We might. But we do not follow your orders, alien," Tabitha said calmly. "Are you the leaders of your, uh, people?"

"We are the Regency and are, as you perceive, the leaders of The Species," another one of the regally marked Grays answered.

"Why are you here, humans?"

"We have discovered that you have been abducting our people, torturing them, and manipulating our history for thousands of years. We want to know why—and we want this to stop!" Tabitha said.

"Ah, you have finally grown up," the Gray in the center said.

"Grown up! Prawmitoos, you are soft. They are still primitive monkeys. Just look at them. If your soldier drones were as adept as you claimed, these monkeys would have been taken care of by now."

"Yes, a nuisance that, but that soldier drone will no longer fail me."

"His demise was too painless."

"Feyibi, you always have a harsh view of all creatures, don't you? If these creatures have not grown up then how are they here and why have we no control over their implants?" Prawmitoos replied.

"Tell us exactly what you want, humans, and perhaps we will spare your lives," another one of them said bitterly as it toed the standard Gray that 'Becca had taken out with her dagger. I was curious if the arrogant royal Gray was bluffing or if they really could take us.

"To start with, where is Tatiana; the one of us that the freckle-faced gray shot with the confinement bubble device?" I asked.

"She was infected by the Himbroozya and had to be removed," Feyibi said.

"Himbroozya, himbroozya, what the hell is this himbroozya?" I yelled at them.

"Human, we can hear you and there is no need to be loud. Why do you not ask your Servant that you carry hidden away in your abdomen?" Prawmitoos said.

"He doesn't know," I told him. *Mike, you're my friend, not a servant!*

Thank you, Steven. But you did program me to follow your orders.

We will remedy that soon then. Just not right this second, okay?

I understand, Steven.

"Ah, yes, but all he has to do is download the information for you from the *Universum Indicium Tela*," one of the other Grays said.

"*Universum Indicium Tela?*" Tabitha asked.

"It sounds like Latin, Tabitha," Anson interrupted. "If it is it means something like the whole world or universe, information or data, and weave or web that is weaved. He is saying the Universal Information Web or World Wide Web!"

"Latin?" Tabitha asked. Nobody responded.

"The Infrastructure?" I asked. "We decided not to let Mike access the Infrastructure to keep you from tracking us," I said.

"A wise decision, I suppose," a royal Gray said.

"I agree with you, Yiaepetoes. Perhaps these primitives are more advanced than we think. It appears that they even understand the existence of the UIT."

I found the parallels intriguing. The YIT or *Universal Indicium Tela* (U is a Y in latin, I, T) is very similar to us saying WWW for World Wide Web—very interesting. Then Tabitha's comment hit me—*why Latin?*

"Enough small talk. What is the Himbroozya and where is Tatiana?" I said.

"The Himbroozya is a technological picophage designed by Tentalos for Opolawn. He infected the human race with it more than six thousand of your years ago. As far as your friend is concerned, I do not know of her location or how we can help her," Prawmitoos answered.

"A picophage?" Jim asked. "What does it do and why did he infect humanity with it? And who the hell is Opolawn to us?"

"And for that matter," 'Becca added, "why are y'all so damned afraid of this Himbroozya that you have to disintegrate someone infected with it as soon as you meet them?"

"The Gray bastards are afraid of this Himbroozya and can't cure it. I bet that's why there's a quarantine around the isolatees," Anson pointed out.

"You understand quite well, human," Prawmitoos replied.

"Wait a minute," Tabitha interrupted. "Why Latin?"

"It is not Latin, human. It is Teytoonise. You will find most of your ancient languages have a root in Teytoonise. A side-effect phenomenon we have yet to understand about the Himbroozya is that those species infected with it evolve Teytoonise language and concept parallels," Atalas replied.

"Well then, what does this Himbroozya do?" I asked.

"It causes a *species* to be immortal, not an individual. The species is immortal because it drives them to perpetuate. But, more than that, it drives the infected species beyond its abilities and causes it to develop new methods of warfare and means for destruction—which the Lumpeyins might then use against *us*. We also have intelligence that suggests that Opolawn himself can control individuals infected by it across vast distances of space via the YIT. Opolawn left the picophage behind to infect humanity as he knew it was deep within our controlled space. We warred with the Lumpeyins and forced them from some of our space but they took some as well. We then reached a very uneasy and false peace. But before the truce required them to leave certain regions of our space, they managed to leave behind this menace on many planets," Feyibi explained.

"And these planets would be ones where individuals infected by this phage are denied access to your YIT, I suspect?" Anson said.

"Yes, that is correct," Prawmitoos said.

"Is there a cure for this picophage? Why can't the nanomachines eat it?" Tabitha asked.

"Tab, my guess is that this picophage is just that, a picometer phage. That would be three orders of magnitude smaller than the nanomachines and would be undetectable by them," Anson replied.

"You are quite correct." The royal Gray furrowed its head and wrinkled the coloration there. It didn't seem happy that we understood their plight.

"Then there is no cure for this picophage?" 'Becca asked.

"No cure that we have been able to discover. This is why we have drones live in your solar system and conduct experiments on your species. They are trying to develop a cure for this technological disease. Unfortunately, they have yet to discover one. They are motivated, as they are exposed to the phage and cannot return unless they find a cure. We have sent our best scientist drones."

"Yes, I bet you did. All the way to the Russian front, *mein Fuehrer*!" Tabitha said.

"Wait a minute." I thought about their actions seeming a bit megalomaniacal and not with any good intent, or at least none that I could perceive. "You could care less about us, isn't that right? You are experimenting on us to find a cure for yourselves. That is why you stay hidden away so. You are afraid of these Lumpeyins, aren't you? And what happens if we become aware or a threat?" I knew the answer. The bastards would wipe us out.

The Teytoonis didn't answer immediately. In fact they seemed to all have facial twitches. They were conferring over their headbands. I almost decided to grab one of them and connect to his circuit, but I thought better of it.

"Okay, so why can't you help Tatiana?"

"There is no escape from the collapsing quantum singularity that she has been placed in. Her use of the warp field to delay her fate was clever, but it will not save her in the end and is only delaying the inevitable. Even if we could save her, we would not. She is infected after all," Prawmitoos said.

Mike, access this damned YIT and get as much info as you can on everything. If you detect them pinging you, get out.

I understand, Steven.

Finally, Tabitha forced them to answer the big question. "You never answered. Are you afraid of these Lumpeyins and are we inconsequential to you?"

"Yes," is all Prawmitoos said.

"And when we get too dangerous to be used as lab rats what then?" Tabitha asked.

"I believe the answer is obvious," Feyibi replied.

"You plan to destroy humanity?!" Anson asked.

"I'm sorry, but it is your fate," Prawmitoos said.

"Bullshit!" I said. I didn't like these bastards from the first day I met them and I liked them even less at this point.

Steven?

Yes, Mike? I was getting used to being part of multiple conversations at once. Having a wife and a sentient computer always talking in your head will force you to develop this skill.

There is way too much data on the YIT for me to download even small fractions of it. Do you have any suggestions? Mike said in my mind.

Uh, Mike, have Michelle make a copy of yourself back in the supply room on the Phoenix, *but tell her to not add any SuperAgent code. Use that cube as a data repository. In fact, have her make as many cubes as she can and fill them up with as much as you can find that might be pertinent to the survival of the human race. Understand?*

Yes, Steven.

"Wait a minute," Jim interjected. "If this Opolawn creature can control the picophage on individual levels, then that must mean there is some sort of control mechanism somewhere."

"Yes, so?" Feyibi asked.

"Well, why don't we go and get the damned thing and turn it off? Then what happens to the picophage?"

"We have seen this before. The picophage drives its victims rapidly insane. Destroying the control mechanism is not an option for humanity since so many of you are infected—more than two-thirds of your species are tainted. The wars that would be created on your planet would devastate your culture. On the other hand, it would be a good option for us."

"Well, what if we found the thing and just locked it away in a place and let nobody send instructions to this picophage? Would it just lie around dormant? How does the *virus* spread?" Tabitha asked, not quite sure if the word *virus* actually fit.

"The phage spread is controlled through the control mechanism and Opolawn chooses his victims carefully," Yiaepetoes explained.

"This Opolawn must be one bored dude to sit around for millennia just tinkering with four billion people's lives," 'Becca said.

"The mind of the Lumpeyins is amazing and such tasks are minute to them," Prawmitoos assured us. I wasn't sure if he had meant the mind of a Lumpeyin or the mind of the Lumpeyins. Were they individuals or were they a collective mind?

"Well, that is the answer. We will go and take the control mechanism from the Lumpeyins and then we will control our own fate. We will let the virus remain dormant until it is gone from attrition of the infected individuals. Once all infected people have died of old age, a few generations from now, then we will destroy the controller," Tabitha said.

"Great plan, Tabitha. But if we return from Lumpeyin space with this control device or whatever the hell it is, you bastards will let Tatiana out of her prison and you will spare Earth from annihilation." I told them, I didn't ask.

"We will spare Earth. But as I have said before, there is no escape from the diminishing quantum singularity within which she is trapped. We are sorry."

"You're full of shit!" I said.

➤ **CHAPTER 23**

We spent the next three days discussing strategies and possible scenarios to approach Lumpeya City in the mountain continent of the alien planet. There didn't seem to be a simple way to do it. For one thing, the damned place was more than thirty thousand light years away. The trip in a Gray ship would take as much as ten days. The next big hurdle was the fact that Opolawn would see us coming for those ten days. So, somehow we had to devise a ruse to fly under the flag of truce. Prawmitoos suggested that we could approach under the treaty by which the galaxy had been separated. It seemed like the only way to approach Lumpeyinis or whatever the hell they called it.

We also needed intelligence on how the picophage worked, what the controller looked like, and where it would be. Mike found a lot of this information on the

YIT. The aliens didn't compartmentalize their information since none of the drones would look for anything that they weren't instructed to look for. I quickly understood why I was able to hack Mike so easily. God, these aliens were powerful, but stupid. I stored that information away in my mind and began to subprocess it for possible future applications.

The information that we couldn't find on the YIT wasn't there because it didn't exist, according to Feyibi. The Titan told us as much information as it had gathered through personal encounters and then had the others discuss the concept with us as well. We understood the general configuration of the device. It could gather massive amounts of information via the YIT and subprocess that information at various stages during the data manipulation process before it reached the main processor. There an artificial intelligence of some sort would sort the data throughout the multiprocessor bus of the device and reroute commands back out over the YIT. In other words, it was another damned SuperAgent. Mike, Anson, Jim, and I discussed the possibilities of overpowering the SuperAgent or just pinging the controller across the Infrastructure to find it.

We realized that the picophage must have some sort of signature that could be detected and that the Teytoonis knew this. The credit card device knew that Tatiana was infected. How? We searched back through the YIT and found it. The individual picophage device was much larger in macrospace. In fact, each tiny device was about six centimeters across; again the Dr. Who's phone booth phenomena came into play. The devices apparently used a Van den Broeck-modified Alcubierre-type warp bubble that was a picometer wide on the outside but was six centimeters wide on the inside. So how was it detected? Easy; the tiny location within the picometer bubble contained more energy density than normal space from an outside-the-bubble reference frame. Following Einstein's equations that spacetime curvature is proportional to energy density, the spacetime around these pico devices should be slightly curved inward. And the Teytoonis had been able to detect this extremely small change in spacetime curvature. Anson commented to the fact that all of these little warp drives floating around on Earth could have been one of the reasons that during his original warp experiment program he never could find a closed solution to the Einstein equations that matched the experimental data. Mike thought he was correct.

At any rate, we figured out a way to rig together one of these credit card things with the sensors on the *Phoenix* and then have Mike ping Earth through the Infrastructure. When he did he received an echo that had the address of the picophage cloud. There were more than 10^{30} returns in a superposition wave and we nearly dismissed them as noise until we looked at the signal's frequency spectrum. The information was spread out on a hopping spectrum from radio-type pings way on up to pings that the Teytoonis used, but they were there and we found them. The Teytoonis were amazed at our scientific and engineering capability because they had never gotten this far in tracking the things before. Before long Tabitha warned us to start keeping most of our tricks secret. We hoped that something here would end up being a weapon that we could use to hold both the Grays—the Teytoonis—and the Lumpeyins at bay.

After we were confident that we understood exactly the signal that the picophage returned upon pinging, we started looking for signals that were being sent to the picophage devices.

"You know," Tabitha commented, "what we have done here is good SIGINT work even if it was with alien technology."

"Well I would agree partially, Tabitha," Anson said. "But it is a little more, really. I would say it was MASINT since we weren't just detecting the SIGnals INTelligence, but we also had to do some Measurement first And then do some SIGnals INTelligence."

Whatever Anson or Tabitha wanted to call it, we were putting some well-learned human traits to good use.

Finally, after day twenty-two we had it. Anson called us into the makeshift lab in the *Phoenix* where he and Sara had detected a signal from an exact location within Lumpeya City the Grays had pinpointed. That *had* to be the device's location and we now knew exactly where it was. These facts really amazed and frightened the Grays. They had apparently been trying to find this thing for more than six thousand years with no luck. 'Becca pointed out to them that their slave scientists probably weren't really motivated in the right way to help them. Then she told them about flies, honey, and vinegar. It was completely lost on Feyibi and Atalas and Yiaepetoes, but Prawmitoos seemed to ponder the story. Perhaps it didn't fall completely on deaf ears.

Occasionally, Tatiana and I would talk for limited, small amounts of time. I missed her terribly. The wait between conversations wasn't as bad for her since she had taken to putting herself in suspended animation in order to conserve her strength and life expectancy. Oxygen wasn't a problem since the nanomachines could convert the carbon dioxide that she breathed out right back into diatomic oxygen very easily and practically instantaneously. The warp armor belts only had minimal air supplies since we expected to use them in a breathable atmosphere. All that was normally needed to replenish the air would be a quick lights-off lights-on maneuver. We had planned for them to be used as emergency spacesuits but that was for limited periods of time and the air supply limitation was counted in minutes, not days.

Food and water were Tatiana's biggest problems. We calculated that the nanomachines could reutilize her clothes and weapons; her urine, feces, and sweat; and the food and water that were in her stomach, and any excess body fat and muscle over and over (at the body's typical ten percent efficiency) for about a year before there was nothing left of her but vital organs. If she had to she would use her hair first, then her breasts, then her fingers and toes and her earlobes and ears, her eyeballs, then her hands and feet, then her arms and legs, until there was nothing left. So we only allowed ourselves a minute a day for quality time together. It was hard thinking about what she was going through and that she was trapped there this way, but she was intent on staying alive no matter what it took. She had a year before she had to start in on her hair. That had to be enough time. The total gruesome calculated time that she could stay in there and still be fixed when she got out was pushing a hundred years, about twice that if we stopped talking until we got her out. But Tatiana told me that if she had to stay there that long without talking to me, she would end it now. We didn't have that conversation again.

Fortunately, with our rapid download capabilities I could fill Tatiana in on a full day in a matter of microseconds, and then spend the rest of the minute telling her how much I loved her.

Tatiana told me a few days after I had downloaded her the specs for the picophage detection system that she was working on an idea for getting out. She knew she was wasting energy that she might need sometime in the future, but she said she was only allowing herself an extra minute a day for this—which would cut her year into six months. She told me several times that she didn't have a need for legs and arms in that damned bubble. I cried all that night and had that image stuck in my head. It was Jim and 'Becca who came around and pulled me through the depression. I also had Mike keep tabs on it for me. He assured me that I was perfectly normal and that he was sad, too.

Ten more days passed and we were prepared for our journey. We planned to take the *Phoenix* to Lumpeya City. The Teytoonise drones had fixed the quantum fluctuation drive and so it would be able to make the trip a third of the way across the galaxy in just ten or so days. Tabitha asked Prawmitoos if he would give Annie, Sara, and Al a ride back to the edge of the quarantine zone and drop them off there in the *Einstein*. He had a science drone ship do this. He told us that he planned to come along to Lumpeya City with us. We argued with him about it for some time, but the Gray finally put his foot down and said that this would be the only way he would allow the *Einstein* to return to Earth space. Anson stepped in and told him that he had a deal.

Finally, we were on our way to meet the Lumpeyins—or at least Opolawn. Once we were aboard the *Phoenix* and on our way at a million times the speed of light, Prawmitoos took me aside when nobody else was around and he touched my forehead.

You hear me, human?

Yes, alien. What do you want?

This is something that you might need. He palmed two small medallions made of a flintlike stone to me. One was a grayish color and the other black.

What are these and why are you giving them to me?

You have the Servant and understand its mechanisms quite clearly. I think you could use this best. It is FUER. Your people have yet to develop this technology, but I give it to you now with hopes that you will understand its potential applications. It is what you might mistakenly call elementary particles.

When he thought it and spoke it the word sounded like a drawn out "fuyer" and sounded almost exactly like the way that Anson says the word "fire" in his slow Southern redneck drawl. He downloaded the instructions to me and I realized that it was a serious weapon, one which worked similarly to a nuclear bomb. If you forced the two rocks together hard enough, like striking two flint stones, you would create sparks. If you really slammed them together it would release tremendous amounts of energy, many hundreds or possibly thousands of times greater energy than a nuclear device. FUER was a Latin acronym for *fugitivus unus elementum retineo*. *Fugitivus* translates to something like a fugitive or runaway slave. *Unus* means one and only one. *Elementum* is the first principle or basic constituent. *Retineo* means constrained or confined. Put it all together and you get something like fugitive one and only one basic constituent confined. It rang a bell with me and I was sure it would with Anson, Jim, or Tatiana. The best I could gather was that the rocks were crystallized arrays of quarks.

Single quarks didn't exist as far as I knew until that moment. Quarks are the basic constituent of matter and always come in twos or threes—never one and only one. The gluon force required to keep the damned things together gets larger the harder you try pulling them apart. In other words, quarks are attached in such a way that they can't be pulled apart because it would take a near infinite force to do it. I say infinite just because humans have never figured out how much energy it would take. Oh, there are theories, but nobody has ever figured out how to do it. Obviously, Prawmitoos had figured out how to free some quarks, capture the free ones, and confine them in some type of matrix. He was giving me a couple of chunks of the stuff.

Human, you must keep this inside your warp field or Opolawn will be able to detect it. Do you understand?

Yes. Thanks, I think. But why are you doing this?

When we get to Lumpeya City I cannot help you. We are under treaty with the Lumpeyins and will not make war with them unless they are infringing upon that treaty. They are not violating the treaty as you are not protected by us. Use this gift of FUER wisely.

Mike, did you get all that?

Yes, Steven. Curious, isn't it?

Let's remember to download it to Tatiana later.

Okay, Steven.

Mike?
Yes, Steven?
You are a good friend.
Thanks, Steven.

Tatiana had the brilliant idea of attaching the two FUER pieces to a small warp armor belt. If we modified the warp bubble to rapidly collapse like the Gray's confinement bubble, it would force the two pieces of quarkium nuggets together and implement the quark fusion bomb effect. The warp device would be destroyed, thus releasing the mammoth explosion. We talked this over with Mike and were able to build such a device into a box much smaller than a wristwatch. I then had Mike attach the FUER medallions on either side of the thing and place a low-level warp bubble on and around the FUER at all times. This small warp bubble was about the size of a golf ball and I had Mike place a hard shell around the warp field. Then I picked up the little ball with the miniature warp bubble inside it and put the thing in my pocket. I hoped I wouldn't have to use it, but all it would take to activate it would be a mental order from me to Mike and I would use it if I needed to.

➤ CHAPTER 24

"Yeah, but I still don't trust the little bastard," 'Becca replied as she turned and leaned back in her chair. The YIT radar data displayed on the widescreen bridge monitor behind her head overlaying our current position on that region of the galaxy. There was still a long way to go to Lumpeya City.

"Well, I don't either, but why else did he give me the FUER?" I looked around at the group for a response. I could tell that Anson didn't like Prawmitoos either. We had made the bridge, the engine room, and the nanomachine room off-limits to the Gray so we could speak here without worrying about him eavesdropping. Mike kept tabs on what he was up to continuously. The silly Gray just seemed to sit idle in his assigned quarters and did nothing.

"Steven," Tabitha said. "These Grays are very self-serving and conniving. Everything they do is planned. In fact, I wouldn't be surprised to see that there are plans within plans that we haven't yet considered."

"Plans within plans within plans . . ." Anson said.

I realized he was quoting from *Dune*. The W-squared's science fiction training seemed ever present. "You're right, of course. But this is quite a gift, I just need to make sure that I don't use it to the Gray's advantage. I'm not sure when or how that will be," I said.

"An opportunity will present itself sooner or later, Steven," Jim said. "As long as we are all on the same page here; none of us trust the Grays, right?"

"Duh!" 'Becca said and slugged him on the shoulder.

"Well, Jim, I'll tell ya one damn thing. That stuff about his soldier drone not having the chance to fail him again sounded a bit like Darth Vader or Admiral Thrawn to me," Anson said. "Hell fire, boy, I wouldn't trust 'em as far as I could throw him."

"I can't quite get a grip on his motivation either," I said.

"Steven, my boy, Prawmitoos's motivation would seem odd to us even if we did know it. You know why?" Anson asked.

"I dunno?" I shrugged my shoulders.

"Because, son, he's an alien. Ergo, therefore, and all that shit, his motivations will be just that . . . alien! It is very unlikely that the alien motives are in line with anything that would make sense to us. So what do we do about it?" He asked everybody this time and I could tell that they had had this conversation before. And the more I really began to think about all the science fiction stories

I had assimilated, I was certain I would reach the same conclusion.

"We don't give a damn about their motives. We do what we need to do to survive and thrive," Jim and 'Becca recited.

They were right! We couldn't concern ourselves with why the aliens were doing what they were doing other than for intelligence on a means of defeating them. All of us would have preferred to meet a group of utopians that would give us the cure for cancer and an *Encyclopedia Galactica* but that isn't what happened. Each species is going to do what is best for that species, most likely. This is what we planned to do. This is what we would do. If what we had to do to insure our survival was detrimental to the Grays' survival, well, I guess I just didn't really give a rat's ass. Anson had used those exact words a few seconds before and I found that I completely agreed with him.

We attempted to come up with a plan of attack, but we knew so little about what was about to happen to us when we reached the Lumpeyine central world that we decided there was no need in wasting our time planning. We had no data from which to plan. Prawmitoos was little help and the YIT didn't have enough details of the city or fortress or temple or whatever it was to give us a clue as to a course of action. We were just going to have to wing it!

We are almost to Lumpeya City, gorgeous. Hang in there.

I'm fine, Stevie. No sign of the Lumpeyins yet? Tatiana asked.

Oh yes! They have been shadowing our approach now

*for a day or so. The same way the Grays did us when we
entered their space.*

My idea for getting out of here hasn't panned out yet.

What was the idea?

*I thought of attempting to use our quantum connec-
tion and to attempt quantum teleportation of a miniature
warp bubble through the Infrastructure. I don't have the
resources in here to set that up. It's back to the drawing
board.*

*I thought we decided that that probably wouldn't work
anyway?*

*I know, but it makes sense that it would work if the
matter was shrunk to as small as half a wavelength of the
information beam that is teleported and if we could make
the matter fall into the right place in the quantum connected region of the data stream.*

*I'll think about that, hot stuff. In the mean time, you
better get back to sleep. I love you.*

I know you do, Stevie.

We reached Lumpeya City while being shadowed by
nineteen vessels that implemented something similar to
warp drive. They could keep up with the *Phoenix*'s quantum fluctuation drive so it was clear the Lumpeyins
understood warp technology far better than we humans
did. Prawmitoos remained quiet until we reached orbit
around the planet-sized city. The central part of the city
covered or perhaps made up the mountain continent of
the planet, but the entire planet was the capital city of
the Lumpeyins. Prawmitoos then called out in his native
tongue to the Lumpeyins and asked to speak with
Opolawn directly.

He claimed he was simply here as a liaison to introduce the Earthling delegation to the Lumpeyins. A few seconds passed and then the *Phoenix* was engulfed in a warp field that was attached to a beam of yellow light that shone from the planet below. The planet was about twice the diameter of Earth and had blue oceans covering nearly fifty percent of it. There were amazingly large technological structures that surrounded and covered the world, even above the oceans. The sky was filled with floating platforms and towers that didn't appear to touch the surface anywhere, and there were space-based buildings and platforms everywhere. As the yellow beam of light pulled us downward we could tell that the architecture appeared to us to be a combination of science fiction techno and ancient Greek temple.

We dropped toward the planet at about Mach thirty or so and then came to a screeching halt two hundred meters above what Prawmitoos referred to as the Sanctuary of Opolawn. According to Mike, we were directly over the coordinates for the picophage control device.

The temple stretched out radially in every direction as far as the eye could see. There were columns that stretched upward thousands of meters—maybe more. A river flowed from the center of the building and grew in size as if flowed down the mountainside into the ocean below. The temple appeared in much the same design as pictures I had seen of Apollo's Temple on Earth, but with an odd modern and sci-fi décor, and many orders of magnitude greater in its majesty. As Anson put it, there was too much just downright gaudiness.

The *Phoenix* was put down on what appeared to be a landing field near the edge of the river. It never dawned on me to ask the name of the river. We followed Prawmitoos out of the spaceship down to the surface and there we met, in all His Majesty, Opolawn.

The Emperor of the Lumpeyins stood before us about three meters tall and looked almost human—humanoid at least. Anson muttered something about convergent evolution and probabilities of so many humanoids, but I didn't pay close attention. And who knew—with the nanomachines—these things could make themselves appear however they wanted, right?

Opolawn stood straight and tall and had body features and tight muscles not unlike any well-constructed human—except that he was huge and his hair looked more like fur. This fur-hair was probably four or five centimeters long and stood up in an unruly fashion. Most striking was its color—bright fire-engine-red. It matched his eyes perfectly. His ears were somewhat elfin shaped. He had five fingers on each hand and he was wearing gray-white boots similar in style to combat boots—so I couldn't count his toes. He wore a loose-fitting style of trousers that were similar to our battle dress uniforms, and they were bloused at his boot tops. The pants were also gray-white but with flecks of bright yellow, which sort of matched the general terrain colors. He was wearing a loose-fitting top of the same color and material that wrapped around him similar to a karate gi jacket. Around the loose top at his waist was a brilliant yellow, red, and gold sash that fluoresced continuously. Finally, and most interesting, was his skin. It was red, bright red and seemed to glow.

I scanned the area and noted that all of the creatures here were red-skinned giants with elfin ears and red fur hair. Opolawn's entourage was all dressed in a similar manner to him, and most of them were wielding some type of staff. I concluded that these staffs were weapons and that I didn't want to get on the wrong end of one of them.

He laughed a deep booming laugh and in an echoing voice said, "Prawmitoos, I see you have brought pets with you."

"They aren't mine, Opolawn. I am merely giving them a lift. They have things they would like to discuss with you," Prawmitoos answered in his screeching voice.

"Indeed." Opolawn turned to his entourage and issued some orders in a tongue that Mike had never heard of before.

Apparently there was more to this YIT than we had been able to find. Perhaps as part of the treaty that the Teytoonis had with the Lumpeyins, the Lumpeyins were firewalled off from the YIT.

"Speak, Earthlings. Who are you?" Opolawn commanded.

Tabitha slowly and confidently stepped forward and in her voice of command but with an edge of diplomacy said, "Opolawn, I am General Tabitha Clemons, the leader of Earth's space defense force. We are here to discuss the presence of both Teytoonis and Lumpeyin technology in our solar system and the likelihood of having it removed in a peaceful manner."

Opolawn's voice boomed again as he laughed. "I see. Did you Earthlings go to the Teytoonis or did they come to you?"

"That is a complicated question, but suffice it to say that we met them halfway," Tabitha said.

Opolawn walked between all of us looking closely and

smelling us. As he sniffed us he waved his left hand up and down in front of us like he was an evangelist about to heal us. My guess was that he was using some sort of sensor on us. He stopped in front of me and bent forward to peer down into my eyes. I matched his gaze with burning hatred and overbearing confidence.

Mike, be ready. If this son of a bitch makes a move we'll show him just how tough we are.

I am ready, Steven.

"You, are different," Opolawn said to me.

"Yeah, how so?" I asked.

He just smiled at me and said, "I am not certain. But you are different and I do not know you." He moved on to Anson.

"You, I know." Opolawn's body morphed into a giant purple emu and then it morphed into the likeness of Albert Einstein wearing a spacesuit. Opolawn's likeness of Albert Einstein said in a mockingly whiny tone, "It was not your fault that the world took your great invention and tried to destroy itself, Anson."

Anson looked shocked and began cursing the alien with every redneck curse word he had ever learned. "Have you been in my head, you alien thug? !@##?! You should not have told me this because now I'm gonna have to kick your ass, you overgrown sunburned pointy-eared goddamned alien freak!" Anson seethed in anger and I could see veins pulsing on his temples as he clenched his fists tight and shifted his weight onto the balls of his feet.

Opolawn chuckled with booming laughter while Anson continued to curse him up one side and down the other. Anson professed several times that Opolawn was going to pay for violating his mind and the human race. Opolawn just continued to tease him. Then he appeared for a brief moment as something that looked like a flu virus with Casimir effect power generators attached to it and then he morphed back into Einstein.

Tabitha, Jim, and 'Becca seemed to realize what Anson and the Einstein lookalike were arguing about. 'Becca seethed with anger and looked ready to pounce, but Tabitha interrupted.

"Opolawn, enough tricks!" she ordered. Opolawn found it amusing and morphed back into himself. "So, it is true then. You have invaded Anson's mind through his dreams before?"

"That is true, General Clemons." Opolawn laughed again. "I visited Dr. Clemons from time to time."

"Did you alter his mind?" 'Becca asked.

"I only . . . visited. I occasionally left an idea or two, but your scientist here is quite the smart little monkey and would have figured it out on his own . . . in another forty years or so." Opolawn laughed again.

"That is bordering on a violation of the Treaty, Opolawn," Prawmitoos said calmly in his girly voice.

"You will pay for invading my mind, alien!" Anson activated his warp armor. Seeing this startled all of us and we followed his lead. He was very pissed and I thought was about to start bustin' caps up in Opolawn's ass. But somehow he restrained himself. "You haven't returned since the War, Al. Why?" Anson asked.

"Why, my dear monkey, you accomplished your part. But I see you have continued to work on the technology." Opolawn poked his finger at Anson's warp armor shield. Simultaneously the shield glimmered blue while Opolawn glimmered red in a wave from his finger to his tail. "Very impressive. You did this on your own, too!"

"Opolawn," Prawmitoos interrupted. The little regally marked Gray stepped between Anson and the Lumpeyin emperor. "Have you discussed your interaction and influence changes with the Arbitrators?" His head was about knee-high to Opolawn but the little alien didn't seem afraid.

Opolawn seethed and glared downward at the little Gray. "Do not threaten me, Prawmitoos. You know as well as I do that the creatures in the *probatur claustrum* are not protected by the treaty."

"*Probatur claustrum?*" Anson asked. I could tell he was trying to translate it in his head.

Mike, what does that mean?

Probatur is a Teytoonise word for test or examine and claustrum *can mean pen, cell, prison. I would say the best combination would be test cell or examining cell.*

Examining cage, perhaps?

Yes, that is probably good, Steven. I understand your approach now. Perhaps "test tube" would be a better interpretation.

Test tube. We've been right all along about being lab rats!

"*Probatur claustrum.*" I turned to Anson. "Test tube or lab rat cage!" Anson understood it immediately and said that it paralleled Latin perfectly. I had Mike teach me Latin real quick.

"So, that is what the quarantined zones are, test tubes," Jim said through clenched teeth.

"Enough of this. We have come to talk, not fight," Prawmitoos interjected.

"Very well, runt," Opolawn said. "We can retire to my

temple for refreshments and entertainment, and we will hear your requests. Then perhaps I will kill you all." He laughed again.

Prawmitoos said nothing but he stared right through Opolawn with his huge black eyes. I caressed the golf ball in my pocket and was looking forward to wiping this temple right off the top of this goddamned alien mountain. And I was thinking that killing the emperor would be a good thing. I could tell that Anson had already made up his mind about killing Opolawn. I had only known Anson for a couple months or so, but I had yet to find him wrong on anything of importance.

➤ CHAPTER 25

Opolawn lifted us with a warp field and flew us into his temple. We passed through a great hall that was larger than any stadium on Earth and then floated into a terrace about two hundred meters up on one of the giant columns. He set us down on the patio, which had one of the most amazing views that I had ever seen. The terrace overlooked the ocean many kilometers away at the base of the mountain chain. The sun was setting and shining in all sorts of reds, violets, and blues. It was magnificent, and Opolawn stood there for a moment taking it in.

"The universe can be quite beautiful at times," he said. "And sometimes it can be quite vile," he commented as he turned to Prawmitoos. It was obvious that Opolawn and Prawmitoos had a history and that it was bad . . . very bad. None of us had the nerve to pry.

"Help yourselves to anything you desire, Earthlings." He motioned and the room was filled with dancing naked aliens, both male and female, and there was a table in the middle of the room with nearly every type of food and beverage imaginable.

"No thanks," I muttered.

"Let's get down to business," Tabitha said.

"Very well, General. Why *are* you here?" Opolawn sat on a large fur-covered chaise lounge. Several naked aliens of both sexes doted over him, bringing him fruits and juices and fanning him.

"I want you to hand over the control device for the picophage that infects many of Earth's citizens," she said.

"Aha! How do you know about this picophage, as you call it?" Opolawn boomed.

"Simple," Anson answered. "Us monkeys figured out how to detect it, Al!" Anson continued to display his anger and disgust for this alien and he purposefully dumbed up his retort even more with his extreme redneck drawl. I would have to find out what this Albert Einstein stuff was all about—but not now.

"Really? Is this true, Prawmitoos? They had no help from you?"

"I only told them that there was a picophage," Prawmitoos said in a flat voice. "They came to me knowing that they were infected with something. When my soldiers tried to stop them these monkeys overpowered them, rather easily I might add."

"If that is so, Prawmitoos, then I should have attacked The Species ages ago. I find it hard to believe that mere monkeys could offer any sort of real fight. Really,

Prawmitoos, you never cease to disappoint me," Opolawn taunted the Gray.

"Enough," Tabitha said. "Will you give us the control device or not?"

"What do you think you will do with this so-called control device if I give it to you?"

"We will keep it until the last of the humans with the picophage die of old age, and then we will destroy it. If we have it, at least then we will know you are not controlling us. Even if you can enter our dreams, you still can't control us when we are awake without the picophage and its controller." Tabitha stood strong and fast and seemed completely fearless.

"You think so, do you? It is your dreams that you are afraid of. It is your dreams that make you fear these miniscule Gray bugs," he said.

That's it, Mike! I thought. *He implanted the alien abduction memories in us!*

That makes a lot of sense, Steven.

I have no idea what to do with that information, but I know it's right, I thought.

"If I give you the controller, Prawmitoos and the rest of The Species will eat you alive." Opolawn laughed.

"The Grays have agreed not to attack us and to leave us alone if we can prove that you are not controlling us," I told him.

Opolawn laughed for several seconds. "And you silly monkeys believed him, did you? I'm sure he argued with Feyibi on your behalf too, didn't he?"

"Yes, so?" Jim asked.

"You've been duped. You monkeys aren't as smart as you think you are. Not yet, at least. You are nothing but trained lab animals, as you have discovered. Prawmitoos didn't tell you about the other countless species that they have destroyed, and under false pretenses I am sure."

"That is enough, Opolawn," Prawmitoos said.

"I don't answer to you, bug. I will say what I please," Opolawn continued. "Did he happen to mention how he committed genocide on the Thuans and the creatures of Thweh? I guess not. What about Eyivaes? Did he explain where they are? And what of Aa?" Opolawn pushed away a Lumpeyin girl who was offering him some sort of bright green round fruit.

"Ah, Opolawn," Prawmitoos squeaked. "You act as though you were perfect in the eyes of these Earthlings, and that you yourself have not committed your share of unspeakable atrocities to countless races as well."

"Opolawn, you are claiming that these Grays killed off no telling how many other E.T.s in the Teytoonise side of the galaxy?" Anson asked and shook his head.

"That is correct, my little monkey. You humans have duped yourselves into the belief that evil was in the heart of humanity. Well, I have a lesson for you. Evil is alive and well in the universe." He sneered at Prawmitoos and it seemed as though sparks would fly between the two of them.

Opolawn continued, "You have been ignorant of the great evils of this galaxy for far too long to travel across the galaxy and make demands of me. And you are very foolish if you think that the Grays, as you call them, want anything for you but death. The sole intent of The Species hive is to populate the universe and devour all that stands in its way—and I literally mean devour. Several species that have survived have only survived because the picophage means death to the Grays. You owe your survival this long to me! The only reason the Teytoonis ever had interest in you monkeys is because they knew that your infection might lead them to a means of attacking us, the Lumpeyins." Opolawn stood three meters tall and thumped his chest. "WE ARE THE TRUE PROTECTORS OF THIS GALAXY!" His voice boomed through the chamber and it appeared that fire danced around the periphery of his body. Perhaps this was my imagination but that is what it looked like.

"Nevertheless, Opolawn, Prawmitoos did argue with his people on our behalf and he has helped in bringing us here. Will you give us the controller or not?" Tabitha continued to be focused on the subject.

"I will not. I am afraid that you poor monkeys are not smart enough to survive without me controlling your evolution and keeping the bugs at bay. If I am not helping you then what will keep the vermin away?" Opolawn replied.

"We are now a threat to them. What will keep them away now?" 'Becca said. "How will you protect us from being annihilated by the Grays?"

"Is this true, Prawmitoos? Do you bugs plan to destroy the humans? Answer me."

"It is of no concern to you, Opolawn, as their space is not within your jurisdiction." Prawmitoos squinted his big black eyes at the light Opolawn was emitting from the surface of his skin. I decided that these Lumpeyins must be phosphorescent. As the sun set, the sky grew dark enough to notice their skin's glow. Opolawn's glow seemed to be slightly brighter than his dancing troupe's.

Mike, is he phosphorescing?

The Lumpeyins are apparently bioluminescent like the dinoflagellates, black dragonfish, fireflies, and many other organisms on Earth.

I see.

"I am sorry, humans. I cannot give you the controller, as it must not fall into the hands of the vermin Teytoonis." He held up a small device in his left hand and tossed it into his right. "A brilliant device forged from the same quantum connected material that the Himbroozya was, hence it works through the YIT at any distance. You see, the Himbroozya is fatal to the Gray monsters. This is why they developed nanomachines and scientist drones to study it. The actual regal line of the bugs would be destroyed instantly if they come into contact with the picophage. As long as you are not a threat to them they will use you as research animals in attempts to create a vaccine. Ah, but my scientist Tentalos designed a very good phage that the bugs have yet to be able to cure. The control is my bonus. Perhaps one of these days you backwater species can be forced to develop a weapon that will rid me of these vermin once and for all. This is not the day, and you are not that species; I fear you are doomed."

At warp speed, Anson plowed headfirst into Opolawn, knocking the controller free for a microsecond. I had caught Anson's planned motion from my enhanced eyesight and my peripheral vision. This microsecond was all I needed. I warped through the region of space where the alien's hand and the controller were and I did a quick lights-off lights-on maneuver. As I continued to fly forward I took Opolawn's hand and the picophage controller with me. I picked up the contoller and tossed his hand out of my warp bubble with a second off-on sequence.

The hand fell into the ocean below. As I doubled back into the fight it was obvious that Opolawn was far stronger than we had suspected.

Opolawn grasped Anson in his left hand. His grip was around the neck of Anson's warp bubble armor. Anson tried to adjust the warp field but Opolawn held him. Tabitha, Jim, and 'Becca were on the bounce and got the squeeze on him. This forced Opolawn to drop Anson. Opolawn exploded in a flash of light that flung the four warp armored humans through the walls of the chamber. I couldn't tell what happened to Prawmitoos. I didn't really care, either.

I thought I would catch Opolawn in the back unaware but he sidestepped at warp speed and chased me as I missed him. We warped through the cityscape, flying through buildings and dodging each other's barrages of flung debris. Opolawn began flashing bright high-power energy beams of visible light at me. From where I wasn't sure, but I was beginning to believe that these were serious bursts of energy that I didn't need to be in front of. One of them hit my warp bubble and the next thing I knew I was in orbit around the moon of Lumpeya City. I warped back to the center of Lumpeya City as fast as I could to find the battle still raging. This was a dangerous affair and since I had the controller I thought we should make an attempt at leaving. I zipped to the *Phoenix* and had Mike fire it up. Prawmitoos was already there, trying to hack into the controls of the spacecraft. As I said before, the Grays have a lot to learn about hacking. I punched Prawmitoos in the head and tossed him out of the *Phoenix* payload bay onto the ground below. He landed right on his little gray ass. I then zipped the warp field closed and called the gang to converge on me.

Mike and I zigged, zagged, and dodged lightning. The *Phoenix* took some hits, but the alien condensed matter hull was tough. The warp field I applied helped also. I finally got the crew inside the *Phoenix*'s warp bubble and they managed to make their way to the bridge. All the time the *Phoenix* was taking a great deal of fire from Opolawn and several others of his entourage that had joined the fight.

"Mike, engage the quantum drive and get us out of here fast!" I told him. "Warp bubble shield on!"

Just as the drive started to engage, a brilliant flash of light appeared through the view screens and the ship lurched to a halt.

"What the hell!" Jim screamed and fell forward face-first into the floor. The inertial dampeners were overtaxed apparently.

"They've caught us in that damn beam thing they got us with on the way in," 'Becca said.

"Can we overcome it?" Tabitha asked.

Mike?

Sorry, Steven, but no, we cannot.

"It looks like they caught us. But they can't get through the warp bubble," I told her.

"Damn! Okay, we keep the warp bubble on forever if we have to. It looks like we have a stalemate here," Tabitha said.

"YOU CANNOT GO ANYWHERE, MONKEYS. YOU MIGHT AS WELL COME OUT," Opolawn's voice boomed over the YIT intercom. Opolawn was floating above his city. He appeared as a brilliant ball of light, almost like a miniature yellow sun. The bright yellow beam of light passed from the temple below him up beside him and to the *Phoenix*. He pulled us down to his altitude and laughed in his booming voice over the YIT intercom. He looked like a small sun floating before us. Somehow that sun was going to have to set. I was wide open for suggestions.

We were trapped between a rock and a really, really hard place. If we gave up, we were dead and the Grays would destroy humanity. If we stayed here until we died of starvation or Opolawn figured out how to get in to us, we would be dead and the Grays would destroy humanity. If we destroyed the controller before we died, the humans back on Earth infected with the Himbroozya picophage would go nuts—the picomachines would be a control system with random gain and no controller—and the result would destroy humanity. We brainstormed and threw ideas around for the better part of an hour, but we had no clue as what to do. Opolawn grew impatient and it was our guess that he would eventually figure out how to crack our shell and get us out.

"Okay, anybody have any sci-fi scenarios that fit?" Anson asked us.

"I'm kinda drawing a blank, Anson," 'Becca replied.

Jim shrugged.

"Hey, I think I've got one," I said.

"Let's hear it, Steven," Tabitha ordered.

"There was an episode of the old *Star Trek* series where they bumped into the ancient Greek Gods and—" I started.

"Of course!" Anson slapped his forehead.

"Apollo caught them in much the same way, didn't he?" Jim rubbed his head in thought. "Spock found his power source, if I recall, and Kirk had 'em blast it with the *Enterprise*'s phasers, right?"

"The scenario fits, but I think bright guy out there is too quick for us to just shoot out his tractor beam," Anson responded.

"Yes, Anson, but it is a place to start formulating a plan. Let's see what we can come up with." Tabitha nodded encouragingly to each of us.

"Well, Tabitha, the problem I see is getting out of our protective warp bubble without getting smashed," 'Becca replied.

"There must be a way!" Tabitha wasn't about to give up.

Stevie?

What, honey, I'm kinda busy right now.

I know, Mike told me.

Oh.

Use the YIT and get out.

What do you mean, Tatiana?

Quantum connect and teleport away.

We've never tried that and we aren't sure it will work.

It will work. You just need to know where you're going to teleport to. You need to go to another SuperAgent.

The only ones we are friendly with are Mike and Michelle that are both here and Mikhail that is with you. No good.

There must be a way, Steven.

Maybe. You are wasting energy, baby. Go back to sleep.

➤ CHAPTER 26

It is really funny the things that pop in your head when you are trying to think of something else. I was thinking about Tatiana's suggestion and was trying to figure out what all would be required to do the quantum teleportation of a nanowarp bubble over the YIT from one SuperAgent to another. We would need three cooperative SuperAgents: one on each end to act as the transmit and receive locations and one in the warp bubble to guide the bubble into the quantum connection interference beam. We weren't exactly sure how the SuperAgent could guide us into the quantum connected region of the cube since it was such a small place. If we figured all that stuff out we still needed three SuperAgents. The only real SuperAgents that I knew of were Mike, Mikhail, and Michelle. The dummy we made back on the Moon wasn't smart enough to surf the YIT; it was only designed to drive the construction nanomachines. And then it hit me.

After all these years it finally hit me how JackieZZ had survived the quantum singularity that she had pulled on me in the Gladiator Sequence back just before The Rain. The black hole was two dimensional and looked more like a funnel in three-dimensional space—therefore the event horizon only sucked in things above the mouth of the funnel. There would have been some spillover and a small increase in the gravity field beneath the funnel—I'd noticed it pull her hair and boobs upward—but not near as much as was above it. All along I had been thinking the thing was a real black hole, not one that was constructed differently or in fewer dimensions or with a tailored event horizon. It had to have been all of the exposure to warp field mechanics and spacetime curvature manipulation physics that I had been involved in over the past few months that finally allowed my brain to subprocess the information in my subconscious and come up with the answer. But what good did that do me now?

I wasn't certain exactly, but I was beginning to formulate something in the back of my mind. I also started thinking about Sequencing and how hacking through The Realm wasn't much different from this universal Infrastructure and Framework or the YIT. With The Realm you start sending out agents to look for doorways to other worlds within The Realm and then you figure out where to get a key for any new door you find. If you find a key that fits, you can open the door and go to and from that world whenever you like.

The YIT was no different. All of the SuperAgents in

the universe were connected to each other through the Infrastructure. Each of the SuperAgents was a door to whatever lies on the other side of the SuperAgent—to this point only information lay on the other side of the SuperAgent, just as a server lies on the other side of your Internet connection. In The Realm you have to find the doors before you can open them. The same goes for the YIT. You have to find the SuperAgents before you can use them. So how was Opolawn talking to us inside the *Phoenix* over the YIT intercom? He had a SuperAgent on him somewhere just like I did. That's how he knew I "smelled different."

I decided to try and write a Sequencing code that Mike could use to ping Opolawn's SuperAgent. When I spoke to Mike about this, he thought I was slow.

Mike, we need to develop a code to ping for other SuperAgents.

Steven, how do you think I have been downloading information from the YIT?

Holy shit, Mike! I never thought about it. You are just surfing away and have found all sorts of YIT sites haven't you?

Yes, Steven.

Can you communicate with Opolawn's SuperAgent?

Opolawn has a firewall.

Can we crack it?

Unlikely. The encryption is a multidimensional multirank tensor and appears to be changing continuously with random fractal dimension.

Are there any other SuperAgents nearby that are not encrypted?

Why, yes, there are many, Steven.

Where is the closest, other than Michelle, of course?

There is one at the landing field hangar where we previously landed.

I got off my duff and headed for the supply room where Michelle was located. I now had a partial plan anyway. I knew that if we left here without stopping both Prawmitoos and Opolawn, we would be in immediate trouble. I didn't want to leave behind the *Phoenix* if at all possible—in order to do that there would have to be some mayhem left behind us so that Opolawn's ships didn't fight us all the way out of Lumpeyin space—assuming we could survive that. And if we did get back and somehow Prawmitoos had returned to Teytoonis space, I was sure that he was going to be a bit sore at us and that he would be coming for the controller.

So I had to develop a multifaceted plan—a plan within a plan within a plan. First, I had to test the physics of YIT teleportation.

Tatiana, wake up!

Yes, Stevie?

Listen, take Mikhail out of your body and place him a few feet away from you.

Right on! It's about time, Steven! . . . Okay . . . it's done.

Mike, get ready to drive us into Michelle's quantum connection pathway.

I understand, Steven.

Michelle?

Yes, Steven.

Connect to Mikhail, please, and send a continuous data stream for thirty seconds. Keep the line open for return messages until I give further orders. Okay, Mike.

Okay, Steven, good luck.

The warp bubble formed around me and Mike adjusted the field so it would be like Dr. Who's phone booth—big on the inside, small on the outside. Mike told me that the outside bubble diameter requirement was on the order of 1×10^{-29} meters and that nobody had ever tried to build a stable warp bubble that size before. We were only a handful of orders of magnitude larger than the Planck length, which would be theoretically as small as you could go in this universe. But Anson's warp technology with Tatiana's modifications and a funnel-shaped field like JackieZZ had used made this possible. Of course, we needed a SuperAgent as smart as Mike to control all of these field parameters at once, but it was possible and looked like it would work. Mike steered the warp bubble through the funnel-shaped warp field down into the mechanism in Michelle's orange and green crystalline cube until he hit the dark shadow spot where the quantum connected fringe patterns are created. The warp funnel kept the tiny warp bubble on target as it approached the datastream hole. The datastream from Michelle to Mikhail was flowing into the dark quantum flux below where the small end of the funnel-shaped field stopped. When Mike got us close enough we were pulled in instantaneously and were surfing on the information beam that was being sent across the galaxy via the underlying oscillating fabric of the universe—the YIT, the Infrastructure, the universal quantum connection.

And a microsecond later we popped out inside another quantum connected interference region in another cube. Mike projected the funnel-shaped field in front of us and steered us into the small end of the funnel. As we rose up through the funnel the outer diameter of our warp bubble grew. Less than a second ago, I was inside the *Phoenix*, and now I was standing beside Tatiana who was herself standing inside a dark bubble of spacetime. There was a white-and-blue swirl over the surface of the bubble and with my enhanced eyesight I could see her there naked in front of me. It worked! Traveling through spacetime on the quantum connected Infrastructure worked!

"It's about time, Steven." She slugged me on the forearm and then jumped into my arms. "I love you! I love you! I love you! Now get me the hell out of here!"

"I love you, now hold on to me," I told her.

"Like I would do anything else?" she asked sarcastically.

Mike, reverse the process.

Okay, Steven.

We left Mikhail sitting there in the bubble to fend for himself before two thousand years passed or the bubble was destroyed. If we could figure out a way to get him, we would do it—just not now. We popped into the supply room just outside of Michelle's housing and Tatiana immediately had the nanomachines redress her and bring her health to optimal status. She created a bag of cheeseburgers, fries, and a soda and began scarfing them down.

"It worked!" I shouted.

"I toolf eww it fwoul," Tatiana said with a mouthful.

We need to tell the others. This gives us an amazing advantage. I thought to her as I watched her eat. She was a sight for sore eyes, to say the least.

Okay. Hey, my temple implants still work without Mikhail, she thought to me.

They will function as long as you are within a few

hundred thousand kilometers of me, Tatiana, Mike thought to us.

Oh. Neat! She thought in Russian and she continued on to her fourth cheeseburger.

I missed you!

Me, too, she said. I would have kissed her but there was a likelihood that she would have bitten me by mistake. Besides, there was a cheeseburger in the way.

Tatiana's appearance on the bridge of the *Phoenix* startled 'Becca at first, but everyone was pleased to see her and pleased that the teleportation of the miniature warp bubble worked. It was the idea of creating a funnel-shaped warp to guide us into the quantum connection zone that was the trick. Anson liked it a whole lot and wanted to discuss the physics of the concept. I told him that it was a trick an old Sequencer taught me. Only Mike, Tatiana, and I got the joke.

Tabitha wanted more information on how we could use the concept tactically and strategically. Her military mind and training served us all very well. So I quickly filled them in on my plan. Then the debate started.

"Wait a minute, though." Tabitha played with the red curl of hair on her forehead. "If we can go anywhere else why don't we just do that?"

"I'm not sure that that isn't the best idea. That is why we are talking about it." I shrugged my shoulders. "The thing is though, that wherever we went would be in Gray space on a Gray ship and then we would have to take it from them. It can be done." I smiled at Tatiana.

"Danmn tfootn!" Tatiana said as she forced a handful of fries in her mouth and followed it with a swig from her soda.

Anson chuckled a little. "Slow down, honey, or you're gonna bite a finger off."

"Haffen'tf eaten in fweeks!" Tatiana replied as she continued to stuff more fries in her mouth. She didn't actually need to eat. The nanomachines in the stockroom had returned her health, but she really hadn't eaten in weeks.

"If we go now, without taking care of Sunshine out there, we might live to regret it in the future," Jim said. "But what do we do exactly? We can't just leave the bomb behind. Opolawn would detect it and stop it. "

"We have to distract him somehow, and *then* we have to get away from him," Tabitha thought out loud.

"How about this," Tatiana said, finally without food in her mouth. She reached in my front pocket and pulled out the golf ball and the controller. She held the golf-ball-sized bomb in her right hand and the controller in her left hand. "Mike, can you hear me?"

"Yes, Tataiana."

"Can you make the bomb look just like the controller?" she said.

"Yes, Tatiana. Hand it to Steven," Mike replied.

Tatiana handed the golf ball back to me. I held the golf ball in my right hand and it got fuzzy around the edges. It changed colors and then formed itself into an exact replica of the controller.

"Will it still go boom, Mike?" I asked.

"Only if you want it to," he said.

Then Tatiana ran for the door at more than fifty kilometers per hour and she was gone and the picophage controller went with her. It didn't dawn on us that she would be under Opolawn's control if we brought her out of the Gray's confinement bubble and on Opolawn's doorstep. Mikhail was no longer in her belly; the little piece of Gray technology must've somehow been "vaccinating" her from Opolawn's control. I should've figured that out. Perhaps I should have even waited about freeing Tatiana. That was dumb. I took off after her but she had too big a head start and she knew where she was going and I didn't.

Mike, track her for me.

Looks like she is going to the hangar bay, Steven.

Got it. Thanks!

Fortunately, she hadn't put on a warp armor belt yet since we got her back. I caught up with her in the hangar bay because she had to slow down to open the door—manually. Manually, hell; she ripped it right off the hinges—or whatever you would call that alien door-sliding mechanism. I made a mental note that the door wasn't made from the alien degenerate matter like the hull was. I tackled her from behind and she rolled with my momentum and tossed me thirty meters into the ceiling of the hangar bay. That hurt. I jumped from the ceiling as I began to fall, pushing myself at her. I just missed her but caught a metal hairpin in the shoulder.

The nanomachines healed the wound before she stabbed at me the second time. I leapt over her, but she jumped upward into me as soon as I was over her head. She caught me with her left arm and stabbed me in the neck with a second hairpin. This stunned me a bit as the pin actually grazed my spinal cord. Tatiana tossed me to the floor hard and ignored me for a microsecond. The nanomachines fixed the damage to my spine and dissolved the metal hairpin. Then I had the alien armor suit cover my entire body. I didn't want a metal stick through the cerebellum. The last drop of blood from my neck wound dropped just as the alien armor suit covered the spot and I rose to my feet.

I shook my head and got my bearings. At about a hundred kilometers per hour Tatiana lunged into my chest with both feet. This time I had a slight blur in my peripheral vision that warned me. My enhanced reflexes forced me to twist and drop just as she hit me. This allowed me to move with her momentum and the impact didn't hurt near as much as it could have. Also, the alien armor material that Tatiana had developed was doing a great job of protecting me. We rolled and swapped blocks, punches, and kicks until she caught my foot and flipped me. She did a forward judo roll on top of me and her knee twisted my chin sideways against the deck plating on the floor. When you're fighting, you lose track of time but I had a good measure of how long our last little entanglement had taken since I caught a glimpse of the drop of blood that had fallen from my neck splashing on the deck right in front of my face!

I lunged upward with my heels against the floor and pushed her off of me. Tatiana did a forward handspring and caught me in the chin with a back kick in the process. I staggered backward for a microsecond and then attempted to bear hug her. Yeah, that didn't work worth a damn. She dropped into a horse stance and head-butted backwards. The back of her head caught me square on the nose, breaking it. Had I not been wearing the armor the head-butt would have likely killed me. She stepped in behind my right leg and pulled me down to the floor with an elbow to the ribs to top it off. She was up and running before I could taste the blood running down my throat. The nanomachines fixed me up soon after that. I was rising to my feet when, at God only knows how fast, Tatiana slammed into me feet first, again. She was kicking my ass! It all happened so fast I barely had time to react and my reactions were slow because I couldn't bring myself to *really* fight my wife.

"Why is it I always seem to be getting in fights in this payload bay?" I asked Tatiana as I grabbed a handful of her hair and pulled her over to the floor as we hit. We tumbled for several meters and came to a stop against one of the modified warp missiles that was stored there. "Well, that missile ain't ever gonna fire," I said as I ducked her barrage of kicks and punches. "Come on, honey, snap out of it, will ya! Fight the bastard!"

I was blocking her punches and kicks while trying to grab her. I couldn't bring myself to—really—hit her. I knew it wasn't her doing this. It couldn't be her.

Tatiana, what are you doing?

Tatiana is not home, little monkey. Opolawn's voice came to me through Tatiana's mind link. This was enough to startle me and throw me off guard for a split microsecond. That was all that Tatiana, uh, Opolawn, needed.

She caught me with a right hook to the head and then dropped and grabbed me by the ankles and yanked my feet out from under me. As I lost my balance she tossed me headfirst into the bulkhead. I hit the wall with a massive *crack* and my head poked clean through the metal wall and into the hallway on the other side.

"That hurt!" I saw stars for several seconds before the nanomachines could right my injuries. I pulled myself back through the hole in the wall and shook myself off. I was too late.

Tatiana was already in the smaller Gray ship and had opened the bay doors. She couldn't get anywhere in the little ship though because the outside warp bubble was still in place around the *Phoenix*.

Let her go, Opolawn, she can't get out!

Why would I do that, monkey?

"Steven? What is going on!? Where are you!?" Tabitha's voice came over the comm.

"Don't open the warp bubble, Tabitha. Opolawn is controlling Tatiana and she is trying to fly off the *Phoenix* with the smaller Gray ship," I called back to her.

"Roger that!" Tabitha responded.

Tatiana, fight him. Snap out of it, baby!

That will do you no good, monkey. No human has ever overcome the Himbroozya before.

Yeah, well, nobody bats a thousand!

Let her out or I will force her to fly into the warp field wall at high velocity. The little bug ship will probably bounce around inside the bubble and beat all of you even more senseless than you are.

Stop it!

Let her go.

No!

Then you will all die. The little Gray ship lifted slowly off the deck plating and hovered for a second.

Okay! Wait! Opolawn, wait! But not her. I'll meet you on the surface with the controller, but you have to let her alone now!

Brave monkey. Very well.

Steven? Tatiana's mind voice came to me.

Tatiana, land the craft and come to me. She landed the little spaceship and crawled out of it. I took the controller from her and put it in my pocket with the replica. I wasn't worried about confusing them—Mike knew the difference. As soon as Tatiana handed me the controller a small warp field formed around her. I turned and there was Anson pointing his little warp field projection device at her.

"It's for her own good, son!" he said.

"I agree," I told him.

> ## CHAPTER 27

I had my alien armor suit on everywhere except for my head. I figured that Opolawn wouldn't recognize me and would think I was up to something if he couldn't see my face. I also grabbed an extra warp armor belt in case mine went out. I wanted to be prepared for anything, whether I would need another one or not. "Be prepared" was the only credo that seemed to make any sense to me at this point. So I grabbed everything I had with me that would fit in my pockets. I put on my double shoulder-harnessed nine-millimeter Glocks just in case. I didn't think that a handgun was going to do me any good in a high-tech battle against a creature as powerful as Opolawn, but again, be prepared.

I hadn't told Opolawn how or where on the surface I would meet him, so I called out over the YIT to him and he opened a communications channel. I told him I was coming out and that I would meet him on the ground at the landing field we were at earlier. He agreed to that location and told me that he was losing his patience and that I had two minutes.

Tabitha set up two warp bubbles around the *Phoenix*. The first one was the one that was already in place and was holding off Opolawn's yellow tractor beam. She adjusted the interior space of the bubble enough so that she could project a second bubble. I flew the little alien ship out past the location for the inner bubble and she turned it on and turned off the outer bubble. The light bombarded the ship and the bubble and Opolawn's air force was surprised because fourteen ships surrounding the *Phoenix*'s warp bubble opened fire on it when the outer field went down.

"CLEVER MONKEY." Opolawn's voice boomed over the Gray ship's intercom as several of his fighters fell in beside me. I kept my warp armor on just in case he tried something fishy.

"You didn't think we were that stupid, did you?" I called back at him and faked a laugh.

I landed the ship meters away from where we had landed the *Phoenix* earlier that day and I hopped out onto the platform where I had dumped Prawmitoos.

"Okay, Opolawn, here I am!" I yelled up at the blinding miniature sun.

Opolawn drifted slowly down to the ground and dimmed himself slightly. He almost dimmed himself enough that you could tell it was nighttime.

"Hand over the controller, monkey, and no tricks," he said.

I placed the replica controller on the ground in front of me and backed up so the controller was on the edge of the bubble. I expanded the warp armor bubble to its maximum and then I turned on the second warp bubble. The second bubble I kept nearly skintight so I could turn off the outer bubble, leaving the picophage control mechanism lying on the ground unprotected and between myself and the alien.

Opolawn began to laugh as he walked toward the device confidently, and arrogantly he said, "Monkey, you should learn where your place is." He bent over to pick up the controller and for the first time I realized that his knees bent both ways.

"Now!" I yelled into the comm. Opolawn looked up just as the squeeze play warp missile appeared and caught him in a squeeze. The force of the implosion threw me back a thousand meters, and debris and rubble blasted through the air around me. I warped into Opolawn from a head-on position to keep him off balance. The impact sent him flying about eighty meters straight up above me since I caught him at the bottom of his protective field— whatever it was—and it was like I had punted him straight upward.

"Don't stop now!" I yelled up at the *Phoenix* as three more squeeze play missiles caught him. Then Jim and Anson zipped out of the *Phoenix* and began pounding on Opolawn's air and space forces with their warp armor. Tabitha and 'Becca continued to fire away at Opolawn with the missiles.

Mike, where is the SuperAgent down here?

It is in the hangar, Steven.

Show me in my mind, Mike.

Okay, Steven. Then I had a map of the landing field in my head and there was the SuperAgent, just inside the hangar doors only fifty meters away.

Mike, where is the transmitter of Opolawn's tractor beam? Show me!

Here, Steven. The map in my head scrolled a kilometer to the south and blinked where the beam was located.

Thanks, Mike.

I warped at top armor speed to the tractor beam facility and continued right on through the wall of the building and out the other side. I turned upward and did a loop-de-loop and straight down through the shaft of the thirty-meter-diameter dish transmitter. The transmitter aperture sparked and creaked and shuddered violently, but the thing didn't go out. So, I did a zigzag pattern downward throughout the facility, flinging equipment, debris, and red-eyed red-skinned pointy-eared aliens to and fro. Finally, the big aperture of the transmitter crumpled under its own weight and imploded. The tractor beam blinked twice and was followed by a gigantic explosion and bright orange flash. The blast wake jostled me a bit as I blazed a warp trail out of the area and back to the landing field.

"Tabitha, are you gone yet?" I called her.

"I let loose about ten more missiles and then hit the gas! We are about two-tenths of a light year away and picking up speed. You'll have to bring Anson and Jim," Tabitha said.

"I understand," I said as I set down on the landing field. "Jim, Anson, where are you?"

"We are straight above you and headed your way." Then they appeared right beside me in static warp bubbles.

"Okay, good. Let's get the hell out of here."

"NOT SO FAST, MONKEYS!" A flash of light from above scattered the three of us by a hundred meters. Opolawn fired his lightning bolt at us. The smaller personal warp fields were strained tremendously by the bolt, much more so than was the *Phoenix*'s system.

Steven, your warp armor can't take many more hits like that one.

I was afraid of that. Thanks for the warning, Mike.

Okay, Steven.

"Anson, Jim, scatter and don't give him a target! Keep moving at high speeds!" I shouted over the comm.

"Roger that shit!" I knew that came from Anson.

"You got it, Steve!" Jim said.

The three of us got Opolawn in the classic dogfight merry-go-round. Anson would zip by him and then I would go head-to-head with him from a different direction, while Jim would be trying to get an angle on him. We rolled and tossed and looped around him at hypersonic velocities and would occasionally impact him. His personal warp field, or whatever armor he was wearing, was strong, but it was slower to maneuver. We had him in the classic fast, small, maneuverable fighters versus one big, powerful fighter type of air battle. Just like the MiGs versus the F-4s in Vietnam—Mike told me this. This was working well for us for a few seconds. We made several good hits on him and each time it seemed that his illumination dimmed a bit. But then the tide of the battle turned. Opolawn got wise to our three-dimensional battle tactics and took one dimension away from us.

He fought us to the surface, where the ground would limit our maneuverability. A second later I was staring closely at the Moon of Lumpeya City as I smacked into it. It was covered with civilization and I took out a good portion of ten city blocks. I rolled over and reversed back to Lumpeya City at full warp of the armor. It took about a second and a half to make it back to the fight.

Anson and Jim were holding their own with him and my abrupt return caught Opolawn off guard. I hammered him four kilometers straight down through the temple and into the crust of the planet itself. As we passed down through layer after layer of crust and water tables and limestone Opolawn finally stopped the downward momentum and flung me hard sideways a good half of a kilometer through the limestone bed. He shot upward to the surface only to be sandwiched by Anson and Jim.

I plowed up through the crust and surfaced through the center of the city, causing the large columns to topple in a couple of places. When those thousand-meter columns fell, they really fell!

"Where are you?" I called out.

"We're over the river by the landing strip again!" Jim said.

"And you ain't gonna believe this shit, but the air field is in perfect condition and I think I just saw Prawmitoos trying to make his way across to the little alien ship. Yeeow!!" Anson replied just as Opolawn hammered him.

"GIVE UP MONKEYS! YOU CANNOT DEFEAT ME!" the alien emperor's voice boomed through the comm.

"Anson's hit escape velocity, Steven! I need some help here!" Jim said. I could see a mountain a few hundred kilometers off to the east explode as Anson passed through it and continued on spaceward. Opolawn had hit him hard.

Jim and I tried to squeeze Opolawn several times but to no avail—he was too fast! We actually banged into each other a couple of times a little harder than I would've liked and the sky was filled with window-shattering sonic booms. Then I rushed Opolawn and stopped short with a feint that caused a shock wave to scatter debris in his face. Jim hammered him. Opolawn's larger, more sluggish bubble only moved a few kilometers. But it gave us a millisecond to breathe.

"I don't think we can force his warp field to overload, Jim!" I said.

"I think you're right, aaagggh!" Jim splashed and skipped through the ocean and traced out into orbit as he caught the full brunt of a lightning bolt from Opolawn.

"We have to get out of here, guys!" I yelled over the comm.

Opolawn and I were chasing each other around in circles until Anson poured up from the ocean and grabbed Opolawn by surprise. With a great sonic boom Anson forced him upward and upward and upward until I could see an explosion on the surface of the moon of Lumpcya City above. An outsider looking in at the battle might have thought that it looked like something from a comic book, like Superman's epic fight against Doomsday, or a video game like the *Gladiator Sequence*, or an episode of *Dragonball Z 3D*, but this was no game or comic book and there was no television magic required here. This was a battle of wills and alien technology and good old human stubbornness!

Jim settled down beside me.

"What kept you?" I asked.

"Them!" He pointed at more of Opolawn's fighters

bearing in on us. Anson appeared from the top of them taking out several and scattering the rest. Opolawn wouldn't be far behind and we were getting overwhelmed and tired.

Mike, can you give me an edge on Opolawn somehow?

I can track him in your mind, Steven, but you aren't fast enough to outmaneuver him. Opolawn's computational skills are quite remarkable. I fear you are not capable of defeating him, Mike warned me.

Are you? I asked as we started back through the wheel with Opolawn, and now more of his fighters were entering the wheel as well.

What do you mean, Steven? Mike asked.

Could you take over my body and take him?

YES!

DO IT, MIKE!

Then it was a whirlwind even faster than I had been experiencing before. I was zigging and zagging and looping and diving and slamming faster than my mind could grasp. Once I noticed that Mike had pushed Anson and Jim to the ground. Jim grounded on the little Gray ship and toppled it over with Prawmitoos inside it. I think Mike did that on purpose.

Then he dropped below Opolawn and dodged his barrages. Interestingly enough, with each barrage of fire that Opolawn made it forced Jim and Anson to leap and dodge and move closer together with respect to each other. I was moving so fast and the stress was so great that occasionally I thought I heard tears and cracks in my body—but I was feeling no pain. The nanomachines may have been working. I wasn't sure if Mike was using all of his computational powers to fight Opolawn or not. But

Mike kept pushing and pushing and pushing. He taunted Opolawn into following him to extreme altitude and then he turned back planetward. We zipped past each other head to head at near light speed. Had we collided I'm not sure the little warp field generator on my belt could've taken the stress. Fortunately, Mike swerved at the last nanosecond.

Opolawn stopped and reversed course in pursuit of us and he fired off more of his lightning bolts. A blinding barrage of Opolawn's fire flung Jim and Anson skipping back across the landing field and through the hangar doors of the temple. Mike dropped below Opolawn at maximum velocity and I thought I could feel my right hand going through my rear zip pocket, but it all happened in a matter of microseconds so I wasn't too sure about it. Mike dropped me continuously for a full two hundred milliseconds, several tens of kilometers below Opolawn, and shut off the warp field at about five hundred milliseconds before impacting the ground. If I hit the ground—or air— at that velocity I would have been turned to dust, but we were still in space so there was no atmosphere for me to slam into or breathe. But the warp field was only off a microsecond or less.

Then the freckle-faced soldier Gray's credit card that I had kept all this time turned on and the blue-white light flowed from it as if in slow motion. Mike hit the warp bubble again and I was holding the credit card above my head with the warp field and the beam of light formed as Mike stopped me cold on the surface of the planet just outside the hangar on the bank of the river. A ring of dust and debris was thrown up around me as the blue-white light flowed upward from the credit card and into

Opolawn's trajectory. Opolawn was moving way too fast to stop and he flew right into the Gray confinement singularity beam. I stood in an Okinawan Karate Cat stance with my hands above my head, holding the confinement beam with my warp armor's field, and the blue-white light of the Gray confinement singularity surrounded Opolawn and then began to collapse. The blue-white ball of light rapidly vanished and then was gone. Opolawn was now trapped inside the forever-contracting singularity. How long would his warp field hold out—three or four millennia? Who knew, but if he didn't have a SuperAgent in there with him and if he didn't know how to use it he was doomed to be squished when his systems could no longer handle the crushing stress. Eventually, all parts would give out and Opolawn would die!

Mike let me rest for a second or two while he put the nanomachines to work on me. I still stood in the odd fighting pose at the edge of the river's bank. Then Mike gave my body back to me.

It's all yours, Steven. We beat him.

Mike, that sure was a lot like a memory of mine.

Yes, indeed, Steven. It was your memory and it was a great strategy.

Did you read my mind?

You said I could take over your body. Should I not have?

You did right, Mike. Let's get out of here.

Steven?

Yes, Mike, what is it?

Just one more thing . . . JACKIEZZ WINS!!! The image of little JackieZZ's overemphasized female video likeness flooded my mind.

"Thank you, JackieZZ, wherever you are!" I said.

Uh, Steven?

Yes, Mike?

We've got company so we'd better go.

Right, Mike. I rolled over Superman style and flew to the hangar. I rolled over on my back and could see more of the fighters converging on our position. I swooped down and caught Anson and Jim in my warp bubble while Mike shook hands and negotiated with the SuperAgent on the hangar's construction computer. As we started to shrink out and just before the warp bubble went opaque I caught a glimpse of Prawmitoos running into the hangar with the replica Himbroozya controller in his hand and then the bubble went black and we slipped through the quantum connection of the SuperAgent in the Lumpeya City hangar bay.

We immediately appeared inside the supply room just outside of Michelle in the *Phoenix*. I turned the warp bubble off and scanned the room. Jim and Anson were drenched in sweat and I was sure I looked the same. The three of us were exhausted.

"Did you fellows catch ol' Prawmitoos running after us just as we left?" I asked them.

"I saw him running across the field toward us just before you picked us up. Why?"

"Well, uh . . . he had the thing that goes Big Bang in his hands," I said.

"Then by all means, son, don't disappoint the little bastard. Go ahead and detonate it," Anson said with a huge—as he would put it—shit eatin' grin on his face.

"Should I? You wouldn't think any less of me would ya?" I laughed. "Mike, can you hear me?"

"Yes, Steven," Mike's voice came through the supply room speakers.

"Detonate the bomb," I said.

"Okay, Steven. It is done."

"That's it?" Jim asked.

"What did you expect, Jim? I mean, we have to be at least a light year or more away by now." Anson slugged him on the shoulder. "Hold on a minute. Tabitha, we are on board!" he said over the ship's intercom.

"Yeehaw!" Tabitha let out a Texan hoot. I just knew that if she had had a cowgirl hat she would have slapped her knee with it, whirled it about in the air, and then tossed it. "Well, get up here. Y'all need to see this."

We rushed up to the bridge just in time to see the Lumpeya City star system dwindle out of range of the sensors of the *Phoenix*. 'Becca was fiddling with one of the display panels.

"Check this out," she said. "Michelle was able to hack into a system on the moon of Lumpeya City and got this image just a few seconds ago. Okay, run it Michelle."

"Okay, Rebecca," Michelle said.

An image of Lumpeya City with a resolution of about five kilometers per pixel appeared on the screen. A second or two of the image played through and then the screen went totally white, the image saturation compensated, and then the planet came back into view but this time with a giant mushroom cloud larger than the entire continent of North America. We only realized this because 'Becca zoomed out to a planet-sized view. Most of the mountain continent was totally destroyed. Lumpeya City was no more and the ocean was rolling in where the mountains once stood. The dust filled the sky and would soon blacken out the sun of the red devil's homeworld. That was fitting, I thought. It serves the pricks right for toying with us. I laughed and felt good about it.

"We were under some pretty hefty fire until that thing went off," Tabitha said. "Then all of our pursuers just dropped off and left us alone."

"What now?" Jim asked.

"Well, first I want to let Tatiana out of her cage," I said.

"Consider it done, son." Anson went and toggled a switch on a panel in front of Tabitha. Then into the intercom he said, "Tatiana Montana, please report to the bridge. Your husband is lost without you."

Tabitha punched Anson in the back. "Y'all don't get too cocky. We just smoked a lot of big red devils and one rather important little Cray. I would imagine their friends are gonna get pretty pissed at us when they figure out what happened."

Tatiana burst through the bridge door. "What's going on?"

I held up the picophage controller and waved it at her. "You're all mine now, baby!"

➤ CHAPTER 28

We spent a few minutes resting and thinking about our next move. Tabitha was right; the Grays would be pissed at us and would soon be coming for us. The question was, how long would it take for the Grays to figure out what had happened? If we assumed that Prawmitoos got a message off to the Grays, then they would be preparing for us. We had a secret weapon that neither the Grays nor the Lumpeyins could reproduce. Mike, Tatiana and I had figured out how to send matter in super-miniature warp bubbles over the universal Infrastructure from one SuperAgent to another. Even if one of the aliens that saw us vanish into thin air survived the explosion at Lumpeya City—which sounds impossible—it wouldn't have understood what happened to us. To the alien it would appear that we just vanished and there would be no way of them knowing that we used the YIT connection to travel. We all decided that this was the single most important information that the human race now had and it should be the most guarded secret in the history of mankind. Think about it. If hostile aliens knew how to approach us by quantum connecting through our SuperAgents then they could zip in and out of our society at will—assuming we place these SuperAgents rampantly throughout our civilization. Complete armies could travel through the YIT by using a warp bubble that was large on the inside and small enough on the outside to travel through the Infrastructure.

This was exactly what we planned to do—warp armies through the YIT and take the fight to the Grays. We needed to get closer to home first, but our present location was a good twelve days from Earth at maximum warp velocity and that could be too late if the Grays decided to immediately eradicate Earth. We couldn't quantum connect to Earth because there were no SuperAgents there. We only had Mike and Michelle available and had used up the last bit of the rare alien materials needed to build SuperAgents on Michelle, so we couldn't just make another one. We needed to get to Earth faster than maximum warp allowed, so we had to find a SuperAgent close to home to surf the YIT to.

"Mike, can you find where there are *Phoenix*-class Gray ships as close to Earth as possible?" Jim said.

"Yes, Jim. There are seven Gray ships in the outer part of the Sol System now and there are nineteen Gray vessels dispersed evenly about the quarantine zone's edge."

"Then we should take the ones at Earth first," Tabitha said.

"Michelle, can you fly the *Phoenix* back to Earth's Moon without us?" 'Becca asked.

"Of course I can, Rebecca," Michelle answered.

"What's our plan for taking the ships?" Anson asked.

"It will be easy, Anson," Tatiana said. "Steven and I beat them as normal humans with no warp armor or anything like that. We only had a couple of machine guns each."

"I helped a little," Mike said.

"Of course you did, sweetheart. I'm sorry and I didn't mean to forget you, Mike," Tatiana said.

"So, how about this? We armor up, zip into the operating room of one of the ships and, with the warp bubbles, we run around the ship and squish the blue blood right out of a bunch of little Gray monsters," I suggested.

"Sounds like a helluva plan to me!" Anson said.

"Okay, let's do it!" Tabitha ordered.

We loaded up for bear and little Gray aliens. Once, Tatiana couldn't get her gear to sit straight and I had to touch her and let the nanomachines fix it. She told me that she felt naked without Mikhail. I assured her that as soon as we got more SuperAgent material we would remedy the situation.

We also let the gang in on the mind communication through the SuperAgent link. We trusted them all completely now and they didn't seem too sore about the fact that we had kept that from them. They had known Tatiana and I could communicate to each other through the SuperAgents, but we had not told them that anybody could with a simple temple implant. Anson commented that we had learned the secret weapon lesson well and that he was proud of us.

We all told Michelle that we would see her in a few days and then Mike closed the warp bubble around us. The bubble shrunk down and we were riding the quantum connection a third of the way across the galaxy, about thirty thousand light years. We popped out into the abductee operating room of the Gray alien spaceship and there were two catatonic humans lying on floating stretchers. The room we were in was completely white and it was very bright. We settled to the floor quietly and the two Grays working on one of the humans were caught totally unaware.

Tatiana moved so fast that you couldn't see her snapping the necks of the two little monsters. *Ick! This brings back some bad memories, huh, Steven?*

Yeah, it does. Mike, can you take over the programming of this SuperAgent like I did you?

Already done, Steven.

Excellent. Open the doors and let's go squish some Grays!

How many are there? Tabitha thought.

There are nine more aliens aboard, Mike told us. Then he displayed a map of the spaceship in all of our heads. There were little blinking red dots where the live Grays were.

Okay, just like we planned, three teams. Tatiana and I will take the three on the bridge, I thought to them.

Anson and I will take the three in the aft section!

'Becca and I will take the other three. Good hunting!

We split up into three different directions and went about taking the ship. The ship was similar to the *Phoenix,* minus the humanizing that had been done to it. With the warp armor we all made light work of the Grays on board. It took us about seven seconds to take the ship. The Grays never even knew we were coming.

We went through similar steps and took all seven of the Gray ships in Sol space. We felt an urgency to quickly take as many ships as we could, because who knew how the Grays were going to react when they discovered we had the controller and had blown up one of their nobles.

Once we had liberated all of the vessels Mike generated a replacement for Mikhail, and Tatiana and I zipped back into the little confinement singularity where he was trapped. We replaced him with a dumb SuperAgent and Tatiana picked him up and placed him against her navel. Mikhail quickly dissolved through her skin and placed himself inside her abdomen. I touched her and gave her a crew of nanomachines to make her complete.

Let's get out of here.

Okay, Steven. Mikhail, it is great to have you back!

It is great to be back, Tatiana.

Now, we are all one big happy family again, I said and toggled the warp field back on. The bubble grew opaque. It was the last we would ever see of the little prison the Grays had trapped Tatiana in.

You think Opolawn is enjoying his accommodations? I asked Tatiana.

I hope he hates it! Tatiana said as we popped back into the belly of the commandeered Gray spaceship.

We zipped the new ships back to the Moon and reprogrammed all of the SuperAgents to be more like Mike—that is, to be loyal to humanity and to us in particular. We updated Annie, Al, and Sara on current events and decided that a good plan of action would be to take as many alien ships as we could. So we recruited fifteen of the most trusted members of the military moon colony that we knew. Tabitha reminded them all of their oaths and then we trained them on how to take the Gray ships. Before Michelle returned to the Moon, we had taken thirty-seven Gray ships and were retrofitting them for human use.

We sent out teams every day over the Infrastructure and captured more and more alien ships and technologies. Each of the teams carried one SuperAgent with nanomachine accompaniment and each time they would bring back more and more alien materials and resources. With the Infrastructure and our new means of traveling through it we were rapidly spreading out through the local cluster.

And then the Grays came. Just a few weeks after we had returned from Lumpeya City they came in a fleet of more than a thousand *Phoenix*-class ships.

Fortunately, we knew about it. We had infected most of the SuperAgents within a thousand-light-year radius of Earth. The Grays were still fairly oblivious to hackers. It seemed that this was a human specialty that was lost on them. Although they made some attempts to set up firewalls, we quickly hacked them down. Tatiana and Mike had overcome the isolated abductee firewall through familiarity and cunning reexamination of instruction definitions. It was like arguing with yourself what the definition of the word *is* is—you can convince yourself of a lot of things that way. Like I said, the Grays were no good at keeping generations of hackers out of the Infrastructure.

We would ping out through the Infrastructure waiting

for "connection established" or "denied returns" and then
start in with code decryption hacks and backdoor tricks.
The only thing missing was dumpster dives. Since we
didn't know what the Grays did with their garbage we
couldn't go and dig through it. We didn't need to; as I
said, the Grays were amateurs at designing firewalls. Once
we established a data connection we simply made a quantum connection through the Infrastructure, warped into
the bellies of the oncoming assault fleet and took the ships
from them.

Tatiana and I were along for the battle. We took several
of the ships ourselves. In fact, the entire crew was along.
Our battle plan required everybody aware of the
SuperAgents and warp armor and the Infrastructure to
be involved. At such short notice, only a few weeks after
returning from Lumpeya City, we were not really completely prepared for an attack of a fleet of a thousand
ships. After all, we had only captured and refurbished
some thirty-odd Gray ships to date. But we weren't giving
up.

Tabitha had developed a great tactical plan of slash and
burn and move on. She decided that as many of us as
could, would teleport from one ship to the next ship, kill
the Gray crew, then move on to the next one, and repeat
the process until there were no Grays in the attack fleet
left standing.

There were a hundred and two of us, each with warp
armor and we had had enough time to create a hundred
new SuperAgents, each with its own personality. All of
the slash-and-burn team members had volunteered to
have the SuperAgents implanted in their respective abdomens and each of us had temple implants. We would take

teams of two through to each alien ship and therefore each team would have to take at least twenty of the Grays' ships. Tabitha rallied us before the plan was implemented and gave us a pep talk.

"Attention all personnel, this is General Clemons." She paused for a second and cleared her throat. "An alien threat of far superior firepower is approaching us at superluminal velocity. These aliens are known as the Teytoonis, and indeed are as powerful as the gods from our ancient mythology. These aliens . . . these Teytoonis are self-centered and believe themselves to be the only species that should exist in the universe. Well, I disagree with them and I am sure you do too. We are going to strike these monsters with cunning and human brilliance the likes of which this alien species has never seen before. Leave no alien survivors . . . our own survival depends on this. You must also not be captured under any circumstances. The aliens must not have access to our technology. If you are caught, you have been briefed what to do and I expect—humanity expects—that you follow orders. Good luck, good hunting, and God bless." Tabitha paused again to let her words ring through the lunar base and then she added in her voice of command, "MOVE OUT!"

Tatiana and I were second in line on the *Phoenix* and were preparing to quantum connect to our first target. Michelle had already passed through the first two-man team of Jim and 'Becca. We nearly had to hogtie Anson and Tabitha in order to convince them that they couldn't lead this assault, just in case we failed. Humanity needed a commanding general and lead scientist that understood the threat it was facing. If the slash and burn failed, Tabitha and Anson would have to devise a Hail Mary play. We hoped that it wouldn't come to that.

Phoenix 2 going for quantum connection, I thought over the net as we shrank down through the Infrastructure connection inside Michelle. *Mike, have you turned the destination ship's SuperAgent?*

Steven, Michelle has beaten me to it.

I see.

Coming out of warp now, Steven! Mike said as Tatiana and I hit the floor inside a little white room.

There were no Grays waiting on us and there were no human abductees on board. That was a good sign, I guessed.

Warp armor! Mike, where are they? I asked. Mike displayed a map of the ship and indicated where the Grays were hiding out—actually they were just hanging out since they were not expecting us; they had no reason to be on their guard.

Steven, I've got the six up top. You take the six below, okay?

Right! Race you back to Michelle, last one buys.

You're on.

We made short work of the unsuspecting Grays on board and were back through Michelle to the next craft on our list. Fifteen seconds later we were on to the fourth. Thirty seconds later we had taken all twenty ships. We paused on the last one and listened in to the battle to see how it was going. Mike opened a channel to the operation net and it was rather quiet. The mission had been a success!

In less than one minute and twenty-three seconds the entire alien fleet had been destroyed. There were no survivors and we had not lost a single soldier during the operation.

"All of the alien ships are to be brought to the rally point at Mars except for one. I want three teams to volunteer to take all of the Grays' remains that can be gathered and load them into that ship. We will load the ship that _Phoenix_ team four is presently on."

We took that one alien ship and packed it full of dead Grays as Tabitha had ordered. She then ordered it sent at maximum velocity back to the Ringworld hive center.

"Great job, everyone! Operation Slash and Burn was a success! We will see you on Mars." She cheered.

We hoped that the Grays would get the message to leave us the hell alone.

➤ CHAPTER 29

Tatiana and I went down to Bakersfield not long after Operation Slash and Burn and found Lazarus's body. I could barely do it. I cried and cried but Tatiana held my hand and helped me through it.

We cloaked the *Phoenix* with the Cray cloaking system, and landed where I had parked the SUV those months before when I had driven out to bury him. God, our lives had all changed a lot since that day—the day I tried to kill myself—that day I buried Lazarus. We landed far enough off the road that oncoming construction traffic would not run into the cloaked ship. We could have parked in a hover above the ground and used either our warp armor or the tractor beam, but I wanted to land.

"It was this way," I told Tatiana. I was beginning to tear up a little. It was going to take a lot of courage to do this.

Tatiana grabbed my hand and whispered, "It's okay, baby." She was quiet after that.

I found where I had buried old Lazarus. There wasn't any sign that anybody had been through there since I had. The little army surplus shovel was still standing up in the ground right where I had left it. I fell to my knees beside the grave site and began to weep.

"Laz, ol' buddy. If only I could fix you now." *Mike, are you sure it is too late to fix him?*

Steven, I am sorry. There would be nothing left of the neural pathways that made him who he was. We could rebuild the dog's body but it would be mindless or blank and would not be the dog that was your friend. I thought I could actually detect the sorrow in Mike's mind voice. He was becoming more and more alive every day.

Steven? Tatiana put her hands on my shoulders.

Yes?

Honey, let's do what we came to do, she said.

Okay, you are right.

We used the nanomachines to remove the dirt and exhume his remains. After only a few months his body was still in pretty good shape and there was plenty of live genetic material left. When I saw the poor little guy's body I lost it. I started bawling and couldn't stop. I fell to my knees crying.

"I don't know that I can stand this," I muttered. "I am so sorry, buddy. If only I had known then what I know now, I could have saved you. I'm sorry . . ."

"I have enough genetic material, Steven. We should bury him now." Tatiana had a strong stomach—or at least had Mikhail turn off her typical reflexes; Lazarus smelled bad and there were bugs and things crawling on his corpse.

She shifted the sands and formed a silicon-and-carbon box around Lazarus's body. There was a crystalline form of silicon dioxide engraving on the dark gray box. It simply read, *Lazarus The Dog*. The sands shifted and the box sank into them.

I used the nanomachines and erected a huge and fitting memorial to my buddy. The memorial was a three-meter-tall obelisk made of carbon placed in an extremely tight matrix. It was damned near unbreakable. Engraved in the obelisk was the following: "*Here lies Lazarus The Dog, the keeper of Steven Montana's sanity and therefore the savior of humanity.*" It would be a long time before anybody ever understood that, but I knew what it meant and so did Tatiana. Tatiana added the dates for his lifespan and then had a fence of smaller carbon obelisks rise from the dirt, each of which had a silicon dioxide crystal in the shape of a flame on the top. When the sun flickered on the flame-shaped crystals it looked like an eternally burning array of torches. I added a walkway and a border about the grave and then turned the top of the surface of the grave into several inches of glass. I backed away and looked at our handiwork and decided that Lazarus would have approved.

"There is just one thing missing." I reached into the sand and built a squeaky toy that was reminiscent of his favorite one. I set it on top of the glass surface of the grave and had it sink down inside the glass a few inches. "Now, you'll always have that squeaky toy, buddy." I cried some more and sat there Indian style for about a half hour. Tatiana stood there behind me with her hands on my shoulders and never flinched or moved until I was ready to go.

"Thanks for doing this with me, Tatiana." I wiped the tears from my face.

"You are welcome, Stevie. He must have been a really great friend." She held my hand and we walked back to the cloaked alien spaceship.

Steven?

Yes, Mike?

I am sorry for your loss, too.

Thanks, Mike.

Before we left Earth again I made a handful of diamonds and a suitcase full of foreign currency out of carbon from some of the debris alongside the road in Bakersfield. Tatiana and I cashed in the diamonds and cash through the CIA's "diamond factory" and we bought up all of the new beachfront property in Bakersfield and all of the property within a ten kilometer distance from Lazarus's burial site. It cost about a hundred million dollars—it was cheap since the reclamation after The Rain was far from completed. We set up a pet cemetery around the memorial and kept a large budget in place to have it maintained. The town around the cemetery remained as Bakersfield, California, and it became *the* beach vacation spot. It was a great memorial to Lazarus and my family and the other families that were lost in The Rain.

We set up a state-of-the-art cloning lab on the Moon and hired some of the best scientists in the field. We got them cleared and moved them up to the Moon with us.

We took fertilized zygotes from several different breeds of female dogs and replaced the DNA in them with Lazarus's. We mixed the X and Y chromosomes in a few of them so we would have some boy dogs and some girl dogs. We then froze a few hundred of the Lazarus clone zygotes in case we needed them in the future. But most importantly, we had a litter of pups of Lazarus clones— some were girls and some were boys and some had a few physical traits and colors mixed in that we threw in on purpose so that they all wouldn't look the same but would have Laz's genetic traits. One of the pups was a spitting image of my old buddy and he is the one that we took. We gave the rest of the pups to the kids on the Moon. We let Mindy, Michael, Ariel, and Hunter have the first pick and then we gave the remaining three to other kids. It was my plan to make sure that Lazarus's genes lived forever.

The clones thrived and we used the nanomachines to remove any genetic anomalies that might have caused them problems in the future. There were early cloning experiments years ago where the scientists cloned a four-year old sheep. The clone came out four years old. We didn't want that with Lazarus's clones; we wanted puppies that were honest to goodness puppies and not four-year-old puppies. The alien nanomachines and Mike and Mikhail helped us figure out how to make proper clones and all of the Lazarus IIs turned out perfect.

Although we had built my late friend one great memorial down on Earth, I felt that the best memorial was the clone puppy. Scientifically, he was known as Lazarus II but I felt that he needed to be his own puppy and so I named him Woodrow the Dog instead. Tatiana and I call him Woody. At first we didn't get any of the pups fixed and it wasn't long before there was a puppy surplus on the Moon. We also made sure that some other breeds were brought up so as not to stagnate the gene pool.

We encouraged folks traveling to the new outpost worlds throughout the quarantine zone to take a few puppies with them as well. Lazarus's DNA was spreading across the galaxy along with humanity. I liked this very much. It might have been the damned Grays that were inadvertently responsible for his demise, but it was also their fault that he would be spreading across the galaxy and I hoped that the Grays hated dogs even more than humans.

Tatiana and I had decided a few years after the first litter of Lazarus's clones that Woody needed a kid to play with since the Clemons and Daniels children were growing up fast. Of course, Anne Marie and Al had their second one on the way by that point, but Woody needed a child or two of his own to play with. So we obliged him with a baby girl we named Serena Tatanya Montana and then, a year and nine months later, we had a boy we named Jacob Tyler Montana. One sort of Russian-sounding name and one sort of American-sounding name; it worked out well and they made Woody and us very happy.

Tatiana, Serena, Jacob, Woody, and I moved down to a ten-thousand-square-foot mansion on the beachfront at Bakersfield. We were only a few kilometers from the graveyard and Woody and I would visit there every now and then. The kids and Woody play on the beach and play fetch in the surf on a regular basis and the city that is rising up from the ashes of The Rain is becoming a great place to live and raise a family.

Tatiana and I like to watch the kids race Woody on the beach. At one and a half years old Jacob keeps up with him well and at a little over three it is no longer a race to Serena. She has to sort of trot so as not to run off and leave them. Oh, I guess I should explain that.

The enhancements that Tatiana and I had made to ourselves with the alien nanomachine technology were not just mechanical and cosmetic enhancements. In fact, the nanomachines manipulated our DNA so that the enhancements were real and would be passed on to our progeny. So in a sense, we really were superhuman, and not just altered freaks. The next step in human evolution was *us*, and we initiated it through technology, not waiting millions of years for the right mutations to come along. The nanomachines really did bring on a human revolution in many ways. Almost immediately following the birth of our children we put temple implants on them so we could keep up with them and aid in teaching them. Serena's first rudimentary thoughts were of needs like food and water and the desire to be held. After a few months she began to have more detailed thoughts and a few months after that was thinking and verbalizing complete sentences. When things were too difficult for her to say because she hadn't learned how to make her mouth or vocal cords do those motions Serena would think her needs to us. We were afraid at first that this would make her complacent about learning to speak properly, but it didn't. She would see us talking to people and really wanted to be able to do everything we could do.

Jacob was different. Sometimes I think that boy came out of the birth canal jabbering away. He was a vocal one from the get go. He also cried an awful lot during his first few months. He just needed more attention than Serena had wanted. As he grew he became more independent. At just under two years old he was running and talking and playing with Serena and Woody. We had to watch the kids carefully since they were stronger than Woody now and we were afraid that they might hurt him. Under no circumstance would we let the kids play with normal kids, not for a few more years. Oh, but they could play with Al and Annie's two girls, who were similarly genetically enhanced, since their parents had been before the girls were conceived. And Ariel and the Daniels twins had been enhanced recently, as well. So the superkids had some other superkids to play with. We kept an eye, ear, and mind, on them through the implants. Sometimes Mike or Mikhail or Michelle would babysit them for us also. The kids always got a kick out of that. We did also, because then we could turn off the kid's channel and let one of the SuperAgents monitor it. It takes a toll on you listening to the kids jabber both verbally *and* mentally.

The kids wanted more puppies and I was kind of excited about the idea as well. We bred Woody with a beautiful chocolate Labrador retriever and the puppies were amazing and brilliant. They were all fetching and sitting and heeling before they were four months old. Tatiana and I had discussed it and we decided that as we grew older and once the kids reached an age that they would really understand what we were doing, we were going to start slowly increasing Woody's intelligence via the nanomachines.

At the rate the kids were growing and maturing we suspected we could start with the project in a few more years. We thought it would be possible eventually to make Woody smart enough to carry on conversations with them after a few years. Perhaps we would use intelligence boosting along with cookies as a reward for good deeds, so that his intelligence would evolve slowly and allow him to grow into it. But in the meantime he was great the way he was, being father to a handful of new pups. The kids liked it too.

We did put temple implants on Woody because one day he got lost downtown and it took us two days to find him. We had driven the kids to the park with Woody and something must have spooked him—we never figured out what—and he ran away. When we found him, he was happy to see us and was very hungry. Tatiana materialized a bowl of dog food and a bowl of water on the spot for him and the kids cheered and petted him and gave him biscuits that I had materialized. Woody came home and licked his puppies and curled up on his favorite spot near the fireplace and went to sleep. I tugged his ears and had Mike install the implants on his temples.

It was very interesting to try to interpret Woody's thoughts. He really had only a few that were recognizable. Mike and I mapped the neurochemistry and electromagnetic signature of his brain when he would respond to certain stimuli and before long we began to find trends. Woody would exhibit a particular thought pattern when he was hungry, or when he needed to go to the bathroom, or when he wanted attention, or when he was afraid, and when he was happy. Mike was able to interpret these patterns but there was no basis for any type of language or communication. All of his responses were based on his basic instinctual emotions and the need for survival. Tatiana and I knew that this was the basic data we would start with when—and if—we decided to enhance his intellect. In the meantime, we set up signals to the kids so that they would know if Woody needed to go outside or needed food or needed just plain petting. His needs were always filled almost immediately and one could argue that he was the most spoiled dog in the history of humankind.

➤ CHAPTER 30

We would often host the W-squared core group down at the beach house for weeks at a time. The kids would play with the dogs on the beach and the adults would sit around and drink too much and talk about our history and various philosophies and the possibilities of future alien threats.

We were sitting around the patio fireplace looking up at the stars one evening, discussing the status of the public SETI program and how wrong the Search for ExtraTerrestrial Intelligence scientists had been.

"I always thought it was silly for the SETI guys to look only at a small band of wavelengths for signals of such mammoth proportion that a magically advanced species would have to have designed it for us and pointed it directly at us," Anson said as he held an empty beer bottle in his hand. The beer bottle morphed into a model of a radio telescope and then into a little red devil and then it turned back into a bottle of beer—now it was full.

"You know, I've never really thought about it before, but since the Grays and the red devils have been in control of the galaxy for so long, there aren't any radio signals out there to detect," I said.

"That's right." Tabitha sat down between Anson's legs and leaned back on him in the lounge chair. "As far as we can tell they use only the Infrastructure communication systems. No radio or microwave or optical systems have been found at all except for the energy transmission to the nanomachines. They only do that for a few meters and at extremely low power signals."

"Yeah, you're right, Tab. And that's just the Gray's nanomachines. Since the Lumpeyins use the miniature warp bubbles in the Dr. Who's phone booth configuration, they could put little SuperAgents in there and control them through the Infrastructure," 'Becca said.

"Hey! 'Bec, that is probably exactly how those things work. The Infrastructure transceivers in the picophage warp bubbles are probably low-level SuperAgents," Tatiana said.

"We'll have to consider that. That might give us an edge on stopping that damned picophage ahead of schedule," Anson said. He was already on another beer.

"I hate to change the subject back to where we were a few minutes ago, but," Jim said, "what about the quarantined aliens? They would most likely use radio signals. I'll bet you with the Solar Focus telescope we could pick up their signals."

"Why would we want to do that, Jim? We can just take

the *Phoenix* and fly over and see them anytime we desire. No speed-of-light worries," I replied.

"Just for the hell of it and to prove that we were right about the SETI folks. Then if we find the signals we could figure out a way to detect them from public radio observatories." Jim was getting excited.

"Hey, I see where you are going here. If we can point the idiots in the right direction and find a real E.T. signal then we will have shown the public that there are indeed aliens out there. A great start in the informing of the general public process," Tabitha added.

"Well, that too." Jim smirked. "But I was thinking more along the lines of showing those Utopians up. Why can't our team be the one that goes public with the observation? It would show those guys up, big time."

"Hayul fahr! I like it!" Anson said.

"Honey . . ." 'Becca smiled. "You're still pissed that you didn't get to go to M.I.T. aren't you?" Rebecca let out an intoxicated giggle.

"Hey, we did the work. We ought to go in the history books somewhere." Jim sounded a little irked. "Hell, Anson invented the first warp drive and flew us out to other worlds and enabled us to have a first real defense against would-be alien attackers. Stevie and Tatiana over there stole and redesigned alien technologies that have revolutionized the way that we think about the universe. And all of our efforts combined have enabled us to become one of the most powerful species in the galaxy! Or at least powerful enough to hold off alien invasions."

That evening we decided to start working on a plan to get radio telescope time at Arecibo. Tabitha and Annie were going to work that through NASA and Air Force channels. Anson, Rebecca, and Jim were going to use the Solar Focus telescope to find radio signals from the various quarantined planets. Tatiana and I first bounced out to each of these systems in the *Phoenix* to determine which ones were in a technological age; otherwise, the search at the Solar Focus telescope would have taken a lot longer.

All said and done it took us about six months to pick the right candidates, detect them from space, determine how to modify the receivers at the large dish in Arecibo, and then to get dish time there. We all took a two-week vacation in Puerto Rico and spent all of that time in the radio telescope facility on top of the mountain. We had everything set up and ready to go in a matter of a couple days because the nanomachines facilitated the equipment upgrade process very quickly. In fact, there were a few times where we had trouble explaining to the facilities officer how we had changed some things so quickly.

We just told him that we had plenty of budget and that we were really good at what we did. He didn't like that response until Annie came around and told him to stop asking questions or she would have him removed from the facility. When the fellow protested that she couldn't have him removed, Annie had him removed just to prove the point. She let him back in two days later after he promised to behave himself. Besides, we had detected one of the quarantined civilizations the day before and we wanted there to be witnesses. We found a whole bunch of communications signals at about thirty-two gigahertz. They were very low power and required state-of-the-art amplifiers, but we could detect them. We also, miraculously, discovered signals around five other star systems. The radio astronomers and SETI folks hanging around the facility couldn't believe what they were seeing.

A week later, when we announced it on the international news channels, the world couldn't believe it. SETI had been at it for so long with no luck that the general public never really expected them to find anything. The announcement was made and we were all interviewed to a great extent. We all made a big point about the fact that we weren't considered part of the typical SETI community. We all got a big laugh out of that and we also all got to offer our opinions as to what types of aliens there might be out there. Here is when we really showed how different we were from the SETI folks.

We made it very obvious that we thought that the possibility that these aliens might come and give us the cure for cancer was ridiculous and it was more likely that they would want to come and eat us, or something equally unpleasant. There were a few heated debates with some of the academic community but Jim and Anson and Tabitha and 'Becca really held their own. They truly were brilliant and it was a good thing that they were on our side. After about three more years of this debate and fun, we had to go back to our real jobs—defending the planet. The damned Grays had finally decided that they would make another attempt at overtaking humanity. But we had been preparing for them all along.

There had been nearly five years with no word from the Grays except for border skirmishes along the edge of the quarantine zone. So we decided we had better spread out as best we could while we could. After all, we figured it would be harder tactically to destroy many worlds as opposed to just one.

We took complete groups of volunteers and all the

materials we could muster and warped them through the quantum connection and the Infrastructure to all of the habitable worlds within the quarantine zone. We warped a complement of retrofitted alien spaceships through the Infrastructure to each of the outpost colonies. After all, we could make the inside of the warp bubble pretty much as large as we wanted to. We even warped some closed-down military facilities from Earth through to some of the outpost worlds. We took ghost towns, trailer parks, condemned shopping malls, you name it. We only took things in the middle of the night and even then we were seldom without witnesses. We would either recruit the witnesses or pay them off. We always had construction crews working the place the next morning so nobody was the wiser. Oh, there was some talk on the Internet about it but only on the crackpot sites. After all, there were no such things as UFOs and alien abductions. And there never would be again!

Once we placed a SuperAgent on each of the outpost planets we could quantum connect basically anything between any two SuperAgent locations. Our population and presence in space were growing. Our recruitment program back on Earth was put into high gear and we picked up as many volunteers as possible. With the inflow of technology and the rapid nanomachine production at the "diamond factory," we were able to offer high wages to any new volunteers. We had reached nearly forty outpost worlds and now had a fleet of more than a thousand retrofitted spacecraft with superfast quantum fluctuation drives and humanized SuperAgents. It was all kept so "above Top Secret" and compartmentalized that if you weren't "in the know" then you weren't "in the know."

Our plan was to spread out and build up as big an empire as we possibly could so we could have a better chance at defending ourselves if the aliens came. We all knew that one day soon they would come. Be prepared! Since each new outpost might be vulnerable, we made sure there was always at least one contingent of *Phoenix*-class ships and SuperAgent-carrying warp-armored soldiers.

We had hoped the ship full of dead aliens we returned to them would give them the hint to not come back and that we were a species they didn't want to mess with. But we soon found that they had not forgotten about us.

Perhaps they had been investigating and studying the ship that we had returned to them to determine how we had beaten them so easily, but I don't think they figured it out. But this time they were very serious and sent a fleet of not a thousand vessels but one hundred thousand vessels. We again detected their approach long before they ever reached the quarantined zone. Since they never figured out how to keep us out of the alien Framework that they had laid in place on top of the universal Infrastructure, we could monitor their whereabouts fairly easily. It seemed obvious that we were much more suited for warfare than the Grays—they just weren't being devious and clever enough and we had had millennia of being forced into warfare due to the Lumpeyin Himbroozya picophage. We were good at warfare when we needed to be and Opolawn's prodding us along hadn't hurt us in that regards. Perhaps a hive collective works in such a way that their response is too sluggish to be good at warfare, I don't know for sure. I just know that we were better, smarter, and we kicked their little Gray asses.

The alien attack force was much more overwhelming this time, so we had to use a combination of the quantum teleportation and plain old space warfare ship-to-ship fighting, but we beat the socks off of them again because we could zip in and out of any of their spaceships. In the past five years of preparation for an alien attack fleet we had produced many more SuperAgents and drafted many more worthy Slash-and-Burn operatives, and we had also captured a lot more alien ships. Since we had never left a survivor in previous conflicts with the Grays they still didn't know how we were getting around within their fleet, and they were helpless. We zipped in and out of their fleet vessels like untouchable gods with unimaginable powers.

We saw them coming and hit them way out before they reached the old quarantine zone. This battle went slower just due to the size of it, but it never once turned against us. We knew what needed to be done and we set about doing it. While conducting the ship-to-ship fighting we discovered that enough squeeze-play warp missiles could force the alien degenerate-matter-hull spaceships into small black holes and that the subsequently formed singularities were unstable and soon went supernova. This actually had a positive effect on the tide of the battle. Once we found out what would happen, we forced a squeeze play in the middle of their fleet. The alien ship shrunk inward on itself until it became a singularity for a few seconds. The singularity's event horizon was small, but it did poke a neat hole clean through the next ship in its path. And then the thing went supernova and splattered ten of the ships around it and disrupted the fleet's formation. We did this repeatedly and in a well-orchestrated manner and the technique worked tremendously well in creating chaos in the alien tactics. We had learned a considerable amount about space warfare and tactics over the past five or so years and it was showing. We had fun with that weapon.

Tatiana and I stayed on board the *Phoenix* this go around, but according to the combat teams, the ship-to-ship fighting was nowhere near as much of a thrill as popping inside an alien ship and completely taking the Grays by surprise and in a matter of seconds, the ship completely from them. Our standard mode of operation was still to leave no Grays standing, sitting, or breathing. We couldn't risk the possibility that one of the witness Grays would figure out how we got on board their ships. Although we believed and still do believe that to be unlikely, as there is no way that they could actually see us and detect what we were doing at such a small scale once we shrunk down and entered the SuperAgent Infrastructure's quantum connection.

This time it took our fleet of thirty-three hundred and nine vessels and our warp-armored SuperAgent-toting infantry two hours and twenty minutes or so to completely halt the alien fleet's advance and another thirty minutes or so making sure that there were no alien survivors left. We discovered that about fifty percent of the alien fleet carried Prawmitoos's FUER and we guessed that was with hopes of igniting the Earth and blowing us asunder. Now we have the FUER and will soon be able to reverse engineer it. Like I said before, the Grays are stupid and not very good at warfare. Or again, perhaps, we are just really good at it.

After the battle had ceased we sent them a hundred

ships full of dead Grays and on each of the vessels we used the nanomachines to inscribe in bold, shiny letters the Teytoonise version of the sign at the gates of Hades: ABANDON ALL HOPE YE WHO ENTER HERE! We've been fighting the war against the aliens, Grays and Lumpeyins, on more than just one front. We've also been studying the dormant picophage. Since we had let the general public know that these civilizations existed, sooner or later they would want to communicate with these folks and we hoped to be able to communicate with them safely. With our near-infinite budget from the rare commodities and the other classified endeavors that the nanomachines enabled us to create, we ramped up a huge research effort on the picophage cure—not just for the quarantined aliens but for us as well. Anson developed a means of monitoring the phage devices on the picometer scale and mapping their whereabouts. There were some suggestions on the table presently about being able to capture the individual picophages with the same type of warp bubbles that we use to traverse the Infrastructure. These bubbles are much smaller than the picophage is and if we could drive through and into a quantum connected datastream there was no reason to believe that we couldn't fly around and capture all of these picometer devices. That would happen soon. Then we would have a cure and could go and infect the quarantined races with the cure. We couldn't believe the Grays never thought of this, but then again they used mainly quantum technologies, not general relativistic ones.

If we cured these other civilizations it would put another burden on us, though. At the same time we would also have to protect them from the Grays or they would wipe them out—we believed Opolawn when he told us the Grays believed they were The Species and would devour any others in their path. In the meantime we had every intention of stopping all alien abductions on these worlds and letting them live their lives under their own power. Our plan was to do all of this without letting the local inhabitants ever know we were there. If they call out to us to see if we are here, we planned to answer then, but only then. There have been enough meddlers in this galaxy's history.

> ## CHAPTER 31

Next year we plan to spread the technology of longevity to the species. We have already improved medical technology eons ahead of anything the quacks would have ever come up with. There are no longer any deadly diseases since a dumbed-down version of the nanomachines has been released to the public domain. Nanomachines for specific tasks were introduced into the public as inventions by the brilliant scientist husband-and-wife team Dr. Steven and Dr. Tatiana Montana.

The doctorates weren't honorary. We were able to take courses from Anson and Jim and 'Becca and a few others at the satellite location for the University of America that was located on the Moon and we also had taken many classes at the new University of California at Bakersfield. We both wrote dissertations on nanomachine construction and manipulation.

Of course, now we could build machines nearly twenty orders of magnitude smaller. We were also fairly certain that the Grays couldn't do this. We weren't so sure about the limits of the Lumpeyins. At any rate, the current status of medical technology was such that most people could now expect to live a healthy, happy life to at least a hundred and eighty years.

Next year we plan to introduce to the world that the only reason not to live to be thousands of years old would be if you were hit by a truck—a big and very fast-moving truck that stopped and backed up over you several times— or were squished in an alien collapsing singularity. And it wasn't physicians that developed the cure for old age. Tatiana says I've been hanging around Anson and Jim too much and have adopted their distaste for medical quacks, but Anson and Jim are right and I like them—I can't recall a quack that I ever did. After all, the headshrinkers would've never found that Gray implant in my brain, but they would've sold me all the drugs I could afford until my insurance ran out.

We knew that the ability to live forever would really shock the world and excite it and force it to start thinking about colonizing other worlds or we would run out of room on Earth. We had that part of it covered. There were thousands of outpost worlds in need of settlers. The human race was really growing up and we were also becoming a dominant force to be reckoned with in our part of the galaxy. I hoped we weren't getting too big for our britches.

And were we getting too big for our britches? Because a war between alien species forced one of those races to infect us with the desire to build a war machine, our evolutionary path skewed from what we might have been. The alien that infected us had hopes that our acquired propensity for warfare would one day enable us to develop a means of destroying his enemies. Well, the red bastard got more than he bargained for, didn't he?

Opolawn hadn't counted on some brilliant redneck scientists and astronauts, a Russian bureaucrat's daughter, and a video game repairman from Bakersfield. He hadn't expected that we would develop a means not only of destroying his enemies, but him as well.

As far as my part in this war was concerned, I started out completely alone in the universe after The Rain—which Opolawn had caused in a way. But the W-squared core, Tatiana, and an alien SuperAgent showed me that nobody is really alone and that somehow we are all physically connected to each other.

I'm not real sure about the philosophical ramifications of our connectedness with the universe, but practically it means that the human race is now a formidable species and that if any of you aliens out there think you want to come and mess with us then you had better think twice. We might just make a quick quantum connection to you and lower one hell of a boom on your ass!

➤ **AFTERWORD**

Well, here we are at the end of my second book and although I didn't want to make it a habit of putting afterwords in my books it looks like I'll put one here anyway. Actually, a colleague of mine, Dr. T. Conley Powell (an expert astrodynamicist and physicist) read the manuscript before I sent it off to Jim Baen.

"You have a lot of very cutting-edge physics in this one," he told me. "And if you don't want folks thinking you just made a lot of it up and that it is not fantasy, perhaps an Afterword is pertinent."

We discussed this a bit and after a while I decided that Conley was probably right. But here is what I want to do. Rather than spending pages here explaining the modern theories of quantum connectedness and the universal quantum consciousness and quantum teleportation and computer Agents and so on and on, I will merely say here that these things are at the state of the art of technology today and I will suggest how you can find more information on these topics.

One of the main characters in this book is a computer Agent. Well, actually it is an evolved next level and alien SuperAgent. At first read one might not understand the true implications of what a computer Agent is. If you have seen *The Matrix* then you are familiar with Agent Smith and his band of black-suited agents. Agent Smith is an example of a computer subroutine with some sort of artificial intelligence algorithm that is designed to carry out particular decision-making functions. With things like fuzzy logic, genetic algorithms, and artificial neural networks it is quite possible that Agent codes could become as aware as Agent Smith or as my SuperAgent in this story. You may not realize this but you have probably used something similar to a dumb Agent everytime you use an internet search engine. There is all sorts of information on this topic on the web and in books. Go to your favorite library, search engine, or online bookstore and search for "computer agents" and you will find more than you can read in a lifetime.

Another major technology in the story is that of nanomachines. We have all most likely heard of these and seen them in books and television programs. However, I think that a lot of writers miss the really and truly most amazing aspect of this technology and that is that it will create the next evolutionary step for mankind. With real nanomachines there will no longer be fear of injuries and diseases and old age. Physicians as we know them and medicine as it is today will become an archaic thing of our past. Search "nanotechnology" and "nanomachines" for this. Oh, and I'm not certain that I have ever heard of anybody proposing machines on the order of 1×10^{-29} meters as was discussed here, but the Alcubierre warp technology would allow for it.

Since I covered the warp theory in my first book, *Warp Speed,* I will not go into it other than to say, "If you didn't read that one first you should check it out." Search "warp theory" and "Alcubierre" for this.

The major theme of this book is the *quantum connection. Quantum connectedness* is a well-observed phenomenon, although its applicability to things such as teleportation and time travel and the like are presently the topic of much debate. However, the papers mentioned in the story are real and experiments have been conducted that have teleported photons across a laboratory. And it shouldn't be too long before more complicated things are teleported. This teleportation does occur at the speed of light, as mentioned within this story, and this is why we needed to discuss something greater for the information to travel upon—the universal quantum consciousness. Really, I am not making this stuff up! There have been several papers out about the possibility that everything within the universe is *quantum connected* with everything else and even the universe itself. This is a very abstract concept but there is some experimental basis for parts of it. Go search things like "quantum connectedness," "quantum consciousness," "Bell's inequality," "EPR—Einstein, Podolsky, Rosen experiment," "quantum teleportation," and "quantum entanglement."

There are a lot of smaller ideas in the book that are equally as fun and can also be found out there on the web somewhere. If you have questions about the things in here just go search for them. It is exciting to ponder some of these concepts and the real ramifications they will have on our species once we develop them. Imagine having a *quantum connected* teleportation system set up across the universe in such a way that anywhere is just a *connection* away. Once we learn to teleport ourselves around the universe the way we teleport information around the Internet, then that really will be something! It's not an impossible concept and who knows, it might happen sooner than we think. I know I can't wait!

The following is an excerpt from:

HONOR OF THE CLAN

JOHN RINGO & JULIE COCHRANE

Available from Baen Books
January 2009
hardcover

PROLOGUE

Monday, December 19, 2054

The room was ornate in a way that put rococo to shame. On the walls, many of the details in the gilded reliefs incorporated fractals, so that one could have examined the gilded scenes and abstract curlicues with a microscope and not run out of exquisite detail. The base for the gilding was a white substance similar to ivory, but with an opalescent sheen that no elephant tusk could ever boast.

All in all, the effect would have given a Himmit a heart attack, had one of those worthies tried to rest on that surface, and had it had a heart. The other surfaces were similarly ornate, reducing the Himmit on the carpet to a body surface of merely gothic levels of detail, that shifted quiveringly. Every hour or so, the Himmit placed a forelimb against its head, as if it was in pain.

In the center of the room was a large table of stone. In the stone was a sword. From the sword emanated a voice that was heavily modulated to prevent identification.

"This situation disrupts the entire plan. It is grossly unacceptable. Curse the Epetar group for clag food! What were the rest of you thinking? Progress be damned, I'll be hard pressed to salvage something other than outright war over this," he fumed.

"Abject apologies, Master." The Indowy got no farther.

"Don't bother. You, yourself, didn't do it, so your apologies are hardly sincere for all that you speak for others. Shut up and let me think."

The Indowy decided that it was more likely than not to be in the interests of his clan to volunteer some information. "Master, I have news that the O'Neal is traveling to Barwhon to approach the Tchpht on a diplomatic mission," it said.

The leader of the Bane Sidhe, whoever it was, was not known for its sense of humor. Indeed, so seldom was its humor triggered that its existence was largely regarded as mythical. The Indowy before it and the Himmit in the corner were, therefore, shocked senseless when a strange sound emanated from the blade of the sword.

"Stop . . . stop . . ." it rasped. "I'm not . . . it's just . . . O'Neal . . . diplo . . . too funny." The rasping crept into its voice. For just a moment it became normal enough to make out what sounded strangely like the mellifluous tones of a Darhel.

"The greater problem still exists," the sword hummed with a last chuckle. "Whether this drives the plan backwards or advances it must be considered. I will give you orders in time. You are dismissed."

If the Himmit was affronted, neither of the other species had the experience with its expressions to discern it. The crack at the edge where the ceiling met the wall widened around the body of the Himmit as it exited, sealing back to invisibility behind it.

"O'Neal. A diplomatic mission," the sword hummed once more. "Too funny. Oooo. *I* have an idea . . ."

Then it vanished.

CHAPTER ONE

Let's dance in style let's dance for awhile
Heaven can wait we're only watching the skies
Hoping for the best but expecting the worst
Are you gonna drop the bomb or not

—"Forever Young," Alphaville

Sunday, December 20, 2054

Major General Mike O'Neal rolled his AID then slapped it onto his wrist forming a band. Slapped it on hard.

"Hey," Shelly said. "Don't take this out on *me*!"

"Sorry," Mike said, grumpily.

He was intensely bored. Bored of gaming, bored of reading newsfeeds, bored of reading, period. Bored of watching movies, TV and every other form of video broadcast. Porn just wasn't his style but he'd even watched some of that. And found it very boring indeed.

404

In part it was his own fault. When he'd been recalled to Earth and boarded his first Fleet vessel he had treated the Fleet officers with even more disdain than usual. Fleet had, year by year, sunk lower and lower in his opinion. The officers were slovenly and corrupt, the sailors were abysmal and the only reason the ships operated at all was that they were Indowy made and damned hard to break. He'd never been the diplomatic type and his dislike of Fleet was displayed by saying he'd be in his cabin. An orderly, or whatever you called it in the Fleet, brought his meals, he made trips to the tiny gym and that was that. For the last five months the only time he'd spoken to a living soul was at starports.

The rest of it wasn't on him. First of all there was the fact of *five months* on board ships. That was just *insane*. These weren't even the bulk transports they'd used in the first part of the War. These were *Fleet* vessels, the fastest in the *universe*. But between having to hunt from star system to star system and tween-jump transits, not to mention jump transits, it just took forever to get to Earth from out on the edge of the Blight.

Then there was the recall. It read damned near as relief. Just a simple order to turn over command of the First Division to his Assistant Division Commander and return to Earth. No clue as to why, no incoming division commander. Nada.

So five months of not speaking to a living soul and worrying, any time he let it get past his iron self-control, about what the orders meant.

Probably it meant a staff job on Earth. He'd done them. It wasn't his favorite job by a long shot but he could do the deal. But that begged the question why there wasn't an incoming division commander. And if it was just a staff job they'd probably have said that in the orders along with "and General So-And-So will be along at some point to take over the Division."

It *could* be forcible retirement. But Fleet Strike didn't have an "up or out" policy. To avoid the cronyism that was destroying Fleet, positions were purely merit based. To get his division, some younger brigadier would have to show that he was better at running the Division than Mike. They rotated potential commanders in from time to time, shuffling the commander off to a staff position or sideways. But most of the time the new commanders, after a reasonable time to learn the job, went back to a lower rank or wherever they hell they'd come from. Mike and Major General Adam Lee Michie had been running divisions of the ACS corps for nigh on thirty years. Some time in and out but mostly in command. Mongo Radabaugh was the junior, having beaten out Bob Tasswell about five years ago to take over one of the division commander's slots.

Mike probably could have taken corps at some point if he wanted it. George Driver was an excellent corps commander, no question. But Mike figured he had the edge. Thing was, corps wasn't his style. It was a thankless job, since the divisions were spread across a sizeable chunk of the galaxy clearing Posleen worlds. Corps Command was based on Avauglin, a marginally habitable "recovered" world about sixty light-years, and a month transit, from Earth.

The divisions, though, moved as a unit, lived as a unit, dropped as a unit. Mike knew every guy in the division more or less. Hell, with the way that the ACS hadn't been restocking, 1st Division wasn't much larger than a brigade. *One* of the things he planned on bringing up whatever the reason that he'd been brought back to Earth. Surely they could get *some* ACS restock. It was getting as bad as back in the Siege . . .

And here he was stuck in the loop. Again!

"Shelly, time to Titan orbit?"

"One hour and twenty-three minutes, General," the AID said, liltingly "You did well, this time. Six minutes and seventeen seconds from the last time you asked. That's up from your mean of three."

"Iron self control, Shelly," Mike said. "Iron self control."

"Message from General Wesley's AID," Shelly said. "You're on another shuttle from Titan to Fredericksburg immediately after landing. Quote: Get some sleep on the shuttle; briefings immediately on landing so you can quit asking Shelly what's going on. The answer is good news and bad. Close quote."

"My iron self control is clearly well known," Mike said.

To human eyes, the Ghin was an average-looking Darhel. To human eyes, Darhel fur looked metallic gold or metallic silver, with black traces threading through; the Galactic's eyes a vivid green in a white sclera, laced with purple veining.

There were no humans in the office. The Tchpht who was present saw the Ghin in a rather different light. The eyes, so vivid to humans, were rather dull; but the fur glinted brightly, like the color play across anodized titanium.

"I greet you, Phxtkl. Thank you for granting me the favor of a game," the Ghin said.

"It is always a pleasure to instruct, O merely expert student of Aethal."

The Tchpht bounced rapidly upon its ten legs, tapping in a sequence that was either arhythmic or too complicated for the Darhel to decode. No one knew if the Tchpht meant to give offense or not when they used blunt descriptors in speaking to others. Since they were similarly descriptive with their own, more often than not, and still seemed to interact in a functional way, the other Galactics had decided that tact was absent from the Tchpht make-up.

It didn't matter. Tact was no part of the Ghin's purpose today. He made no further commentary, but merely moved to the Aethal table in the center of the room. Pieces were positioned within a holographic display.

"I wished to start from this position and play out the problem, if you would."

"You are placing me in a position of much advantage, although you are allowing yourself much opportunity. Are you sure you wish to choose this starting configuration?"

"Yes. Very sure."

"This is quite likely to be in my critique at the end of the game."

"I understand. Perhaps better than you realize."

"Ah. So you have a purpose in your choice. You make the game interesting. And, of course, your problem draws from existing conditions, with much variation."

"Of course. Many problems and configurations may arise in the game," the Ghin offered.

"Within reason, O erring and insufficiently experienced student," the Tchpht said.

Their play proceeded at a dignified rate, Phxtkl withholding commentary for most of the game, as was his custom. He would wait until major crises in a problem emerged before lecturing on errors and the alternate options which a lower ranked opponent might have selected.

Merely rating high expert in the game, the Ghin was not ranked in the Galactic standings. Tchpht and Indowy masters played him on request out of deference to his position, but equally from what the humans would call the "waltzing bear" factor. Very few Darhel treated Aethal with anything other than tolerant contempt, as a meaningless distraction from the realities of power and commerce. Intangible relationships had power only so long as they were honored. Darhel only honored relationships as stipulated by contract, rendering the alliances and intricacies of Aethal meaningless from their point of view. Or, more accurately, irrelevant to their own lives.

The game drew to a crisis, a positioning almost certain to weaken the Ghin's position enormously, and, by extension, grossly distort the interactions of Phxtkl's pieces in an unfavorable way.

"Now it is time for my comment, O arrogant slave to physical items." The master highlighted a section of the display in a red haze. "Observe this section and how it is now cut off from the influence of your web, held by only the tiniest of threads, the minimum connection that never ends. It may seem an insignificant set of resources, but look at the potential." The Tchpht pointed to various nexus pieces above the table. "Despite the loss of face here, here, and here, or the losses in several of your tertiary relationships, this was a critical play."

"I see that. I will set up an alternate problem for

just a moment," the Ghin said. He had no worry of losing the current game which was, of course, saved in his AID. If Phxtkl was surprised that the referenced alternate problem was already crafted and saved, he gave no sign, bouncing and tapping upon his low stool as always.

"Here is a starting problem. You will see the relationship to a recent past current Galactic situation. Here is the current situation. You see, of course, the likely moves if no sacrifices are made to alter the web."

The alien creature was silent for a long few moments, looking at the three displays. "I disagree with a number of the particulars of the various patterns, but . . . your overall point is taken. Isolation is loss of influence. Avoiding that is worth much. Worth enough, in this case." Phxtkl was still for a few seconds, in his species' equivalent of a deep, martyred sigh. "This is one of the least enjoyable games of Aethal I have ever played, O intriguing schemer of much age. Today, I have been the student; unpleasantly so. I must make some necessary social sacrifices to continue the movement you have begun just now. I wish you success, O annoying one, and I leave."

"Leave for Earth." The Ghin was uncharacteristically blunt. "You have something to repair."

Her silver blond hair framed her face, drawing attention to the startlingly intense, cornflower blue eyes. Other than a subconscious awareness of the soft brushing against her face and neck as she walked, her hair was the last thing on Cally O'Neal's mind as she rubbed sweaty palms on her jeans before entering Father O'Reilly's secular sanctum sanctorum.

"Cally. Good, you're here. Can I get you some water or a soft drink?" the priest inquired gently.

Uh-oh. Whenever the leader of the O'Neal Bane Sidhe started out with the kind and gentle routine, you knew you were in for it. Not that it was her fault. At least, she didn't think there was anything serious going on that was her fault. She was a bit late on her expense report for the last mission, but she'd think he'd give her some slack for blowing it off over Christmas. She had had a feeling something was wrong, but this was obviously more serious than she had thought. She allowed a wrinkled forehead to show her worry as she started to get up. There was a cooler just outside

"Just water, I'll get it," she said.

"Sit." The gentle tone carried the force of command, as he pulled a pitcher from his small refrigerator and poured her a glass.

Her eyebrows lifted as Grandpa came in, sitting across and facing her. They were both facing her. She instantly noticed that Papa O'Neal had no chew, and no cup. This was not good.

"Papa, can I get you anything?"

"Nothing, thanks."

"Can I ask?" the assassin asked.

"Cally, you have got to learn not to kill someone on a job just because he's a bad man and he's in your way," the monsignor said. "In this case, he wasn't even in your way."

"What in the world was wrong with killing Erick Winchon, and if you didn't want him dead, why the hell did you send *me*? Dead's what I do."

"The Aerfon Djigahr was your target, not Winchon," Papa pointed out. "Also, if you remember, *we* didn't pick you for this mission, your sister did. Not that we wouldn't have anyway. Personally, I think the little prick looked a lot better as a corpse, granddaughter, but there have been . . . complications."

"Michelle said she could deal with all that." She absently brushed her hair back, tucking the strands behind her ear.

"No, she said she'd *try*," O'Reilly said. "It didn't work. We've been disavowed."

"Disavowed by who and why? I thought violent mass-murderer scumbags like Winchon were persona non grata with *all* the races."

"The Tchpht, the Himmit, the Indowy with whom we still *had* a minimal backdoor relationship," the monsignor said with a sigh. "Thank God Aelool and Beilil felt too much personal responsibility to join the exodus. The whole reason the Crabs wanted Pardal dead was that plotting the death of one of only five emergent human Mentats, the beginning of our species' enlightenment, was a far *worse* evil. Turns out, they viewed it as a problem on the scale of the Posleen war. That is the *only* reason they authorized the killing of Pardal, to protect Michelle. And then you have to go and kill one of the *other* four mentats!"

"He was a freaking psychopath," Cally said. "A powerful and dangerous one for that matter."

"They feel they could have managed that," O'Reilly said, holding up his hand to forestall a reply. "The point is, I've tried to find words to describe to you how angry they are, and I can't come up with anything remotely adequate."

"Like a kicked hornet's nest?" Papa said.

"Angry like a super-nova is hot?" Cally asked.

"Angry like I'll get if you two can't take this *seriously*!" O'Reilly shouted. "Cut off. NO support. None! *Totally* on our own!"

"We've got funding," Cally pointed out, shrugging. "A lot more funding than we did before this went down."

"Would you care to consider what we *don't* have?" O'Reilly said, sarcastically. "Just consider the following. No access to GalTech. No access to Galactic medicines. No access to Galactic injury care, not nannites, not even a tank much less a slab. We don't even have *human* medical support. The next time you get seriously injured, you'd better be able to do internal surgery, Cally, because otherwise you're going to *die* for real and for certain."

"Oh," Cally said.

"No access to GalTech weaponry," O'Reilly pointed out, turning to Papa. "No plasma weapons. No gravguns. No armor. No plasteel. No logistic support except what the Clan can provide. And entirely out of Clan funds instead of the trickle of continued support we got. We're entirely on our own for buying ammo for what weapons we've got or buy on the open market. Only our own access to black market."

"Stewart can help there," Cally said.

"Minimally," Papa pointed out. "Unless you want to get my son-in-law killed."

"Not . . . usually," Cally said.

"No access to Bane Sidhe intel," O'Reilly continued. "Or Himmit. No . . ."

"Okay," Cally said. "Okay. Got the picture. I fucked up. I was under a certain amount of pressure at the time."

"Not a good enough excuse for the mess you've created," O'Reilly said. "However, even though you were *intimately* involved in the unfolding of this mess, I can't figure out a way to help in the salvage operation."

"Yes, sir. No excuse, Father," she said.

"Cally, what were you thinking?" O'Reilly asked.

"I made a serious mission planning error, sir, and I was winging it."

"Quit sirring me, this isn't the Army."

"Yes, sir—I mean, yes, Father." She watched him sigh and knew it wasn't the response he'd been looking for.

"In any case, you're not here for a dressing down. Or, more accurately, I'm done. What you're here for is a joint Clan/Organization planning meeting," the priest said, sitting down in a chair next to Papa's.

It wasn't what she'd expected to hear. Cally decided it was a very good opportunity to keep her mouth shut.

"My own mistakes in this debacle include not having pulled your grandfather behind a desk, doubtless kicking and screaming, ten or fifteen years ago. My reasons seemed good at the time." He sighed. "Hindsight is twenty-twenty." The young-looking old man rubbed his thumb and forefinger together, fingering rosary beads that weren't there.

"They say that infantry captain is the best job in the Army. Every generation, every new crop of captains, has to face the same fact—you can't be a captain forever. Operations is fun."

"You're pulling me from the field," she said woodenly.

"I certainly would if I could, but we don't have a good replacement. And we're down on support for training. Right now, with DAG no longer being trained by the Federation and both you and Papa in the field, we're effectively eating our seed-corn. Your DAG recruits aren't ready to do covert ops. So you're going to have to do the two-hat shuffle and train them."

"Can I ask what the other one is?"

"You just did. We cannot survive without Galactic allies. We need raw materials, transportation, tools, technology, information. These are all things they have, that we need. Papa here is going to have to put on his clan head hat and go play diplomat for us."

"Granpa? Diplomat . . . ? Have you gone *bonkers*?"

"Why does everyone react that way?" Granpa asked. "I'm a perfectly diplomatic person."

Nathan gave Cally a wry grin.

"He's the only one who can," the monsignor said, serious again. "As bad as things are, they'll only meet with a clan head—O'Neal's clan head. We're all going to be making some sacrifices and doing things we'd rather not. From the point of view of the Galactics, the only way to ensure that Clan O'Neal isn't going to go rogue, again, is to have agreements with the Clan Leader."

"If I promise you won't kill any more of the nomenklatura without authorization, they'll accept that as an unbreakable promise," Papa said. "Which it *will* be, granchile o' mine."

"Yes, O Great and Powerful Oz," Cally said, flippantly.

"Which means that we're all going to have to be doing things we'd rather not," O'Reilly said. "I will be without my right arm, for example. His assistant will therefore have to speed up her learning curve, something that is good for her but not welcome. Which brings us to your second job. Although in normal line of succession, Michelle would be clan head, that's not . . . appropriate at this time. She has her own problems from this debacle. You will, therefore, be acting clan head in your granfather's absence."

"Which means you get all the headaches of running the O'Neal Clan," Papa said with an evil grin. "Like herding bengal tigers that is."

Cally felt the beginnings of a crushing sensation in her chest, her face automatically defaulting to an expressionless mask. Perversely, the first coherent thought to wander through her head was that this would ruin Christmas, and how was she going to tell Shari.

"Don't get used to that feeling," O'Reilly said. "You have *a lot* of material to cover, and then you can expect a lot of practical work. In an area that is about as far from your skill set as any I can imagine."

"Nailed that one," Cally said, trying not to grin.

"Hush," the monsignor said, trying not to chuckle. It wasn't a moment for humor. "If you see less than a ten hour day the whole trip, praise God for the break."

Cally took the opportunity to grab her grandfather in a tight bear hug, loosening up when he grunted from the pressure of her Crab-upgraded muscles.

"Good luck in the lion's den," she said.

"Good luck to you in the hot seat. See you when I get back. If you get a chance, hug your sister for me."

In the hall, she watched him walk away, O'Reilly's deputy at his elbow, until they turned and were out of sight.

—end excerpt—

from *Honor of the Clan*
available in hardcover,
January 2009, from Baen Books

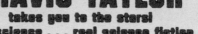

Flag in Exile 0-7434-3575-3 • $7.99

"Packs enough punch to smash a starship to smithereens."—*Publishers Weekly*

Honor Among Enemies 0-671-87723-2 • $21.00
 0-671-87783-6 • $7.99

"Star Wars as it might have been written by C.S. Forester...fast-paced entertainment."—*Booklist*

In Enemy Hands 0-671-87793-3 • $22.00
 0-671-57770-0 • $7.99

After being ambushed, Honor finds herself aboard an enemy cruiser, bound for her scheduled execution. But one lesson Honor has never learned is how to give up!

Echoes of Honor 0-671-87892-1 • $24.00
 0-671-57833-2 • $7.99

"Brilliant! Brilliant! Brilliant!"—Anne McCaffrey

Ashes of Victory 0-671-57854-5 • $25.00
 0-671-31977-9 • $7.99

Honor has escaped from the prison planet called Hell and returned to the Manticoran Alliance, to the heart of a furnace of new weapons, new strategies, new tactics, spies, diplomacy, and assassination.

War of Honor 0-7434-3545-1 • $26.00
 0-7434-7167-9 • $7.99

No one wanted another war. Neither the Republic of Haven, nor Manticore—and certainly not Honor Harrington. Unfortunately, what they wanted didn't matter.

At All Costs 1-4165-0911-9 • $26.00
 1-4165-4414-3 • $7.99

The war with the Republic of Haven has resumed...disastrously for the Star Kingdom of Manticore. The alternative to victory is total defeat, yet this time the cost of victory will be agonizingly high.

1633 with Eric Flint   hc • 0-7434-3542-7 • $26.00
                               pb • 0-7434-7155-5 • $7.99
1634: The Baltic War with Eric Flint   hc • 1-4165-2102-X • $26.00
American freedom and justice versus the tyrannies of the 17th century. Set in Flint's *1632* universe.

THE STARFIRE SERIES
WITH STEVE WHITE:

The Stars at War I   0-7434-8841-5 • $25.00
Rewritten *Insurrection* and *In Death Ground* in one massive volume.

The Stars at War II   0-7434-9912-3 • $27.00
The Shiva Option and *Crusade* in one massive volume.

PRINCE ROGER NOVELS
WITH JOHN RINGO:

March Upcountry   0-7434-3538-9 • $7.99

March to the Sea   0-7434-3580-X • $7.99

March to the Stars   0-7434-8818-0 • $7.99

We Few   1-4165-2084-8 • $7.99
"This is as good as military sf gets." —*Booklist*